Praise for Terri Reed and her novels

"Terri Reed strikes a good balance
between the suspense and relationship[s]."
—*RT Book Reviews* on *Double Deception*

"In the exciting *Double Jeopardy…*
Reed does a terrific job…"
—*RT Book Reviews*

"[An] attention-grabbing story that delivers a
fascinating and pulsating conclusion."
—*RT Book Reviews* on *Double Cross*

"Reed's fast-paced action
will keep readers wondering…"
—*RT Book Reviews* on *The Cowboy Target*

"A good mystery and plenty of suspense…"
—*RT Book Reviews* on *The Innocent Witness*

WWW.THRIFTYOWL.COM

TERRI REED

Double Deception

and

Double Jeopardy

⟨H⟩HARLEQUIN® LOVE INSPIRED® CLASSICS

Recycling programs
for this product may
not exist in your area.

ISBN-13: 978-0-373-60649-8

DOUBLE DECEPTION AND DOUBLE JEOPARDY

Copyright © 2014 by Harlequin Books S.A.

The publisher acknowledges the copyright holder of the individual works as follows:

DOUBLE DECEPTION
Copyright © 2007 by Terri Reed

DOUBLE JEOPARDY
Copyright © 2008 by Terri Reed

Printed in U.S.A.

CONTENTS

Books by Terri Reed

Love Inspired Suspense

*Double Deception
 Beloved Enemy
 Her Christmas Protector
*Double Jeopardy
*Double Cross
*Double Threat Christmas
 Her Last Chance
 Chasing Shadows
 Covert Pursuit
 Holiday Havoc
   "Yuletide Sanctuary"
 Daughter of Texas
†The Innocent Witness
†The Secret Heiress
 The Deputy's Duty
†The Doctor's Defender

†The Cowboy Target
 Scent of Danger
 Texas K-9 Unit Christmas
   "Rescuing Christmas"
 Treacherous Slopes
 Undercover Marriage

*The McClains
†Protection Specialists

Love Inspired

Love Comes Home
A Sheltering Love
A Sheltering Heart
A Time of Hope
Giving Thanks for Baby
Treasure Creek Dad

TERRI REED

At an early age Terri Reed discovered the wonderful world of fiction and declared she would one day write a book. Now she is fulfilling that dream and enjoys writing for Love Inspired Books. Her second book, *A Sheltering Love,* was a 2006 RITA® Award finalist and a 2005 National Readers' Choice Award finalist. Her book *Strictly Confidential,* book five in the Faith at the Crossroads continuity series, took third place in the 2007 American Christian Fiction Writers Book of the Year Award, and *Her Christmas Protector* took third place in 2008. She is an active member of both Romance Writers of America and American Christian Fiction Writers. She resides in the Pacific Northwest with her college-sweetheart husband, two wonderful children and an array of critters. When not writing, she enjoys spending time with her family and friends, gardening and playing with her dogs.

You can write to Terri at P.O. Box 19555, Portland, OR 97280. Visit her on the web at www.loveinspiredauthors.com, leave comments on her blog, www.ladiesofsuspense.blogspot.com, or email her at terrireed@sterling.net.

DOUBLE DECEPTION

Be strong and courageous,
do not be afraid or tremble at them,
for the Lord your God is the one who goes with
you. He will not fail you or forsake you.
—*Deuteronomy* 31:6

To my husband, my hero.
I love you always and forever.

ONE

Brody McClain hated storms.

The pounding rain and swirling wind off the Nantucket Sound were relentless, like the nightmares that had plagued him for five years.

Old anger resurfaced and burned in his gut.

With a shake of his head, he pushed the memories aside and focused his attention back on the small cottage. *Concentrate.*

Lightning streaked across the sky and reflected off the windowpanes of the dark house, making the dormer windows glow like large, luminous eyes.

Brody crouched behind the branches of an ancient rhododendron. The blood in his head thudded in tempo with the rapid beat of his heart. He gritted his teeth, forcing his breathing under control.

After a moment, his vision cleared and his eyes adjusted to the night. Drops of rain streamed down his back, plastering his cotton shirt to his skin. *Should have grabbed a jacket, McClain.*

From beyond the house, above the roar of the churning surf crashing against the cape, a seagull's high-pitched squawk protested the downpour.

I'm with you, buddy.

Blinding lightning pierced the midnight sky. More rumbling thunder nipped at its heels. Brody narrowed his gaze, staring at the large multipaned window near the front door, waiting impatiently for another flash to confirm what he thought he'd just seen.

Finally the light came. In that second of stunning brilliance he saw the silhouette.

Someone *was* in the house.

His fingers tightened around the grip of his Glock. He'd drawn his sidearm as he'd approached the house, heeding the familiar, gentle nudging he'd learned to respect. Only once had he ignored that inner signal. That mistake had cost him everything.

But that was then. Now… Brody moved soundlessly along the wraparound porch toward the back door. He tried the knob. Locked.

He pulled out a ring of keys and skimmed his finger along the flat surface of each, searching for the correct raised letter. He found the key marked with a *K*. He slipped it into the lock and opened the door.

A noise beyond the storm outside caught Kate Wheeler's attention. Just scraps of sound really, like a hinge in need of oil. The noise went perfectly with the eerie shadows that played along the covered furniture, making the white sheets appear ghostly. Musty staleness mingled with the salty scent of the Atlantic Ocean permeated the air.

She shivered in the darkness, her imagination wreaking havoc on her nerves with thoughts of some unknown assassin stalking her.

Outside, the wind howled across the Nantucket Sound, a forlorn noise that echoed through the house.

Fighting to keep her anxiety from turning into panic, Kate leaned against the wall.

Lord, I'm really scared. I need Your courage.

She never should have come here tonight. She should have done the smart thing and waited for morning before coming to the house she hoped held answers to her husband's death. But patience wasn't one of her virtues.

Now she was stranded. The airport limousine service had disappeared long ago and the cell phone tucked in her purse was useless, the battery dead and the recharge cord forgotten at home. Given the circumstances of Paul's death, she should have been more cautious.

Ever since his funeral the previous month, she'd had the uneasy feeling someone was watching her.

The sensation followed her everywhere, the constant impression of eyes observing her every move, taking stock, waiting for the right moment to attack.

I told them you have it.

Paul's dire words rang in her head. If only she knew what "it" was.

Her condo in Los Angeles had been ransacked twice, which led her to believe that they—whoever *they* were—hadn't found the mysterious object. She hoped she'd find answers to her questions here in this small Massachusetts town, starting with this place— a house she'd known nothing about.

She glanced around as hurt burrowed in deep. How long had Paul owned this oceanfront cottage? Why had he bought a house when he'd refused to purchase one with her, his wife?

Once she would have expected the trappings of a normal marriage.

Paul's courtship had been the epitome of romance. They'd met at a Chamber of Commerce mixer. She'd been taken with his blond good looks and professional demeanor. He'd wooed her with candlelit dinners, roses at her door every Friday and touching love letters. She hadn't been able to resist his hard press. He'd represented stability and security: everything she longed for, everything that had been missing in her childhood.

But after the wedding, he'd changed. Even though he'd championed her career, urging her to advance rapidly through the ranks of the bank where she worked, he'd become distant at home. At first she'd attributed his withdrawal to difficulty adjusting to marriage.

As time wore on, she'd become more confused. She didn't know what she'd done to make him pull away. Throughout their four-year marriage, they'd been both physically and emotionally separated. The lack of love, respect and affection had cut her to her soul.

She'd tried everything to keep the marriage intact. She'd prayed every day. She'd sought professional help. But Paul had refused to go to counseling. He'd refused to talk to their pastor. He'd even stopped attending church. When people asked about him, she didn't know what to say. They'd become strangers living in the same apartment.

Now he was dead and she was left to clean up the mess.

She pushed away from the wall. Though she'd never been afraid of the dark, the lack of electricity in the little seaside bungalow unnerved her. She moved to the rustic side table and finally located matches and a candle in the bottom drawer.

With shaky hands, Kate struck the match. Nothing. On her second try the little stick sputtered to life with a small burst of flame and she held the fire against the candle's wick. But if she'd thought the light would quell her uneasy feeling, she was mistaken. Beyond the circle of light, the glow flickered, deepening the shadows and adding to the spooky feel of the room.

The wind increased in tempo. A branch grated along a wall and a chill darted over Kate's flesh, raising goose bumps along her skin. A gust of air blew through the living room and the candle's flame careened crazily out of control before sputtering to a silent death. Inky darkness once again descended, enveloping her.

Suddenly, the familiar sense of being watched became acute, wrapping around Kate like greedy hands, stealing her breath. She shuddered. She glanced about the room, the blackness overwhelming, menacing.

Nothing's there. No one had been there for a month. She was safe here. She had to be.

Moving quickly toward the entryway where she'd left her suitcases and purse, Kate decided to find a bedroom where she could curl up beneath the blankets and wait for morning. Answers would be found in the daylight.

A flash of lightning exploded and threw the ebony night into stark relief. Her world appeared like a photo negative.

The harsh light illuminated the retreating figure of a man as he moved away from her through the kitchen.

A man with a gun.

The blood drained from her head. For a split second she wrestled with the sensation of dizziness. Her heart clutched before pounding in large, booming beats. The roar of blood rushing back to her brain flooded her ears, blocking out the sounds of the night.

He would see her if she moved to the front door. Her gaze darted in the direction of the bedrooms. If he found her there she'd be trapped. But what choice did she have? The bags slid from her slackened fingers to land soundlessly on the small area rug beneath her feet. *Please, Lord, protect me.* Because no one on earth would.

Then all was black again.

Once inside the cottage, Brody listened for any telltale sounds of the intruder, but the nocturnal noises beyond the walls of the house taunted his caution. Not wanting to announce his presence yet, he kept his flashlight attached to his belt.

Silently, he moved from the kitchen into the dining room. A large wooden table and several chairs made the area difficult to negotiate in the dark.

He breathed in. Beyond the musty, rank smell of disuse, an out-of-place scent drifted past his nostrils. The acrid smell of a burnt match.

On heightened alert, Brody moved forward, leading with his firearm. Once free of the dining room, he entered the living room. Another smell. A fragrance he recognized from his mother's garden—the sweet scent of lilacs.

Light flashed. A sharp, loud bang exploded into the stillness and ricocheted off the walls.

Brody dove for cover. His heart hammered in his chest. Adrenaline pumped through his veins and his nerves stretched taut. For a beat of time he was back in Boston, seeing the flare of gunfire, reliving the agony of betrayal.

The sounds of his own breath wiped the memory

away. *Thunder, you idiot.* The storm was playing games with his mind.

Crawling to the wall, he pressed his throbbing hip and back against its cool surface. He took a deep, calming breath and focused on the one constant in his life, his job. He could never forget what he had to do.

Peering around the corner into the entryway, he caught sight of a dark shape. He froze, his heart picked up speed again. Though his vision was 20/20, the darkness made it difficult to see. Brody expelled a harsh breath. He had no choice. He had to get closer.

Lying prone and using his forearms to move his body forward, Brody crept across the threshold between the two rooms, over the cold hardwood floor toward the dark form. Three feet away, he released the breath he'd been holding.

Luggage. Black leather, two large and one small carry-on type. He frowned and moved closer. He nudged them. Full.

What was going on?

A fragment of noise came from down the hall, toward the bedrooms. He slowly rose and in a low crouch, proceeded into the gloom of the long hallway. He stopped to listen for more sound to direct his way. None came.

He paused at the first door he came to and listened for a moment. No noise. Still he braced himself, fisted his flashlight and turned the knob. The door swung open. Brody flipped on the flashlight. His gaze swept the room. Nothing beneath the bed. But the closet…

Out of habit, he glanced over his shoulder, making sure no one was behind him. He pressed his back into the wall, closed his hand over the closet doorknob and slowly turned.

Kate had to find a way out of the house.

She stood in the middle of the second bedroom. A bed, a dresser, a nightstand and a closet. There was nowhere to hide. Forget the closet. She couldn't take being in the small, confining space. Better to face her enemy and die in the open than wait meekly in what very well could be her coffin.

Chills slid over her body.

She didn't dare go back down the hall, so that left the window above the bed. Stepping up onto the mattress, she grasped the handle and pulled upward.

The window wouldn't budge. She tried the lock, but it refused to give. Using all of her strength, she managed to turn the lock, and yet the window still wouldn't move. Running a hand over the wood, she found the problem. The window had been nailed shut.

She gritted her teeth in frustration as she fought desperate panic. The logical part of her mind that had always ruled her life clamped down on the urgent impulse to dive head-first through the glass and hope she got away in one piece.

An idea formed in her mind. Something she'd seen in a movie or read in a book.

Lord, let this work in real life.

Kate snatched the brass bedside lamp, yanking the cord from the wall. Taking a deep breath, she raised her arm and threw the lamp with all her might at the window. Glass shattered in a shower of chunks and slivers, mostly landing in the dirt on the outside of the house, some falling inward onto the bed.

She cringed at the noise, then jumped from the bed and ran across the room to press her body against the wall beside the hinges of the door bare seconds before it burst open. The doorknob connected with her hipbone and she bit her lip to stifle a cry.

In hypnotic terror, she watched as the broad back of a man appeared within her line of vision. *Please, don't let him find me.*

She squeezed farther into the corner. The man stopped in front of the open closet door, his head cocked to one side. He moved out of her view and she heard the barely perceptible creak of the mattress and a powerful beam of light lit the room. Kate closed her eyes and prayed her ruse had worked and he thought she'd escaped.

The light went out and she heard a soft thud. He'd stepped off the bed. A second later she heard him move toward the doorway. Tensing, she waited.

Through the crack between the door and the jamb she saw him pass by, a dimmer shape against the darkness. Relief coursed through her, making her knees weak. She hadn't been found. *Thank You, Lord.*

Minutes ticked by. She heard the solid click of the front door being closed, the sound of the man retreating to take his search into the night. The waiting seemed eternal before she gathered enough nerve to emerge from behind the door.

Should she go through the house to escape? She turned to look at the broken window. The jagged edges would cut her to shreds. She didn't have any choice. She had to go through the house.

Brody stood poised with his back against the wall at the mouth of the long, dark hallway. Clever trick, breaking the glass to make it look as if his prey had jumped out the window and escaped.

The second Brody had entered the bedroom he'd known he wasn't alone. A tightening of his senses had made him aware of the other's presence.

Even if his instincts hadn't alerted him, he still would have known. No one could have gone out that window without cutting themselves and leaving a trail of blood. Besides, the lack of footprints in the soft, mossy dirt below the window, visible in his flashlight's beam, had been a dead giveaway.

So he waited. Waited as a honed patience calmed his heart and readied his body. It was only a matter of time.

* * *

Inch by inch, Kate made her way down the pitch-black corridor, her hand guiding her past the doors to the other rooms. As she neared the living room she stopped. A familiar, yet strange sensation tickled her spine. She wasn't alone.

On some deep, basic level she felt the man's presence, sensed his heartbeat. She pressed her back flat against the wall and balled her hands into tight fists. It wasn't fair. But then, God never promised life would be fair, only that He'd be there.

Her gaze slid from the grayer light of the house back to the darkness of the windowless hall. Was he behind her in the dark, inching his way toward her? Taking her lip between her teeth to keep tears and welling panic at bay, she stood immobile, unsure what her next move should be.

Tension coiled, her stomach churned and her lungs burned. She couldn't go back. She had to go forward.

With a deep breath, she pushed from the wall and forced her legs to move fast. Adrenaline coursed through her limbs and her heart raced. She could see the front door. She just had to make it across the open entryway. Three more feet…iron cords wrapped around her, stopping her momentum with a jerk. She screamed as she was tackled to the ground.

Her head smacked against the hardwood and spots of light exploded before her eyes. A huge, muscled body landed on top of her, effectively pinning her beneath his hulking figure, and drove the air from her lungs.

Fear blasted up her spine. She was going to die, and it was all Paul's fault.

With a grip of steel, the man yanked her arms over her head and held her wrists captive while another probing hand ran over her body. Numbing shock rippled through her, then the roaming hand stilled.

The man swore in a deep hiss near her ear and eased off her.

She took a shallow breath.

"You're a woman," a deep, rich voice accused.

The observation seemed ridiculous. Of course she was a woman. Did Paul's murderer think Paul had been married to a monkey?

The ridiculous thought brought fear raging headlong into her consciousness. This man was here to get something she hadn't a clue about, and then he would probably kill her the way he'd killed Paul. Then another thought flittered across her mind: what if he assaulted her before killing her? *Oh, Lord, take me home quickly.*

No. Not yet. Sheer terror spurred her into action. She twisted and turned, her body bucking in an effort to throw him off balance. Her hands pulled against the restraint of his grip, her legs struggled to find leverage on the floor, pushing and kicking wildly. The toe of her shoe made contact with a shin, eliciting a grunt of pain from her attacker. A moment of satisfaction brought a tightening to her lips.

Her knee flew upward but he rolled slightly, deflecting her hit to his hip. She ground her back teeth. She wasn't going to let him win. She wasn't ready to die.

"Hey, lady. Calm down."

Calm down? He wanted her calm so he could kill her. Her grandmother had taught her that God hadn't made women to be passive, but proactive. She'd fight with everything she had before she'd calmly let this man do her in.

Arching upward, she used her forehead as a ramming device. She connected with his chin, causing his teeth to come together with a snap. Pain shot through her.

For a moment his grip lessened and she took advantage of the opportunity. Freeing a hand, she lashed out, aiming for his eyes. She fell short, her nails raking sharply down his face, evoking a yowl of pain.

"That's it!" The harsh words echoed through the house. He held her hands in a grip so tight she knew she'd never get free.

"No!" But still she fought, determined not to give up until the last breath left her body. Too many questions remained unanswered, too much pain still lived in her heart. Blind fear made her body convulse, desperate to break free.

The chink of metal somewhere above her head made her close her eyes. She didn't want to see the torture device he would use on her and she prayed for oblivion. Oblivion and a painless death.

She cried out in surprise as he twisted her arm behind her and flipped her over. Cold metal encircled her wrists. A sharp snap filled her ears. And only then, from the far reaches of sanity, did she realize she'd been handcuffed. The man spoke in low, smooth tones, but her terror-fogged mind couldn't grasp the words.

"Do you understand?" The steady cadence of his words, the richness of his voice, washed over her and a sense of unreality set in. Closing her eyes tightly, she readied herself for the journey to heaven.

The man grasped her shoulders and gently shook her. "Do you understand? Answer me!"

"No." She didn't understand why she was about to die. She didn't understand how she'd come to this point in time. And she didn't understand how she could have been so wrong about Paul. Who had she been married to? What kind of man had he really been? And why had he allowed this to happen to her? Unfortunately, she would die without the answers.

"Lady, how hard is it to understand? You're under arrest."

TWO

The woman beneath him stilled.

"Arrest?" The word came out in a dry croak.

"Yes, you're under arrest." Brody couldn't see her face but he heard the rapid labor of her breath, felt the rise and fall of her chest where their ribs connected. And he was all too aware of the fact that his intruder was female. Soft and full of curves. The smell of lilacs he'd detected earlier wasn't a remnant of the owner's last visit, sporadic as they were.

The scent clung to his captive's hair.

Pushing away, he came to his knees and helped her to a sitting position.

"You're…you're not here…to kill me?" Her voice faded to a hushed stillness and Brody heard the fear behind the words.

"I'm not going to kill you," he said in a calming tone. "Do you understand that anything you say can be used against you in a court of law—"

She made an odd noise. "You're a cop?"

"Yes, ma'am. You have the right to an attorney. If—"

"I haven't done anything," she interrupted.

Brody ignored her protest and finished her Miranda rights then helped her to her feet as a bolt of lightning whitewashed the room. He caught a glimpse of an impish face and large, luminous eyes. The tip of her head barely reached the top of his shoulder. So much spirit in one so little. A spark of admiration for the way she'd fought him flared hot.

The light faded and the shadows returned, leaving him feeling unsettled. She certainly didn't look like a criminal.

He heard her test the strength of the metal links between the cuffs.

"Are these really necessary?"

In the blackness, her voice rang cool and clear, yet Brody heard the underlying tension in her tone. Why did she think someone was out to kill her?

"I'll take them off when we get to the station." His natural caution took precedence. Regardless of the gender of his intruder, experience had taught him how deceptive people could be—especially the female sort.

"The police station?"

"Actually, the county sheriff's office. Let's go." His terse answer harbored no room for discussion.

"My purse!"

Brody paused by the grouping of luggage. He picked up the leather bag that he'd mistaken for a carry-on piece of luggage. "This?"

She nodded.

The damp shirt on his back itched and the house grew colder by the minute, making his hip hurt and his limbs grow numb. He resisted the urge to limp by placing a hand on her arm to guide her out of the house. She tried to pull away but he tightened his hold.

Beneath his palm, she trembled as he helped her into his cruiser. Her flowery, lilac scent once again reminded him of his mother's garden. A place where he used to find a sense of serenity. Even if he took up Mom's constant invitations to come home, he doubted he'd find that kind of peace now.

With the heater cranked high, they rode in silence through the small town of Havensport, Massachusetts, the quaint buildings of the New England community surveyed by Brody with a sheriff's eye.

Stores dark and locked tight, no suspicious characters roaming the streets. There never were. Until tonight. Havensport was as boringly safe as a small town could get, but old habits were hard to break.

The sheriff's office kept keys of all the summer homes in case of emergencies. Lucky for Pete Kinsey that Mae Couch, the elderly lady who lived next door, had been looking out her window and seen someone lurking about. So unusual an occurrence was it, Sheriff Brody McClain had immediately responded.

He glanced in the rearview mirror. The woman's face was turned toward the window, but he could make out the straight line of her nose, which tilted upward slightly at the tip and a wide, generous mouth set into a firm crease. She hadn't spoken since they'd left the house.

Within the enclosed space of his cruiser he couldn't tell the color of her hair. The lights of the station would tell him soon enough. He returned his gaze forward as he slowed to park the car in his spot by the door of the station.

The Havensport County Sheriff's Office stood at one end of town like a sentinel on guard duty. Though the redbrick building, built in the early part of the century with a high peaked roof and multi-paned windows, had withstood updates both in and out, it still remained a historical landmark, due mainly to the fact that the first sheriff's family still owned most of the property within a thirty-mile radius around the town.

Brody got out and opened the back door. The woman refused his help and struggled out of the vehicle on her own. With reluctance, he again felt admiration for her grit.

Rain poured from the sky, rolling in rivulets down his face. Quickly, he ushered his charge into the station.

Her hair was copper. He'd always liked redheads. He should have stuck with them instead of being tempted by Elise's willowy blond good looks.

The station's warmth seeped through his drenched clothing, bringing life back to his numb limbs and chasing away the cold reality of Elise.

After settling the woman into a chair, he unlocked the handcuffs. She rubbed at the rough, red marks left by the metal rings. Brody lowered his gaze and busied himself at the antique oak desk, ignoring the uncomfortable twinge of guilt that rose at the sight of her reddened, slender wrists.

Deputy Warren Teal stepped from the bathroom, still drying his hands with a paper towel. "Hi, boss."

Warren's curious gaze settled on Kate as he crumpled the sheet into a ball. After tossing it into the wastebasket, he perched his lean frame on the edge of Brody's desk. "What do we have here? This the perp at the Kinsey house?"

Brody arched a brow at the deputy. The young rookie was overeager at times, but fairly competent.

"Sorry." Warren moved away and sat at the only other desk in the room. "She do that to your face?"

Ignoring the questions and the reminder of his stinging cheek, Brody took a blank report, a pen— he preferred to write out the reports first and key them in later—then turned to the woman. "Name?"

Her gaze pinned him to his chair. Confusion radiated from the depths of her large green eyes. "You don't know?"

Brody's mouth twisted with wry amusement. "Lady, I'm good, but not that good."

She blinked. "Why did you arrest me?"

"B and E is a felony, ma'am." At her blank expression, he clarified, "Breaking and entering."

"I didn't break in," she insisted, leaning forward.

"I own the house. My late husband left the property to me." Her voice wavered. "If you'll let me call my attorney, he'll be able to straighten this whole mess out."

He glanced at her left hand. No band of gold encircled her ring finger. "Pete Kinsey's your husband?" That was a surprise. The womanizing stockbroker had commented often enough how marriage turned men into jellyfish. Not exactly the marrying type.

"My husband's name was Paul Wheeler. He owned the house. Pete Kinsey was my husband's business partner."

Warren turned in his chair, his gray eyes round with interest. "Pete never mentioned a business partner." He shook his head in bemusement. "Wow, can that man party."

Pete Kinsey's parties were legendary on the Cape. Every summer he'd host a big bash with the big society types in attendance—Hollywood celebrities, corporate big shots, political figures. The affair lasted a full weekend and the locals looked forward to the money it brought in. And as long as they didn't break any laws, Brody left them alone.

"Don't you have some work to do, Warren?"

The deputy shrugged and picked up a report.

Intrigued by the situation and by the petite redhead, Brody tapped his pen against the form in front of him as he studied her. "Your full name?"

"Katherine Amanda Wheeler."

Brody wrote out her name. "Address?"

The Beverly Hills address took him by surprise. "You're a long way from home."

She ignored his comment. "Don't I get a phone call?"

"As soon as I have the paperwork filled out." He laid his hand on her purse which he'd deposited on top of his desk. "Is your ID in here?"

"Yes."

He picked up the satchel and unzipped it. "Mind?"

Her deprecating gaze bored into him. "Do I have a choice?"

"No." But still he waited for permission.

"Then go ahead."

He dumped the contents of her purse onto the desktop. A compact, a black tube of lipstick, three granola bars and a thick black wallet spilled out. He unclasped the single snap on the folded wallet and plucked her ID from the first plastic sheath. He wrote down the information on the form. "Your occupation?"

"I work for Valley Savings Bank as the Vice President of Operations. You want to call my boss for a reference?"

Brody cocked his brow. "No. That won't be necessary."

She rolled her eyes. The harsh fluorescent light overhead failed to wash out the sparks of fire in her shoulder-length hair. His gaze strayed to the curling ends where they teased the collar of her pink silk blouse. He tightened his grip on the pen in his hand to keep from reaching out to test the curls. Would they be as silky as they looked?

Her clothing spoke of the kind of money that went along with her address. The tailored suit she wore, though wrinkled and damp, couldn't hide the curves beneath.

"What were you doing there, Mrs. Wheeler?" he questioned, bringing his mind back to business.

"I wanted to see the house." Katherine wrapped her arms around herself. He noticed her shiver while some of the fight drained from her eyes. The coat he'd failed to take with him hung on the back of his chair. Reaching behind him, he grabbed the jacket and handed it to her.

She wrapped the too-large jacket around her shoulders. "Thanks."

He gave a short nod of his head. She looked small and vulnerable and in need of protection. Seeing her in his coat made his chest burn. Irritably, he pushed the phone across the desk. "Make your call."

He didn't have to offer twice. Her long, tapered fingers moved over the keypad. Brody watched her hands and then, like a gawker at a crime scene, his gaze was drawn to her mouth. Pink, soft-looking. Well-shaped lips. Kissable lips.

Yanking his mind away from that treacherous path, he decided he was more tired than he'd thought. The last thing he should be thinking about was his suspect's kissability.

He forced his attention back to the phone, on the

faint metallic sound of a male voice coming through the line. From the look of consternation on Katherine's face, he guessed an answering machine had picked up.

"Gordon, it's Kate. You won't believe this. I'm at the Havensport Sheriff's office, of all things. The number here is…" She raised her brows in question.

Brody gave her the number, which she repeated into the phone before hanging up. Circles of fatigue darkened the skin beneath her eyes, and he shifted uncomfortably in his chair. He dearly wished his mother hadn't raised a gentleman. Despite how much he might want to let Katherine Wheeler go lie down, he still had questions that needed answers.

Swallowing his inclinations, he got back to business. "Why did you think someone was coming to the house to kill you?"

A watchful wariness filled her gaze. "I was alone. You attacked me. What was I supposed to think? That you wanted to dance?"

A spurt of amusement kicked up the corner of Brody's mouth.

She picked up his nameplate and toyed with it between her slender hands. Her manicured nails clicked against the brass. "Where do we go from here?"

"I need to verify your story, check out your ID—"

"And then?" She lifted an auburn brow.

"Then you'll tell me what kind of trouble you're in."

For a brief second her gem-colored gaze locked

haughty indignation that rivaled his younger sister Meghan's. He smothered a smile.

Kate moved into the cell and turned her back on him. An unsettling protest nagged at Brody. He didn't like seeing the petite redhead behind bars. She seemed harmless and innocent, hardly a hardened criminal.

He took a step and pain shot down his leg, reminding him sharply that appearances could be deceiving. He'd learned his lesson and he'd sworn never again to let a pretty face distract him from his job. He shifted his weight and eased the pain.

"Here." Kate slipped the jacket from around her shoulders and shoved it at him. He took it, then closed the cell door, along with the door to his bleeding heart.

Exhaustion overtook Kate and seeped into her bones, making her limbs heavy with lassitude. She grabbed the blanket from the cot and fluffed the pillow with her fist.

Sleeping in a jail cell wasn't exactly how she'd planned on spending her first night on the east coast, especially not on charges of breaking and entering.

She'd probably said more than she should. Her lawyer had sternly told her not to say anything, ever, without his presence. A self-deprecating grimace pulled at her mouth. Of course, if she'd heeded Gordon's advice and not left town, she wouldn't be incarcerated right now.

Sitting down on the narrow, makeshift bed, she muttered, "Better a jail cell than a coffin."

Her hands twisted the rough blanket. The material grew warm beneath her palms. Her lips formed a wry smile. *Thank You, Lord, for giving me such a safe place to sleep tonight.*

She looked at the sheriff. From a distance, his big, male body wasn't nearly as intimidating while hunched in front of his computer screen, his large fingers stabbing at the keys.

The set of his square jaw revealed his concentration and she doubted he realized his dark, wavy hair still glistened with rainwater. His soaked brown uniform emphasized his wide shoulders and broad chest. She could appreciate his masculine appeal with him across the room, but with him up close she'd found herself struggling to breathe evenly.

Abruptly, she shook off the notion of attraction and attributed the thudding of her heart to fear. A tight knot formed in her stomach. Soon, he would learn the complete story of Paul's death and the police's interest in her.

The sheriff had been too perceptive by half, his dark, intense eyes assessing her like an oddity. His questions and offer of help spoken in that much-too-pleasing accent had nearly unhinged her, making her want to open up, to tell him what haunted her nightmares. But Paul's final words echoed inside her head.

Trust...no one.

During the last several weeks, Kate's natural inclination to look for the good had dimmed until she was afraid even to allow herself to trust a man who should be trustworthy. But the police in Los Angeles had made her very aware that trust had to be earned.

The only person she remotely trusted now was Gordon Thomas, her lawyer. The kindly older gentleman had entered her life when her mother had hired him to deal with her divorce. Over the years he'd stayed a part of their lives, becoming a surrogate uncle for Kate, always willing to listen when she couldn't deal with her mother. Kate was grateful he'd taken an interest. Gordon had guided Kate in her college and career choices. She hated to think what path she'd have followed without his tutorship.

But this situation demanded she act on her own. She couldn't ever have the peace and security she craved if she didn't pursue the truth.

Her gaze wandered back to the sheriff. His dark hair fell across his forehead as he shifted in his seat, obstructing her view of his eyes, though she could see the angry red marks running down the side of his cheek left by her nails. She hoped he wouldn't scar, although she doubted even the puckering of wounded flesh could decrease the handsomeness of his ruggedly sculpted face.

Overhead, the lights dimmed and then blinked off and on. The sheriff lifted his head and their gazes locked. For a moment they stared at each other and a shaft of embarrassment darted up Kate's spine to settle in her cheeks. She was staring. She turned sharply away from his hooded, watchful eyes.

"Oh, man."

The sheriff's disgruntled voice brought her head back around.

"What's up?" Warren asked, his wiry form unfolding from his desk chair.

"Computer's down." The sheriff straightened and rolled his massive shoulders.

"You look done in. Why don't you head home? I'll stay here with the prisoner."

Kate stiffened at the deputy's words. Staring hard at the sheriff, she held her breath, waiting for his reply. Don't go. *Lord, please don't let him leave.*

Sheriff McClain leaned back in his chair and laced his fingers behind his head. His lids dropped, hiding the darkness of his eyes. After a heartbeat he replied, "No, I'll stay. But there's no sense in us both being here. You go on home to your pretty wife."

The deputy slanted Kate one last curious look, shrugged and picked up his jacket from the back of his chair. "Suit yourself. See you in the morning."

Kate breathed a sigh of relief as the deputy disappeared through the station door. While probably capable, the deputy just didn't seem as made for the task of protecting her as the sheriff did.

Her attention shifted back to Sheriff McClain. Didn't he have a wife to go home to? A wife waiting, worrying and wondering if he'd return or would this be the day he died for his dedication to his job?

What type of woman would claim the love of a man with a dangerous occupation?

A woman like her own mother.

A woman unlike herself.

She squashed her curiosity. The sheriff's private life was none of her business. If he left his wife alone and lonely while he gave his job the attention his wife craved, what was that to her? Right now Kate needed him to do his job. She was thankful he'd stayed, but she wasn't going to dwell on the sheriff or why his presence was comforting.

Instead, she lay down on the cot and pulled the blanket to her chin. She doubted sleep would come, but closing her eyes and pretending sure beat staring at the too-handsome man who'd arrested her.

The storm's wrath didn't seem to penetrate the station walls and the room fell silent. Feeling relatively safe for the time being, Kate tried to relax. Unaccountably, she felt the sheriff would keep her from harm. God had put her in his care. She'd face her worries again with the new day.

Her body grew heavy and her lids felt weighted down as sleep settled in. Faintly, she heard a rustling of noise. The sheriff finally moving from his reclined position. His quiet footfalls echoed inside her head, but she was too groggy to open her eyes to see what he was doing.

Even when she heard the quiet click, then the slight squeak of the cell door opening, she couldn't muster up enough panic to rouse her from slumber.

She felt the added weight of another blanket being laid across her. With a sigh, she snuggled beneath the cocoon of rough material and drifted completely to sleep.

Brody stared at the sleeping woman.

Katherine Wheeler. No, he much preferred the informal Kate that she'd referred to herself as.

Why did he care if she grew cold? It shouldn't matter. But it did.

There was something compelling about her, something that pulled at him. Maybe it was the vulnerability he saw in her large, springtime eyes or the fact that she'd felt safe enough to allow herself to rest. Whatever the case, it had to stop. He couldn't allow himself to be drawn in by her.

Until Kate's story checked out, he had to think of her as a criminal. He half hoped she did own the house; he'd hate to see her end up in Walpole. Massachusetts Correctional Institute-Cedar Junction was no place for such a pretty woman.

But then again, if what she said was true...what if she decided to become a resident of Havensport? Brody had an uneasy feeling that having her in the same town for any length of time would be hazardous to his carefully tended solitude.

Ha! As if you'd ever let a woman get close to you again, reprimanded his inner voice. *As if this woman, who drips with class, would ever want to get close to you.*

Brody drew back from the sleeping woman on the cot. He rubbed the spot on his hip where he bore the constant reminder of what trusting a woman could do. Old anger and helpless rage roared to life and Brody let out a compressed breath. He spun away and stalked back to his desk to stare at the blank computer screen.

The quicker he cleared up the mess with his guest, the better. Then his nice quiet life could resume the way he wanted it.

Alone.

THREE

Sunshine streamed through the barred window of the jail cell, spilling slanted lines of light across the cement floor and onto the cot where Kate lay. The warmth of the golden rays touched her cheek, and roused her from sleep.

Turning her head fully into the light, Kate frowned at the faint scent that clung to the air. She couldn't place it, but she knew it. A masculine fragrance, which stirred up images of a hard body pressed against her, a handsome face and a tender gesture.

The sheriff.

Kate's lids popped opened, her body tensed on the hard cot. Now she remembered where she was and why. Staring up at the gray ceiling of the jail cell, she listened for movement. Only the sounds of her own breathing met her ears. Was she alone in the jailhouse? She only had to turn her head to see through the black bars, but she stayed motionless, assessing her situation.

Strangely, she hadn't dreamed last night. One would think being locked up in a cold jail cell would bring her nightmares on full force. But she felt rested and ready to tackle the task of discovering why Paul had been murdered.

First she had to deal with Sheriff McClain.

Once Gordon explained about the house, the sheriff would have to let her go. But she had a disquieting feeling her association with the man wouldn't end there. He seemed the type to press, to find challenge in uncovering secrets. Her heart skipped a beat. Maybe the sheriff could help.

She sat up abruptly.

No. She couldn't trust anyone, save God. Even this man who'd sounded so sincere when he'd offered his help, who had cared enough to supply another blanket, who'd…she glanced down.

On the floor, next to her feet, sat a tray with juice, cereal and milk. Surprise and a good dose of pleased warmth suffused her.

Her gaze sought out the sheriff. He sat leaning over his desk with his cheek resting on his forearms. Asleep. He looked boyish, with waves of ebony spilling over his forehead and dark lashes splayed across his cheeks. Kate shook her head in wonder. Just when had Sheriff McClain brought the tray in? She'd heard the squeak of the cell door only once, when he'd brought her the blanket.

A violent shudder swept her body. She'd spent a dreamless night within the cell, lulled to sleep by a false sense of security. Anyone could easily have killed her in her sleep. *Anyone* being the sheriff.

But he hadn't.

Sheriff McClain was not the enemy. He hadn't known Paul. The man was simply a small-town sheriff doing his job. In her heart, she acknowledged that as truth, but her brain wasn't so sure.

Trust no one.

"Get a grip, girl," she muttered as she opened the milk carton and poured the liquid into the bowl of corn flakes. Paul's warning couldn't have extended to the sheriff. There was no reason she couldn't trust Brody McClain.

As she finished the cereal and was about to open the orange juice, a pained grunt split the air. Kate's gaze jumped to the sheriff. His once-relaxed features pulled back into a grimace, his head jerked and a moan slipped from between his lips.

She realized he was gripped within a nightmare. She knew what it was like to feel helplessly lost in the dark swirl of fear, memory and sleep. Compassion filled her chest until it ached with the need to relieve him of his dreams.

"Sheriff McClain?" Her voice bounced off the walls but held no power. "Sheriff?" she tried again, but to no avail. His head thrashed across his bent arms, his big body tense.

Taking a deep breath, Kate used her diaphragm to add more strength to her voice. "McClain!"

Her voice snapped through the station like the slam of a door.

As a wake-up call, it worked well.

Brody jerked his head up and blinked several times before he realized he was at the station, not on a darkened street in the middle of a storm facing the barrel of a gun.

His gaze met that of the woman occupying the cell. Red curls framed her face, emphasizing her large, compassion-filled eyes. She'd witnessed his nightmare. *Great.*

Taking a shuddering breath, Brody composed himself and rose from his chair. Rigid, stiff muscles objected to the stretching. His limbs ached. The need to work out the kinks demanded his attention, but Brody had a job to finish first. The gym would have to wait.

He moved away from the desk to the coffee machine. With each step of his right leg, pain shot into his hip. He refused to allow himself the luxury of limping when meadow-green eyes followed his every move.

By rote, he went through the process of making strong coffee. Soon, the sound and smell of brewing French roast filled the air. Brody inhaled the rich scent for a moment, and pushed away the unease of Kate having witnessed what he worked so hard to keep beneath his heel. He walked steadily to the cell and opened the door. "Good morning."

His charge stared at him. Her head listed to the

side and questions fairly radiated from her expression. "Good morning."

The corners of her mouth kicked up in a tentative smile that sneaked inside his chest and made it difficult to breathe.

"Thank you for breakfast…and the blanket."

He swallowed against both her gratitude and the effects of her smile. He didn't want either one. "I hope you slept well."

"I did, actually." She stood and stepped past him, then stopped in the center of the room. She looked around uncertainly. "Is there a restroom I could use?"

"Down the corridor, on the left." Brody watched her disappear before he shifted his feet and took his weight onto his left leg, easing the ache in his right hip. Why was he bothering? It didn't make sense; vanity wasn't usually one of his faults. But letting her witness his weakness was…out of the question. He didn't want her to look at him with pity.

Most everyone in town knew vague details of how he'd acquired his limp. Few dared approach the subject and even fewer knew the truth of the situation. Taking a bullet was a hazard of the job that every law-enforcement officer faced. Only for Brody it was so much more and so much worse.

Forcing his torturous thoughts to recede, Brody limped over to his desk, sat down and tried to boot up the computer. The screen remained blank. He made a mental note to call the local computer expert and have him take a look at the infernal machine, which was always on the fritz. Somewhat ruefully, he figured he'd have to check out his guest the old-fashioned way.

As he reached for the phone, it rang, the shrill sound ringing hollow in the small station. Picking up the receiver, he answered, "Havensport County Sheriff's Office, Sheriff McClain speaking."

"I understand you have Katherine Wheeler in your custody." The gravelly voice boomed in Brody's ear, the tone sharp, the words clipped.

"And you are?"

"Gordon Thomas, Katherine's attorney."

Figured a Beverly Hills address could buy attitude. "She was caught breaking into one of our residents' summer home."

"The Kinsey residence?"

"Yes."

"The house belongs to my client."

Brody didn't like the condescending tone in the man's voice. "I'll need proof of that."

"What's your fax number?" the man asked curtly.

Brody rattled off the number and a few seconds later the machine in the corner beeped and hissed. Paper rolled out; sheet after sheet until finally it gave one final beep and remained silent.

"Sheriff McClain, I'd like to speak with Ms. Wheeler."

"Sorry, she's indispos..." Brody's voice trailed off as he noticed Kate standing beside his desk. Even with her wrinkled clothes and finger-combed hair, she radiated a quiet confidence. He'd give the lady credit; she was no fragile flower.

"Here she is."

Kate took the phone and turned away. He could hear the urgent note in the low tones of her voice. Picking up the fax, he flipped through the pages and realized Katherine Wheeler, though he liked *Kate* better, had been telling the truth. She now owned the house.

"Here, he wants to talk with you."

Kate's little smile grated on Brody's nerves. So she hadn't been lying. *Big whoop.* The fact that one female had the ability to tell the truth should make him happy, but he couldn't stop the unsettled feeling that something wasn't right. How did Pete Kinsey fit into this?

"Everything seems to be in order. I still have questions."

"I'm sure you do, Sheriff, but first things first. Release Mrs. Wheeler. There's no need for her still to be in your custody."

Brody wasn't so sure about that. He couldn't deny Kate's name appeared on the copies of her late husband's will and the deed to the house. She had every right to walk freely away and go about her life, yet he hesitated.

Mentally, he reviewed what he knew: Kate Wheeler's husband had been murdered, she'd inherited the Kinsey home. According to the paper faxed to him by the lawyer, the L.A.P.D. was investigating Paul's death but had yet to produce a suspect. All in all, the lawyer had supplied Brody with more information than required.

Legally, Brody had no reason to hold Kate, but it didn't sit well just to let her walk out. His protective impulses demanded he take her back to the house himself. For crying out loud, the woman had been terrified that someone was out to kill her, too.

Brody glanced at the blank computer and fervently wished the contraption hadn't gone on the blink. He would have liked to gather a bit more unbiased information.

Into the phone, Brody said crisply, "Mrs. Wheeler is free to go. I assume I can count on you to answer further questions?"

"Of course, Sheriff. Always happy to cooperate with the authorities."

The veiled sarcasm in Thomas's voice rang clear. Brody's hand tightened on the receiver. "I'll be in touch."

As soon as he'd put the receiver back in the cradle, Kate piped up. "I told you I owned the place. You should have given me the benefit of the doubt."

He slanted her a sideways glance. "Just doing my job, Mrs. Wheeler."

"I thought people were considered innocent until proven guilty?"

"Not in any reality I know." Brody's mouth quirked with a self-effacing grimace.

He'd been young and idealistic enough once to believe in the system, to believe that good triumphed over evil, that right always won out in the end, and that justice for all wasn't selective. But it was and he'd spent his adult life dedicated to making sure the innocent received their justice.

"But that's how it's supposed to work."

"*Supposed to* being the operative phrase."

Emotions flickered across Kate's face—anger and a touch of sadness. The impulse to take her into his arms and hold her until only joy reflected in the depths of her green eyes rose up sharply. He clenched his jaw. Been down that road. Not going again.

She shook her head. "This isn't the way God planned it, you know."

Her words poked at an old wound. He raised a brow. "What makes you think God gives a rip?"

Little creases appeared between her brows. "Because the alternative is unthinkable. Without God, there's no hope. Without hope, what's the point?"

"The point is to make it through each day." Refusing to let slip any of the betrayal he felt, he kept his voice neutral. "And if you live to see another day, you make it through that one."

"That's not living."

He shrugged. "It's surviving."

"That's missing out on all that God has to offer."

Her earnest expression tugged at him, but he could never forget or forgive. "Yeah, like heartache and pain. No, thanks."

"Who hurt you, Sheriff?"

The sincerity in her quietly asked question hit him in the chest like the business end of a nightstick. No way was he going to open up to her. No way was he going to allow anyone close again.

"I've seen more than my share of heartache and pain."

Compassion and skepticism warred in her eyes. Tension coiled in his veins. The moment she decided to let it go he released a concentrated breath.

Amusement entered her gaze. "Havensport doesn't exactly seem like crime central."

"Normally, it's not. You're the most excitement this town has seen in a while."

An auburn brow arched. "Oh, really."

Heat crept up his neck. *Real smooth, boyo.*

She was exciting in a dangerous way that had nothing to do with the law and everything to do with attraction. Not a good thing.

He cleared his throat. "I meant the breaking and entering."

Kate smiled and his gaze snagged on the cute little dimple in the middle of her chin. What would she do if he kissed her there?

His expression must have given away his thoughts because her smile faltered and a blush deepened the contours of her cheeks. She didn't look away.

"I'm sorry I scratched you."

Back to business, McClain. Forget about kisses. Kisses only led to betrayal.

"Are you ready to tell me what had you so scared?"

She lifted her delectable chin. "May I leave now?"

She was a tough little cookie. He liked that. "Come on, I'll take you back."

"I'll walk, thanks," she replied and headed for the door.

"I'll drive you."

With her hand on the doorknob, she glanced over her shoulder. "It's not that far."

"Doesn't matter, I'm taking you back."

With her hands on her hips, she glared at him. "I'm perfectly capable of seeing myself to my house."

She was beautiful with her face framed by red curls and those green eyes sparking with fire. He had no intention of getting burned no matter how beguiling the flame.

"Are you always this stubborn?"

"You're the one being stubborn," she declared with a huff.

She reminded him of a rookie cop with a chip on her shoulder. "Humor me, okay? Let me do my job and take you back to your house."

She regarded him steadily for a moment. "All right, fine. Do your job." She opened the door and walked out.

Brody picked up a fax data form and wrote out a request for information on the investigation of Paul Wheeler's murder. He dialed in the number for the L.A.P.D. and sent the fax. He turned to go and his gaze landed on Kate's purse sitting on the floor next to his desk.

Her wallet still rested on the desktop. He picked it up. Maybe it was curiosity, maybe instinct, but instead of returning the wallet to the purse, he flipped it open. Plastic sheaths of photos, including her ID, separated the two halves. One side was lined with credit cards, gold and platinum. The other side held her checkbook.

He thumbed through the photos, a knot forming in his chest as his mind registered what he saw. There was a picture of Kate in a white wedding dress standing beside a tall, blond man. There was a photo of an older woman who he guessed to be her mother. Another picture of an older man in military uniform. Another less formal picture of the blond man. Brody slipped the picture out of the plastic. On the back, someone, Kate he presumed, had written the name Paul and the date of when the photo had been taken.

Brody tucked the picture into his shirt pocket. One question had been answered, but now he had others. He wondered how much Kate knew. And if she didn't know? Dread crept up his spine. He didn't want to be the one to tell her. But it looked like he had no choice.

Stepping out into the morning sunshine, Brody found Kate waiting on the sidewalk, her arms akimbo and one Italian-loafer-clad foot tapping. His mouth twisted. She was doing a bang-up job of looking like a woman used to getting what she wanted, when she wanted it, but the effort she was putting into the display made him think it wasn't her usual M.O.

The brief summer storm left the air with a crisp freshness. But the telltale signs of raindrops still beading on his car reminded Brody of the night before and of what Kate would find when she went back to the house. He stopped in his tracks.

"Kate?"

She looked over her shoulder at him, her steps slowing to a halt and her brows drawn together. "Now what?"

"Did you get everything?"

Her brows rose. "I didn't bring anything."

"This, maybe?" He held up her purse.

She snatched it from him. "Thanks," she mumbled.

She wouldn't be thanking him when he told her what he'd discovered. With a pleasureless twist of his lips, he followed her to his cruiser and held open the passenger-side door. She gave him a tight smile and slid in.

As he headed the car down Main Street, he tried to formulate the best way of saying what needed to be said. But every time he tried to tell her, he couldn't get the words to form.

"Okay, out with it."

"Excuse me?"

Kate sighed. "You obviously have something on your mind. You've looked like a fish out of water ever since we got in the car."

He slanted her a glance. "And how is that, exactly?"

"You keep opening your mouth to say something, then shutting it tight." Kate demonstrated with exaggerated movements.

Brody's rich laughter filled the cab of the car. Kate sucked in a breath. She liked the sound of his laugh: deep and warm…and inviting. She forced the thought away. She couldn't let down her guard no matter how pleasing she found the sheriff.

"So, what is it?"

Brody sobered, his expression turning grim. A sense of impending doom filled Kate. What could he possibly have to say that would warrant such a reaction? Nothing, she decided, now that they'd determined she wasn't going to be arrested.

"How long were you married to your…late husband?"

She frowned. "Four years."

"How do you know Pete Kinsey was his business partner?"

That seemed like an odd question. "Paul told me after I found an invoice for a piece of office equipment. It had Kinsey's name on it."

He slanted her a quick glance. "You never met Pete Kinsey?"

She hated the pinprick of hurt needling her. "No. I didn't even know about him until a year ago. Paul hadn't invited anyone he worked with to our wedding."

He didn't comment, as his hands gripped and re-gripped the steering wheel.

"Why?"

He shrugged, then asked, "How well did you know Paul?"

An even odder question.

"As well as one could, I suppose. Paul wasn't your open and friendly type." Thinking back over the course of their relationship, she wondered how she'd missed his coldness in the beginning. Or had he been just that good at hiding it?

"He changed from when you first met him?"

Unnerved that he'd practically read her thoughts, she replied, "Yes, he did."

"He traveled a lot."

It wasn't a question. "Yes. How did you know?"

Without answering, Brody slowed the vehicle and turned down the narrow dirt drive leading to the house.

In the bright morning sun, the cottage-style home and surrounding area held a charming appeal. A far cry from her impression last night. The blue-gray shingles, quaint dormer windows edged in white, and the wraparound porch were very welcoming. The shrubs and foliage of the yard held a certain rustic charm. And beyond the bungalow, the beach and frothy waves of the Atlantic Ocean gleamed in the sunlight. It was very picturesque and soothing.

Kate wished she'd been able to arrive in the light of day rather than the dead of a stormy night. The late flight out of L.A. and the subsequent drive to Havensport had made her arrival untimely.

She regretted she hadn't rented a car instead of arranging for ground transportation. But at the time it seemed the best thing since she hadn't a clue where she was going. Last night, the driver had dropped her off without so much as waiting to see if she'd made it in the house okay, leaving her stranded without any way to get around.

Brody parked and got out. Just as Kate opened the door, he was there offering her his help. She laid her hand in his. Warmth spread up her arm and around her heart. She hadn't felt anything but coldness in so long.

Quickly, she disengaged from him and stepped away. "You didn't answer my question."

"And what question was that?"

She put her hands on her hips. "How did you know Paul traveled?"

Brody ran a hand through his dark hair. She watched the motion with a good dose of curiosity. How would his hair feel beneath her hand? Uncomfortable with the course of her thoughts, she averted her gaze and concentrated on the unseen bird singing from high in the large birch tree to the right of the house.

"I knew your husband."

Snapping to attention, she frowned. "You did?" Wariness coiled tight in her chest. She looked at the house and tried to rationalize how they could have met. "He did own the house even if Pete Kinsey lived here. They were business partners, after all."

"Not partners, exactly."

Apprehension chilled her skin like a cold wind. "Meaning?"

Brody shifted his feet in a restless gesture before saying, "You see, your husband and Pete Kinsey were, well…"

"Yes?"

"Man." His hard jaw tensed. "I'm botching this up."

The wind turned into a full-blown hurricane. Could he have the answers she sought? "What? What should I know?"

Locking his gaze with hers, Brody stated, "They were the same man."

FOUR

She didn't know what she'd expected, but it certainly wasn't something as ridiculous as that. Relief and disappointment made her laugh. "Excuse me?"

"Paul Wheeler and Pete Kinsey were the same person."

She couldn't see any humor in his expression, any mirth glinting in his dark eyes, but she couldn't believe he was serious. "What kind of joke are you trying to play on me, Sheriff?"

"It's no joke."

"Oh, come on." She gave a nervous laugh. "You can't expect me to believe…that…my husband led some sort of…double life."

Brody shrugged. "Believe what you will. The facts speak for themselves."

"What facts?"

Shifting his weight to his left leg, Brody asked, "Was Paul tall, about six feet, with gray eyes and blond hair?"

Mutely, she nodded.

"So was Pete Kinsey."

She scoffed. "Those are your facts?"

Brody's mouth tightened. "Pete Kinsey had a tattoo."

Kate's eyes narrowed. "So?"

"Did Paul?"

"A lot of people have tattoos."

"On their left shoulder?"

Her mouth went dry. "Maybe."

"Shall I describe it to you, Kate?" he asked, gently.

She shrugged and turned away, not liking what she was hearing, what he was insinuating.

"A small broken match."

Her stomach churned. "Tattoos aren't trademarked, Sheriff." She glanced at him and his look told her he thought she was grasping at straws and soon the whole haystack was going to collapse.

"Did you ever go with your husband when he traveled?"

"No. I have my own career to think about."

She almost groaned as the words left her mouth. The bank. This trip put her job, her career, in jeopardy, but she'd needed to take a leave of absence to find the answers to Paul's death. The not knowing was driving her nuts.

And standing here arguing about something this far-fetched wasn't helping her accomplish anything. "Really, Sheriff. I think you should go. Your job here's done."

"Do you know where he went, Kate?"

She rolled her eyes. "His work took him all over the globe."

"And what work was that?"

"He was a financial consultant."

Brody nodded. "He came to the Cape every Fourth of July."

She couldn't say where Paul had gone for sure, and she'd always wondered why he'd work over that holiday. But what the sheriff was saying couldn't be true. Paul was cold, selfish maybe, but he wasn't…

She was about to say he wasn't dishonest, but she knew in her heart that whatever Paul had been mixed up in, it hadn't had anything to do with honesty. But could he have led a double life? No. She would have known, sensed something. Wouldn't she have?

"Goodbye, Sheriff."

He held out a photo. "This is the man I know as Pete Kinsey."

She took the photo, instantly recognizing it. "You must be mistaken."

"I'm not."

She looked up into his eyes and noticed the way a thin, lighter blue ring circled the near-black irises, reminding her of the wind-tossed ocean off the Pacific Northwest coast. The sheriff had no reason to lie to her. But this just couldn't be, her mind insisted. Paul was many things, but was he capable of this kind of deceit?

And if what the sheriff said was true, what did

that say about her and her judgment? Could she have been that blind? How could she have been married to a man for four years and not know him?

Somewhere inside the house lay the answers. "This doesn't prove anything."

If it were true that Paul had had another existence, then that made her pretty stupid. Stupid for trusting, for believing in her husband. Stupid for trying so hard to save her marriage even after he'd moved out.

"I...it's just not true."

The look of understanding, of pity, that stole over the sheriff's handsome face made her blood boil.

She crumbled the photo into her fist. "You can go now. I don't need or want you here."

His hand closed over hers. Her gaze was drawn to the way his larger, masculine hand enveloped her smaller, more delicate fingers in a protective grip. Her gaze lifted and met his intense look.

His dark eyes simmered. She could easily fall into the blaze that beckoned and allow herself the luxury of soothing warmth.

"Kate." He spoke her name in an oddly hushed tone.

She jerked her hand away, stunned by the connection and longing welling up inside her.

He stepped back, his expression bemused.

Without another word, she fled to the safety of the house. As she reached the porch, she heard him say, "If you need anything, you know where to find me."

Her steps faltered, and slowly she turned around. Yes, she knew where to find the sheriff. For a moment, she allowed herself the indulgence of looking at him. She noticed the way his uniform outlined his masculine shape; broad chest tapering to a trim waist, long, lean legs.

A spark of sunlight caught her attention. Golden rays glinted off his badge, soaked into his dark hair, and caressed his handsome face. Her hand still tingled where he'd touched her.

Absently she rubbed the spot and took a step backwards, as if the more distance she put between them, the easier it would be to forget the odd sensations she'd felt when they'd touched. Animal attraction. Basic human instinct. God had, after all, gifted humans with the ability to connect physically to another. Though she'd never experienced anything this swift and this profound.

The crumbled ball in her hand bit into her palm and her jaw clenched. Regardless of how her hormones responded to this man, she refused to rely on him for help. She had to find out the truth about Paul on her own. "Goodbye, Sheriff."

His expression rueful, he nodded. She watched him stride back to his car and climb in. He waved his hand in a final salute as he turned the car around. Standing rooted to the porch for several seconds after he had disappeared, a deep loneliness crept over her.

She'd been lonely before. The four years of her marriage were the loneliest in her life, but this sudden intense aloneness rocked her because it was desperate and unfamiliar. How could a man have this much effect on her?

Resolutely, she turned her attention to the house. Inside were the answers. She needed to stay focused and not let herself be distracted by the handsome sheriff.

Squaring her shoulders, she went in.

In the daylight, the house didn't hold such a spooky, haunted-house feel as it had the night before. She looked around and moved purposely into the living room.

Built-in shelves lined one wall; big pieces of furniture covered with sheets dotted the large, dark green area rug.

Drawn to the shelves with the framed pictures, her heart throbbed inside her chest. With a shaky hand, she lifted a frame and stared at the picture. Paul smiled up at her, his arm slung carelessly around a buxom blonde. In the background, blue water sparkled in the glistening sun, mocking her with its seductive invitation to partake of the couple's free and easy spirit.

She dropped the picture. It hit the floor at her feet, the glass cracking in two.

Numbness stole through her, surrounding her heart and chilling her soul as she picked up another frame. In this picture, a party by the looks of it, Paul was flanked on either side by recognizable faces. Some celebrities, others political figures.

Grabbing at another frame, she again saw Paul with famous and well-known people. She plucked at another picture and another until her arms were full. *What is going on?*

It wasn't unreasonable that he would know these people in his line of work. After all, he was a consultant for wealthy people. But why hadn't he mentioned he had the kind of relationship with them that was evident in these pictures?

It was clear that all the photos were taken at the beach house. Some even in the very room she stood in. Her throat constricted and tears blurred her vision as bitterness settled around her like a smothering cloak.

Abruptly, she dumped her load onto the couch. A cloud of dust puffed into the air, little bits and pieces floating away and doing nothing but making her sneeze.

Moving in a fog, Kate went from room to room looking at the remains of a life cut short. Of a life she'd known nothing about.

Besides the dust, the rooms were clean, uncluttered and devoid of personality. Guest rooms. She came to the room with the broken window. Before nightfall she'd have to have someone come out and repair the damage. She turned away from the reminder of her terror and continued on.

In what appeared to be the master bedroom, she saw signs of Paul—the scent of his cologne clung to the clothes hanging in the closet, his shirts and undergarments folded with precision in the drawers. She swallowed back the vile taste of betrayal.

She found receipts and notes in the top drawer of the oak dresser. The writing was Paul's, but the signature said Pete Kinsey. She stared at the papers. Pain squeezed her head like a vice. How could she have been so oblivious?

The tremors started deep down inside and quickly worked their way out. She sank to her knees and rested her head against the bed. Sobs clogged her throat and tears burned a salty trail down her cheek. Why had Paul, or Pete or whoever he was, lied? Why had he kept a part of himself from her? Was this other identity the reason he'd been killed?

Her hands curved into fists. Why had he involved her?

Lord, I'm so angry and hurt and confused. This doesn't make sense.

A line of scripture floated through her consciousness. *My presence shall go with you, and I will give you rest.*

Clinging to that promise, she slowly crawled up onto the bed and curled into a ball. So tired, so very tired. Her mind shut down and blessed numbness wrapped around her, taking her away from the hurt and endless parade of lies.

Brody's fingers drummed on the desktop. What was Kate's story? The thought had plagued him since he'd left her at the Kinsey house.

"What's eating at you, boss?" Deputy Teal's voice broke through Brody's thoughts.

"Nothing," he replied, absently.

Nothing, everything…Kate. For more hours than he cared to admit to, Brody had been unable to keep his mind off Kate Wheeler. She'd made her feelings clear. And he was glad. He certainly didn't want to be bothered with a headstrong woman who couldn't accept the truth even when it stared her in the face.

Brody stilled his fingers. He'd wasted enough time today thinking about Kate. She wasn't his problem. She owned the house now, and would eventually realize that what he'd told her was the truth and then she'd go back to where she came from. He nodded to close the subject in his mind, but he couldn't quite banish the nagging terror he'd seen in her eyes.

There were other matters needing his attention. Like the feud still raging between Mr. Haskel and Mr. Moore. The two old codgers each swore that the other was poaching fish. Like you could poach fish from the ocean during fishing season.

He shook his head, knowing that the fighting gave the two widowers something to keep their minds active. Only they sometimes got carried away in their attempts to out-fish each other. On numerous occasions, Brody'd had to settle a dispute over whose fish was whose.

Today it seemed Mr. Haskel had caught Mr. Moore using his lure.

Rolling his chair away from the desk, Brody

heard the crinkling sound of paper caught under the wheels. Teal and his paper basketballs. He bent to retrieve what he assumed would be a stray ball and discovered a sheet of fax paper.

He stared at the contents of the fax for a good thirty seconds before he remembered to take a breath.

He knew it. He just knew it. Below the L.A.P.D. heading, the fax stated that Katherine Wheeler was considered a "person of interest" in the murder investigation of Paul Wheeler and that currently Mrs. Wheeler's whereabouts were unknown and she was being sought.

He hoped they were wrong, but if they weren't…

His lip curled. *He* knew where she was. Sitting back down in his chair, he picked up the phone and called California. The line was picked up on the third ring and after Brody explained to the desk sergeant what he wanted, he was transferred to a Detective Arnez.

"Sheriff, what can I do for you?"

Brody swiped a hand through his hair. "I have information concerning the Wheeler investigation."

"Wheeler. Hold on."

Brody heard the rustling of paper before Arnez came back on the line. "Oh, yeah. Got the file right here. Hey, didn't you request the current status of the investigation earlier today?"

"I did."

"So what's your interest?" Arnez asked.

"I don't have an interest," Brody stated quickly. "I caught a perp breaking and entering last night, only it turned out to be Kate Wheeler."

Arnez's voice perked up. "You've got her in custody?"

Brody frowned. "No...I let her go. Her lawyer faxed over the deed to the house and she's the owner. But... I...know where she is." For a reason he couldn't explain, Brody felt as though he was betraying Kate. But that was ridiculous. If she'd committed a crime, she had to pay the price.

"She's in your town, then?" Arnez asked.

"Yes."

"Hold on."

With his free hand Brody drummed his fingers on the desk again as the detective put him on hold. A tight, wound-up feeling stole over him. Had Kate killed her husband? Would he have to arrest her and send her back to L.A.? Why did his mind rebel against the thought? He shook his head, clearing his thoughts.

Concentrate on the job, McClain, nothing else.

He wouldn't think about her copper-colored curls, her big green eyes. None of that mattered. Nor would he think about the vulnerability in her expression, the feisty spirit that he found so appealing. And he definitely wouldn't think about the little dimple on her chin that even now he longed to kiss.

Arnez came back on the line. "Tell you what,

Sheriff. The powers that be say keep an eye on her. The case is being handed over to the FBI."

"Why the Feds? Thought this was a simple murder investigation."

"Don't have all the details, but seems the hubby had his fingers in a few pies around the country that he shouldn't have. The Feds are playing this close to the vest, so they'll contact you with further instructions. Just keep tabs on the lady."

"Will do." He wouldn't be arresting Kate again just yet, but he could find out what she knew about her husband's dealings.

After he hung up the phone, he delegated the Haskel/Moore situation to Deputy Teal. Brody left the office, walked the short block to his studio apartment where he changed into a fresh uniform and then headed down the main street of Havensport on foot.

Having spent the night and most of the morning at his desk, it felt good to stretch his legs. His hip hurt, but he was used to the biting pain. Welcomed it, in fact, as a reminder of what getting involved with a woman could do. He wasn't going to get involved with Kate Wheeler, he'd keep things strictly business.

Around him, the small town bustled with energy. After the late-summer squall of the night before, people were busy enjoying the sweet freshness left from the rain. The dress shops and specialty stores had their doors wide open inviting the tourists in, the front of the Book Depot was lined with bins of books. He strode by the Java Stand and inhaled the mouthwatering aromas of baked goods and coffee. He smiled and waved at several locals as a sense of belonging swept through him.

Brody surveyed it all with a sense of pride. He loved Havensport and its people. They'd welcomed him openly when he'd run for the position of sheriff. Not that there had been any other candidates, but still, he'd found a place to belong. A place where people didn't look at him with either pity or mockery.

A movement to the right of his peripheral vision drew his gaze.

Sunlight caught fiery sparks on shoulder-length curls as Kate stepped from the grocery store, her arms laden with bags and a black leather purse slung over her slender shoulder.

She wore a simple but fresh-looking white cotton, button-down blouse and blue jeans that hugged her curves. A tension he hadn't realized he held eased in his chest at the sight of her. He couldn't comprehend the strange sensation, didn't know where it was coming from or why. He only knew that on some level he was drawn to her, to her spirit that kindled something deep inside him.

Man, she was beautiful. Not in a classic model way, not the way Elise had been beautiful. No, Kate was the girl-next-door kind of beauty. The type a guy could get cozy with, feel at home with, snuggled up close in front of a roaring fire with, her head resting on his chest... Brody shook off the image. He couldn't let himself fall into that trap. *Keep it pro-fessional, McClain.*

He'd been asked to keep an eye on her and that's what he would do. Nothing more.

The loud screech of tires split the air. A dark blue van barreled down the road toward the mercantile. Abruptly, the vehicle slowed as it neared the shop. The side door slid open and the van halted directly in front of Kate. A man wearing a black ski mask leapt out. His hands closed around Kate's upper arms as he dragged her toward the open door. The bags she held fell to the ground. Milk splattered over the hot pavement, an orange rolled under the van.

Kate's scream ripped Brody's senses apart.

Brody ran with one hand pulling his sidearm from the holster at his hip.

"Stop," he shouted at the top of his lungs.

The masked man paused and looked at him. Killer's eyes. Cold and hard. Brody'd seen eyes like that before. The man who'd killed his father had those same type of eyes.

The frantic motions of the driver, whose face was also obscured by a mask, spurred the first man back into action. Kate struggled against her captor as he continued to drag her toward the vehicle.

Brody raised his weapon. The van's engine roared. Having no other option, Brody planted a warning shot through the side of the van.

The man holding Kate shoved her aside before jumping back into the vehicle just as the van vaulted forward, the tires burning black smoke against the street. The van swerved toward Brody. He dove to the side, his body hitting hard on the sidewalk before he rolled to safety.

Ignoring the explosion of pain in his hip, he raised his weapon, aimed and fired again. A taillight exploded from the impact of his bullet. In frustration, Brody watched the van peel around a corner and disappear.

"Great." He picked himself up off the ground. His hip throbbed, the pain ricocheting down his whole right side. He limped over to Kate.

She sat in the flowerbed in front of the store. The shocked expression on her face didn't hide the terror in her eyes.

Brody painfully hunkered down in front of her. "Kate. Kate, talk to me."

Her gaze lifted. Tears welled in her eyes and her lower lip trembled. "Are they gone?"

"Yes." He gathered her close and helped her to her feet.

"My...my groceries," she whispered, pulling away from him. She bent and picked up the mess lying in the road.

Brody firmly took her hands, stopping her movements. Her body shook violently. Shock was setting in. Brody's gut tightened. She was vulnerable and in need of his protection. He led her to a bench. "Come on, Kate. Over here. Sit down."

"Here, Sheriff." Myrtle Kirby, the mercantile's

owner, handed him a blanket. He wrapped it around Kate's shoulders, his hands lingering, offering comfort.

"Kate, sit here. I'm going to hunt those men down."

"Don't leave." Kate grabbed his hand and held on tightly, her eyes begging him to stay.

Her hand was ice cold. He wanted to pull her close and wrap her in his embrace and tell her everything would be okay. He didn't.

"I'll sit with her, Sheriff," Myrtle volunteered. "But she needs a drink of water after what those nasty men tried to do."

Pulling his hand from Kate's, Brody nodded his thanks to the older woman and watched her walk briskly back inside. Unnerved by Kate's pleading gaze and his own reluctance to leave her, Brody turned his back and paced a few steps away. It was too late to follow the van, anyway. Using the radio attached to his uniform, he contacted Deputy Teal.

"Warren, I want you to get an APB out on a dark blue van." Brody gave the model and make. Not surprisingly, the license plates had been removed.

"Okay, boss. What's up?"

"Occupants attempted to kidnap Kate Wheeler."

"Wow, when did this happen?"

Brody's grip on the radio tightened. "Warren, just do it now."

"Okay, okay."

"Sheriff!" Myrtle cried from the doorway of the little store.

Turning sharply, Brody's heart slammed into his throat. The blanket lay in a heap on the ground and Kate Wheeler was nowhere in sight.

He'd been duped again. So much for the damsel-in-distress routine. He was going to find her and make her talk even if he had to haul her back to jail.

FIVE

Kate kept running despite the stitch in her side.

Run. Run. Run.

Over and over, the single word replayed itself inside her head. Her lungs ached and her muscles burned. And still she ran, her sneakers making a thwacking noise against the still-damp pavement and her purse banging against her side.

The house. She had to get to the house where she could hide and watch, and maybe finally see what it was *they* were after.

With every pounding step, her terror was giving way to anger. Because of Paul and the mess he'd left her in, her life was threatened, her career possibly lost and her heart numbed. To think she'd given four years of her love and her life to him only to have been betrayed so thoroughly. And the betrayal continued, even in his death.

With no sign of the van, she bounded up the porch stairs. Her feet skidded to a halt and she widened her eyes in shock. Wood splintered around the busted lock on the front door. A shiver ran the course of her body.

Idiot, you're too late. You'll never learn the truth.

Kate spun around, her gaze searching the area. No one lurked behind the stand of trees off to the right and the path leading around the house toward the beach lay deserted.

Even the house across the way appeared uninhabited. She seemed to be alone. Should she go in? Should she run back to town? Did it even matter?

She was suddenly overwhelmed with the knowledge that she was alone and so utterly at a loss as to what to do. Were the men inside the house waiting for her? Or had they already come and gone? Her shoulders sagged.

Okay, think. Logic suggested that they'd come and gone. And obviously not found what they were looking for or they wouldn't have tried to kidnap her. She clenched her fists. She wished she knew what she was supposed to have.

She placed her hand over her runaway heart. "Okay…that would mean, for the moment, I'm relatively safe and no closer to answers." She cringed as the last word hung in the salty breeze.

Suddenly, the crash of the ocean was overshadowed with the roar of an engine, the sound of tires eating up the gravel. The hairs on the back of her neck stood up. Kate whirled around, ready to bolt, and nearly fainted with relief at the sight of the sheriff's car as it slid to a halt.

Sheriff McClain leapt out of the vehicle and covered the distance between them in long, angry strides. "Just what do you think you're doing?"

"Don't yell at me."

He visibly reined in his anger, taking a deep breath and slowly exhaling. His too-dark gaze bored into hers. "I told you to stay put."

"I…I just…just couldn't sit there." Didn't he understand? It wasn't in her nature to let life happen. She had to do something, and running for the house was the only thing she could think of.

"What if those men had been here when you arrived?" He made a chopping gesture with his hands. "Did you even think of that?"

"They weren't here."

"But they could have been."

Touched by his concern, she lowered her voice. "But they weren't. They'd already been here and gone."

His eyes narrowed. "How do you know?"

She stepped aside and pointed to the broken lock on the door.

"Oh, man," he muttered.

Striding past her, he inspected the lock. With the tip of his shoe he pushed opened the door while he withdrew his weapon from his holster.

"They aren't here," she repeated.

He shot her a hard look before taking her by the

arm and propelling her back down the stairs to his cruiser.

"What…what are you doing?"

He released her to open the car door. "Calling in a CSI team."

"Don't bother. I seriously doubt they'll find anything useful."

"This a crime scene."

She pinned him with her gaze. "There's no crime if I don't report it."

His mouth twisted. "Consider it already reported."

Exasperated, she spread out her hands. "I couldn't begin to know if anything is missing."

He dipped his chin and gave her a look of disbelief. "You didn't explore the house?"

"A little." She didn't want to confess she'd been so shaken by the revelation of Paul's double life that she'd spent several hours in a stupor before finally shaking it off. To escape the house and its contents, she'd gone for a walk along the ocean before heading into town for supplies.

"I'm not going to have you bring a bunch of people traipsing through here." She jabbed a finger at him, even though deep down she knew she was being ridiculous. She didn't even like the house. "I still have rights, you know."

He gave her a grim smile. "True. You have the right to stay out of the way."

"You are insufferable," she huffed.

One dark brow lifted. "I aim to please, ma'am."

Realizing any more protests would be useless, Kate folded her arms over her chest, leaned against the front end of the car and settled in to wait.

Later, in what felt to Kate like an interminably long time, but which in actuality was two hours, the crime scene investigators had come, done their job and taken whatever information they'd gathered away.

"Satisfied?" Kate asked as Brody rejoined her at the car.

He shrugged. "We'll see. Are you ready to go back in?"

Ready? If she never set foot inside again she'd be happy. But that wasn't to be, so she pushed away from the car. "Let's see what damage has been done."

Careful not to touch the black powder dusted on the door lock and frame, Kate stepped into the living room. The place looked as if a tornado had touched down. The shelves were in disarray, glass littered the rug, white stuffing protruded from the couch and loveseat, and books were strewn about the floor.

Not again. Kate's heart plummeted to her toes. Even though the house had only been in her possession for a short time, she felt violated. The feeling left a bitter taste in her mouth. "Those dirty, rotten…oh!"

She found her nose jammed into the sheriff's broad back. The freshly laundered scent of his brown uniform shirt brought order to the chaos surrounding her.

"Steady there," he said as his hands settled on her shoulders.

He anchored her, made her feel safe. She moved away from him. "Sorry," she mumbled, disconcerted now by her reaction to him.

She preceded him down the hall. Each room looked the same as the living room. Nothing had been left untouched or intact.

Anger grew with each breath she took. How dare those men tear apart what was left of Paul's life? It wasn't fair. But then again, it wasn't fair of Paul to involve her in his shady dealings.

She shuddered to think what would have happened had she been here when the men had come in. She wouldn't have thought it possible, but she was suddenly very grateful she'd spent the night in jail. If she hadn't, she wouldn't now have the sheriff's protection.

"Kate, what were they looking for?"

His sudden question forced her thoughts to focus. "I…I don't know."

Her mind toyed with telling him of Paul's dying words, but the memory of the suspicion in the L.A.P.D. detective's eyes stopped her cold. That man hadn't believed her, had even insinuated that she'd killed Paul. Would the sheriff react the same way?

"Look, Kate. Until you level with me, I can't help you."

Help. The word conjured up a sense of welcomed relief. But how far should she trust this man?

Granted, he'd saved her life and he seemed sincerely concerned, but was that enough? Would he believe her? "Sheriff McClain…"

"Brody," he said, his voice low and husky.

She ducked her head as heat rose in her cheeks and a smile curved her lips. "All right then…Brody." For the life of her, she didn't understand her reaction. She was blushing like a fourteen-year-old.

The hallway became too confining, the sheriff too close and big. Needing some distance, she stepped past Brody and walked back into the living room. Glass crunched beneath her shoes, the sound echoed in her heart.

Behind her, she could feel Brody's presence like a buffer from the storm. She realized she wanted to trust him, to confide in him the horror of finding Paul's body, the terror of not knowing why or from whom she was in danger.

"Kate, talk to me. Tell me what's going on."

Suddenly cold, she wrapped her arms around herself. "I honestly don't know what's happening." She turned to look at him. The heat in his eyes could warm her. "It seems you were right about Paul being Pete Kinsey."

Contrition filled Brody's face. "I'm sorry you had to find out like this."

"Me, too." Kate bent to pick up a torn photo. She stared at her husband. Who had he really been? "I found him."

Brody stepped closer. "What?"

Tears blurred her vision. The image in the photo swam out of focus. "After they...hurt him. I...I found him."

"Who are they?" Brody's gently asked question came from very near her shoulder.

She shook her head. She didn't have the answer to that question. "He...he told me I was in danger. He...he said...he—" A sob clogged her throat.

Warm hands descended to her shoulders and slowly turned her around. "Who are they?" he repeated.

"I don't know," she whispered to the front of his shirt.

The slight pressure of his hand raising her chin sent tremors rippling over her skin. She sucked in a sharp breath when she met his gaze. Deep in the depths of his eyes, just beyond his concern, lurked suspicion. Kate saw it, acknowledged it and hated it. She had to make him believe in her.

"Brody, I don't know what Paul was involved in. I don't know why he was killed or...or who's after me."

His expression shifted slightly, became colder, more remote.

Almost desperately, Kate tried again. "You...you've got to listen to me." She fisted her hand in his shirt. "I want answers just as badly as you do. Don't you see...it's my life that's in danger? Do you really think if I knew who'd killed Paul...I wouldn't tell the police?"

For the briefest of seconds his eyes flickered with indecision. She grasped on to a moment of hope.

"Please…please believe me."

She didn't understand when it had become so important that he believe her, but suddenly it was. God had brought Brody into her life and if Brody, who seemed so sure of himself, so confident and secure, could believe in her, then surely she'd be able to get out of the predicament that Paul's death had left her in.

Brody stepped away from her and her heart nearly crumbled. His demeanor turned rigid and unbending. "I'd like to believe you, Kate. But somehow your words don't ring completely true. You're hiding something. I'd like to know what."

Disappointment rolled in, but she refused to give it any ground. Instead, she shifted the conversation. "I haven't thanked you for saving me today."

His gaze narrowed. "Why did you need saving?"

She clenched her jaw, controlling the rising exasperation. "I don't know, but I'm thankful you were there."

"Doing my job."

"No, it was more than that. You were at the right place at the right time."

He shrugged. "Coincidence."

"I don't believe in coincidence. God put you where you needed to be."

Brody moved to the door with a frown etched in

his forehead. "I'll have someone come out and fix that lock."

She allowed him to dodge her statement. He clearly didn't want to go there. She stepped to the door and touched the bent metal. "I don't think replacing the lock will stop them from coming back."

"No. It won't." His dark, intense gaze bored into her. "Kate, I—"

"Look, Sheriff." She cut him off, resigned to not having his trust or his help. "Your job here's done. You can go."

He stared at her for a long, taut moment, then nodded and left, leaving Kate alone again. Disappointment twisted around her like ivy vines, almost choking her, but she shoved the disappointment away. She couldn't rely on him.

She leaned against the closed, broken door and wished she'd never come to Havensport looking for answers. But without the answers, the unknown would always haunt her and keep her from the things she needed most: peace and security.

"No," she cried to the empty house and kicked the door with her heel.

She refused to give in to defeat. She'd seen what allowing despair and hopelessness did to her mother. No way was she going to let it happen to her.

Take charge was Kate's motto. Don't let life happen to you, make it happen *for* you.

She pushed away from the door and stormed into the living room. Who needed the sheriff anyway?

She certainly didn't. She'd find the truth on her own. She'd prove to him that she was innocent even if it killed her.

She snorted. It just might.

A chill zigzagged down her back. Quickly she spun around, half expecting to see two masked men come bursting through the broken door. No one was there.

She needed to find a weapon, something with which to defend herself with if they did return.

In the kitchen, she found a large carving knife and then headed for the living room.

Staring at the shambles the intruders had left in their wake, she wondered what they'd been looking for. And why hadn't they found it?

The chaos surrounding her made her edgy. She didn't like it when life wasn't in order. It drove her nuts not to have one plus two equal three.

And nothing had been adding up since she'd walked into their apartment and discovered Paul.

Kate laid the knife on a side table next to a brass lamp and pushed the stuffing back into the gaping hole in the middle of the navy-and-white striped couch.

Why couldn't Brody have given her the benefit of the doubt?

She punched the stuffing, the rough fiber rasping against her fist.

Why had he, like the other detective, assumed she had something to do with Paul's murder?

She slammed her fist into the material again, leaving a dent. Flopping back onto the couch, she acknowledged the pent-up adrenaline still pumping through her veins.

Calm down. Take deep breaths. Imagine yourself on a tropical sandy beach.

The self-talk wasn't working. Her muscles were bunched and wound tight. Her heart still beat faster than normal and her jaw ached, giving testimony to the headache brewing.

Sudden footsteps on the stairs broke the stillness of the house.

She sprang up from the couch and swiped the knife off the table.

The footsteps trailed across the porch and approached the door.

Renewed adrenaline flooded through Kate. Blood roared in her ears.

The masked men had returned.

She positioned herself beside the door. Knife ready, she held her breath and waited for the intruder to burst in.

A loud knock reverberated against the wood.

"Who is it?" she barked.

"McClain."

She released a compressed breath and relaxed her stance. Still cautious, she opened the door a crack and peered out.

The sheriff indeed stood there.

Ignoring the ridiculous surge of pleasure, Kate stated flatly, "I thought you'd left."

Brody's expression turned serious. "Until those men are caught, you're under my protection."

"So you're here because it's part of your job," Kate stated. Why did that thought irritate her?

He gave her a bland look. "Yes, Kate, protecting you is part of my job." He inclined his head toward the door. "May I?"

Kate pulled her bottom lip between her teeth. She wanted to say no, go away. She'd already decided she didn't need him or his protection, yet deep inside a little voice whispered, *let him do his job.* Kate opened the door wider and stepped aside.

Brody stepped into the entryway and Kate noticed how much space he took up. It seemed as if the very air around him expanded and grew with the force of his presence. The house didn't seem lonely with him there.

Kate stifled a laugh at her own absurdity.

"Get your things together."

She gaped. "Excuse me?"

"You can't stay here. Myrtle has an empty room she'll let you stay in."

Annoyed at his high-handedness, she huffed. "I'm not leaving."

"Look, you can't stay here." His gaze narrowed to dark, intimidating slits as he closed the distance between them.

Engulfed by his nearness, her pulse accelerated.

She knew the rush of sensation whizzing through her had nothing to do with fear and everything to do with him as a man. An attractive man. She swallowed hard.

In a sudden movement, he clutched her wrist and held her arm upright.

The carving knife glinted between them, bringing reality sharply into focus.

SIX

Mortification flushed through Kate. Her gaze darted to his and locked on. He arched a dark brow. He knew. In the swirling dark depths of his eyes, she saw the thread connecting the knife she now held to the weapon used in Paul's murder.

Deftly, he took possession of the weapon.

"I...I had to defend my...myself. I didn't...you left." She decided the best defense was a good offense. "You left. I was alone. I reached for the first thing that came to mind."

"Interesting that a knife should come to mind."

Kate flinched. "What else was I to do? Those men could've come back and you weren't here."

"I was here, Kate. Just outside."

Her heart gave a little lurch. He hadn't left her. "But I didn't know that."

He nodded slightly, before stepping past her to the dining table where he laid the knife down. "You know a knife isn't a good weapon for anyone, let alone a woman to use," he said, conversationally. "Too easy for it to be taken away and used against you." He met her gaze. "For future reference."

Unnerved by that little tidbit, she frowned. "Look, Sheriff McClain. I…"

"Brody."

He leaned against the table and folded his arms across his chest. His cotton uniform shirt stretched over defined biceps emphasizing his physical strength. She swallowed against the longing to have those solid arms wrapped around her, shielding her from danger. Uncomfortable with her thoughts, as well as once again being given permission to use his first name, she began again. "Brody. I didn't kill my husband."

"Then why did you run from L.A.?"

She frowned, feeling somehow that she was walking into a trap. "I didn't run."

"Weren't you informed that you shouldn't leave town?"

"Well…yes. I mean…right after it happened, that detective told me to stick close to home in case they had more questions. But…that was forever ago. Surely I don't need to still be there."

"You're considered a person of interest in the case and until you're exonerated from the investigation, you should've stayed put."

"I didn't know." That must have been why Gordon had advised her not to leave.

"So what *do* you know?"

"Nothing. I know nothing." *I told them you have it, Kate. Trust no one.*

She'd tried to trust the police in L.A. That had gotten her nowhere. Detective Arnez and his insinuations left her feeling totally stranded.

All right, Mrs. Wheeler. You meet your husband with divorce papers in hand. He's not so anxious to sign. Maybe doesn't want to give you everything you're asking for. You get angry, maybe even a little nuts. You grab a knife and stab him to death.

Kate blinked up at the detective in horror. *No, that didn't happen.*

Oh, come on now. It happens all the time. The wifey gets hacked and then hacks the hubby.

I want my lawyer. Kate stared at the cold metal table then up at the mirrored wall. *I want my lawyer.*

Yeah, yeah. I know. He's coming.

Kate closed her eyes to the scene, trying to block out the bitter taste of the detective's suspicion. It wasn't fair. She'd done everything right. She hadn't touched anything save Paul and the phone. She'd called 911. Why did everyone want her to be guilty?

A tear leaked from the corner of her eye and trickled down her cheek. The roughened pad of Brody's finger glided across her skin and caught the tear.

Kate's eyes snapped open at the unexpected contact. In hypnotic fascination, she watched him rub the wetness between his index finger and thumb. A shiver traipsed down her spine, leaving her breathless.

She met his dark, smoldering gaze. Her knees loosened, and her breathing turned shallow. His full lips drew her gaze.

Abruptly, Brody stepped back. Cooling air filled the space between them. Like a door slammed shut, Brody's eyes became shuttered and his expression closed, unreadable. He spun on his heel and strode into the living room.

Kate sagged against the table. What had just happened?

She forced her breathing to a slow inhale and exhale. No. No. No. She wouldn't allow herself to be attracted to him. No way, no how. Attraction, emotions, feelings. They were distractions that would only keep her from finding the truth.

The tips of her fingers grazed the sharp edge of the knife lying on the table. She jerked away and stared at the prism of light reflecting off the blade. The sheriff didn't believe her.

The man had nearly accused her of murder.

But he'd trusted her enough to leave the knife lying unguarded, and she couldn't deny the yearning inside to lean on him. None of it made sense. She'd never reacted to a man in such a manner before, not even Paul.

She loathed the chaos going on inside her head, twisting up her emotions, making her see things in the sheriff's eyes that couldn't possibly be there.

She forced her feet to move, to carry her to the living room where Brody was stacking the ruined picture frames. His fingers carefully picked through the glass and debris.

Maybe if she concentrated on the chaos of the house and put it in order the rest would follow suit. With purposeful steps she headed to the bookshelf.

"Did you grow up in L.A.?"

Brody's causally asked question grabbed her attention. "No. I grew up in a small town in Washington state."

Brody nodded. "I've never been to that side of the country. I imagine it's beautiful."

"Yes, it is." She started picking up books from the floor. "A beauty that I'd never appreciated until I'd moved to southern California."

"Is that where you met Paul?"

"Is this an interrogation?" she countered tightly.

When no reply came, Kate glanced up to find Brody's intense gaze locked on her.

"No, Kate. I was just curious."

"Oh." She smiled sheepishly. "Sorry."

Brody began picking up the strewn magazines off the floor. "What took you to L.A.?"

"School."

"Where?"

She smoothed the pages of a hardback fiction book. "I received a scholarship to UCLA."

"That's a long way from home." Brody bent to pick up a rectangle of paper from the floor.

She shrugged and watched his blunt fingers rub the edge of a business card. "It got me away from my mother and gave me a purpose. Something to work towards."

He tucked the card into the front pocket of his shirt. "Why did you want to get away from your mother?"

She reached for another book. "My mother…has problems."

There was a moment of silence and Kate was glad he didn't ask for more about her mother.

Brody righted a chair. "Do your parents still live in that small town?"

Kate paused as she reached for more books. "My mother does. My father is retired in Florida."

"Divorce?"

Nodding, she picked up more books and arranged them on the shelf. Maybe if she opened up and let him see who she was, then maybe she could win his trust. "I was fifteen when my father walked out."

"That's rough," Brody commented softly.

"You have no idea." She couldn't quite keep the bitterness out of her voice.

"Messy, huh?" Compassion filled Brody's tone.

"My father was career military. Special Ops. Onward and upward was his motto. Mom and I got tired of the constant moving. Mom pleaded with him to take a post in one place long enough for me to complete high school. His solution was to leave us behind."

"Must have been hard on you."

She shrugged, belying the hurt of her father's desertion. "Not as hard as it was on Mom."

"Meaning?"

She swallowed back the bitterness, the anger directed at her father, at his dedication to the job. "My mom spent so many years living in fear of losing Dad. Years of finding him gone in the middle of the night on some mission, never knowing if he'd return and if he did would he be hurt? When dad finally bugged out, Mom slipped into a deep depression and found solace in the bottle."

The compassion in Brody's eyes sent her heart pounding against her ribs. "I'm sorry, Kate."

With a shrug she dismissed his sympathy. "Yeah, well. I tried to pick someone unlike my father. Someone safe. Risk-free. I mean, how much more stable and normal could I get than a financial consultant?" She laughed at the irony. "Look where that got me."

"Some risks you can't foresee."

"Right." She tracked Brody's movement to the couch. His hand traced the dent in the stuffing left by her fist. Goose bumps raised along her flesh. What would his caress feel like?

She rubbed her arms and pushed the ridiculous question away. "And you, Brody? You a native of Havensport?"

"No."

The one-word answer conjured up a ton of questions, but Kate didn't ask. She didn't want to know this man, didn't want to get too close and start to care. She might not be able to foresee all risks, but there were some risks she could avoid.

"What do you plan to do with this place?" he asked.

She thought about that. She certainly wouldn't be living here, her life was back in L.A. and keeping it as a vacation home didn't seem right. She doubted she'd ever relax here. This was Paul's, not hers. "I'll sell it."

He nodded and made a sweeping gesture with his hand. "And all this stuff?"

"Box it up and give it away. I don't want any of it."

"Sounds like a plan. We can get some boxes from the mercantile." He glanced at his watch. "Let's get you settled at Myrtle's first. We can deal with this tomorrow."

Though she was grateful for his willingness to help, she wondered what he saw as he stared at her with his dark, hooded eyes. Could he see her wounded heart? Did he realize how difficult this all was for her? Could she handle compassion from a guy like him?

Only one thing to do. Shore up her defenses against any compulsion to lean on him. She'd get through this. God would help her.

She lifted her purse from the floor by the front door. As she left the little bungalow by the ocean, she wished she could as easily leave the past behind.

It would be a long while before she could put

Paul's memory to rest. She only hoped she didn't end up following him into the grave.

Myrtle's white lap-sided house with its weathered cedar-shingled overhang sat on a side street right off Main Street. An easy walk from the mercantile store and not far from the sheriff's station. An old Stars and Stripes hung from a pole on the corner of the house. The front door opened and Myrtle stepped out to greet Brody and Kate as they neared the porch.

"Oh, you sweet thing, I was so worried about you." Myrtle slipped an arm around Kate and drew her into the small two-bedroom home.

Brody followed them in and set Kate's suitcases near the door. Amused, he watched color flood Kate's cheeks. He'd been on the receiving end of Myrtle's good-natured mothering before. Watching the gray-haired woman hover over Kate made him think of his own mother.

He made a mental note to call home to check on her and see what trouble his siblings were in because there was always some crisis going on.

"You nearly gave me a heart attack today, young lady," Myrtle gently admonished as she led Kate to the overstuffed flowery couch in the small living room.

Light from the smoldering fire in the stone fireplace caught in Kate's hair and made her curls shine like a bright new penny. She had the grace to look contrite. "I'm sorry. I never meant to alarm you."

"Well, it's a good thing our dear sheriff was able to find you. Whatever made you take off like that?" Myrtle gave her a pointed look, her gently lined face stern, yet concern shone in her intelligent gray eyes.

This should be interesting. Brody arched a brow, waiting for Kate's answer.

Kate slanted him a quick glance. "I wanted to see if I could find out what those men were after."

Brody's jaw clenched. So, she hadn't been running to the house for safety like he'd first thought. Didn't she have any idea how much danger she could have been in?

But then again, maybe she was lying. Maybe she'd planned this whole event to throw suspicion off herself, to cover up the fact that she'd killed her husband. The possibility tied his insides up in knots.

There was something about her. Maybe it was the way she spoke about God with such conviction that made him want to believe her.

He rubbed his chin, ignoring the sick feeling settling in the pit of his stomach. She'd gained a measure of his trust after the attempted kidnapping, but the small grain of trust receded to nothing more than a speck as a strange sense of déjà vu seeped into his bones.

He'd been down this road before and he wouldn't make the same mistake he'd made with Elise. Her innocence had been a sham he'd too easily bought and paid the price for.

Kate's words about God could be just that. Words.

"What *were* those men after, Kate?" he asked, hoping to catch her off guard.

She started at his question, a flash of…something in her expression. Guilt? "I don't know."

"So you've said." His gut told him she was hiding something. His wariness grew, but he was a patient man. Time would reveal the truth. The best way to keep an eye on her was to keep her with him.

But he resisted the idea.

He still had a town to serve and he'd made it a policy years ago not to take civilians on calls. He'd learned the hard way what horrors could be witnessed. The dangers the unsuspecting could be made to suffer or, worse yet, the distraction that could cost a life. She'd be safe with Myrtle. Moving to the door, he said, "Ladies, I'll return later to see how you're doing."

Kate shook her head. "That won't be necessary. You've done your job here. I can manage."

"Just the same. I'll be back."

She shrugged and turned away.

As he left Myrtle's, he decided to have Warren camp out front, in case Kate's kidnappers returned or she decided to run.

A little voice in his head warned him not to be surprised if she did take off. Kate was a woman who had secrets. Was her innocent routine an act? Did she have something to do with her husband's death? Who were the men who'd tried to grab her? Did she have ties to them?

He thought about the story she'd told of her father and the reason she'd married Paul. She'd claimed to want a safe, risk-free life. Yet she'd come clear across the country to find answers about her husband's death.

It seemed to him the safe, risk-free thing for her to do would be to sit back and let the authorities do their job. She was a puzzle he'd like to solve.

So many questions. No answers. Yet. Waiting and watching was the key. She'd trip herself up eventually. Then he'd know whether she was a good actress or an innocent victim.

Too bad he didn't know which to hope for.

"Here, dear. Make yourself at home," Myrtle showed Kate to the spare bedroom. "If you need anything, let me know."

Grateful for the older woman's kindness, Kate smiled. "Thank you so much. I hope I'm not imposing."

Myrtle waved a hand. "Oh, please. Not at all."

The jingle of the phone drew Myrtle away, leaving Kate alone in the small room with a colorful patchwork quilt covering the full-size bed and a dark oak dresser against one wall.

Everything about Myrtle's house was warm and comforting. Very much like Kate's memories of her grandmother. Antiques and lace doilies, things that spoke of a different era, made Kate long for the simplicity of being with her maternal grandmother, the only person whose love she'd never doubted.

On some level, she knew her parents loved her. She was their only child. But her father had been devoted to his career, her mother to her father, then to the bottle. When her husband had left, Constance Hyde had slowly slipped into alcoholic oblivion, leaving Kate feeling helpless and insecure.

Helpless. Insecure.

Feelings she'd fought and had thought she'd conquered. She was an independent woman with an upwardly mobile career that had prestige and responsibility and she'd once had a dream husband.

But that was the problem. Paul had been a dream, an illusion, and she'd been so blind. Looking for the fairy-tale ending of happily ever after that now she suspected didn't really exit. Her parents certainly hadn't found it and neither had she.

Wanting to do something productive to stop her depressing thoughts, Kate went in search of Myrtle. She found her in the living room, just finishing her phone call.

"Myrtle, would the mercantile have empty boxes I could have?" Now was as good a time as any to box up Paul's life.

"Of course, dear." Myrtle smiled. "Let's walk over there."

As they left the house, Kate noticed a sheriff's car parked down the street. The car was slightly different than the one Brody drove and she could see

Deputy Teal behind the wheel. So Brody was having her watched. For protection or because he didn't trust her?

She wouldn't waste her time trying to figure out his motives.

They walked the three blocks to the mercantile. Kate liked the quaint town with its rustic charm and sleepy pace. There were no rushing cars or hurrying pedestrians too busy even to smile as they passed by. The few cars on the street rolled by slowly and the spattering of foot traffic moved at a sedate pace. Kate inhaled the salty scent of the ocean and listened to the soothing sound of the waves.

Life in Havensport seemed uncomplicated and tranquil. She longed for the peace of such a life.

At the mercantile, she gathered up several empty boxes. Myrtle arranged to have the boxes delivered and left on the porch of Kate's cottage. Then as they walked back toward Myrtle's, Kate had an idea. "Would you mind if I walk over to the bank?"

Concern crinkled at the corners of Myrtle's eyes. "You'll be careful?"

"Yes," she replied. She wouldn't be caught unaware again.

"Don't be long, dear. I'll fix us something to eat."

They separated and Kate headed toward the First National Bank. In the style of most of Havensport, the bank had cedar shingles that had been stained to a red-gold color. Baskets of multicolored flowers hung from the large roof overhang. Inside, plush beige carpeting, soothing peach-colored walls and gleaming fixtures made a welcoming atmosphere. Kate headed to the nearest desk and asked to see the manager.

A tall man in a brown business suit came out from a windowed office. He had nicely styled blond hair and a warm smile. He extended his hand. "I'm Andy Sheldon, the manager. What can I do for you?"

"Hopefully, you can tell me if my husband had an account here and if he had a safe deposit box."

The man's brows rose. "Well, let's see what we can do."

Kate followed the man back to his office. She could only hope her quest for answers would stop here. Then she could leave Havensport and the sheriff with his suspicions behind.

"Sheriff?"

Brody pressed the button on the radio attached to his shoulder. "Yes, Teal?"

"The ladybird left the mercantile and headed into the bank. You want me to go in there? See what she's up to?"

Brody shook his head at the deputy's corny lingo. "No. Sit tight."

Shutting off the computer, Brody left the station and headed down the street to the bank. He had run a check on Kate, on Paul Wheeler and on Pete Kinsey and had found nothing new. No priors. No outstanding parking tickets even. On the surface everything looked on the up and up. Relief filtered through him, catching him off guard. He hadn't realized how much he'd been expecting to find something shady in her past.

He walked inside the bank just as Kate was walking out of Andy Sheldon's office. Brody stepped off to the side next to the door beside a ficus tree. Kate and Andy shook hands and then she headed toward the door.

Her shoulders were slightly slumped and her expression pensive. It wasn't until she was reaching for the door that she noticed him. She started. "What are you doing here?"

"Keeping an eye on you."

"Worried I might rob the bank?" she asked sarcastically before pushing through the door.

He caught her by the elbow as they stepped outside. "Worried someone will try to grab you again." He didn't add that he was also having her watched because he didn't completely trust her.

Her mouth tightened at the corners. "I appreciate your diligence in doing your job, but this is overkill. Those men aren't going to come back."

"You don't know that," he countered. Or did she? "What did you find out at the bank?"

She let out a heavy sigh. "Nothing. Neither Paul nor Pete had an account or safe deposit box there."

"Back to square one," he murmured.

She started walking. He fell into step with her. They headed back toward Myrtle's. "Yes. Back to not knowing anything more than I did this morning." She kicked at a rock lying in the road and sent it scuttling into the bushes. "I had some boxes taken over to the house."

"Good. The window will be repaired by this evening. First thing tomorrow I'll take you over and help you pack up."

"Anxious to get rid of me?" she asked drily as she stepped onto Myrtle's porch.

To be honest with himself…yeah, he did want to send her on her way as quickly as possible. He didn't like this conflicted nonsense going on inside of him. "Just trying to be of service," he replied. "I'll see you tomorrow."

She gave him a tight smile and then disappeared inside.

As Brody returned to the station, he thought about Kate's question. He wished he didn't suspect he'd miss her when she disappeared from his life for good.

SEVEN

Kate awoke feeling refreshed from a good night's sleep. For the second time in as many days she'd not had a nightmare. She supposed it was because she felt safe at Myrtle's with Deputy Teal just down the road.

She peeked out her bedroom window that looked out at the street. Sure enough, there was a car down the road, but it wasn't Deputy Teal's car.

It was Brody's.

A tingling of anticipation raced through her system. She tried to subdue the sudden pleasure of knowing that Brody was the one watching over her.

Irritated with herself for such ridiculousness, she quickly dressed and left the room. Being pleased that Brody was watching over her really shouldn't make any difference.

The smell of bacon and coffee scented the air and made her stomach rumble. She hadn't had much of an appetite the previous night and had only eaten a little of the chicken and rice Myrtle had made.

Kate walked into the kitchen as Myrtle was putting a plate piled high with bacon into the oven. "Good morning," Kate said.

Myrtle straightened and wiped her hands on the red-checkered apron tied at her waist. "Morning, dear. Sleep well?"

"I did. Thank you."

"Whenever you're ready for breakfast, there's bacon in the oven, eggs in the warmer." She pointed to a covered silver dish. A flame heated the metal bottom. Obviously Myrtle was used to entertaining. "Cups are there." She pointed to a cup rack on the wall by the refrigerator where several mugs hung. "Would you care to join me at church this morning?"

A longing to be in a place where God was present welled inside Kate. The necessity to replenish her faith was strong. "Yes. I'd love that."

"Wonderful. The service starts in an hour and a half." Myrtle picked up a sponge and wiped down the counter.

"Would you mind if I take a cup of coffee to Sheriff McClain?"

Myrtle's brows drew together creating more creases in her forehead. "The sheriff's here?"

"Outside in his car."

Myrtle put the sponge down in the sink and then went to the front window. "Was he there all night?"

Kate shrugged, trying for nonchalance when she

couldn't deny the pleasure of knowing he'd been out there. "Probably."

"By all means, invite him in for breakfast." Myrtle bustled back to the kitchen.

A nervous ripple shook Kate as she went out the door. He was just doing his job, she told herself. He wasn't looking out for her because he cared and she was only offering because it was the polite thing to do. Plus, Myrtle had insisted. The crisp morning air cooled her skin through her twill pants and light-weight cotton sweater.

Brody rolled down his window as she approached the car. He wore his uniform beneath his jacket and a thermos sat on the seat next to him.

"Care to come in for breakfast?" she asked.

Surprise flared in his eyes before a slow smile spread across his face. "Love to."

Feeling awkward because of the rush of warmth his smile generated in her, she sternly reminded herself this wasn't some sort of date. She stepped back when he opened the door. He moved slowly, stiffly from the car. White lines appeared around his compressed mouth. Concern and guilt coursed through her because he'd spent an uncomfortable night sitting in his car while she peacefully slept.

"After you," he said with a sweeping gesture of his hand. They walked to the house with her slightly ahead of him and, as they stepped onto the sidewalk leading to Myrtle's door, she glanced back. Was he limping? He met her gaze with raised brows and walked past her without a limp. Must have been her imagination.

In the time it took Kate to bring the sheriff in, Myrtle had set the dining-room table for three. In the middle of the table sat the plate of bacon and the warming dish full of scrambled eggs.

Myrtle came out of the kitchen carrying a pitcher of orange juice. "Sheriff McClain. What a pleasant surprise," she gushed, her obvious affection for him glowing in her eyes. "Have a seat, you two."

"Kate." Brody held out a chair and once she was settled, he held out a chair for Myrtle. Kate liked and appreciated Brody's good manners. Paul had never been so solicitous.

It felt strange sharing a table, a meal with Brody. It was as if they were friends or something. She couldn't deny she was grateful for his presence, even if he was there only because he was doing his job. He made her feel safe and cared for.

They ate and talked and Kate enjoyed herself. Because of Myrtle's presence, the conversation never strayed to Paul or his death. For a short time, Kate was able to put all the bad stuff that had happened over the past weeks aside. They talked about everything from movies to politics to sports.

Kate was amused to discover that she and Brody shared similar tastes. She only wished they had similar agendas. His was to protect her, yes, but she suspected he wanted to make sure she truly was innocent of any wrongdoing in order to protect his town. She wanted answers that would prove her innocence, but mostly to give her peace so she could move on with her life.

As they cleared the plates, Myrtle paused and addressed Brody, "Sheriff, Kate and I are headed to church now. Would you care to join us?"

Brody blinked. He hadn't been to church in years. Not since he was old enough to refuse while his mother and siblings still attended. The void inside of him seemed magnified in church. "I…"

Kate laid a warm hand on his arm. "You don't have to go. Myrtle and I will be fine."

He frowned. He didn't like the idea of her going somewhere unattended. He'd go and hang out in front. Just in case those men tried anything. "I'll come with you."

Kate's pleased smile slid through him with surprising ease, making him feel good. As he followed the ladies out of the house and headed toward the little white chapel in the middle of town, he chastised himself for liking how good her pleasure made him feel.

He wasn't out to win her over. His job was to protect her and his town. He couldn't ever forget the job was what mattered. He'd forgotten that important rule once and wasn't about to do it again.

They approached the wide-open doors of the church. Many of the townsfolk milled around the door, chatting, greeting each other before filing inside. Brody took it all in with a jaundiced eye. He didn't see the point. Hadn't seen the point in worship or church for a long time. Not when God had deserted him when he'd required Him most.

Brody stopped on the top stair and moved off to the side.

"You're not coming in?" Kate asked as she stepped to the side with him. She had a Bible she'd brought from Myrtle's securely held in one hand.

"No. I'll wait out here for you." He folded his arms across his chest. He found himself studying the way the sunlight glinted in Kate's copper-colored hair, making some of the strands appear almost gold in tone.

"Suit yourself," she said, but she didn't move away as he expected her to.

"Well, hello, Sheriff."

Brody turned toward the gruff male voice. Mr. Leighton, the great-grandson of the town's founding father, hobbled his eighty-plus-years frame up the stairs. "Mr. Leighton. How are you today?"

"Better now that I see you've decided to join us this morning." The older man's dark blue eyes peered at Kate. "Who's she?"

"Mr. Leighton, this is Kate Wheeler. She's in town for…a while."

Mr. Leighton held out his bony hand to Kate. She shook it. "Hello, Mr. Leighton. It's a pleasure to meet you."

"The pleasure is mine, dear." He released her hand

and shifted his gaze back to Brody. "Well, escort the lady in, young man."

"I'm not coming in," Brody said quickly. "The town's better served if I stay on duty."

Mr. Leighton adjusted his paisley tie. "You're here so there must be a deputy holding down the fort." Mr. Leighton raised a white brow. "Correct?"

Brody frowned, feeling caught in a trap of his own making. "Yes, but I…" He paused when he noticed the amused and challenging gleam in Kate's green eyes. Without a word spoken she asserted more pressure on him than Leighton's direct offense.

His gaze darted between the two. He decided he could tolerate one hour spent inside the church for the good of Havensport's sheriff's department. He didn't want to offend the department's number-one supporting family. "Shall we?"

"Let's," she said cheerily and she took his arm.

Not missing Mr. Leighton's approving smile, Brody escorted Kate inside and through the double doors leading to the sanctuary. The dark, oak walls of the chapel could have been oppressive if not for the large windows on either side of the building that allowed sunlight to stream in.

As they moved down the center aisle between rows of wooden pews, a feeling stole over Brody. It wasn't what he expected. There was no anger or hurt. No gaping void. He didn't feel out of place. He didn't feel unwelcome. Searching inside himself, he tried to decipher what it was he felt.

They took seats in the third row next to Myrtle. Brody nodded in greeting to several familiar faces. He saw Mrs. Kim, one of the elementary school teachers, and her family; Dora Able, who owned the bookstore in town; Deputy Teal and his family. Which meant that Deputy Anderson was on duty.

Kate leaned in close to whisper. "If you're uncomfortable, you can leave. You don't have to be here."

"I'm not uncomfortable."

"Well, that's sure a fierce scowl on your face," she whispered again.

Deliberately relaxing his features, he whispered back. "I want to be here."

And he realized he did. The feeling that he couldn't identify was belonging. He belonged among these people. This was his town. He settled back, enjoying the insight. He'd always felt protective of Havensport but not really connected. A smile tugged at his mouth. He had connected with the people here. They looked to him to keep them safe.

A man rose and went to the pulpit. Brody had met Pastor Sims a few times. The man was average in height, medium build with light eyes and dark hair. Brody had found the pastor engaging on the few occasions they'd crossed paths.

Pastor Sims asked the congregation to open their hymnals. Kate leaned forward to take one from the pocket attached to the back of the pew in front of them. Her graceful fingers leafed through the pages until she came to the opening hymn. Organ music coming from the loft at the back of the chapel filled the air.

Brody recognized the melody and a glance at the book in Kate's hands confirmed it. As voices joined the organ music, the words to the hymn bubbled inside Brody from some long-forgotten place. He clamped his jaw shut.

But the pressure building in his chest physically hurt. He tried to concentrate on anything other than the growing urgency to unite his voice in worship with the others in the sanctuary. On the second refrain he couldn't hold out any longer. The words tumbled out, at first low and weak but gaining in volume and boldness.

As he sang he felt lighter, the pain in his chest receded, leaving him vaguely dizzy.

The song ended and then another began. Again the words came easily. Brody felt Kate's warm gaze, but he couldn't acknowledge her curiosity. This desire to communicate with God was too new, too unexpected. And he wasn't sure how to take his sudden ache to worship.

Later, after several more songs and after the congregation had put away their hymnals, Brody crossed his arms over his chest in defense against anything the pastor might say about God.

"If you have your Bibles, please turn to second Corinthians, chapter twelve, verse nine," Pastor Sims instructed.

Brody watched Kate deftly turn to the page in

her Bible as if she knew exactly where that passage was without having to think about it. She scooted the Bible closer so he could see it better. Though he appreciated her thoughtfulness, he had no intention of looking.

As the pastor began to speak, Brody let his mind wander to Kate's situation. Again he wondered just how involved she was in her husband's death. And what she wasn't telling him.

His mind tangled on something the pastor said. And without consciously deciding, Brody found himself listening.

"The Lord said to Paul, 'My grace is sufficient for you, for My strength is made perfect in weakness.' It's important to realize that the Lord's answer to Paul wasn't punitive. Rather, it affirms that no matter what befalls us, be it a sickness, a loss of a job or the death of a loved one, that Jesus' grace can sustain us if we choose to allow Him into our lives."

What was this grace the pastor was talking about? Brody grappled to understand.

And, as if Pastor Sims had a direct connection into his thoughts, he said, "Grace is God's undeserved favor that can bring us healing, both physical and emotional. God's grace can protect us, guide us. In our deepest pain, deepest weakness, God's goodness and faithfulness are revealed."

The pastor went on to give examples from various Bible passages. He spoke of Noah. Of Jacob and Joseph. David and Paul.

And Brody sat there in the third row feeling as if God was talking directly to him. He felt that he was on the brink of…he didn't know what.

Something inside him wanted to respond, wanted to seek this favor, this grace the pastor spoke of. Brody wanted God's strength.

But the questions rose. Why did his father have to die? Why hadn't God protected his father? Why hadn't God protected Brody? The clamoring in his head drowned out the rest of what the pastor had to say.

When the time came for the pastor's prayer, Brody's gaze wandered over the people with their bowed heads and closed eyes. Did they really believe their prayers would make a difference?

His gaze rested on Kate. Her lips moved with silent words. Could a woman who'd killed her husband sit in church and pray like that? Could she find absolution when he couldn't even find God?

Focus on the job, boyo. Time would tell him of Kate's innocence or guilt.

Soon they were filing out with the rest of the Havensport's townspeople. Brody shook hands with several people, ruffled the hair of a toddler and found that sense of belonging firmly taking up residence in his heart.

He and Kate walked Myrtle back to her home and then taking his cruiser, headed first to the mercantile to collect more boxes and then to the Kinsey house.

Brody was thankful Kate didn't ask any questions

about his thoughts on the church service or the pastor's sermon. He wasn't prepared to delve into what he was feeling or thinking about God and grace and unanswered questions.

He doubted he'd ever be.

The boxes she'd had delivered the day before were stacked near the front door. Brody had also had the lock on the front door fixed. Kate liked his thoroughness. They went inside and Kate was overwhelmed with the task at hand.

"You know, you could call the local donation center. I'm sure they'd have people willing to come take care of this," Brody suggested, his tone gentle as if he could sense her reluctance to dive right in.

"That's a good idea. I'll do that with the furniture and stuff. But I want to go through his personal items. Maybe I'll find some closure. Something."

They worked together as a team. Brody would dump the contents of drawers into a box and she'd sift through the items, looking for something to tell her who Paul really was and why he'd been killed.

Several hours later, with nothing significant to show for their efforts, Kate's head pounded with frustration. They'd gone through every drawer and bedroom closet. They'd stripped the beds, emptied the linen closet and looked through the toiletries in the bathroom. Brody had stacked the now-full boxes in a corner of the living room and was dragging stuff out of the entryway closet.

She pulled an empty box closer. Rubber boots, a duffel bag full of tennis gear, an empty briefcase. Brody handed her the coats. She searched the pockets of each as she had every other piece of clothing in the house. From the inside pocket of a black leather jacket, sharp edges of paper poked at her hand. Her heart rate accelerated. She tugged out the folded envelope.

She ran her fingertip along the edge of the envelope. It had already been opened. She pulled out the sheets of paper. Letters. Only letters. She released the air trapped in her lungs and breathed in a sickly, sweet scent of perfume. She looked closer. The words were written in a flowing handwriting and in a language she didn't recognize.

"Kate? You okay?"

She glanced up to meet Brody's concerned gaze. "This isn't in English." She held up her find.

He moved to her side. She handed him the bundle and watched as his big capable hands shuffled through the pages. "Looks Cyrillic."

Her brows rose. "What?"

"Russian."

"How do you know?" she asked.

"One of the locals, Mr. Waskasky, is from St. Petersburg. He used to teach Russian studies at the university. I've seen writing like this in his house. He'll be able to translate these."

Russian. She shivered. Who was this man she'd been married to for four years? The doubts, the questions and insecurities swelled and bubbled, buffeting her like the crashing surf outside. Once again she was reminded that the only way she'd find any measure of peace was to find the truth.

"Can we go see him now?" she asked Brody.

Brody took her hand, his grip strong and reassuring. Warmth suffused her arm and chased away her chills. She wanted to hang on to that warmth, that anchor, but she let go and moved toward the door ahead of him.

Though she was thankful that at the moment he was dedicated to helping her, she couldn't allow herself to depend on him in the long run, no matter how much her heart wanted her to. She couldn't forget that he was a man dedicated to a dangerous career. They could never have a future together.

Mr. Waskasky wasn't home when they went by his condo in a newer development at the edge of town. Brody left his card with a note, asking for the older man to call him when he returned.

Disappointment showed bright in Kate's green eyes but she didn't say much as Brody drove her back to Myrtle's.

They were walking into the small house when the radio attached to his shoulder crackled and hissed. Teal's voice came through. "Sheriff, we've got a situation at the high school."

Brody reached up and pressed the respond button. "Serious?"

"No. But the principal wants you there."

"Copy that. On my way."

He met Kate's wide-eyed stare.

"You're leaving?"

"I have a job to do."

Myrtle laid a hand on her arm. "You'll be fine here, dear."

Kate gave her a wan smile before turning back to Brody. He narrowed his gaze at the slight pallor of her complexion.

"I'll be back," he offered.

She nodded, her expression bleak and vulnerable. Something in Brody shifted, softened, making him want to take her hand again and reassure her. Making him think of the way he'd almost kissed her less than forty-eight hours ago. He forced himself to remember his resolve to remain unaffected by her act.

He couldn't risk paying more for believing in her. She was a job. He wouldn't let it get personal. He turned to go.

"The letters!" Kate thrust the sheets of paper toward him.

"Right." Caution warned she could be setting him up with her false trust. He reached for the papers. "I'll drop them off with Mr. Waskasky when I'm done. He should be home by then."

She didn't let go. "I'm going with you."

"You can't."

"I'm going with you," she repeated, her expression determined.

"Kate—"

"What if you don't come back?"

Reacting to the urgency and desperation in her tone, Brody sought to reassure her. "This is a routine incident. I'll be back. Then we can go see about the letter together."

Her gaze searched his face as if she were deciding whether to trust him or not. Finally, she gave a short nod. "Fine."

Brody left, shutting the door firmly behind him. As he heard the click of the lock slide into place he couldn't shake the unsettled feeling that no matter how much he tried to protect himself, he was still vulnerable to a red-haired woman with worry in her wide green eyes.

EIGHT

Kate gathered up the remains of the clam chowder dinner she'd shared with Myrtle and headed into the kitchen. Though she enjoyed Myrtle's company, she couldn't shake a restless disappointment. Her life hadn't turned out the way she'd planned. She'd so wanted a normal, all-American life. How had she ended up with so much deceit?

Myrtle smiled as she entered. "Thank you, dear. Just put those dishes on the counter. I'll take care of them later."

"I'll wash them. It's the least I can do for all your kindness." Kate went to the sink. Nervous energy made her edgy and she needed something to do. She glanced at the old wooden cuckoo clock hanging on the pale yellow wall of the kitchen.

Three hours. Where was Brody?

Kate washed the dinner dishes, her hands working automatically, scrubbing and wiping. The simple task left her mind to wander.

Trouble at the high school. Teenagers with too much time on their hands was Myrtle's guess.

But what if it was something more? What if Brody was hurt and didn't return? An ache tightened in her chest. She recognized the sensation. Only this time it was more acute.

She scrubbed harder at the soup bowl in her hand. She didn't want to like Brody, much less worry about him. But the ache, full of anxiety, fear and dread was the same she'd experienced every time her father went off on one of his missions.

As a child, she hadn't understood why her mother was so anxious every time her father left. Sometimes he disappeared in the middle of the night. Her mother would lock herself away in her room and cry, leaving Kate alone and confused.

It wasn't until Kate was nine and her father was hurt, a wound in the shoulder from an explosive of some sort, that she'd begun to grasp the nature of his job. And though Brody wasn't a covert operations specialist like her father, he was a cop. And a cop's life was as iffy and dangerous. Anything could happen.

What if he didn't come back? The question played like a broken record in her mind and an invisible band across her chest squeezed tighter. She was only concerned because he had the letter, concerned that he'd have it translated without her. She picked up a dish towel and dried a blue plate.

No. He'd said he'd wait, that she could go with

him. But could she trust him to keep his word? He hadn't given her any reason not to, but Paul's whispered warning not to trust anyone lurked in her mind.

She scoffed out loud. Hadn't Paul proven he was the one not to be trusted? He'd lived a double life, lied to her and endangered her. No, she wouldn't compare Brody to Paul.

"Did you say something, dear?" Myrtle asked as she tidied the counters.

"I was wondering where Sheriff McClain was."

"Oh, I'm sure he'll return soon."

Kate nodded and stacked the dishes to the side.

"Thank you for helping." Myrtle put the clean dishes in the cupboards.

Kate leaned against the sink. "Thank you for your wonderful hospitality."

"I must confess it's good to have company. My late husband, Fred, used to say I lived to entertain, but it's been years since I had a guest."

"How long ago did your husband die?"

"Fred passed on about ten years ago now. He was a good man." Myrtle stared off into memories. "So full of life. He found humor in everything and he made our years together blissful. He was my soul mate, created by God to love me and me him."

Touched by the sentiment, Kate wondered if she'd ever find that kind of bliss, find her soul mate, the one created by God for her. She doubted it. She'd never risk her heart again.

Looking back, she knew bliss hadn't been there

with Paul. He'd been safe, steady, which was what she'd wanted. What she still wanted, but she knew better now. Paul hadn't come close to giving her the security she craved. She couldn't imagine loving someone so deeply that you knew they were a gift from above.

An image of Brody rose in her mind. His dark probing eyes, his strong jaw and his mouth with its devastating grin. Would his kiss be as devastating?

Whoa! Kate shook her head to clear her mind. Not what she should be thinking about. Instead, she thought about how he made her feel so safe and cared for. He really listened. He never talked over her the way Paul had. The sheriff was a gentleman. But she had no intention of becoming his lady.

Myrtle's gaze pinned her to the counter, as if she could see into her heart, laying bare her doubts.

"To completely love another person is to experience the essence of God."

Myrtle's words seeped deep into Kate's soul. "I doubt I'll find that kind of love."

"Love isn't something that can be planned or scheduled. Love is a choice."

"Love is full of risks," Kate countered.

Myrtle laughed softly. "Life would be boring without risks."

Growing uncomfortable with the direction of the conversation, Kate broke eye contact to glance once again at the clock. She hated this waiting and wondering and worrying. She could never, ever be a police officer's wife.

"Would you care for some tea, dear?" Myrtle asked.

With a sigh, Kate resigned herself to waiting. "That would be lovely, thank you." She walked to the French doors leading to the wooden deck. "I'm going to step out for some fresh air."

"Good idea. After the last few days you've had, with those nasty men trying to grab you, you need a little rest and relaxation."

She gave Myrtle a half smile. Myrtle had questioned her during their meal and Kate had given her as vaguely truthful answers as she could. She didn't want to worry the kind older woman. She didn't want anybody else to be drawn into this mess.

She stepped out onto the deck. A slight breeze ruffled through her hair and sent a chill down her spine.

The sound of the surf drew her attention to the path that led between the shrubs surrounding the yard. She longed to walk down to the water's edge, to feel the soothing sand beneath her feet.

Instead she wrapped her arms around her middle and leaned against the railing. On the horizon, the blue-green water met the soft pinks and oranges of the setting sun like a watercolor canvas, serene and lovely.

Her mind turned to the problem at hand. She had to make plans in case the sheriff didn't return. She swallowed against the panic that thought brought.

She needed to be logical, practical. She couldn't rely on anyone else.

If she didn't get the letters back, then she'd head to New York state. She'd memorized the return address: 425 W 5th, Brighton Beach, New York. She hoped she'd find the answers to her questions there.

And if Brody did return?

She had a feeling he wouldn't leave her to do this alone. And she didn't know how she felt about that.

A whisper of movement came from the bushes to her right. Her throat constricted and terror reared up with lightning speed. She whirled around.

A seagull stared at her through the green leaves of the bush.

She laughed at her own paranoia. She was safe on Myrtle's deck.

She'd turned to go back in when a movement in her peripheral vision alerted her seconds before a hand clamped harshly over her mouth. She grabbed at the arms that dragged her across the deck, down the stairs and through the bushes.

Dear God, please save me!

Where was Brody?

Brody pulled his cruiser up to the curb behind Warren's vehicle and threw the gearshift into Park. The trouble at the school had taken longer than he'd anticipated. A group of teens, some local, a few out-of-towners, had broken in and vandalized the halls. Brody had to track down each kid's parents and then he'd stuck around to supervise the cleaning that the principal had demanded the kids do rather than pressing charges.

It was growing late, and he knew Kate would be disappointed when he told her he'd heard from Mr. Waskasky, who wouldn't be able to help until the morning.

Brody got out of the car and walked toward Warren's car. He frowned. Warren wasn't in the driver's seat. His gaze narrowed on the cottage. Warren was going to get an earful. He'd told the young deputy to stay outside, not to make his presence a bother by bugging the ladies.

He charged up the stairs and knocked on the door. A moment later Myrtle answered.

"Sheriff, you're back." She waved him in. "I was just getting tea and a cake ready to take out to Kate."

"Where's Deputy Teal?" he asked.

"I haven't seen Warren this evening." Myrtle looked over his shoulder and frowned. "I hadn't noticed his car."

His senses went on the alert. "Where's Kate?"

"On the deck out back."

He palmed the radio attached to his shoulder and radioed the station.

"Anderson, here."

"Have you heard from Warren?"

"No, not since he left this afternoon."

Brody clenched his fist. "Come to Myrtle Kirby's. I need your help."

"Should I call Sheriff Talbot?"

"No," Brody barked, irritated that the older deputy would automatically suggest calling his old boss. He wasn't going to call in the retired sheriff. It was bad enough that Warren had gone missing. He didn't need to add to the questions and scrutiny that would come from Sheriff Talbot. "Just get here."

He clicked off the radio. He'd started back down the stairs when he heard a low moan coming from under the porch. Brody found Warren facedown in the dirt, blood, still sticky and wet, smeared on the back of his head.

Brody dragged him out. "What happened?"

Warren blinked and struggled to sit up. "Two men. I got out, they asked for directions. One hit me from behind."

Greg Anderson's car screeched to a halt behind Brody's car. People emerged from neighboring houses, obviously curious about the police cars in front of Myrtle's.

Brody and Greg helped Warren to a chair on the porch.

"Oh, my," exclaimed Myrtle when she saw the state of the deputy. She turned her troubled gaze on Brody. "Kate?"

Brody left Warren to Greg's care and stormed around the house to the back deck. Empty. Dread gripped his gut.

Myrtle stepped out from the house. "She was here

just a bit ago. Maybe she went down to the beach."
The worry in her voice was unmistakable.

Brody gritted his teeth and charged across the
grass. He skidded to halt when he came to one of
Kate's shoes lying near the bushes. He cursed as terror slammed into his chest. He'd failed to protect her.

Or she'd gone of her own free will.

In which case, he'd failed to do his job. Again.

"I'll find her." He was determined to figure her
out. And when he did he'd send her back to Los Angeles, back to be someone else's problem.

He moved more cautiously toward the path leading through the bushes to the beach. His heart rate
picked up speed when his gaze snagged on the telltale signs of a struggle where the grass met the sand.
Large indentations—like those of men's boots—
marred the sand and deep grooves—like that of
someone being dragged— ran down the path and
around the bushes.

Dread seized him. He *had* failed her. His hand
reached for his sidearm as he emerged from the path
onto the beach. His gaze swung about, searching the
growing darkness. The beach was empty.

She could be anywhere by now. To the right, the
bushes gave way to the backyard of Myrtle's neighbor and to the left, the bushes ended at drainpipes
that dumped the town's rainwater, creating a rocky
inlet. Logic and gut instinct told him to go left.

He ran toward the drainpipes. He skidded to a halt
as a figure stumbled out from behind the bushes.

"Kate!"

In her hand she held a big stick. Her clothes were wet and dirty. Her eyes widened, and then she went down in a heap at his feet. His breath froze and he dropped to his knees.

Flashes of his father's lifeless body threatened to cripple him. He forced himself to stay focused on Kate. In the waning light he saw the ugly gash at her temple and the bruises on her face.

"Kate, Kate!"

She didn't wake.

Strangling with panic, Brody fought back the fear gripping him and did something he hadn't done since he was ten years old.

"Lord, please don't let her die."

Kate struggled from the drifting, floating sensation that held her body and her mind. Her eyelids fluttered open. Dull light stung her eyes and she blinked.

Where was she?

Sterile walls, a firm mattress, the hanging bag of fluid with a tube running down to a shunt stuck into her right hand. A hospital.

Aches on various parts of her body made themselves known with dull intensity. She closed her eyes again, trying to sink back to the sweet ignorance of slumber, but the images flicking through her mind like a projector on high speed wouldn't allow her ease.

Instead, fear built within her chest as she remembered the hands around her. Terror clawed at her throat, cutting off her air as she replayed being dragged away from the shelter of Myrtle's house. She fought to breathe, her body thrashed as she tried to sit up, to run.

Pain exploded in her head causing bright light to blot out her vision. She gritted her teeth. She had to leave. She wasn't safe.

Suddenly, strong hands pushed her back into the pillows. Fresh panic swelled. The restraints holding her down were too strong. She couldn't break free. "No."

"Shhhh, Kate. You're safe."

She recognized the voice. She stilled. "Brody?"

The hands holding her down gentled to a calming caress. "Yes. I'm here."

Slowly, she opened her eyes to assure herself he was real. His face came into focus, and relief cascaded swiftly through her like an early-spring waterfall, powerful and refreshing.

She sighed and drifted as the tension eased from her body. Her head throbbed as adrenaline left to be replaced by oxygen.

She wasn't sure what to make of Brody's presence. The thudding of her heart took on a different beat, less frantic but just as wild. She felt safe, yet threatened. Comforted, yet panicked. And none of it had anything to do with her situation and everything to do with the man beside the bed.

She didn't want to need him, she shouldn't want to rely on him. Even so, she was thankful he was there. And she knew in her soul that he was the reason she was still alive.

God had answered her prayers by providing her with a protector here on earth, though Brody wouldn't appreciate that title. A smile played at the corners of her mouth. A spasm of pain radiated through her head for her effort. She closed her eyes, letting the ache wash over her and ebb away as the smile fell.

There was still so much to do and so many questions that needed to be answered. And as much as she hated to admit it, she couldn't chase down the answers on her own. She needed Brody, needed his strength, his intelligence and his protection. She needed him to trust her. But she had to keep her heart safe. She couldn't allow herself to fall for him. He was the opposite of the stable, secure life she longed for.

But for now she could use his help.

Her gaze sought him. He'd taken a seat next to the bed. He no longer wore his brown uniform; instead, a light blue button-down shirt and faded jeans hugged his big body. Lines of tension framed his ebony eyes. His clean-shaven cheeks emphasized his hard jaw.

"Hi." The word came out as a croak.

Brody immediately moved to pour her a cup of water. Gently he held the cup to her bruised and swollen lips. The water hit her mouth, cool and flowing. She greedily drank, relieving the parchedness of her throat. When the cup was drained, he sat.

"Better?"

"Much." She tried not to wince. Talking stung her lips and her jaw was sore. She ran her tongue around her mouth, noting thankfully that she wasn't missing any teeth. "How did I get here?"

"I found you unconscious on the beach."

He definitely was sent by God. "You saved my life. Thank you."

"If I'd have been doing my job better, you wouldn't have been in that situation."

His tone of self-recrimination pulled at her heart. She reached for his hand. He enfolded hers in his capable fingers, the pressure reassuring and thrilling. "You couldn't have known they'd be so bold as to take me from Myrtle's deck."

"What happened?"

She took a deep breath and strove for logical, unemotional. "I was grabbed from behind and dragged down the beach. I struggled, one of them hit me. I went down hard. I managed to grab a piece of driftwood. I got a few good hits in. They must have heard you coming because all of a sudden they left." She ran her tongue over the tender lump in her lip.

"Did they say anything?"

Gaining his trust needed to start now. It was her move. If she expected him to continue to help her and protect her, she needed to be honest with him and put some trust in him, as well. "They kept asking me where the disk was."

Two little grooves appeared between his eyes as his brows lowered. "A disk?" His demeanor shifted, becoming remote, distant. Coplike. "Tell me about the disk."

She swallowed, hating the suspicion in his dark gaze. "I don't know anything."

"Where's the disk, Kate?"

"I don't know."

"Then why do they think you have it?"

"I… When I found Paul, he was still alive. He asked for Gordon, our lawyer and then he…before he died in my arms, he said, 'I told them you have it.' He didn't tell me what 'it' was."

Brody stared at her for a long, taut moment. His eyes searched her face, peeling away the layers of her heart, looking for hidden secrets. She wanted to lift her chin and dare him to disbelieve her.

Instead she allowed herself to be laid bare and vulnerable beneath his steel-eyed gaze. She didn't have any secrets. Not now. What he saw was what he got.

"Will you help me find that disk, Brody?" she asked, her voice a notch above a whisper. It was so hard to ask for help. But she needed it. She needed him. She tensed, waiting, hoping for his answer of yes.

His gaze came to rest on her battered lip, his expression softened ever so slightly before he spoke. "Yes, I'll help you."

A stone of worry lifted from around her neck. Fatigue overwhelmed her. She sank back and melted into the bed.

"But I need a promise from you, Kate."

She stiffened, wary. "What?"

"From now on you have to be completely honest with me."

"Of course," she answered quickly and a bit sheepishly. "Before, I...I didn't know if I could trust you."

"And now?"

She swallowed. For all his gruff and bluster, she sensed a good man lurked deep inside. She jumped in with both feet and prayed for a soft landing. "I trust you. God sent me the guardian angel I prayed for and you're it."

NINE

"I'm no angel," Brody scoffed.

"I said you're my guardian angel, as in protector. Not that you're angelic."

Her humor sliced through him. She still had spunk. He liked that. Admired it, too. "There's a difference?"

"Hmmm, angelic equals perfect and heavenly."

His mouth quirked to one side. "Perfect, I'm not."

"No, you're very human," she agreed, with a smile in her voice. "The only real angels I know of are in the Bible." Her eyelids fluttered. She was losing it, but trying so hard not to give in.

Then she focused her gaze and the undisguised trust in her eyes caught him off guard. No one but his sister had ever looked at him like that.

But his reaction to Kate was far from brotherly.

He wanted to take her into his arms and soothe away the hurt she'd suffered. He wanted to run his fingers through her red curls and feel the texture slide against his skin, he wanted to fill his lungs with her sweet scent and lose himself in her embrace. He wanted to shield her from the world.

But none of those things were possible.

Instead, he focused on her battered face, on the bandage over the gash at her temple. He hated seeing her so bruised and vulnerable. He wanted to beat something, someone to a pulp. He'd failed to protect her. It wouldn't happen again.

"You're flawed in a good way," she said.

Her words stung. How could Kate see his flaws as good? With Elise, he'd had a major lapse in judgment, had allowed his emotions to rule his actions. And he'd paid the price. His career effectively snuffed out, his ego shredded and his body left damaged. There was nothing good about any of his past.

"Kate, I don't know what you think you know…" he trailed off as her eyes closed and she sighed.

"I know you're here and that's all that matters." Her words were slurred as the fatigue she'd been fighting overcame her.

His heart twisted in his chest. He didn't deserve her trust. He couldn't live up to her expectations. He should call the Feds and let them deal with the situation.

Her eyes opened, panic shining in the emerald depths. "No. You promised you'd help me."

He hadn't realized he'd spoken his last thought out loud. "Kate, the Feds are better equipped to protect you."

"Please, no one else."

Her plea was an arrow to his heart. And a reminder of what happened before. "Rest, Kate. We'll talk about this when you're stronger."

"The letters?"

"Safe. I'll ask Mr. Waskasky to come here to translate them tomorrow."

She relaxed. "Thank you."

"Did Paul give you any strange keys or anything out of the ordinary?"

She thought for a moment. "No. The last thing he'd given me was a birthday present a year and a half ago."

"And that was?"

She gave a small wry laugh. "My very practical, very useful purse." She glanced around. "I suppose it's still at Myrtle's."

"I'll have it brought over."

"I'd appreciate it. A lady feels naked without her purse."

Brody blinked and tried to banish the image her words conjured up. He smoothed a curl behind her ear, his knuckle grazed her cheek. Her skin was soft, her hair silky. His stomach muscles clenched. She didn't deserve this pain. "Rest now, okay?"

"Hmmm." Her eyes closed as she nuzzled against his hand. "You'll stay?"

Tenderness bloomed, tightening his chest. He leaned in and kissed her forehead. "Yes, I'll stay."

Saying those words was like hitting the rewind

button on his life. He'd promised Elise he'd help her, too. And the result had been disastrous.

Kate made a soft little sound deep in her throat. Then her breathing became even and rhythmic. Watching her sleep, Brody released the tension he'd held since he'd found her on the beach.

His gut-level instincts told him she was telling the truth when she said she didn't know anything about the disk. Which left them with another uncovered piece of the puzzle as to why she was in danger.

The situation was becoming more complicated by the minute. And his attraction to Kate was only making matters worse. He had to get a grip. He knew from experience he couldn't protect Kate and care about her at the same time. In doing so he compromised his judgment and jeopardized his focus.

Keep your mind on the job.

His father's motto slapped him upside the head. He wished he'd listened last time. This time he would.

He had a tough decision to make. Helping Kate meant leaving the town unprotected. That was unacceptable. He didn't take his pledge to protect and serve the community of Havensport lightly. He knew what he had to do—call old Sheriff Talbot. The one person in Havensport who knew the truth. The one person who would demand to know why Brody needed to do this.

And the answer had Brody tied up in knots.

* * *

Kate awoke to voices in her head.

She had no way to distinguish time, no way to know if she'd slept for a moment or for hours. Turning her head, she listened. Brody's distinct, velvet-coated tones sent waves of comfort over her, and then another voice. A burly, masculine sound that stole her calmness away. She lay still, tense. The two men spoke at a hushed level, but she made out the words. Was the other man Brody's father?

"How long do you need?"

"Don't know." Brody's voice suggested the shrug Kate could envision.

"This is way too risky. Let the Feds handle her."

Kate nearly bolted upright in protest, but Brody's quick response soothed her panic.

"I gave her my word."

"Why are you doing this to yourself again?"

"Look, Sheriff—"

"No, you look, *Sheriff.* I'm no longer sheriff here, you are. You have a responsibility to this town."

Kate stifled a groan. She hadn't realized she was jeopardizing Brody's job by asking for his help. But what was she to do? She wished she had the courage to handle this alone. But she didn't. She needed Brody. Needed his protection.

"I'm entitled to a vacation after three years without."

A long silent moment stretched taut through the hospital room.

Kate wanted to open her eyes. She wanted to see the two men, but they might notice she was awake and halt their conversation. She had to know what helping her would cost Brody. Though how she'd ever repay him, she didn't know.

"A vacation then," the other man said with grudging reluctance.

"Effective immediately."

"Son, I just don't want you to get hurt again."

Kate noted the paternal caring to the other man's tone and wondered what he meant by his words. How had Brody been hurt? She realized she knew very little about Brody yet she was putting her life in his hands.

Brody cleared his throat. "I won't."

The swooshing sound of the door opening stopped the conversation.

"Gentlemen. How is our patient?" asked a deep, kindly voice.

Kate took that as her cue to "awaken." She deliberately stirred and slowly opened her eyes. Brody sat beside her bed, his handsome face a welcoming sight, though the strained grooves outlining his smile gave away his tension. Guilt pricked at her conscience. She was using Brody for her own gain.

The doctor stepped forward. Midforties, brown hair, hazel eyes behind horn-rimmed glasses. His expression was friendly yet professional.

A few steps back stood an imposing figure with thick, salt-and-pepper hair, chiseled features and a grim set to his square jaw. She swallowed as the disapproval in his blue eyes crashed over her like the surf at high tide. She saw little resemblance between Brody and this man. Who was he?

"Kate, the doc wants to examine you and then we can find out how soon you'll be released," Brody said.

She nodded.

"I'll be back in a while. I have some things I must take care of." He covered her fisted hand, his touch reassuring and agonizing.

He'd be back, wouldn't he? She had no choice but to trust in that. She turned her hand in his and gripped his fingers, giving him the reassurance that she'd be okay. With one last squeeze he left, taking her trust and leaving her with hope that he'd keep her safe.

But at what cost?

Later, Kate awoke with a start as the shadows deepened from the afternoon sun spilling through the little rectangular window. There were no voices this time. She was alone.

She found the controls to the bed and raised the back to a sitting position. For a moment the room spun before landing in perfect alignment. She tested her lip. Still painful, less swollen. The doctor had said he wanted to keep her for a few more hours for observation because of her head injury. She had a nasty bump and a slight concussion.

In the quiet of the room she took the opportunity to spend a peaceful moment with God, thanking Him for her rescue, thanking Him for Brody.

The familiar swoosh of the door sounded, then immediately she felt the energy in the room crackle to life as Brody strode in followed by a short, silver-haired man with thick bifocals.

Brody's gaze skimmed over her. "You look good."

Heat flushed her face at his compliment. "Thanks."

She eyed the stranger with curiosity. He was small and round in his brown slacks and tweed coat. His countenance was unassuming and kind.

Brody introduced her visitor. "This is Mr. Was-kasky. Do you feel up to listening to the letters?"

The letters. Her heart rate picked up. "Yes."

She steeled herself for the inevitable, for more distressing knowledge about her husband the letters were sure to reveal. For how could perfumed letters, hidden away like love letters, be anything but bad news for the stable, secure life Kate had once thought she had?

She extended her hand. "Hello. Thank you for coming."

The man bustled forward and kissed the back of her hand, his bushy mustache tickling. "My pleasure," he intoned in a heavy accent.

Brody pulled the letters from his pocket. "I waited to have these read until you could hear them."

"I appreciate that," she said. His thoughtfulness

and integrity touched her deeply, giving her the courage to hear whatever the letters revealed.

Mr. Waskasky took the envelope and extracted the folded sheets of paper. He cleared his throat. Kate tensed.

"'Petrov, my love, the waiting is killing me. I miss you and can't wait to be with you again. Please, tell me you will come to me before the new year.'"

Each word cut deeper and deeper still. Kate focused her gaze on the textured blanket covering her legs. She wrapped her arms around her middle, trying to hold in the pain, because deep in her gut she knew that Paul was also Petrov.

Page after page of love letters written by a woman named Olga shattered what little remained of Kate's world. Her heart bled until she thought she'd never feel again.

Any love, even the tiniest speck, that she'd held for her dead husband disintegrated. She'd been so blind. Her husband had not *one,* but *two* other identities.

Why had he married her if he had this other woman waiting for him? Who was he really, and what plans had he had for Kate? She felt used, yes, but to what end? Why? Why? The questions spun around her head until she wanted to scream.

Her fingers curled into tight balls. She had to know the answer or she'd never find any peace, never be able to move on with her life.

Brody's big hand closed over her fist. Seeking

his steady comfort, she turned her hand until their fingers were entwined. She lifted her gaze to meet his. The compassion evident in his ebony eyes tore at her heart.

Brody's gaze sharply shifted back to Mr. Waskasky. "Read that last part again."

"'You're too naughty, not letting me open the package you sent. Must I wait? My curiosity grows.'"

Kate squeezed Brody's hand. This package could be something. Finally, they had a clue. Brody nodded to her as if he'd heard her thoughts and then quickly thanked Mr. Waskasky before ushering him out.

Brody returned, his expression grim and thoughtful.

She couldn't contain the excitement building inside. "We have to go to New York."

"Yes," he said, his tone distant.

"Brody?"

"Hmmm?"

"Something's bothering you. I can tell."

He rubbed his chin, his fingers rasping against the dark stubble growing along his strong jawline. Kate's gaze followed the movement. She realized with a little start that she was beginning to learn his mannerisms and could sense the shifts in his mood. Their growing closeness was another worry she wasn't sure how to handle.

Finally, he spoke. "Why were the letters left behind?"

She blinked. "What?"

"The letters. We found them pretty easily. If the men who'd broken into the house had found them and could read Cyrillic, they'd know that Pete had sent a package to this woman. Yet, they came after you a second time. If they couldn't read Cyrillic, why'd they leave the letters? This doesn't add up."

Kate gestured wildly with her hands. "*None* of this makes sense. But we can't let this opportunity to find out more go by. We have to leave now."

Brody checked his black-leather-banded watch. "I'll speak with the doc." He strode from the room, his broad shoulders and slim hips moving with a masculine grace that never ceased to impress her.

She picked at the polyester fabric of the blanket as the questions about Paul/Pete/Petrov surfaced again, swirling faster and faster like a whirlpool pulling her under.

"Stop it!" Her voice bounced off the walls and echoed in the sterile room, effectively smoothing out her agitation. She had a goal now. Something to focus her energies toward. Her life depended on finding this woman and the package.

But she had two calls to make.

The first to her boss at the bank, who was more than willing to extend her leave of absence after hearing about her assault. Kate was thankful she hadn't had to reveal the true reason for wanting the extended leave—to unravel the mystery of her husband's death.

The second call was to her lawyer.

"Gordon, it's Kate."

"Kate! I've been calling the house. Where are you?" Gordon Thomas's concerned voice boomed over the telephone wire.

"I'm in the hospital, but I'll be leaving soon."

"Hospital? Are you all right?"

"A little black and blue, but nothing that won't heal."

"Tell me what happened."

"Paul's killers came after me."

"Came after you? How did you know it was them? What did they hope to accomplish?"

"They wanted something I don't have, but I think I know where it is."

"Really? What is it?"

"A computer disk. I don't know what's on it, but I have to find it."

"And you know where it is?"

"Maybe. I'm hoping so."

There was a moment of silence. "Kate, I'm coming out there."

"No, don't." She didn't want to complicate the situation more by having her lawyer show up. Brody might take that as a sign she didn't trust him or worse yet, that she was guilty of something.

"Kate, don't you think it would be better if you had an ally? Someone to help you in this quest? I am your lawyer. I'm on your side. Let me help."

She had help. Brody. He was here and willing. She didn't want to analyze why she preferred Brody over

Gordon. She just did. She tightened her grip on the phone. "Did you know about Pete Kinsey?"

"What is there to know? He was Paul's business partner. You knew that."

Closing her eyes against the hurt of Paul's lies, she stated, "There was no Pete Kinsey."

"Kate, are you sure you're all right? Maybe I should speak with your doctor."

"No! Paul and Pete Kinsey were the same man."

The silence coming from the other end of the line unnerved her. "Gordon? Did you hear me?"

"I heard you, Kate." A note of indulgent sympathy laced his deep gravelly voice. "Come home now. We'll get you some help."

"Help?"

"I know this has been a trying time for you. Guilt can play games with the mind."

Kate raised her brows in shock as the meaning behind Gordon's words sank in. "I have nothing to feel guilty about. Do you think I killed him?"

"Of course not, Kate. Don't be ridiculous."

Kate pinched the bridge of her nose with her free hand. "I am not going crazy and I do not have anything to feel guilt about. Didn't you help Paul with some of his business contracts?"

"Are you questioning my integrity? After all I've done for you and your mother? I assure you I would have told you if I suspected anything inappropriate going on."

Contrition brought tears to her eyes. "I'm sorry.

You're right. I know you would. You've been such a rock for me my whole life." She wiped at a stray tear. "We found a letter. Gordon, Paul had yet another life."

"What other life?"

"I don't know yet. Does the name Petrov ring any bells?"

"No. Is this person one of Paul's clients?"

She let out a bitter laugh. "Hardly. We're going to New York to see if we can find the disk there."

"We?"

The door to the room swooshed open. Her doctor stepped in followed closely by Brody, pushing a wheelchair.

"I've got to go. I'll call you later." She hung up before Gordon could reply. She met Brody's gaze. "My lawyer," she said quickly to alleviate the wariness in his eyes.

He gave a sharp nod and remained stonily silent as the doctor did a final cursory exam. Satisfied that she was well enough to leave, the doctor signed her discharge papers and left her in Brody's care.

When the second doctor left, Brody asked, "What did he have to say?"

"He didn't know about Pete or Petrov."

"Did he know anything about the disk?"

"No. He was ready to come here, but I told him not to."

"Why?"

"I think it's better if only you and I go to see this

woman. If we show up with a lawyer in tow, she might get spooked."

"You don't think a cop will spook her?" he asked with wry amusement.

"Not if she doesn't know you're a cop."

"Ah." His mouth kicked up one corner. "Undercover it is, then." He walked to the closet. "Myrtle sent some fresh clothing from your suitcase."

Touched by the combined care of Brody and Myrtle, she smiled. "Thank you, Brody, for doing this. I hope it won't cost you too much."

He laid the garments, khakis and an aqua-blue silk blouse on the foot of the bed and gave her a quizzical stare. "Cost me?"

"I overheard you speaking with…your father?"

The corners of Brody's mouth tipped down. "Sheriff Talbot is not my father."

"Oh." Kate blinked. She'd hit a nerve. She opened her mouth to ask, but he was already moving toward the door.

"I'll find a nurse to help you dress, then we'll go find answers about your husband."

She knew the questions she wanted answered, but what questions did Brody have? And would the answers condemn her or absolve her?

TEN

They took an uneventful commuter flight from Hyannis to JFK International Airport. From there they hailed a taxi. Kate sank back into the cab's distressed, red leather seat next to Brody and tried to relax as they traveled down the scenic route along the edge of Jamaica Bay. Anxiety kept her from enjoying the view of sandy beaches, glistening water and strands of trees springing up out of little islands dotting the bay.

She tried not to think too much about what they'd find in Brighton Beach. She hoped this would be the end. And feared that it wouldn't.

The taxi slowed as the traffic became more congested. They inched through various neighborhoods of Brooklyn. Soon they were entering the area known as Little Odessa. She tried to see everything at once yet her heart pounded so loudly in her head it was hard to concentrate and process the interesting sights, so different from those of Los Angeles or the Pacific Northwest where she'd grown up.

"Hey, stop the car," Brody said, his attention riveted on something to his right.

Kate started as the cab abruptly pulled to the side of the street.

"What is it?" She grasped at his sleeve.

Brody pointed out the window to a large, two-story gray concrete warehouse with the words Lanski's Imports emblazoned across the front.

Puzzled, she stared at Brody.

He tugged his wallet from the back pocket of his navy twill pants and pulled out a business card. He flipped it over so she could see the writing. "What's that from?" she asked.

"I found this among Paul's things in the bungalow. Wasn't sure if it meant anything."

Then she remembered.

Brody opened the car door and said to the driver, "Wait. We'll be right back."

A car horn blared and Kate stiffened. The cabby cursed at the black Lincoln Continental waiting impatiently behind them. Another honk. They sure weren't in Havensport anymore. The quaint little town with its friendly and relaxed pace had grown on her in the short amount of time she'd been there.

As Kate slid out of the cab behind Brody and stepped onto the sidewalk, the sun bounced off the pavement and scorched her skin. No cooling summer breeze here.

She followed Brody to the black metal front door of the business. Brody pushed open the door and they stepped in. Men of various builds and ages moved about at a quick pace. Boxes and crates lined the walls. At the other end of the building a large bay door was rolled up. Trucks were being loaded by men driving forklifts burdened by huge crates.

A big burly man with a shaved head and handlebar mustache met them as they moved farther into the work area. He looked impassable in his worn denims and red work shirt straining to contain bulging muscles. "What do you want?"

"I'd like to see the owner," Brody answered, his tone crisp, authoritative.

The man's narrowed gaze raked over them and a chill slithered down Kate's spine. Her senses went on alert. She'd experienced the same type of chill the times she'd thought she was being watched.

"This way," he finally said and walked away.

"Stay close," Brody whispered. "Keep your eyes open."

She nodded, though she didn't know what she should be looking for.

They were escorted to a staircase that led to a windowed office. The small room was messy and the furniture old. Behind a large scarred oak desk a man in his late fifties with a full head of white hair regarded them with little warmth in his light-blue eyes. His brown suit was well tailored, its obvious cost at odds with the shabby conditions of the office.

He steepled his well-manicured hands. "What can I do for you?" he asked, his accent heavy and foreign.

Brody's tense posture had Kate's nerves jumping.

"Are you Mr. Lanski?" Brody asked.

"I am. What do you want?"

"We're looking for information on a man named Paul Wheeler," Brody asked.

The man shrugged, his mouth pulling down at the corners. "I know no one by this name."

"How about Pete Kinsey?"

The older man's brows dipped together. "Again, I know no such person."

"Does the name Petrov ring any bells?"

The man waved a hand. "Petrov is a common name. I know nothing of these men. Now, I am a busy man. You go."

"Thank you for your time," Brody said as he ushered Kate out of the office and back through the warehouse to the street.

Kate breathed a sigh of relief to see the cab still sitting at the curb. As they slid into the backseat, she said, "That was a waste of time."

"Not so much. I think Mr. Lanski recognized all three names. Whether he knows the three are the same man remains to be seen."

She stared at him in surprise. "How can you tell?"

"It was in his eyes."

She processed that as the cab reentered the steady flow of traffic. Brody asked the driver to take them to their original destination.

The taxi stopped in front of a five-story walk-up brownstone building. Kate climbed out of the cab and gazed around as Brody paid the fare.

Off in the distance, the concrete skyline of New York City rose sharply to the clouds. Kate took in the sights and sounds of the colorful neighborhood. Old men with round, craggy faces peered at them as they shuffled by. Several men wore medals attached to the lapels of their shirts.

Her heart stuttered at a long-forgotten memory. She had found a star-shaped medallion by accident once in Paul's belongings when they were moving into their shared apartment. He said the medallions had been given to those who'd fought for Russia long ago.

At the time she hadn't thought twice about how he knew this. She'd asked how he'd acquired the piece and had accepted his answer, that a client had given it to him. But his knowledge and his possession of the medallion made sense now that she knew he had some connection to that country.

Possibly a close connection.

That medallion now rested in a shoebox along with Paul's watch, wedding band and gold money clip. Anger moved through her, weakening her desire to go any further.

Two young women pushed past her. They spoke in Russian, as did most of the residents of Brighton Beach.

Bold letters splashed across signs over stores and

the sides of buildings: Cyrillic writing that she didn't understand.

She clutched her purse tighter to her side as if the small black leather bag could protect her in some way from the inevitable—facing the other woman in Paul's life. Had he given her the love and tenderness, the security, Kate had craved?

"Ready?" Brody asked.

Somewhere inside the building before her was a woman who might possess the answers they sought. She wondered if her quest for the truth was about to end. Would she finally be at peace or left more adrift? She gave Brody a tight smile. "I don't know if *ready* is the right word, but let's do this."

"You can handle it, Kate. You're strong."

His words warmed her heart. With him by her side she *could* do this. God had known she'd need someone to lean on. She said a silent prayer of praise and asked for God's strength.

Together they moved up the stairs. Brody pushed the button next to the name of the woman who'd written the letters. A garbled noise came from the intercom. Brody spoke into the square box. "We're looking for Olga."

A moment later, the front door buzzed. Brody opened the door and they stepped into the building's small foyer. Peeling blue paint and water-stained linoleum attested to the age of the place.

A television droned somewhere and the smell of cabbage sent Kate's nose twitching. Above them, a door opened with a squeak and then a blond woman leaned over the dark wooden stairwell railing. She was too far away for Kate to make out her features.

"Olga?" Brody asked.

"Yes." She stared at them warily. "What do you want?"

"We were hoping you could help us with something. May we come up?"

The woman didn't answer.

Kate tried to give a reassuring smile, though her insides were knotted up. She didn't want to do this, didn't want to face the woman Paul had had an affair with. But Kate would face her and the situation. She'd come this far; she had to see things through.

"We'll only take a few moments of your time," Kate offered.

Still, the woman only stared, as if trying to decide. "It's about Pau…Petrov," Kate said, past the lump in her throat.

The woman's eyes widened and she waved them up.

Kate glanced at Brody as they climbed the stairs. "Do you think she knows he's dead?"

"I hope so," he muttered.

"Me, too." She also hoped the woman already knew about her because Kate didn't want to be the one to deliver two devastating blows at once. His death would be enough of a shock.

On the fifth floor, they walked toward the open doorway of the last apartment. Music drifted out, teasing Kate's memory. She knew the tune. One of Paul's favorites. She swallowed past the hurt tightening her chest and sought Brody's gaze.

He placed his hand firmly on the small of her back, infusing her with the power necessary to walk into Paul's third life.

The apartment was a surprise. The muted burgundies and blues splashed throughout the living room created a homey and inviting atmosphere. White lace curtains hung over the single-paned windows, the mixture of Mission-style, sixties retro furniture and a smattering of antiques giving a hip, garage-sale impression, so unlike the rest of the building.

But it was the woman standing by the scarred, round oak table in the dining room who drew Kate's attention. Willowy and fragile, the tall blond blinked at them with trepidation. Her statuesque build and coloring were so different from Kate's. She didn't know if she'd have felt better about the other woman if they'd resembled each other.

"Olga, my name is Kate Wheeler and this is…my friend, Brody McClain."

"You know my Petrov? Is he safe? I have not heard from him in a long time." Her heavy accent rolled off her tongue in a lyrical cadence.

A sick feeling settled in the pit of Kate's stomach.

Shuffling footsteps came down the hall of the apartment. A tiny elderly woman, wearing a worn, faded orange housecoat and powder-blue slippers, stopped at the doorway to the living room.

The woman had Olga's blue eyes, but her stooped shoulders and wizened face led Kate to guess this must be Olga's grandmother. The woman eyed them curiously, then spoke to Olga in Russian. Whatever Olga said in return earned them a scowl.

"My grandmama does not approve of Petrov," Olga explained and then said something more to her grandmother, to which the elderly woman made a face and shuffled back down the hall.

Kate wished her own grandmother had been around to warn her away from Paul. Though she couldn't honestly say she'd have listened, as Olga clearly hadn't. Paul had been so charming. Had appeared to be the kind of man who would give her the stable and secure life she'd dreamed of. If someone had warned her that he'd turn out to be such a louse, she'd have laughed. She wasn't laughing now.

Brody stepped forward. "Maybe you should sit down."

Olga frowned, her blue eyes wide with worry. "Tell me, please."

Brody glanced at Kate and she saw the same dread in his eyes that crept up her own spine.

"Olga," Kate said. "Petrov sent you a package. Do you still have it?"

Confusion entered Olga's eyes. "Yes. Where is Petrov?"

Kate hesitated, then said, "We have some bad news. The man you know as Petrov is…"

"Is dead," Brody finished for her, his tone expressionless. But his eyes held an anger toward Paul that touched Kate. Brody was angry on her behalf and on behalf of this young woman. She couldn't deny how good his support felt.

Olga blinked as huge tears welled in her eyes. "No. No, I don't believe you."

Kate forced the feelings Brody stirred within her to a far corner of her heart and took Olga by the hand, leading her to the dark blue couch. "I'm sorry we have to be the ones to tell you."

"Who are you? Why do you tell me this? Petrov cannot be dead. I'd know. My brothers would have told me. His mother would know."

Kate blinked, stunned by this revelation. "His mother?" She turned to Brody, who'd sat in a chair across from them. "Paul told me his parents were dead."

"Who is this Paul?" Olga's lower lip trembled. "What have you done with my Petrov?"

Pushing aside her own hurt and anger over her dead husband's deceit, Kate took a deep breath. "Your Petrov was also Paul Wheeler, my husband." She didn't even try to explain about Pete Kinsey.

Olga dropped her chin and drew back. Her gaze darted between Kate and Brody. "You lie. This cannot be."

Kate dug in her purse for her wallet and pulled out her wedding picture. With shaky hands, she handed the photo to Olga.

Olga stared at the photo without taking it. Tears slipped down her face. "I do not understand."

"Nor do I." Kate sympathized with Olga, understood the pain of realizing she'd been deceived.

"Olga, we need the package that Petrov sent to you." Brody's words brought the situation back in focus for Kate.

"Please, Olga. It's very important. It may be the key to why Paul…Petrov was killed." She hated the way her voice wavered when she said his name.

"Why should I trust you? I should call my brothers." She rose.

Brody made a gesture of entreaty. "There's no reason why you should trust us. We're strangers to you. All we can say is that whoever killed Petrov is now after Kate. Will you please help us so we can stop them?"

Olga's gaze searched Kate's face. No doubt she was wondering about the bruises and the cut. It occurred to Kate that she and Brody could be putting Olga in danger now, as well. But the bad guys hadn't found the letter so they didn't know about Olga. At least so she hoped.

Olga gave a slight nod and then left the room, disappearing down the hall. They heard Olga speaking with her grandmother, their voices low, yet from the intensity, Kate guessed Olga was informing her grandmother of Petrov's death.

"You okay?" Brody asked.

Kate felt as though she'd hit a brick wall. Numb,

dumbfounded, shocked. "I don't think I'll ever be okay again."

Brody took her hand. She sent up a silent prayer of thanks again for this man. She didn't know if she could have done this without him.

Olga returned carrying a small wrapped box. One that could easily hold a computer disk. "I was waiting for Petrov to return before I opened this. Those were his orders." She handed the box to Brody, who quickly dispensed with the paper. He opened the box and pulled out the contents.

A feminine gasp filled the air and Kate wasn't sure if it were her own or Olga's. As Olga reached for the stunning piece of jewelry that Brody lifted from the box, Kate turned away.

Just when she thought she couldn't hurt any more, Paul still managed to reach out from the grave and slice a fresh wound to her soul. The jade-studded gold pendant was identical to one Paul had given to her on their wedding night.

"It's not here." Brody's frustration was evident in his tone.

Kate shut off her emotions and refocused on why they were there. "Olga, we're looking for a computer disk. Did Petrov have a computer here?"

"No. He did not work with computers."

"What did Petrov do?" Brody questioned.

Olga's slim shoulders rose and fell in a stiff shrug. "He worked with my brothers. He traveled."

Brody's dark eyes took on an intense light.

"What's the name of the business and what is Petrov's family's name?"

"The company is Lanski Imports and Petrov Klein is…was his name."

Kate's brows rose in surprise. She glanced at Brody. He gave her a meaningful look and a slow nod. Brody'd been right that Mr. Lanski at least knew the name Petrov and most likely had known of his aliases.

Olga sniffed back more tears. "We were to be married next year. My brothers promised Petrov could stop traveling."

As soon as the divorce was final and he could leave Los Angeles, Kate thought sourly and swallowed hard against the fresh taste of hurt.

"Do you have an address for his mother?" Brody asked.

She willed herself not to care as Olga gave Brody the information he wanted. Paul/Pete/Petrov was a rat and she would not waste any more pain on him or his memory. She hated hurting like this, hated that she'd so easily allowed herself to be sucked into this horrible mess.

Never again. Never again would she allow anyone close enough to hurt her so much.

Brody recaptured her hand and Kate turned to stare into his eyes. She wondered bitterly which was worse: being used by her dead husband or the pity so clear in Brody's gaze.

* * *

Brody watched the shuttered look come over Kate and an ache deep inside twisted and squirmed. They'd received as much information as they were going to get from Olga. He rose and pulled Kate to her feet then quickly led her out, leaving behind a tearful Olga in the arms of her elderly grandma.

Once outside, Kate stepped away from him, her arms wrapping around her middle as she stared up the street. Brody sensed she wasn't seeing the hustle and bustle of pedestrians or taking in the ambiance of Little Odessa.

He touched her arm. She looked at his hand before lifting her gaze. He sucked in a quick breath at the desolate expression in her eyes. She couldn't be acting.

"I was such an imbecile," she said, her voice full of self-loathing.

"No. *He* was the imbecile." If the man weren't already dead, Brody would've taken great joy in torturing him.

"I don't understand. Why did he marry me? What plans did he have for me? For the woman up there?"

"I don't know. We may never know."

"That's unacceptable." Her hands clenched at her sides and her expression turned hard, unyielding. "I have to know."

Brody understood her frustration, her anger. The only advice he could give her was the same advice he'd heard and eventually had to learn to live with.

"You have to let go of the questions and make peace with the unknown."

She scoffed softly. "How do I do that? How do I live with the knowledge that I trusted him, gave everything I had to my marriage, and there was never any hope? It was a sham from the beginning. How do I live with that?"

He grazed a knuckle down her soft cheek, wiping away a lone tear, the wetness hot against his skin. "You learn to live with it. Learn to focus instead on the needs of each day. You can't change the past and you can't control the future."

Her hot glare seared him. "That's easy to say. You've never had to go through something like this."

He let his hand drop to his side. "I have, Kate. I know what you're going through." Only too well.

"You do?"

He wasn't ready to open that particular door. "Come on, we should go."

She spun away from him. "You'll have to see his mother alone. I can't do that."

"I wouldn't ask you to."

He hated seeing the hard edges going up around her, hated knowing that she was cloistering her heart behind a stone wall composed of anger, hurt and mistrust. He knew how lonely that place was. He hated that the fire and sparkle that had first drawn him to her were dwindling.

He stepped closer and gently grasped her shoulders. She felt stiff, yet fragile, beneath his touch.

"Don't do this, Kate. Don't let him hurt you any-more."

"I'd have to be able to feel to hurt."

Her icy tone sent a shiver moving along his spine like a storm blowing in from the Atlantic Ocean. He wasn't going to let her do this to herself. He wanted to see the spirited woman who'd fought him so bravely not that long ago. He turned her to face him. "Come on. I know you still feel something. Tell me you don't feel the sparks between us."

His words startled the coldness in her eyes back a step. Good. He wanted to chase that freezing bitterness as far away as he could. He refused to look too closely at why he felt the need to do so. "Tell me you don't wonder what it would be like to kiss me."

She blinked. Twin stains of pink spread across her cheeks. "Kiss you?"

"I've wondered, Kate. Would your lips be as soft as they look? Would you taste as sweet as the lilacs I smell in your hair?"

She tried to move away, but he held her firmly. Her gaze lifted. Beneath the hurt, an underlying current shimmered in the depths of her eyes. Her vulnerability stabbed at him, making his chest ache.

He silenced the voice inside his brain that warned he was getting in too deep. That warned he shouldn't trust.

His lips descended and met Kate's. Ripples of shock washed over him. She wasn't soft and pliant, she was hard as steel and just as strong, and she held herself at a distance from the flame ignited between them as if she were afraid of being burned.

He understood because he felt the same way. Drawn, yet terrified of the conflagration searing the air around them, between them. But he couldn't have pulled away even if the fire department had arrived to spray them with cold water.

He slid a hand from her shoulder to tangle in the mass of curls at the back of her head. Gently he caressed and massaged the tense muscles at the nape of her neck while he gentled his kiss.

She met his kiss with one of her own. His mind nearly exploded when that melting turned into a caress, her lips now receptive and sweet. He'd have sworn he could hear fireworks filling the sky.

Cement chips hit his legs with a sharp sting. Not fireworks. Gunfire.

ELEVEN

Deeply ingrained instincts kicked in and a familiar flood of adrenaline rushed through his blood. He pulled Kate down to the ground, covering her body with his own as his hand reached for the weapon holstered at his back.

A woman screamed, pedestrians ran for cover. Another round hit the pavement inches from his head and he flinched away from the flying shards of concrete. Time to move.

He pushed upward. "Come on!" In a low crouch, Brody hustled Kate to the shelter of a car. "Stay down!" he ordered.

Ignoring the swelling pain in his hip from the uncomfortable position, he peered over the back end of the tan sedan. His gaze roamed over the opposite sidewalk, along the storefronts and to the roof. There. Sunlight glinted off metal. Another round buried itself in the trunk of the car.

They had to get out of there. Brody looked for

an escape. The B and Q subway station was a half block away. If they could make it across the street, the sniper wouldn't have as clear a shot.

The rumble of an approaching train reached him. Brody squatted beside Kate with his back leaned against the car's door, putting his weight mostly on his bent left leg. Kate was tucked in a ball. She peeked up at him through a veil of red curls.

"We've got to make a break for it, cross the street and go to the subway. Think you can do it?"

She blinked rapidly. Her chin lifted and she gave a shaky nod. Admiration arced through him. He knew she was scared, but she wasn't giving in to her fear. *Atta girl.*

Taking her hand, Brody pushed away from the car, aiming his weapon at the man on the roof. "Go! Stay low!"

He squeezed off two rounds as he ran. Kate followed closely on his heels. More shots hit the ground, but they reached the other side of the street unharmed. Side by side, they ran toward the metal staircase leading up to the raised platform of the subway station. Their labored breaths mingled, drowning out the sounds of the approaching train.

People moved aside, giving barely curious glances as they ran past. With more finesse than he thought himself capable of, Brody jumped over the turnstile and then helped Kate scramble over.

"Hey!" shouted the token booth clerk from within her enclosed stall.

"Shots fired! Call 911!" Brody yelled.

With a loud swoosh and forceful current of air, the silver train roared into the station. Still clutching Kate's hand, Brody pushed their way to the last car and into the corner facing away from the station. He remained standing, while she sat on the bench.

Long moments passed as they waited for the metallic ding-ding that announced the imminent closure of the doors. Brody's watchful gaze searched for the unknown enemy through the window. Hopefully, the gunman on the roof had been alone. He didn't see anything that would lead him to believe they'd been followed. Who had known they were in Brighton Beach? Had they been tracked from Havensport?

The door closed and the train moved forward, picking up speed to rush over Brighton Beach toward Manhattan. Brody sank onto the seat beside Kate, his tension receding slightly even as his hip throbbed a sporadic beat. He glanced at Kate. Her chalky complexion and wide eyes as she stared out the window made Brody gather her into his arms. She shook violently and he expected hysterics. "Are you hurt?"

"No." She tilted her head back to look up at him, her gaze clear and sharp with intelligence. "And I thought things couldn't get any worse. Thank You, God, for my protector."

"Some protector," he muttered. If he'd been paying attention instead of kissing Kate, she wouldn't have come so close to being shot.

Kate twisted around to face him fully. "I'd have been toast a long time ago if it weren't for you."

Grateful to see her pluck returning, Brody gave her a grim smile and tightened his hold. "You're one incredible lady."

And if he wanted her to stay that way he had to start doing his job and control his attraction to Kate. Otherwise, he might just get them both killed.

Kate followed Brody from subway to subway until they reached Penn Station. She looked around with interest. She'd never been to the fabled train depot before and was surprised to see it had the same grime and grit as any station, only with a greater number of people filing in and out due to the commuter and Amtrak trains.

On the walls were pictures of how Penn Station had looked before the deconstruction in the sixties. Kate felt a pang of regret for the architecture and beauty of the old station. Brody ushered her quickly to the ticket agent's booth.

He purchased two tickets for a private compartment on a train bound for Boston. She kept glancing over her shoulder expecting to see armed men bearing down on them.

She urged Brody to call N.Y.P.D. in case the subway attendant hadn't, and ask for someone to check on Olga. Kate couldn't live with herself if the danger following her harmed someone else. He led her to a pay phone where he made the call, because he had no cell phone service in the station.

They boarded the train and settled in the private compartment: a small cubicle with a window, two red-leather benches facing each other and an overhead storage area. Soon the rhythm of the steel wheels vibrated through the floor and lulled Kate's frazzled senses.

Somebody had shot at her.

The frightening reality was much worse than any melodrama she'd ever imagined.

She sank back onto the cushioned bench, which was more comfortable than she'd thought it would be when she'd entered the compartment. For one person, the space would have been roomy, but Brody's presence filled the small cubicle. Now an intimate atmosphere charged the close quarters.

He sat opposite her, his long legs stretched out between them, his big body leaned back and his strong arms, arms that had held her so close, so gently, folded across his broad chest. He studied her with hooded eyes. Her gaze dropped to his lips and heat crept into her cheeks.

She felt awkward after their kiss. *Explosive* didn't do justice to the kiss and the connection she felt. She *had* wondered what it would be like to kiss him, and it was more wonderful than she could have imagined. Brody's touch had awakened a yearning she'd never known before. A yearning that, if she gave in to it, could destroy what little remained of her self-respect.

Deep down, the craving to be loved and cherished sat with her like a stubborn child refusing to give up a favored toy. Brody had undoubtedly kissed her to distract her from her pain over Paul, not because he cared. She had to remember that.

She fidgeted under his regard and couldn't take the silence anymore. "Why Boston?"

"I have friends in Boston who will help us," Brody replied, his expression unreadable.

She remembered he wasn't from Havensport. "Are you from Boston?"

He nodded.

When he didn't offer anymore, Kate pressed, "There's someone there you trust?"

"My ex-partner."

Kate absorbed that tidbit. "So you were on the force in Boston?"

"Yeah."

"What took you to Havensport?"

One solid shoulder rose and fell. "They needed a sheriff."

Frustrated by his lack of cooperation in keeping the conversation going, she prodded, "So you decided to give up being a…detective?"

He nodded. "Homicide."

Kate drew back. Everything inside her flinched. Homicide. Murder. Her husband. Thoughts tumbled around her head. A flutter of panic hit her stomach. Surely he couldn't suspect her after all that had happened. She had to believe that her trust wasn't misplaced because if it were…she'd be certifiable. Just lock her up and throw away the key.

No, she was being paranoid. Brody wouldn't be helping her if he believed she was guilty of murdering her husband. With effort she continued the conversation. "So you gave up being a homicide detective to become sheriff of a small, sleepy, coastal town?"

His mouth quirked. "Something like that."

"Why?"

His only response was a raised brow.

Obviously, she wasn't getting anything more out of him. Ever since they'd made it safely to the subway, Brody had been quiet. He seemed more withdrawn than she'd seen him before.

One moment he was holding her in a safe and secure cocoon and the next he was sitting stiffly beside her, his gaze barely touching her. And when it did, the reticence in his dark eyes made fresh tears sting the back of her throat.

She didn't blame him for resenting her. He wouldn't have almost been killed and wouldn't be running now if she'd just agreed to let him call the FBI. Though she knew if Brody had really wanted the FBI's help, he would have called them regardless of her wishes.

He wasn't a man who let others make decisions for him. He was a man of action. A lawman. Living a risky, unsecured life. Even as a small-town sheriff, he faced the unknown every day.

Her mind replayed the events of the last few hours. The woman her husband had been involved with wasn't some tramp. She'd been in love, planning for a future. Paul had used Olga, too. Kate felt sorry for her. The young woman didn't deserve to be lied to. But then, neither had she. Bitter anger rooted around, trying to find a spot to plant itself.

As she stared at the man across from her, his intense eyes unreadable, his jaw set in a firm line, she remembered his words.

You have to let go of the questions and make peace with the unknown...learn to live with it. I have... I know what you're going through.

He'd indicated once he didn't trust in God to care, so how could Brody really have any peace? What kept him from leaning on God? Only one way to find out. "What happened to you, Brody? You said you know what I'm going through. How? What unanswered questions have you tried to make peace with?"

He didn't move. The only indication that he'd heard her was his slight, indrawn breath. Kate studied him, learning his face, seeing the subtle changes as he thought about how to answer. He blinked, a slow sweep of black lashes over high cheekbones. Kate's gaze rested on his mouth, the strong, hard lips that could be so tender.

She wanted Brody to let her in, to open up to her, to prove that he trusted her and believed in her. She wanted to be friends.

Friends were all they could ever be.

She'd just have to make sure her heart understood that she was never going to fall in love with Sheriff Brody McClain. The life of a cop's or sheriff's wife was the antithesis of what she wanted—security, peace.

Too bad the rest of her longed for the comfort and care she'd found in his arms.

Suddenly Brody had the distinct feeling that the private compartment had been a mistake. They were too close, too alone and all of his senses were on alert. He was attuned to every move, every breath she took. It would be too easy to forget his job and take up where they'd left off before the bullets had started flying. He'd never protect her that way. The latest near miss was proof enough.

Now Kate was asking him pointed questions about his past that he had no intention of answering. He couldn't let his guard down; he couldn't succumb to the connection arcing between them because the only way never to risk getting hurt again was not to love again.

He remained motionless under her emerald gaze.

Her eyes narrowed. "Does it have anything to do with your limp?"

He forced himself to remain expressionless even though her question seared him clean through. Of course, she'd have noticed his limp, which had become more pronounced over the course of the day.

But had she noticed it before then? He stretched nonchalantly and shifted on the seat, taking some of the pressure off his sore hip. Why was he trying so hard not to reveal his injury to Kate?

Pride.

He didn't want her to view him as weak. How could she trust him to protect her if she knew he could no longer pass muster as a detective?

Kate moved from her seat and sat beside him on the padded bench seat. "You told me not to let Paul win by allowing him to hurt me anymore. Don't you think it's time you stopped letting your past win?"

His own words were coming back to haunt him. He gave her a hard glance. "You know nothing about my past."

"And you know everything about mine. Doesn't seem fair." She made an impatient gesture with her hands, her knuckles brushing against his leg.

Running a hand through his hair, Brody tried to ignore the prickles of awareness coursing through him at Kate's unintentional touch. "Telling you won't change anything."

"No, probably not."

Surprised by her bluntness, he turned to face her. Her eyes were closed, her head leaned back against the wall, her lips slightly parted as if waiting for his kiss.

Abruptly, he stood, his head hitting the low ceiling. He winced. "I'm going to find some food."

Kate opened her eyes and regarded him steadily,

her gaze telling him she knew exactly what he was doing. Running away from her uncomfortable questions, running away from her.

"Why are you doing this, Brody?"

He raised a brow. "I'm hungry?" he said, trying for levity.

Her lush mouth quirked. "I mean, why are you helping me? What's in it for you?"

Good question. A question that Brody had ignored from the get-go. Part of why he felt compelled—and that was a good description—to help Kate stemmed from some twisted need for redeeming his judgment. Somehow, by helping Kate, he could prove he wasn't a sucker for a pretty face and that he was now capable of determining the innocent from the guilty.

Then there was Kate herself. Her kind and gentle spirit, the spark of fire in her eyes, the way she looked at him with so much trust. Maybe it was because it felt so good to have her call him her guardian angel. If there were such a thing, Kate deserved one.

But so had his father, and there hadn't been one around. Brody steered his memories away from the night his father had died and from the thoughts of faith Kate stirred within him.

Her trust in him made him want to answer, even if his answer wasn't the complete truth. He sat down and braced his elbows on his knees. "I'm helping you because it's my job to."

She leaned forward. Red curls bounced on her shoulders, her expression was determined. "That's not why. Maybe at first, but it doesn't fly now. You could have handed me off to the FBI. Why didn't you?"

"And miss all this fun?" He blinked at her innocently.

Kate gave an exasperated shake of her head. "Is your family in Boston?"

"Yes." Brody's mouth quirked in amusement at her change in tactics. She was a tenacious lady. He had a feeling she wouldn't let up until she got the answers she wanted both from him and from her dead husband. He admired her determination even as he deplored the foolhardiness of treading on dangerous ground. She shouldn't be here, putting herself in the line of fire, searching for shadows.

"Talking to you is like talking to a brick wall," Kate muttered.

Brody chuckled. "You sound like my little sister."

Kate arched a brow, encouraging him without words to continue. He never talked about his family or his life. In his job, he was the one to ask the questions. He felt awkward. It occurred to him that there was safety in his role. He mentally shrugged. Telling her about his family could only deepen her confidence in him to protect her.

"My mom still lives in the house I grew up in. I have three siblings. My older brother, Patrick, teaches at Boston College, my little sister, Meghan, runs an art gallery in New York City and my baby brother, Ryan, is an investment broker."

"Your dad?"

Brody stiffened.

"Divorce?"

He relaxed slightly at the tenderness in her tone. He remembered what she'd told him of her parents. "No, my parents had a happy marriage." The need to confide in her caught him by surprise and he couldn't hold back. "My father was a cop."

Kate swallowed hard. A sinking feeling pulled at her. "Was?"

Pain deepened the darkness of his eyes. "He was killed."

Compassion tightened a knot in Kate's stomach. "I'm sorry."

"Yeah, me, too."

He splayed his fingers through his hair. A wayward lock fell across his forehead. She resisted the urge to push it back in place. "Was he on duty?"

The corners of his mouth tightened. "No. He'd just come off his shift." Brody's eyes took on a faraway glaze. "I'd missed the bus, so Mom called Dad and had him come pick me up at school. We were on our way home."

The realization of where this story was going filled her with dread.

A sad smiled touched his lips. "He teased me about liking school so much that I'd want to spend the night. We both laughed because my older brother Patrick was the one passionate about school."

The smile faded. "A call came over the radio. Another cop was in trouble, needed backup. We were just around the corner. I remember he hit the steering wheel with the palm of his hand and I nearly jumped out the window. He had this expression on his face that I'd dubbed his cop look…angry, intense. He jerked the wheel. We shot down a side street. We were the first to arrive. The other cruiser was empty, the door wide open. He told me to stay put and lock the door. Then he got out."

The dread squeezed her insides. "You didn't stay put."

"I was twelve. I wanted in on the action, wanted to see my dad take down the bad guy." He clenched and unclenched his fists. "Only I saw the bad guy take down my dad. The scum shot him in the chest. He died…instantly."

Her heart ached for the little boy who'd seen such violence, for the man who lived with the memory. No wonder he thought God didn't care. She touched his arm. The muscles beneath the cotton of his blue chambray shirt tensed. The naked anguish in his eyes hit Kate square in the chest.

"I'm so sorry, Brody. No one should witness that, let alone a child." She blinked back tears. "Why did you become a policeman?"

"To honor my father. To give to the department that gave so generously to our family." His jaw tightened. "To make sure the bad guys in this world paid for their crimes."

She squeezed his arm. "I admire you for that."

His hand closed over hers with unbearable tenderness. The expression in his fathomless eyes shifted. The pain receded. The inner light now in his eyes stalled her breath. She licked her lips. His gaze tracked the motion. Her heart hiccupped.

"I don't know why I told you." The husky timbre of his voice slid down Kate's spine, cementing the specialness of the moment. His story made her want to weep. His confidence moved her.

"Sometimes…it's good to talk," she murmured.

One side of his mouth cocked upward. "I've talked to more head doctors over the years than I have toes."

"That's a lot of doctors." Had he moved? His lips seemed so close.

"You should see my toes."

The vibrant tone in his whisper zinged through Kate. She dragged in a ragged breath. "As long as your feet don't smell."

Brody's rich laughter wrapped around her, releasing the pent-up energy charging the air between them.

Kate scooted away, allowing a cooling space to bring sanity back to the situation. "Did you say something about food?"

His amused gaze let her know he realized she was using his avoidance tactic. Embarrassment flushed through her. He stood and held out his hand. She allowed him to pull her to her feet and told herself to let go of his hand, but she couldn't quite find the power to release her hold on him as they went in search of the dining car.

She questioned her sanity. It was one thing to want the sheriff to believe her, to believe *in* her. And it was an entirely different thing to allow herself to bond to him. She would not fall for him, a man whose very job created insecurity.

TWELVE

Brody watched Kate from the corner of his eye. She stared out the window of the taxi, her eyes wide, taking it all in as they traveled down Summer Street.

"What a beautiful city," she commented as they crossed the Fort Point Channel.

His mouth twisted into a smile. He thought she was beautiful. Her hair, her eyes, her smile. There was no question the whole outside package was a work of art. But the real beauty lay within. There was beauty in her determination to see this ordeal through. Beauty in the resilience that kept her on her feet and moving. Beauty in her compassion and generosity to a woman who by all rights she should resent.

And her faith shone like a brilliant star, bringing light to even his darkened soul.

They were entering the area of Boston referred to as Southie. His part of town. The traffic slowed, became a crawl as they passed by heavy construction equipment and men wearing hard hats and orange vests. The work area seemed endless.

At her questioning glance, he said, "The Big Dig. The city's way of solving the increasing traffic problems. They're taking the highways underground."

The taxi moved forward, picking up speed as the traffic cleared. Brody watched his old haunts roll by. There was McGlinty's Tavern, the after-shifts hangout for several local precincts. On the corner was the movie theater, now expanded into a multiplex.

He'd known these streets so well. Grown up here, walked the same beat as his father before making detective. But all that went up in smoke one stormy night. His career stalled. His heart betrayed. His thoughts zeroed on the woman sitting beside him.

She'd gotten under his skin. That was the only explanation he could find for telling her about his father. He never spoke about that. Not even to Elise.

An uneasy feeling settled in the pit of his stomach. He shouldn't have let his guard down, he shouldn't have opened up to her, risking his heart. Risking betrayal. He wouldn't make the same mistake again.

No, he had a plan.

With the help of his ex-partner, they'd solve the mystery of Kate's husband and then he could get on with his life as sheriff without her.

But the thought of going back to his little studio apartment with its white, unadorned walls and cold hardwood floors didn't hold much appeal. Not when he could easily envision a home with Kate. A place where she would add feminine touches to make it cozy and warm, where her concern and affection would be his.

He frowned, not liking the direction his thoughts were taking him. Playing house was not an option. Emotions wouldn't dictate his moves. He had a job to do. The job must always come first. Kate was a job. Nothing more.

"Is something wrong?" Kate's anxious whisper shook him from his thoughts.

"No. Everything's great." Even to his own ears he didn't sound very convincing. He gave her what he hoped was a reassuring smile.

Moments later the taxi pulled up in front of the South Boston police precinct where Brody and his father before him had once served the public. Brody's chest grew tight. He hadn't been back since the day he'd become sheriff of Havensport. Suddenly he missed the serenity of his small town.

He helped Kate from the car. The pulsing beat of the city filled his senses and the afternoon sun made the cotton of his shirt stick to his skin. Kate's hand gripped his tightly. He saw the worry in her bright-green eyes. He squeezed her hand as he led her up the concrete steps toward the glass doors of the red-brick station house.

Once inside, Brody took a moment to absorb the familiarity of the precinct.

The soothing salmon tones of the marble-tiled walls reflected the light coming through the windows. His gaze took in the black-and-gold plaques spread out across the walls. His father's name was on the plaque near the top left-hand corner. He'd looked up to his dad when he was alive. It only seemed right that he could still look up to him.

Brody took a step forward. A twinge of pain shot up his leg, acutely reminding him he'd come close to having his own plaque etched with his name on that wall.

"McClain!" A gray-haired uniformed police officer charged forward with an outstretched hand. "As I live and breathe…I'd given up thinking we'd see you here again."

"Captain." Brody clasped Sean O'Grady's hand and was unceremoniously pulled into his father's old friend's embrace.

"Does your mother know you're in town, boy?"

"Not yet, but I'm sure she will soon."

From the twinkle in Sean's eyes, Brody had no doubt Colleen McClain would be receiving a phone call within minutes of her son's arrival. Though his father had been gone for years, the sense of family and community in the department continued for the widow and children when one of their own died in the line of duty.

Sean's gaze settled on Kate, who stood quietly to Brody's left. The curiosity and speculation glinting in the old man's eyes brought heat creeping up Brody's neck.

"This is Kate Wheeler," Brody said.

"Ma'am." Sean inclined his head and then turned questioning eyes to Brody.

"She's…uh…in my protective custody."

Bushy gray brows rose. "Your custody, eh? Didn't know sheriffs did that sort of thing."

Irritation burned its way into Brody's chest. Everyone on the force knew why he'd left; he didn't want them thinking history was repeating itself, that he was falling for another suspect. "Is Gabe around?"

Sean gestured with his hand toward the back of the station. "At his desk."

"Thanks." Brody grasped Kate by the elbow and pulled her with him away from Sean's scrutiny.

As they moved through the station, a sense of welcome wrapped around him as he acknowledged shouts of greeting and waves from fellow officers he'd once served with. He forced his mind not to dwell on why he'd left or on how good it felt to be back.

At the rear of the station house, past several rows of desks, sat his ex-partner, Gabriel Burke.

At one time Brody had been closer to Gabe than he'd been to his own two brothers, until Brody's stubborn defense of Elise had wedged a wall between them. A wall that remained today, five years later.

Brody braced himself as they approached Gabe and he met his ex-partner's wary hazel gaze. Gabe had aged. There were lines on his chiseled face that hadn't been there before and a few distinctive gray hairs at his temple.

Pleasure crowded Brody's chest. He quickly forced his emotions under control as he said, "Hey, Gabe."

"McClain." Gabe's gaze slid over Kate, over the hand with which Brody still held her elbow and back to meet Brody's eyes.

Brody stiffened at Gabe's silent reprimand, but he didn't release Kate. He'd stand behind his decision to help her without apology. "We need your help."

"Picking out china?"

"With a police matter," Brody stated firmly.

Gabe sat back and crossed his massive arms over his barrel chest. "Just can't keep yourself from getting mixed up with women who can ruin your career, now, can you, Brody?"

The air swooshed out of Brody's lungs as if he'd taken a shoulder in the gut. Apparently, securing his friend's help wasn't going to be as easy he'd anticipated.

Kate felt Brody flinch. She glanced up to see his strong jaw tighten and his eyes narrow with suppressed hostility. Nervousness roiled in her stomach. What was going on? Why were they so angry at each other? Who was this other woman Gabe mentioned? Brody's career ruined?

"Don't start with me, Gabe," Brody warned.

Gabe raised his hands, callused palms facing out. "Hey, I'm just stating the obvious."

"This is different."

Curious, Kate held her breath as the two men stared at each other for a long charged moment, then Gabe's gaze shifted to her. He was a good-looking man around Brody's age—midthirties, she'd guess—with a square jaw and light blond hair, though there was a hardness to Gabe that made her shiver. She lifted her chin beneath his uncomfortable scrutiny.

Gabe shrugged his massive shoulders as he once again turned his attention back to Brody. "Not according to the FBI."

Brody jerked his hand away, leaving Kate slightly off balance. A flutter of panic sent ripples up her spine.

"The Feds contacted you? Why?"

The thread of suspicion in Brody's voice made Kate pull her bottom lip between her teeth.

Gabe's gaze narrowed. "They know she's with you. They figured you'd contact me." One corner of his mouth curled upward. "And here you are. Seems they think *she*—" he nodded his blond head in Kate's direction "—possesses the information that could blow apart an international money-laundering scam."

A hot wave of shame and anger hit Kate. Not only had Paul been a liar but also a thief. And she'd never known.

Brody's gaze locked with hers. She couldn't read his thoughts; he'd put on that impassive cop face that she didn't like. She shook her head. "I don't have any information."

"The disk," Brody said sharply, his expression intent.

Her defenses kicked in. "I don't have it," she replied just as sharply.

His expression softened and he took her hand. "I know."

The comfort from his touch and the relief his unexpected words produced made her thankful she was firmly anchored to him or she'd have floated to the ceiling. She gave him a grateful smile.

Gabe sat forward. "What's this about a disk?"

Brody explained what had happened in the last few days. As she listened, Kate marveled at how good it felt to know Brody trusted her, believed her. She was truly blessed to have had God bring him into her life, even if there was no future for them together. As a couple.

She couldn't contemplate living the life of an officer's wife. She just couldn't. It was too risky and uncertain. Law officers faced death on a regular basis. And one day, death could win.

Gabe blew out a harsh breath. "What do you want me to tell the Feds? They want her brought into custody."

Gabe's question brought Kate's attention back to the situation. Her throat constricted, trapping her breath. For a moment the room spun. She held on tightly to Brody.

"Nothing yet." His thumb rubbed her palm in a reassuring manner. The panic quieted, but a whole other maelstrom of sensation started sliding through her blood as air filled her lungs. She really liked how easily he was able to calm her fears. She took a quick breath.

"I need your help to look into this import business her husband was involved with," Brody said.

Gabe studied her, but addressed Brody. "Are you sure you want to do this, Brody? You could hand her over to the Feds and be done with it. They'd protect her, they'd find the answers." He released Kate's gaze to turn to Brody. "You sure you want to go down this road again? Remember where it led last time."

A quick parade of anger and bitterness crossed Brody's features before he subdued his reactions into his normal impassive demeanor. "Like I said. This is different."

"Yeah." The corners of Gabe's mouth lifted into a humorless attempt at a smile. "Let's hope so."

Brody's jaw visibly tightened.

Gabe turned to the computer, his fingers tapping at the keys. "What are we looking for?"

Brody turned to Kate and indicated an empty desk adjacent to Gabe's. "Have a seat."

Feeling out of place and unneeded, she sat and watched the two men. One dark, one light. Both were big and strong-looking and exuded an air of confidence that she guessed came with the badge. She didn't much like the way Gabe assessed her as if she were gum stuck to his shoe, something he wished his friend would avoid.

She knew Brody wouldn't tell her what their coded conversation was about. She gathered a woman had hurt Brody once. The thought twisted inside her chest. He was a good man, and the more she knew of him, the more complex and interesting he became. And the more threatening to her heart.

Kate rested her elbow on the desk and placed her chin in her hand. The adrenaline from the day seeped out of her. She blinked several times, trying to fight the exhaustion, but she was losing the battle, just as she was with her growing feelings for Brody.

"Hey, your girlfriend's falling asleep at my desk."

Brody yanked his gaze away from the information on the computer screen and swung around to look at the dark-haired female officer he didn't recognize. She stared back at him with a raised brow. He shifted his gaze to Kate, who was slumped over the desk, her red curls spilling in disarray around her shoulders, her face relaxed and unguarded.

"She's not my girlfriend," he said even as something warm and tender expanded in his chest. He frowned at the unfamiliar sensation and checked his watch. He and Gabe had been at it for a long time, and what they'd found had him narrowing his gaze back on Kate. How could she not have known?

"Well, you going to move her or what?" the woman said.

"Cut 'em some slack, there, Angie," Gabe said.

Brody stood, taking his weight on his good leg. "We'll be out of your way in a sec."

He went to Kate and gently shook her shoulder. Her hair slid over his hand like a caress. His insides clenched and if they weren't in a public place he would have been seriously tempted to slide her hair farther away from her neck and kiss the spot where her pulse visibly beat beneath her pale skin. Instead, he said, "Kate, wake up."

She stirred and raised her head. Her unfocused gaze looked frantically around before she blinked up at him. "What happened?"

He reflexively touched her cheek. "You fell asleep."

She straightened and looked over his shoulder to the female officer standing behind him. "Sorry."

Angie shrugged. "No big deal."

Brody helped Kate to her feet. She adjusted the strap of her purse and gazed up at him expectantly. Since they hadn't planned on an extended trip to New York or the need to travel to Boston, they hadn't packed any clothes. He made a decision. "I'm taking you to my mother's."

A scoffing noise behind them set Brody's nerves on edge. He turned to glare at Gabe, who arched an innocent brow.

"We're not returning to Havensport?" Kate asked.

"Not yet." He turned again to Gabe. "Contact me if you find out any more info."

Gabe's intense gaze bore into him. "And the Feds?"

Brody couldn't ask his friend to lie for him. "Do what you will."

Gabe rolled his eyes. "I hope you know what you're doing."

Brody inclined his head but refrained from letting loose with the words *me, too.* He knew he was doing the right thing by trusting Kate.

And if he wasn't? What then?

As Kate followed Brody back through the station and out to the sidewalk, she couldn't help noticing there was something on his mind. She'd caught a glimpse of uncertainty in his dark gaze at Gabe's parting comment. She didn't appreciate Gabe resurrecting doubts in Brody's mind that she'd been working so hard to banish.

With his hand to the small of her back, Brody steered her around a few pedestrians and guided her toward the park across the street. The warm, late-summer air pressed in on her. Beads of perspiration formed on the back of her neck beneath her hair and soaked into her shirt. "Could we stop at a store so I can buy some clothes?"

One corner of Brody's mouth raised in a small smile. "I'm sure Meggie has something you can borrow."

"Meggie?"

"My little sister."

"Oh, right." Nervous butterflies kicked up their wings in her stomach. She was going to meet his family. What did that mean?

She tried not to let her imagination run amok with thoughts that he cared for her and wanted his family's approval. More likely he didn't know what else to do with her, where else to take her and keep her safe. Because she didn't doubt for a minute that Brody would continue to protect her. He'd given his word. Brody was a man full of honor and integrity.

But the thought of meeting his family still sent anxiety weaving around her heart. She had enough vanity to want to make a better impression on Brody's family than she had on Gabe.

"Where is your mother's house?" she asked, wondering why they were walking through the park.

Off to one side, a playground teeming with children filled the air with merry noise. A woman walking a poodle passed by and the little white fluff sniffed at Kate's feet before moving on.

"Our house is on the west end of the park."

They neared a small stream that flowed beneath a stone footbridge. As they crested the slight rise in the middle of the walkway, Brody captured Kate's hand and pulled her to the side. Her breath tripped and her senses perked up.

Releasing her hand, Brody said, "I have to tell you what I found out about your husband."

She leaned her hips against the railing and stared out over the lush green meadow, cut down the center by the trickling stream. A gentle breeze sent the leaves of the trees swaying into motion.

Kate watched the way the sun peeked in and out through the tree branches. She didn't want Brody to continue. Her quest for the truth was wearing her down. Why couldn't it all just go away? But it wouldn't. She knew peace would only come with the truth, so she braced herself for more. "Okay, what now?"

His gaze narrowed slightly. Watchfulness stole into his expression. "With the information Olga gave us, Gabe and I were able to find out more about Paul Wheeler. His true name was indeed Petrov Klein. He was born in Brighton Beach to Russian immigrants."

So Olga had known the real man.

Kate had been thoroughly conned. She shook her head in disgust and anger. She worked hard to keep the bitterness at bay.

"The Klein family and the Lanski family are both linked to what the media refers to as the Russian Mob."

Kate blinked. "Mob?"

"The *Organizatsiya*. Russian organized crime. Similar to the Italian Mafia, only worse in some ways. More educated and technically skilled. Petrov went to Yale, learned how to manage money and was put to working with the Lanskis' import business. The company is just this side of legit so the Feds can't shut it down.

"Petrov disappeared from the Feds' radar about

six years ago and apparently reemerged three years ago as Pete Kinsey, aka Paul Wheeler. The Feds think Petrov was getting tired of the game and wanted out. Maybe he threatened to expose the operation he was involved in. So they killed him. Now the Russians want the disk he'd put the incriminating information on."

Her mind reeled. Russian Mafia? A tight fist of rage lodged itself in her middle. She gazed up at Brody, beseeching him to make all this comprehensible. "I don't understand. How do I fit into this?"

"The bank you work for is connected through various channels to a Russian bank."

Kate put her cold hands to her face and looked away. "The bank?" It made a twisted kind of sense. "No wonder he'd been so gung-ho about my career. But how could my working for the bank help him? Them?"

At Brody's silence, she raised her gaze back to his. His guarded expression forced the breath from her lungs. She dropped her hands and faced him fully. "You can't possibly think I have anything to do with the Russian Mob."

His gaze searched her face. "Did you suspect anything at all? Did he ever slip into Russian when angry?"

"No!" She felt like she was treading water in a whirlpool. "I thought you believed in me."

"I want to, Kate."

She balled her fists at her sides as helpless fury

volleyed with indignation. "Then do. It's a matter of choice, Brody. Don't doubt me now, please." She had to have his reassurance. Though her faith would sustain her, she needed Brody's trust to hang on to as an anchor in the storm her life had become.

She prayed Brody wouldn't let her drown.

THIRTEEN

"It's not you I doubt, Kate. It's my own judgment."

Kate's fists relaxed slightly as an anxious ripple began somewhere in the vicinity of her heart. "Because some woman once betrayed you."

He flinched. "How did you…?"

"It wasn't too hard to read between the lines. Gabe's worried you're making the same mistake. What mistake?"

He frowned. "It doesn't matter."

"Yes, it does. This is my life that hangs in the balance. We've come this far, don't shut me out." Her heart ached in her chest. Her heart also hung in the balance.

He let out a heavy breath, his expression shifted, revealing his torment. "I became…involved with a suspect."

"Involved how?" she asked softly.

He met her gaze straight-on, his eyes full of bitter recrimination. "I fell hard."

Deep inside she responded to his pain. She also felt the sting of self-reproach for falling in love with Paul. "She didn't share your feelings?"

He laughed, a caustic noise that burst from his chest. "I thought she did, up until the moment she shot me."

She gasped, the air trapped painfully in her chest. He'd faced death at the hands of someone he'd loved. "Oh, no."

Her shocked response seemed to make him angry.

His lips, lips that could be so gentle, twisted into a harsh grimace. "Don't feel sorry for me, Kate. It's my own fault. I was too blind to see what everyone else saw so plainly. Too stubborn to listen."

She put a hand on his arm. The muscles flexed beneath her touch. "We're quite a pair. Here, I thought I'd cornered the market on bad judgment. Never looking beyond the surface. Seeing only what I wanted to see. Paul used me and I didn't even know it."

He ran a gentle finger down her cheek. The caress made her long for more of his touch. "You took your husband at face value, trusted him, as you should have. He's at fault, not you." His hand fell away. "I, on the other hand, should have known. It was a mistake that nearly cost me my life. It cost me my career."

She frowned. "They asked you to leave?"

He stared off into the distance, his expression drawn, showing the hurt that still lingered. "No, not in so many words. I was taken off the street. Relegated to a desk job."

She knew how devastating that must have been for a man who'd gone into law enforcement to honor his father. It hit her that he'd lost his father and his career for not heeding the warnings given. Had those warnings come from God? Was that the wall that stood between Brody and God's grace?

She ached for Brody in a way she'd never ached for anyone else. She wanted to heal him, to help find his way back to God. She want to love him.

Shying away from that last dangerous thought, she reached for him, wrapping her arms around his middle and laying her head against his chest.

He stiffened for a moment and she froze, thinking he'd push her away. But then his arms enfolded her in a warm embrace. She listened to the beat of his heart, took comfort from his embrace. Breathed in the mingling mix of scents clinging to him: the musky scent of man, the remnants of his aftershave and the smell of sunshine and earth from the park.

She leaned back to look up into his face. "You haven't lost everything, Brody. You're still sheriff, that's got to count for something."

His tender smile played across her senses like fingers strumming a guitar, making her body hum. "It does." A shadow passed over his face and the smile faded. "As long as I don't make the same mistake."

A shaft of hurt streaked through her. She drew

back, slipping her arms from around him. Her hands came to rest palms-down, flat against his chest. "So, if this woman betrayed you, used you… If she was so bad…then all women must be, is that it? Is that how I should feel, what I should think? That because Paul was such a rat, that all men are?"

The moment the words were out she realized that she could easily fall into that trap. Had started down that exact road. But Brody wasn't like that. He was good; he was sent by God to protect her. And she trusted him with her life. He'd already proved his honor to her.

He breathed out an audible breath. "No. I mean… it's not that simple."

"But it *is* that simple—and that complex at the same time. People have choices. God gave humans free will so we could choose. Choose to do right or wrong, choose to love Him or not. Choose to hurt others or not. It wasn't God's plan for you to be betrayed. It wasn't God's plan for your father to die. I know in my soul that God wept with you, Brody."

His heart thudded against her palms. In his gaze she saw his skepticism, his hurt and anger. Sadness rose up and choked her with tears.

Lead by example, Katie. The words spoken by her grandmother so long ago rang true in her head.

If she wanted Brody to believe in God's faithfulness then she needed to show him her own faith. "It wasn't God's plan for Paul to deceive me. I know

He's as angry as I am. But He promises to use all things for good for those who love Him. I love Him, Brody, and I know there will be some good out of all this muck. I choose to believe that."

He shook his head, his gaze shifting away. "I don't have that kind of faith."

"You can choose to." She wanted to help him find his way to God, to healing because he'd always be running from his guilt and shame otherwise.

He nudged her arms up so that she entwined them around his neck and then he pulled her closer as he leaned back against the stone railing of the footbridge. She nearly cried with the need to be loved, to be cherished. Her heart pounded so hard in her chest she figured any second a rib would snap.

He closed his eyes for a moment and when he opened them they were clear and focused on her. "You are an amazing lady, Kate Wheeler. You know just how to make a guy squirm."

A nervous laugh escaped her. "I'm not sure if that's a compliment or not."

He lowered his head. "It is."

His lips hovered above hers. His warm breath fanned out across her face. She dropped her gaze to his well-formed lips, and her own breath held somewhere between her heart and her throat.

She sensed he was waiting for her to make the next move, to meet him halfway. Did she dare? Did she want to deepen the connection between them when she knew she'd never allow it to go beyond a single kiss, beyond the point of needing his protection?

Because she wouldn't ask for his love.

He may not be an officer on the Boston police force but he was a lawman, a sheriff. She understood why he was an officer of the law, and she could never ask him to give that up. Nor could she live with it. She wanted normal, stable. No risks, no surprises. Peace and security.

But she also wanted Brody.

The dilemma left her head reeling. And with Brody crowding her senses, her rationale for not giving in to the moment paled to a paltry nuisance, like a mosquito flying about her head.

Lord, what do I do?

She searched her heart, hoping for some sign, some message telling her to back off or go ahead. There were only her feelings, her wants clamoring to be heard. But giving in to them would put her heart at risk. "Brody, we shouldn't…I can't. You're…"

"I'm what?"

His deep voice rasped across her senses, weakening her resolve. She took a shuddering breath. She wanted there to only be honesty between them. "There's no future for us, Brody. Your life is too full of danger. I can't be like my mother, always wondering, worrying if you'd come home at the end of the day. I want peace and security. You can't offer me that."

"No, I can't," he agreed, though his lips still hovered close, beckoning.

Yearning welled, urging her to take what he offered, if only for the moment. "We really shouldn't start something that we can't finish," she mused more to herself than to him.

He made a noise of agreement in his throat and then lifted his chin to softly press his lips to her forehead. The chaste kiss left her frustrated and yearning for what could never be.

"Like I said, an amazing woman." He released her and stepped away. "Let's go. I'm sure my mom is anxiously waiting for us."

She told herself she should be relieved and grateful he'd let her go so easily, but she couldn't help feeling as if she'd just let something wonderful slip through her grasp.

It wasn't God's plan.

Brody chewed on that statement as he eased Kate along the park's paved path toward his childhood home. Though his pulse had slowed to a normal rate, he had to force his mind to concentrate on the tidbit of wisdom Kate had doled out and not on the kiss they'd almost shared.

If it wasn't God's plan that his father die, that Brody would be betrayed by the woman he'd thought he'd loved, then why had they happened? Why did any of the bad things in life happen? Where was God's grace?

Kate talked about choices. Somewhere inside his soul he knew that to be true. Probably some long-forgotten Sunday-school lessons hidden deep in the recesses of his being. Church had been a constant in the McClain family for as long as he could remember. His mother still attended, but after his father's death, Brody couldn't go. He'd felt too hurt, too guilty to seek God.

But ever since Kate had stepped into his life, the faith he'd turned away from kept nudging at him, reminding him of the truths he'd learned as a boy. Reminding him of the betrayal he'd felt when his father died.

He still didn't understand God's plan. He wasn't sure he ever would or even if he wanted to. He didn't want his guilt confirmed. Didn't want to know that had he obeyed his father, his father would still be alive. He didn't deserve God's grace.

Kate stumbled on a rut in the blacktop path. Brody gripped her elbow tighter as she leaned into him for a moment. He caught a faint whiff of her lilac scent and thought of the freshness of spring. Her curves pressed into his side for a split second before she straightened and continued on. His mouth went dry.

He vividly remembered the feel of those curves,

soft and yielding. She'd felt so good, so right in his arms. She made him feel alive.

She was right to call a halt to…he didn't even know what to call that moment on the bridge. Another lapse in judgment? How many times was he going to ignore his vow not to let her in, to let her close?

Kissing her again would have been a huge mistake. Because this time it would have been from wanting her rather than hoping to distract her. And wanting her was not something he intended to let happen. Not again.

He looked up and found they'd come to the edge of the park and stood on the sidewalk facing the two-story home he'd grown up in. His chest tightened. As a boy running home from the park he'd never taken the time to notice how colorful his mother's flowers were, nor how comforting it was to have a place to come home to, to feel safe in.

Comfort welled up and clogged his throat. All the good memories in his life were here in this house. It had taken time away for him to really appreciate the life his mother had worked so hard to provide for her children after his father's death.

"Brody?" Kate's uncertain, tentative expression tugged at his heart.

He smiled with reassurance. "The white house with the green shutters and the tall oak in the front yard. That's where I grew up." He pointed to the second-story window on the right. "My brothers and I shared that room."

"Is that one of your brothers there, by the black car?"

Noticing the black BMW sedan parked on the street, Brody raised a brow. His younger brother leaned against the side of the car, dressed in his uniform, a dark blue pin-striped suit and red tie. He held a cell phone to his ear in one hand while the other hand gestured wildly to punctuate whatever he was saying.

Brotherly love gripped Brody. He hadn't realized how much he'd missed his siblings. "Yes, that's Ryan, the financial mogul. He's also the baby in the family." His little brother who'd followed him around, dogging his steps. "Only don't let him know I said that. The last time I referred to Ryan as the baby, we both came away from the ensuing scuffle with black eyes and bruised egos."

Kate chuckled. "I won't tell."

They crossed the street. Brody's first inclination was to guide her straight up the front stairs and into the house to avoid the inevitable questions from his little brother about the pretty woman on his arm, but Ryan waved to him and Brody resigned himself to engaging with his gregarious younger sibling.

Brody didn't know why he'd thought he'd be able to bring Kate home without being grilled like a fish on the barbecue. His family was all about sharing the details. Something he'd not relished growing up.

Kate stepped off to the side by the gate as Brody moved closer to the black car.

"We'll close at half a mil and no less." Ryan made a face at the person on the phone. "Think about it. We'll talk tomorrow. Gotta go." He clicked his phone closed and shook his head before slipping the small silver technological wonder into the breast pocket of his suit jacket. Pleasure lit up his brown gaze. "Well. Are my eyes deceiving me or is that my big brother?"

"One of them," Brody responded drily.

Ryan came off the car in a flash, his facing breaking into an easy smile as he engulfed Brody in a bear hug. "Mom's going to be beside herself."

Brody returned the embrace. Ryan was no longer the scrawny kid who used to trail after him. His little brother had filled out and grown nearly as tall as himself. Brody felt a pang of guilt for not having kept in better contact with his siblings and for not having helped their older brother Patrick more.

Patrick had stepped in as head of the McClains after their father was killed. Brody had been too traumatized at first even to be aware of how their father's death affected his siblings. Then he'd put all his energy and effort into becoming an officer to carry on in his father's place.

He clapped Ryan on the shoulder as they parted. "You don't look worse for the wear."

Ryan nodded, his chest puffing up slightly. "I do well for myself."

"I know. I've heard. Wheeling and dealing." His mother had told him of his younger brother's passion for accumulating. Brody hoped it wouldn't lead Ryan down a bad path.

He decided when this thing with Kate was over, he'd sit his little brother down and have a long-overdue chat about how money didn't solve problems. Though he doubted Ryan would listen to him. He certainly never had growing up. Why would he start now?

"Wheeling and dealing is what I do best," Ryan said.

Brody couldn't deny that. Ryan had always had an entrepreneurial spirit. Even as a young boy, he'd found ways to make money. Mowing lawns for the neighbors, washing cars for the officers at the station, setting up a lemonade stand. Not just on the sidewalk in front of their house or even the corner of the street. No, Ryan would trudge deep into the park and put his stand near whichever sporting event was taking place. He always came home with his pockets filled with coins. His success probably had more to do with his charm than his lemonade. A good-looking kid, he'd been a big hit, especially with the ladies.

Something that hadn't changed over the years according to his mother. Ryan was the charming one.

Always bringing around different girls but never sticking with one for very long.

On the heels of that thought Brody noticed the curious and assessing stare Ryan was giving Kate.

"Who's this lovely lady?" Ryan asked.

"A friend."

Ryan raised a brow. "Mother *will* be pleased. You don't often bring home 'friends.'"

Brody ground his back teeth together. He should have anticipated the assumptions his family would jump to. All he'd been thinking about was keeping Kate safe and getting her somewhere to rest. "It's not like that."

"What a shame," Ryan murmured and moved toward Kate. Brody didn't like the predatory gleam in Ryan's eyes or the grin spreading across the face that had captured and broken many hearts.

"Hello, I'm Ryan McClain." He offered his hand to Kate, his voice charming, smooth.

Brody frowned.

She took his hand, pink brightening her cheeks.

Brody drew back, not liking the way she was reacting and definitely not liking that he even noticed.

"Kate Wheeler," she said, sounding bemused.

"It's a pleasure." Ryan pressed a kiss to the smooth skin on the back of Kate's hand. Her eyes widened and her blush deepened.

An abrupt blast of possessiveness hit Brody like the potent sting of pepper spray. He moved to Kate's side and placed his hand on the small of her back in a purely territorial way. Both Kate and Ryan stared at him in obvious surprise.

"We should go in," Brody said to cover his reaction.

The knowing glint in Ryan's eyes clearly stated he wasn't fooled. Brody chose not to meet Kate's gaze as he ushered her up the front stairs and into the house.

Brody's mind tried to get around what had just happened. He'd never felt anything like this before, not even for Elise. Protectiveness was one thing, but possessiveness? He mentally turned a deaf ear to the warning bells in his head. Now was not the time to try to deal with his foolishness. He needed to keep focused on his purpose for coming to Boston—to protect Kate and find out the truth about why her husband had been killed.

There couldn't be anything more between them than that. He just didn't have it in him to trust anyone that much.

Kate followed Brody as he pushed open the heavy oak front door with the stained-glass windows.

"Mom?" Brody called out.

"Probably in the garden," Ryan stated from behind Kate.

She tried to control the nervous ripple along her limbs at the prospect of meeting Brody's mother. She told herself it was natural to be wary of meeting someone new, but deep down she wanted Mrs. McClain to like her. Though it shouldn't matter. She wasn't Brody's girl.

But Ryan had said Brody didn't often bring home friends. Which meant Brody hadn't introduced his mother to many of the women he'd dated. Had he brought home the woman who'd hurt him? Jealousy stirred, taking her by surprise. She had no right to feel possessive of him. She held no claim on his affections. No matter what her fanciful heart wished.

She stepped into the foyer and was struck by the bright cheerfulness of the home.

A gleaming hardwood floor stretched beneath her feet and extended into the living room to the left and the formal dining area to the right. A staircase with a polished mahogany banister led to the second floor. She could see the tiled floors and granite counters of the kitchen straight ahead.

The living room was a profusion of color against dark fabrics and wood-paneled walls. Throw rugs and pillows of assorted shapes looked artlessly placed, yet the whole effect was very welcoming. All sorts of fresh flowers in vases of various styles filled every available space.

Her gaze was drawn to the gilt-framed oil painting above a beautiful mantel and fireplace. The McClain family stared back at her and a sense of awe filled her.

A handsome, uniformed man stood in the background. Dark hair, intense ebony eyes. Brody's father. Kate wondered what type of man he had been. Flanking him on either side were two dark-haired sons. Kate immediately knew which was Brody.

She recognized the earnest smile and wavy hair. She guessed him to be nine. The other boy was taller with a proud tilt to his square jaw and just a hint of a smile as if he hadn't been sure he wanted to relax.

Seated in front of Brody's father was a striking woman with long black hair and crystal-blue eyes. A young girl stood beside her mother, their resemblance uncanny. Both possessed high cheekbones and fair skin. Meghan McClain had also inherited her mother's blue eyes.

A small boy sat on Mrs. McClain's lap. Ryan. Even as a child, his grin was devastating and there was no mistaking the impish light in his dark eyes. Such a lovely family. Sadness touched Kate's heart. This family had lost their father and husband not too many years after this portrait had been done.

"Kate."

She blinked back the tears threatening to escape and turned to find Brody's gaze searching her face. Aware that Ryan stood casually poised by the door frame watching them, she said, "Your home is beautiful."

"I don't live here anymore."

"But it's still your home." Her gaze and her pronouncement included both brothers.

"You hear that, Brody? Sometimes I think you've forgotten." Ryan's softly spoken words held a bit of reprimand but also a dose of hope, as if reminding his older brother that he was still welcome at home might bring him back more often.

A hint of a smile curled the ends of Brody's mouth. "I haven't forgotten."

The men exchanged a silent communication that excluded Kate. Yet, she didn't feel slighted. Instead, a warm glow spread through her. She'd witnessed the bond being strengthened between the two brothers. She'd always wished she'd had siblings.

Then Brody shifted his gaze back to her. Eagerness and tenderness mingled in his expression and melted her heart. "Come out back. I'd like you to meet my mother."

Her mouth went dry. What was she doing? Meeting Brody's mother and being in his childhood home went against the idea of not getting too involved. But she was here and she wouldn't be rude, not after all that Brody had done for her.

She took Brody's offered hand just as the ringing of a phone startled her. Her hand convulsively tightened around Brody's at the jarring noise. Ryan withdrew his small silver cell phone from his pocket and headed up the staircase.

Brody gave her hand a reassuring squeeze. "A little jumpy?"

She smiled sheepishly. "After the day—no, make

that the last month, or year, even—I've had, I think I'm allowed."

His dark eyes twinkled. "You are indeed. You're holding up well, Kate. I'm proud of you."

His words made her feel empowered and pleased. She liked that he'd think of her that way. She *was* holding up well, considering someone was trying to kill her and she was growing attached to a man who'd eventually have no more reason to be in her life.

She didn't want to consider why that thought left her more scared than thoughts of her unknown assassins.

FOURTEEN

Brody tugged her hand, urging her to follow him through the kitchen and out the back door into an incredible yard. A brick patio extended from the door about five feet, then a lush lawn, broken only by wood-rimmed flower beds and four distinctive trees ended at the dark-stained fence encircling the whole area.

A woman with a trowel in her gloved hand knelt beside a multi-colored rainbow of perennials. She was dressed in blue denim overalls, a red shirt and green rubber garden shoes. She flipped a long, dark braid over her shoulder as she turned her head at the sound of their approach.

Bright, clear blue eyes widened for a fraction of a second before unabashed joy spread over the older woman's face. Mrs. McClain gave a cry of glee before she scrambled to her feet and hurried to throw herself into Brody's arms.

Kate hung back, feeling uncomfortable watching

the affectionate reunion. She'd never had that kind of reaction from her parents. Her father might go as far as to shake her hand and her mother…well, if she were sober she might give her a stiff hug. But certainly not with the kind of happiness Brody was receiving from his mother.

"Let me look at you." Brody's mom held him at arm's length. Though she wasn't as tall as her middle son, her carriage and presence made her a statuesque woman. "I scarcely believed Sean when he called to say you'd been at the station."

Mrs. McClain's gaze captured Kate over Brody's shoulder. Kate straightened under the curiosity and was relieved to see the smile now directed at her was genuine.

Mrs. McClain turned wide eyes to Brody. "Don't be rude, son. Introduce me to your friend."

Brody's neck reddened, but the expression on his face was tender.

Kate swallowed back the choking guilt for using him so ruthlessly.

"Mother, this is Kate Wheeler."

Mrs. McClain peeled off her garden gloves and tossed them onto a wooden bench before holding out her hand. "Hello, Kate."

She took the offered hand, liking the woman's forthright way. "Hello, Mrs. McClain. It's a pleasure to meet you."

The older woman held on to her hand for a moment. Her blue eyes searched Kate's face before she responded. "I'm happy you're here. And please, call me Colleen."

Kate's heart spasmed. It felt good to be wanted. Colleen gave Kate's hand a squeeze, as if she could sense the emotion welling inside her, before letting go.

Colleen slanted Brody a glance. "You're staying for dinner?"

He nodded. "Yes. I was hoping Meggie might have some extra clothes here that Kate could borrow."

Kate inwardly cringed. What kind of impression was she making on Colleen by being so needy?

"Of course she does." Colleen looped her arm through Kate's. "Come with me, dear. We'll get you set up nicely."

Overwhelmed by Colleen's kindness, Kate met Brody's gaze. He smiled reassuringly and urged her on with a tilt of his head. Clutching her purse to her side, she allowed Colleen to lead her back into the house. The feeling of welcome and comfort surrounding her formed a knot in her chest. It wasn't right that she was here, that Brody's family was opening their home to her when she was using Brody so horribly for her own protection.

But what choice did she have?

After Kate and his mom left, Brody sat down in a cushioned patio chair and allowed the quiet of the garden to ease some of the tension from his body.

He'd always loved to come out here when life had become too much. The shrink he'd been forced to see after his father's death, and again after Elise, had suggested he find a place where he could think. He'd known his mother came to the garden when she wanted to talk with God. So he'd come back here.

Brody had tried talking to God a few times, but the guilt and anger riding him would always become overwhelming. As he'd grown older, he'd learned how to keep the accusations and the self-recriminations at bay, but a deep emptiness kept him from finding peace.

Still kept him from finding peace.

God wept with you.

Brody scrubbed a hand over his gritty eyes. Kate's assurance, her rock-steady faith, gave him some comfort. And yet the cavernous space inside his chest seemed to expand and press on him, urging him to…to what, he didn't know.

Grace.

The word reverberated around his head and his soul, frustrating him because he didn't get how God's grace applied to his life.

He forced his thoughts to the present situation. They had to find the disk. That was the only way he could guarantee Kate's safety. The only way they could figure out the future.

Tension slammed through him. Did he want a future with Kate?

He stood and restlessly paced the brick patio.

He liked Kate. Liked her humor and her spunk. Enjoyed her company. He was attracted to her as all get out. Warning bells of alarm erupted within him, sending his heart rate through the roof.

He cared for her, that much was true. But he'd been down that road. And until he'd met Kate, he'd never thought he'd go again.

But Kate was not Elise.

The situation was different. *She* was different.

He rubbed a hand through his hair. They had to find that disk before he could even analyze his feelings. Or, he mentally added with a rueful twist of his lips, overcome the obstacle of his career. Kate had said she couldn't live with the danger his career put him in. But upholding justice was more than a career to him, more than a job. It was his life.

He couldn't see any way around that.

Kate's eyelids fluttered open. Dusk was closing in, making her vision tough to focus in the graying light. She took a moment to absorb the unfamiliar room. The tall dresser to the right of the door, the desk and wooden chair by the window. The shelves filled with dolls collecting dust. The four-poster bed beneath her with its frilly comforter and ruffled pillow shams.

In a rush she remembered. She was in Brody's childhood home, lying on his sister's bed.

When Colleen McClain had brought her upstairs, she'd insisted Kate rest after pulling out some leggings and a cute long tunic blouse from the white dresser drawers. Colleen had clucked over her like a mother hen, much as Myrtle had. It warmed Kate to feel so cared for even as guilt pricked her conscience.

She'd been nothing but a burden to Brody since they'd met. It wasn't fair that she was clinging to him for protection when there was no future for them. No matter how much she'd grown to care for him. She didn't want to hurt him or his family.

She wondered where Brody was now. She sat up and dropped her feet to the ground. A plush rug covering the hardwood floor tickled her uncovered toes. Reaching down, she found her shoes and socks and quickly donned them.

Her gaze stalled on the white princess-style phone on the desk. It was time to take Gordon up on his offer of help and time to shift her reliance off Brody.

She called Gordon's office and was told to try his cellular phone. He picked up on the first ring.

"Kate, where are you?"

"In Boston. At the house of…a friend."

"Did you find the disk?"

"No. But we found out Paul's real name."

"Real name?" Surprised showed in his tone. "Kate, I'm confused. What are you talking about?"

She sighed. "We found out he had connections to organized crime."

There was a moment of silence. "I'm shocked. I had no clue."

"He had us all snowed."

"Have you told the authorities what you've found out?"

"That's why I called. I need your help. The FBI are looking for me. They also think I know where the disk is. But I don't."

"My advice to you, Kate, dear, is to return to Los Angeles as soon as possible. You can sell the Havensport property and put this all behind you."

"But Gordon, I have to find the truth. I have to know what Paul was doing and why he dragged me into this mess. I have to find the disk."

"Sometimes the truth does not set us free, Kate."

Frowning at the ominous message, Kate said, "That's not encouraging."

"Where are you?"

She gave him the address.

"I'll be there as soon as possible," he promised.

She hung up and was gripped with the urge to see Brody. Somehow she was going to have to find a way to explain to Brody why she'd called Gordon and why she couldn't continue to use Brody. She prayed that when the time came, inspiration would hit.

Grabbing her purse from the top of the dresser, she opened the door to the hall. She stepped out of the room and instinctively headed left toward the light traveling up the staircase. A fragment of noise coming from her right caught her attention. She spun around and collided with a rock-hard obstacle.

Hands grabbed her shoulders. Her blood froze. They'd found her.

The thought sent panic roaring through her system like a dam bursting loose. A scream tore from her lungs. Her purse dropped to the ground with a clatter, the contents spilling at her feet. She clawed at the hands holding her.

"Take it easy." A deep masculine voice rasped into her panicked mind. The hands released her abruptly. She staggered back and pressed herself against the wall. The man remained motionless in the shadows.

Pounding feet stormed up the staircase. "Kate?"

She flung herself at Brody as he crested the top stair. His strong arms wrapped around her, secure and comforting. She took deep gulping breaths trying to calm her pulse.

"What's going on?" Colleen McClain pushed past Brody and flicked on the hall light. "Is she all right?"

From behind Brody, Ryan's amused voice cut through the tension charging the air. "I think Patrick gave Kate a good scare."

"Patrick?" Kate lifted her head and stared back at the man standing down the hall.

With the light illuminating him, she saw he was indeed tall, with wide shoulders and long legs. He looked like the professor Brody said he was, not a killer. He wore a brown tweed coat and tan slacks. From behind his wire-rimmed glasses his gaze bored into her with dark intensity.

"Who's she?" Patrick asked.

"Brody's friend," Colleen answered.

Patrick's brows rose as his gaze shifted from Kate to Brody. "Really. How interesting."

Brody tensed and Kate expected him to release her but his arms tightened slightly. Pleasure moved through her and guilt made her want to cry. He was silently claiming her and if he didn't live such a dangerous life she'd rejoice.

She looked at Colleen McClain. How had she survived the life and death of her police officer husband?

Though Kate's father hadn't been a law officer, he'd put his life in danger every time he went on a mission. He'd put his military career ahead of his family. When he'd left, it was as if he'd died, he'd so completely disappeared from their lives. It wasn't until Kate was in her midtwenties that he'd made contact with her again. And Kate's mother hadn't fared well. Still wasn't coping with the loss of her husband, her marriage.

Kate wanted the ideal. A normal husband who worked nine to five with weekends off, the house with the picket fence, two point five kids and a dog. She wanted normal.

A sick feeling settled in the pit of her stomach. She'd thought she had that with Paul. Everything had seemed to be lining up with her plans. But in the end she did end up like her mother—betrayed, abandoned and alone.

Only the strong arms and big body surrounding her belied that thought. She lifted her gaze up to

Brody's handsome face. A face so familiar she doubted she'd ever forget a single detail. The sloping flare of his nose and those ebony eyes so full of life. His lips that could be so tender were now pressed into a grim line as he faced his older brother.

Her heart pounded against her breastbone. Maybe she needed to rethink her idea of normal. The possibilities that thought opened up weakened her knees. She leaned into Brody, distracting him from his brother. Their gazes met and his expression softened. She gave him a shaky smile.

Patrick cleared his throat, drawing their attention. "I didn't mean to scare you."

"It's okay."

"Patrick, this is Kate Wheeler. Kate, my older brother Patrick."

Patrick extended his hand and stepped forward, his loafer-clad foot sending a lipstick tube scuttling across the hall floor.

"Oh, no." She'd forgotten about her spilled purse. After disengaging herself from Brody, Kate bent to retrieve her scattered belongings, aware of three sets of male eyes taking inventory of her cosmetics, flowered wallet and other feminine items.

"Boys, why don't you go ready the dining room for dinner?" Colleen took command of the situation. "Kate and I can take care of this."

"Gladly," Patrick said as he stepped around Kate and stopped beside Brody, clapping him on the back. "Welcome home."

"Thanks," Brody said.

"I want to hear how you met Kate," Ryan piped up.

"Yes, do tell," agreed Patrick.

Kate glanced up and met Brody's wry half smile. "It's complicated," he said.

That was an understatement. Kate grinned back at Brody.

He winked and then led his brothers down the stairs.

"You'll have to excuse my sons' curiosity about you. I can count on one hand the number of girls Brody has brought home since he was old enough to date. He was always so focused on his career. You must be pretty special."

Not special enough for Paul to tell her the truth. Daunted by Colleen's pronouncement and unsure how to respond, Kate reached for her purse.

"Ryan, on the other hand, has been bringing girls home by the dozen since he could talk them into coming with him. But he can't seem to commit to just one." There was amusement and sadness in Colleen's voice.

"And Patrick?" Kate asked.

A pensive expression settled on Colleen's face. Tiny fine lines bracketed her bright blue eyes. She picked up Kate's flowered wallet, her long elegant fingers toyed with the edge. "Patrick has always been serious, even as a child. After my husband died, a great deal of responsibility was heaped onto Patrick's young shoulders. He hasn't let that go yet. I keep praying the right girl will come along one day and he'll realize it's time to start living his own life."

Kate scooped up a handful of items and stuffed them into the purse as she blinked back the sudden tears. One life cut short and so many other lives affected. Guilt for his father's death clung to Brody, Patrick still carried the weight of family responsibility and Ryan couldn't commit. Kate wondered how the fourth child, Meghan, had fared.

"Here." Colleen handed over the wallet.

"Brody still blames himself for his father's death," Kate said gently.

Colleen's hand shook as Kate relieved her of the wallet. She sat back on her heels, her blue eyes round. "He told you."

Kate nodded. Her pulse picked up speed and the few remaining items at her feet were momentarily forgotten. The enormity of Brody telling her about his father was not lost on Kate. Obviously, he didn't share himself with many people.

"Wow." Tears formed in Colleen's eyes making the blue brighter, more vibrant. "He's not to blame, you know."

"I know. But he can't see that. All he sees is that his choice to get out of the car killed his father."

"No!" Colleen wiped furiously at the tears tumbling down her cheeks. "It was Robert's choice that got him killed. He should have never gone there with his son in the car."

Kate couldn't refute that and her heart twisted with sympathy for Brody's mother.

"I'm sorry. I don't usually go off like that."

Reaching out, Kate touched Colleen's hand. "It's okay." She bit her lip and gathered her courage to ask, "Do you regret marrying a policeman?"

Colleen cocked her head to one side. The speculative and knowing look in her gaze sent heat creeping into Kate's face. "Never. It was who he was." Colleen squeezed Kate's hand. "The only thing you can be sure of in life is love. And when you find love, hold on to it."

Kate took a shuddering breath, wishing she could be alone to analyze and decipher her feelings for Brody. She could no longer deny that her feelings for him ran deep. But she didn't know if she had it in her to love a man with such a risky job. "Thank you."

Colleen's smile was wide. "I think I'll be the one thanking *you* someday."

Afraid Colleen would see the conflict going on inside her, Kate ducked her head and quickly gathered the last of the items and stuffed them into the purse before standing.

"Oh, no," Colleen exclaimed as she stood beside her.

"What?" Kate held up her purse. The hard-sided bottom hung at a crazy angle. She sighed. "When I dropped it, it must have broken. Oh, well." She'd actually be glad to get rid of all reminders of Paul.

"Here, let me see." Colleen took the bag and fiddled with the extending piece. Under her manipulations it slipped back into place with a slight click. "I thought so. I have a purse that has a compartment like this one."

"A compartment?" Kate examined the bottom as her pulse leapt. "How does it work?"

"Press under the edge."

Kate did, and the bottom moved. Why hadn't she ever noticed that? Paul must have known, since he'd given her the thing. Her mind raced to a conclusion that made her tremble with excitement. Could it be? She pushed the stiff plastic piece farther aside and stuck her hand into the dark interior to the bottom of her purse.

Nothing.

Disappointment crashed over her, making tears burn the back of her eyes. Of course, it wouldn't be that easy. She closed her eyes for a second to gather her composure. Deep masculine laughter from downstairs reached her ears. She found comfort in the noise.

"I love the sound of my boys filling the house," Colleen said. "I wish Meggie were home, too." The jingle of a phone sounded from somewhere downstairs. "Better go get that." Colleen moved toward the stairs. "Oops." She bent down and picked up something. Holding out her hand, she said, "Is this yours?"

Kate gaped at the small flat silver disk lying in Colleen's palm. With a hand that shook, she took the disk.

Colleen started moving again. She paused on the top step. "Kate?"

Dumbfounded, Kate lifted her gaze. "I...uh. I'll be right there."

"Okay. Don't be long." Colleen disappeared down the stairs.

Kate's legs felt like rubber. She leaned against the wall.

She had the disk. In her hands was the key to her future. It must have dropped out when the compartment first opened.

"Thank You, Lord," she whispered, grateful that an end was in sight.

They'd hand the disk over to Gabe or the FBI and then it would all be done. The truth would be out and she'd be set free from the prison of not knowing. She'd find the peace she craved.

Brody. She had to tell him she'd found the disk. She pushed away from the wall and raced down the stairs. She skidded to a halt in the foyer. Brody was on the phone.

"Brody," she whispered urgently to get his attention. The news of the disk threatened to burst from her.

He held up a hand and shook his head indicating she needed to wait. He turned his back and spoke low into the phone. Kate frowned, wondering who he was talking to. She moved closer.

"I know my job. I'll bring her in."

Kate drew back her chin. The edge of the disk

cut into her palm. She backed up a step as disappointment rolled through her, a deep hurt quick on its heels. Though why she'd care that she was nothing more than a job to Brody, she didn't know. She'd made it clear they had no future together and he'd agreed. It was as simple as that.

She continued to retreat, putting distance between them. Her gaze dropped to the disk in her hand, the light from the chandelier reflected off the silver coating. People were willing to kill for the information on the disk. Willing to kill *her*.

Deciding it would be wise to be forewarned before she handed the disk over to the police, Kate turned, intending to run up the stairs to the den where she'd seen a desktop computer. Instead she found herself once again slamming into Patrick's chest.

She backpedaled and blinked up at him. "Do you always sneak around like that?"

He raised an imperious brow. "Don't you ever look where you're going?"

Without commenting, she slipped the disk into the opening of her purse and made to move around him toward the stairs.

"The dining room is this way," he said, making a sweeping gesture with his arm.

Behind her Brody hung up the phone, effectively cutting off her chance to slip upstairs to view the disk. With a tight smile at Patrick, she marched ahead of the two brothers into the dining room.

"Sit here, dear." Colleen patted a high-backed, dark cherrywood chair.

Brody edged around Kate and pulled out the chair. She took her seat, shaking with guilt for not sharing her find with him. She almost stopped him as he moved to help his mother bring out the food.

Instead, she folded her hands in her lap over her purse in a protective gesture. For now, the disk lying inside her purse would be her little secret.

She glanced up and caught Brody's gaze. She tried to smile but nausea churned in her stomach.

She hated breaking her promise to Brody.

FIFTEEN

Concern arched through Brody. Kate's complexion had gone pasty and she ate very little as she moved his mother's beef stew around in her bowl. After dodging bullets, running for her life and finding out about her dead husband, he wasn't surprised her scare with Patrick had rattled her.

Just as Gabe's call had rattled Brody. Gabe had said the Feds were checking into Olga and Mrs. Klein. But they'd warned Gabe that they were still seeking Kate. Gabe had rather forcefully suggested Brody bring Kate in so that Brody wouldn't come under any scrutiny for aiding and abetting.

Brody's jaw tightened. He'd told Gabe he'd bring Kate in. But first he had to know who was trying to kill her and make sure they were stopped.

He couldn't live with himself if anything happened to her. He'd promised to help her and he would live up to his promises.

* * *

As soon as an opportunity arose to make a polite exit, Kate left the confines of the dining room with the wonderful chatter of Brody's family echoing in her ears. Her heart throbbed with yearning—to belong, to be a part of the McClains. But that possibility didn't exist.

Brody was committed to his job above all else. She wanted a safe and risk-free life. And she was hiding an important piece of evidence from him.

Three outs. Game over. Loser goes to jail.

She didn't want to go to jail. She shuddered at the thought of living day in and day out inside a small concrete cell.

Better jail than death at the hands of the Russian Mafia.

Kate went into the den and sat down in the plush leather office chair. The masculine accents on the desk and gracing the walls led her to believe the room must be used primarily by Patrick.

Colleen had explained that both Ryan and Patrick had apartments but that Patrick spent a great deal of time still at the house. She'd never met a man so controlled and cold. So unlike either of his brothers. Though there was a calculated gleam to Ryan, he oozed of charm, while Brody brimmed with energy and compassion.

A pang of longing plucked at her heart. She'd grown used to relying on Brody's strength. She turned her attention to the computer. When Gordon arrived, he'd know what to do.

The computer took precious moments to boot up. "Come on, come on," she muttered.

As soon as the desktop screen appeared, she deftly slid the disk into the CD-ROM holder.

With a few clicks, the disk downloaded. A security screen box requiring a password popped up. Her mind raced with possible access codes. She typed in the obvious. Paul's name. She tried all three names. Nothing.

She tried the name of the import business Olga talked about. Access denied. She typed in Olga's name. Again denied. Frustrated, she clenched her fist.

"I could use a little help here, Lord," she prayed.

Her hands hovered over the keys. Her mind replayed Gabe's words. The FBI believed she had the information to blow apart a money-laundering scam. Okay, so she did have the disk, but what if she had more? What if…

Her fingers tapped at the keys. She tried her name. Didn't work. She tried variations of her name and Paul's name. She tried the name of her bank. Again access denied.

An idea formed in her mind. She sat straighter, her blood pounded in her ears. Her hands began to shake as she typed in the word *Lillian,* her grandmother's middle name. The word that she used as a password at the bank.

With growing horror she watched the screen shift. Continuing to use the personal numeric codes and passwords that she'd used on her job, she was soon navigating her way through financial spreadsheets, complete with names of businesses, contacts and account numbers. And all of this was being passed through her bank.

She'd never revealed the security codes to Paul, so how had he gotten them? She covered her face with her hands. Had he drugged her? Hypnotized her? Brainwashed her? The depth of the violation sent a shudder racking her body. A panicked flutter hit her stomach, making her ill. Brody would never believe she didn't know about this.

She dropped her fingers back to the keyboard, closing the information and then ejecting the disk. No one knew she had it. Only the bad guys knew what information it contained. She could easily destroy the evidence that implicated her and no one would be the wiser.

She tapped the nails of her right hand on the desk while in her left palm the disk lay ready. All she'd have to do was run her nails over the CD, rendering it useless.

Anyone would believe the scratches happened while bouncing around inside her purse. No one would think she'd done it. Then the Feds wouldn't have anything on her and the bad guys would no longer have a reason to try to kill her. Her pulse picked up speed.

She could walk away scot-free.

She frowned, struggling against what her grand-mother had raised her to believe. There was no gray area when it came to right or wrong. God's word was clear. If she truly believed in God and His word, she wouldn't give in to fear and self-protection.

A line of scripture came to her, from Proverbs, she was pretty sure. *The fear of man brings a snare, But he who trusts in the Lord will be exalted.*

If she truly believed, she'd trust Jesus to protect her. He'd sent Brody to protect her, after all.

God had proven Himself worthy of her trust.

She took in a deep calming breath. She wouldn't let her fear of jail lure her into doing something she knew was wrong. She wouldn't deface the disk. She wouldn't destroy Brody's trust.

"Destroying that would solve all your problems, wouldn't it?"

She jerked around to find herself face to face with Brody, who stood in the doorway. The hurt in his dark eyes knocked the breath from her lungs. Slowly, she laid the disk on the desk and backed away. Her soul screamed in despair.

She'd never be able to convince him she wasn't one of the bad guys.

Betrayal pressed in on Brody's chest with crush-ing intensity. She'd sucked him in, with her pretty face and talk of faith. She'd made him believe in himself, in her. Had made him want to believe in

God again. He'd been such a fool. Bile churned in his gut. He clenched his back teeth.

"I know this looks bad, but it's not what you think," Kate said with measured softness.

He arched a brow. "Really. What is it, then?" he ground out. He stalked forward to stand directly in front of her. He swallowed against the tightness in his throat. "You lied to me, Kate. You had the disk all along."

"No. Yes." She shook her head. "I mean...I did have the disk, but I didn't lie to you. I swear." The distress in her eyes seemed so real. "When I dropped my purse in the hall a secret compartment in the bottom opened and the disk came out. Honestly, I didn't know it was there."

"You expect me to believe that?" He curled his lip in a sneer.

But he had. Over and over again.

Every time she'd claimed to be innocent, he'd lapped it up just like a lovesick puppy. He hadn't kept his focus on the job. He hadn't used good judgment. "You used me."

Her blue eyes beseeched him to believe her. "Brody, please. I've never lied to you."

"Save it. I'm not going to believe anything you say." He moved to the desk and picked up the silver disk. Amazing something so little, so ordinary could cause so much chaos.

"What do we do now?"

Kate's voice, so vulnerable and full of anguish, sliced through his chest.

He momentarily closed his eyes against the pain and hardened his heart. He opened his eyes and met her unflinching gaze. "I do my job."

Her mouth twisted ruefully. "That's what I admire most about you, Brody. Your honor and your integrity."

A single tear crested her long lashes and fell to her cheek, doing more damage to him than a bullet ever could.

Because he loved her.

Even more than his job.

Kate's heart was breaking.

Brody believed she was guilty.

And he didn't even know the worst of it yet. But he would soon and then there'd never be a way to bridge the abyss between them. Though they couldn't have a future together, she couldn't stand the idea he'd go through life believing the worst of her.

She tried to be strong, tried to hold back the tears, but they wouldn't cooperate. With jerky movements, she wiped at the wetness on her cheeks. Taking a deep breath, she silently prayed, *God, what do I do now?*

However futile the effort, she had to try to convince Brody that she hadn't used him. But she didn't know what to say. Every word that popped into her mind seemed contrite and useless.

Suddenly, Ryan appeared in the doorway, his face flushed.

Brody glared at him. "Ryan, we're in the middle of something here."

Ryan stepped inside and pulled the door closed. "There are two Federal Agents downstairs and they want Kate."

The urgency in his voice sent panic ricocheting around her chest. If Brody didn't believe in her, how would she ever convince the FBI she wasn't a party to her husband's dealings?

Brody's silent, grim expression didn't bode well. His eyes drilled her to the floor. She forced herself not to squirm under his scrutiny. She had to trust that God would protect her.

In a swift movement, Brody pulled Kate toward Ryan. Her heart withered in agony in her chest at the cavalier way he was dismissing her.

"Here." Brody shoved the disk at Kate.

Surprised, she reflexively closed her hand around the edge. "What…?"

Brody's voice dropped to a low whisper as he spoke to Ryan. "Do you remember how Meggie used to sneak out of the house?"

Ryan's brows lowered. "Yes."

"Take her out that way," he instructed his brother. Then he turned to Kate.

Her breath hitched at the hurt in his ebony eyes.

"I'll keep the Feds distracted as long as I can." He

dug in his pocket for his wallet, pulled out the bills and handed her the cash.

She recoiled in bewilderment. "No."

He opened the door, pushed the money into her hand and then firmly steered her out into the hall. "Go. Just go."

He pivoted and stiffly disappeared down the stairs.

"Come on," Ryan urged.

Why wasn't Brody arresting her?

Too shocked to react, she allowed Ryan to nudge her into Meghan's bedroom and over to the window. He lifted the window sash. "The trellis is sturdy. There's a small drop at the end but you'll do fine. Go through the garden to the back gate. From there head west to the end of the block. You can catch a cab to the train station or the airport." He dug in his pocket and produced a wad of green bills, which he handed to her. "Here, better safe than sorry."

Confused, she shook her head. "Why are you doing this?"

His grim expression matched his brother's. "I trust Brody's judgment. You'd better hurry." He reached for her hand and gave it a quick squeeze. "God go with you, Kate."

Unnerved, she climbed through the window and clung to the trellis. Slowly, she made her way downward, her feet testing each rung as she descended. The drop to the ground jarred her knees and she stumbled forward before regaining her balance.

With a furtive glance at the house, she hurried toward the back gate and stepped out into the alley that stretched behind the row of houses. She stared down the alleyway to where it ended at a busy street. Cars whizzed past in a blur of color.

Still reeling, Kate tried to make sense of Brody's actions. He'd accused her of lying to him. He clearly believed she was guilty of something, yet he'd let her go. She knew him well enough to know that not turning her in went against everything he was made of.

He was jeopardizing his career for her. Her heart thundered in her chest. Could he care for her, even believing she was guilty? Her mind grappled with that thread of thought. He cared. But did he love her?

And what if he did? Could she allow herself to love a man whose life was constantly in danger?

She tightened her jaw and started forward with purpose. She knew what she had to do.

As Brody came down the stairs, he found Patrick and his mother barring the doorway to the house. Brody hung back for a moment to give Kate a few more seconds and to watch.

Though his older brother was an academic, Patrick cut an intimidating figure when he chose to. His six-two, two-hundred-and-twenty-pound body was an effective blockade and combined with his mother's Irish fire, the Feds didn't stand a chance. His family stood together. He was going to stand by Kate no matter what.

Finally, Brody stepped forward to face the consequences of his folly. "I can take it from here, Patrick. Mom."

"What is going on, Brody? What kind of trouble is Kate in?" demanded Colleen McClain.

"I'll explain later." Brody met Patrick's gaze over his mother's head. "Could you?"

Though Patrick's firm mouth was set in a disapproving line, he nodded. "Of course. Mother, this way." He propelled Colleen away from the door toward the kitchen.

Brody settled himself against the door frame as if he didn't have a care in the world, when inside, his heart ached in a way he'd never experienced before.

He'd known that letting Kate go would cost him his job and his self-respect, he just wasn't prepared for the pain of knowing he'd never see her again. He loathed the thought that she was out there running for her life alone.

But he'd done what he could by giving her time to get away.

Brody hated the way the two Federal Agents looked down their condescending noses at him as if he was some scumbag perp they'd like nothing better than to bust upside the head. Each agent flashed a badge.

"Where is Mrs. Wheeler?" the short agent, Tumbolt, asked.

Brody shrugged off the question. "I don't know. She left."

"She was last seen with you," the tall one, Heinsfled, said.

"Hey, if you want to search the house, feel free. She's not here."

"Where is she?" Heinsfled asked.

He hoped she was safely on her way to the airport. "I don't know. She didn't say."

"You do understand you are obstructing our investigation. As a fellow officer of the law, one would think you'd be more cooperative," Tumbolt said.

Brody thought he might be sick all over the Feds' shiny black shoes.

"Are you looking for me?"

Brody's blood froze at the sound of Kate's voice.

The two agents turned as one and then stepped down the stairs, moving quickly toward Kate. Brody blinked, hoping his mind was playing tricks and that Kate wasn't standing there on his mother's front lawn handing the silver disk to the FBI. He rushed down the stairs and gripped her arm. "What are you doing?"

Her big springtime eyes bored into him with clarity and honesty. "I would rather live wrongly accused than let the man I love sacrifice all that he is for me."

Brody's jaw dropped as her words reverberated through his brain. She was turning herself in because she loved him. His heart squeezed then seemed to expand, filling him with a deep abiding warmth.

Tumbolt stepped forward. "Sheriff McClain, step

away from Ms. Wheeler. We are taking her into custody."

Shaken by her admission, he stared at the man, trying to understand what he'd just said. Then Kate's hand covered his on her arm, drawing his attention. Her beautiful face was composed and serene. "It'll be okay," she said as she pried his fingers loose. "God will protect me."

He snapped out of his momentary stupor and scowled. "I'm coming with you."

"That won't be necessary," Heinsfled said as he took Kate's arm and began to lead her away.

Tumbolt stepped in front of Brody as Brody moved to follow. "Sheriff, this is no longer your concern."

Brody fought the urge to plant his fist in the agent's face. The last thing he needed was to be detained for assaulting a fellow officer. He wouldn't be able to help Kate that way. "I'll call your lawyer," he assured Kate.

Her smile was grateful. The agent cuffed her and then helped her into the dark blue sedan parked next to the sidewalk behind Ryan's black car.

Within moments, Kate was gone and Brody felt as if his heart had been ripped from his chest.

She loved him.

Unbelievable.

Kindhearted Kate, with her giving and compassionate nature, loved him.

Moved to the depths of his soul by her selflessness, Brody couldn't deny his feelings for her any longer.

He loved her.

Innocent or guilty.

And he wasn't about to let her throw her life away without a fight.

Lord, You know Kate's heart. I'm asking You for Your help here. If not for me, then for her.

He rushed back inside the house and placed a long-distance call to Gordon Thomas's law office.

On the third ring Gordon's secretary answered. Brody identified himself and asked to speak to the lawyer. He was informed that Mr. Thomas was away from the office but could be reached on his cellular phone.

Within a few moments, Gordon Thomas was on the line. "Sheriff. To what do I owe the honor?"

"Kate Wheeler has been taken into custody in Boston by the FBI. She needs her lawyer."

There was a prolonged silence.

"Did you hear me?" Brody demanded. "Kate needs you."

"Does the FBI have the disk?"

Gordon's calm tone grated on Brody's nerves. What was wrong with the man? Brody frowned. "Yes."

"I'm leaving now," Gordon said abruptly and then hung up.

Brody returned the receiver to its cradle. He should feel better knowing that Kate's lawyer was on his way. But the man still had to fly clear across the country, which would take time. Time that Kate would spend behind bars.

There had to be something he was missing.

Maybe he was looking at this all wrong. Instead of trying to find Petrov's beginnings, he should have been concentrating on Paul's ending. There had to be someone else involved.

Brody would pick apart Paul Wheeler's life. He'd work backwards through Paul's life until he found the connection that would unravel the web of deception surrounding Kate. Because only then would he be able to think about their future together.

His brothers and mother entered the room.

"What now, Brody?" asked Ryan.

Brody didn't have an answer to that.

"Would you please tell me what's going on?" Colleen asked.

Brody headed toward the door. "When I come back I'll tell you everything."

"Where are you going?" Patrick asked.

Brody paused with his hand on the doorknob. "I'm going to find some way to help Kate."

He left the house and hurried through the park back to the station. He blew through the doors and headed straight for Gabe's desk. "I need your help again."

Gabe's eyes narrowed. "What? Someone empty out your pension fund?"

"Worse. The FBI took Kate into custody."

Gabe rolled his eyes. "Back to her, are we?"

Brody didn't have time for his friend's cynicism. "Look. I want to dissect her late husband's life. This time I want to work backwards starting with Paul Wheeler. I want to run background checks on anyone he or Kate had dealings with, starting with their lawyer. I want to tear this identity apart."

"That's a big order." Gabe set his elbows on the desk and steepled his fingers. "You sure she's worth it?"

Gabe's question wasn't surprising. He'd seen what had happened with Elise. But even before that, Gabe had been the perennial bachelor. Always scoffing at others who had found love. Predicting every relationship's demise. And on the occasions when his predictions came true, he gloated, feeling proven right.

"I love her," Brody answered simply, honestly.

Gabe raised a skeptical brow. "It's different this time?"

"Yeah, very different." He was willing to lay down his own life for her.

Gabe groaned. "Save me from romantic fools."

"You going to help me or not?" Brody snapped.

"Yeah, yeah. Grab a seat."

Brody dragged over a chair. For the next hour, he and Gabe surfed through the police network of information. They sifted through Paul Wheeler's life, then shifted their focus to Pete Kinsey. The two identities shared one common thread. Gordon Thomas was the active lawyer for both men. Heart racing with anticipation, Brody had Gabe delve into Petrov Klein's life and the Lanskis' import business.

After digging through layers of misleading and miscellaneous information, Brody found what he was looking for. One of the lawyers acting on behalf of Lanski Imports in a small claims case was none other than Gordon Thomas. The connection was slim, but still there.

If nothing else, it would give the Feds someone else to focus on.

Armed with this information, Brody left the station and took a cab to the new federal courthouse. The Moakley Courthouse located right on Boston Harbor had a stately presence with its redbrick exterior, glass atrium and brass appointments.

At the door, Brody showed his identification and was directed to the fourth floor where two agents, one with dark hair, the other with brown hair, both wearing dark blue suits, approached him. These weren't the same agents who'd taken Kate away. He identified himself.

"I'm Agent Brewster," said the dark-haired man.

"Agent Foster," the brown-haired man said curtly. "Sheriff, what can we do for you?"

"I want to speak with whoever is handling the investigation of Kate Wheeler."

"Right this way." Foster pivoted and led the way down a carpeted hall to a small office with a view of the harbor. Agent Foster preceded Brody into the office. Behind the desk sat a balding man in his sixties who rose as the men filed in. Agent Brewster brought up the rear, shutting the door behind him.

"Sheriff McClain, Special Agent in Charge, Frank Monroe." Foster inclined his head and stepped discreetly back.

Brody held out the file folder with copies of the information Gabe had printed off. "I have information in here that links a lawyer named Gordon Thomas to Paul Wheeler and the Lanskis' import business. I think you should check him out."

Agent Monroe raised a brow. "We know all about Mr. Thomas."

"Then why is he free and Kate Wheeler in custody?" Brody asked sharply.

Agent Monroe shook his head. "We have not secured Kate Wheeler's whereabouts. We were under the impression that she was with you."

Brody blinked. "What? Wait a sec." He fought the tightening in his chest. "Two agents took her into custody over an hour ago. She's here somewhere."

Monroe exchanged glances with the other two agents. "What kind of game are you trying to play here, Sheriff McClain?"

A very bad feeling gripped Brody. "This is no game. Two agents. Tumbolt and Heinsfled. They have her."

Monroe frowned. "We have no agents by that name in this office. Did they show ID?"

Gritting his teeth, Brody managed to contain his

anger at the insinuation that he'd failed to protect Kate. "Yes. They did."

Monroe picked up the phone. "Get me Quantico." A minute later, he hung up the phone. "I'd say we have a problem," Special Agent in Charge Monroe said grimly.

A fist of panic slammed into Brody's midsection, effectively pushing the air from his lungs.

Recovering his breath, his forced his emotions to a far corner. *Stay focused*. He had to save Kate.

And he had a good idea where to start.

SIXTEEN

Kate sat in the backseat of the Feds' sedan, her hands cuffed uncomfortably behind her. She'd done this once before. The night Brody had arrested her in Paul's home. Little did she realized then that she'd fall in love with the sheriff.

Or that she'd cause him so much grief.

The look in his eyes when she'd stepped out from the side of Colleen McClain's home would forever be engraved in her mind. His stunned disbelief had given way to pain. On her behalf. His concern for her moved her deeply and had prompted her to admit why she was turning herself in.

She'd shaken him with her declaration of love. She prayed he didn't think her words were some ploy to garner sympathy from him. She prayed he understood that her feelings were true. And she hoped that someday she'd have a chance to reaffirm her words.

Through the side window she watched the buildings, the neighborhoods, roll by. When the car headed for the on-ramp to the freeway heading north, Kate sat up straighter. "Uh, excuse me. Where are we going?"

When no reply came, she leaned forward. "Hey. Where are you taking me? Why are we leaving Boston?"

The taller agent sitting in the passenger seat glanced over his shoulder. "Headquarters," he said succinctly.

They were driving all the way to Virginia? Kate sat back and settled in, as best she could with her hands cuffed behind her back, for the long drive.

She must have zoned out, because the blast of a horn startled her upright in her seat. Heart pounding in her ears, she blinked at the sight that met her through the window. The Statue of Liberty rose like a beacon from her place on Ellis Island. They were back in New York. Kate craned her neck to read the passing sign. They were on the Staten Island Expressway approaching the Verrazano Narrows toll bridge that would take them into Brooklyn.

"Hey, why are we here?" she demanded.

Silence met her question. A tight ball of apprehension gathered in her chest. She would not be kept in the dark. She kicked the back of the front seat.

The man in the passenger seat whipped around to glare at her. "Be still," he snapped.

"Where are you taking me?" she asked again as droplets of fear began to rain all over her, prickling her skin and raising the hairs at the nape of her neck.

"You'll see." His mouth twisted into a menacing smile. Then to the driver he said something in a foreign language that sounded suspiciously like Russian. The two men laughed at some shared joke.

The muscles in her throat constricted. For a moment, she choked on fear. What had she gotten herself into now? She tried to think clearly. Obviously, she was in the hands of Russian mobsters, on the way to some mob headquarters. How could she escape? She had to keep her mind focused and watch for an opportunity.

But for now, the only thing she could do was pray because whatever path God had set her on, she wanted to face it with the same honor, integrity and bravery that she admired so much in Brody. He'd lost so much, yet he'd persevered. He hadn't let the anger of betrayal turn him into a bitter man. Instead, he'd worked hard to overcome his past and make peace with it.

The car pulled to a stop in front of Lanski's Imports.

Somehow she wasn't totally surprised. Since Paul as Petrov worked for Lanski, it would stand to reason that Mr. Lanski would be involved with the Russian mob.

She was pulled out of the car and led through the warehouse doors. She looked for an opportunity to escape, but being wedged between the two men with each of her elbows firmly within their grasp, she had little hope of getting away. Yet.

She tried to catch the eye of one of the workers but the men working in the warehouse went about their business as if these two thugs strolled in with a hand-cuffed woman every day. Acid churned in her gut.

Instead of being taken up the stairs to Mr. Lan-ski's office, she was led to a large storage room with a concrete floor and no windows. In the center of the empty room was a single metal chair.

A hot jolt of fear hit her square in the chest. She backed up as gruesome thoughts of torture assaulted her imagination. The men holding her by the elbows dragged her forward, their fingers digging painfully in to her flesh. Taking quick gasps, she forced herself to hold it together the way Brody would.

"Sit," ordered the man who'd driven the car. He planted his meaty hand in the middle of her back and shoved her forward.

Kate stumbled, but quickly regained her balance. Figuring it safer to comply than to resist any more until she had a better idea what they intended to do with her, she sat on the cold chair, her knees knocking together.

The men left, shutting the heavy metal door behind them. The ominous click of the lock sliding into place sent a chill rippling over her flesh. She tried to take deep calming breaths, but the musty stale air made her gag. What did they use this room for? Just to hold people against their will? How often did they do that? What were they going to do with her?

After a few minutes she rose from the chair. Sitting like the proverbial duck wasn't helping her to stay calm. She had to find a way out. She looked around. Knowing it was futile, she strode to the door, turned her back and tried the knob. No miracles there.

With the heel of her foot she kicked the door. The metallic echo rang inside her chest, emphasizing the emptiness in her heart. She ached deep inside for Brody, longed for his steady presence. His protection. Did he know she wasn't with the real FBI? Tension tightened the muscles in her neck and shoulders. Her head throbbed.

So many questions still unanswered. So much danger threatening her life.

Suddenly tired of all the intrigue, she sat back in the chair, closed her eyes and prayed. Prayed for rescue, prayed for Brody and prayed to understand why all this was happening to her.

Brody had once said she'd learn to live with the unknown, the questions. As he had. Focus on the needs of the day, he'd also said. An overwhelming desperation clawed at her throat, choking her. How could she do that when she had no control over her present situation?

But wasn't that the crux of her faith? She had no control. God was in control. So instead of asking why, she needed to focus on God's goodness. His faithfulness. And if she died today, she'd be going to Heaven and the answers to all her questions wouldn't matter.

Softly, she began to sing every song of praise she could remember.

What seemed like hours later, the lock on the door rattled and the door swung open. Bracing herself, Kate straightened. The two fake Federal agents walked in, followed by Mr. Lanski and the two men who'd taken her from Myrtle's deck.

Then another man walked in, and Kate gasped with stunned relief. His dark hair, salted with some gray, was styled back away from his lined, aristocratic face. He stared down his patrician nose at her.

"Gordon? What… How did you get here?"

Gordon Thomas tsked as he moved to stand over Kate. "Ah, my dear. This breaks my heart."

With a quick flick of his wrist he addressed the others in the room in fluent Russian. Kate's relief evaporated into shocked disbelief. She couldn't have felt more betrayed. She'd always assumed he was of Latin descent with his dark hair, dark eyes and olive complexion.

One of the thugs stepped forward and uncuffed her hands. She rubbed at the red welts forming on her wrists and rolled the pain from her shoulders.

She stared at Gordon. He was tall, reed-thin and immaculately dressed in a dark suit that screamed designer label. A look more appropriate for a Beverly Hills lawyer than a Russian mobster. Or so she thought.

She remembered what Brody had said about the

Organizatsiya being well-educated. Obviously, they'd recruited law-school grads into their fold.

"I never meant for you to end up here, Kate. I'd hoped you would find the disk and relinquish it without any trouble. But alas. You were so determined to discover the truth. I did warn you that the truth wouldn't always set you free."

"I don't understand. Why did you ruin my life?"

"Oh, now. Don't think it was personal. You were a convenient way for us to gain access to the bank. You and your mother were so needy. It was really an innovative plan. We waited for you to grow up and I very carefully steered you toward banking. You had such potential. We knew you'd do well at the bank. You exceeded our expectations. Vice President of Operations. Very nice." He smiled in the fatherly way that had brought her such comfort over the years. Bile rose in her throat.

"It was such an easy thing to plant a camera in your home office to obtain your passwords which gained us access to the bank." He shook his head, his expression rueful. "Only, poor Petrov fell in love."

For a second, old dreams stirred, but were instantly obliterated by reality. Her stomach clenched. "With Olga."

Gordon nodded. "True. And he could have had her if he'd just stayed with the program for a bit longer."

Kate hated being referred to as the program, as if her life meant nothing more than a means to their end. They'd orchestrated her marriage and her career.

And she'd danced merrily to their tune like a puppet on a string. "Why did you kill him?"

"The disk. We found out he'd been compiling information and recording it all. He'd said he wanted out and the disk was insurance. Ha! No one threatens us and gets away with it."

"Who is us? You and Lanski?" Her gaze swept over the other men in the room. The thugs stared at her dispassionately and Mr. Lanski's scowl deepened. "Are you two the heads of the Russian Mob?"

He tsked again. "Really, Kate. You ask too many questions."

"You're going to kill me anyway, right? So why not tell me everything?"

He sighed. "Come." He held out his hand. "I'd like to show you something."

She stared at his hand, hating the sense of doom seeping through her. After all this, she was going to die. But at least now she had closure where Paul was concerned. And she'd known Brody. Her heart squeezed with sadness and regret that they'd never have a life together.

She allowed Gordon to help her to her feet. He tucked her hand into his elbow and escorted her out of the small room ahead of the other men whose disdain she felt like a thousand pinpricks.

Gordon stopped as Mr. Lanski stepped close and spoke harshly in his mother tongue. The two men argued for a moment before Mr. Lanski waved a hand of dismissal and walked away.

Gordon continued on up the stairs to the office where she and Brody had first met Mr. Lanski. He shut the door behind them. He pulled her over to the computer where the disk had been loaded. She wondered if she should tell him she'd already seen the contents but decided to remain silent. If by some miracle she got away, anything he said might prove useful.

"See, here," Gordon said, "Our business flourishes."

"Business," she scoffed. "Money laundering, you mean."

He frowned. "No need to be rude, Kate."

She rolled her eyes. She had every right to be rude.

"We have many legitimate businesses." He went on to explain the workings of their operation.

Kate listened with growing astonishment. The scope and ingenuity of the operation must have taken years to build. Assets from several legitimate companies were being used to fund several more illegal operations ranging from selling drugs to smuggling diamonds.

Gordon went on to explain how Petrov's parents were immigrants who owed their allegiance to the people who supplied them with a home in America. Petrov had done well in his American school and had been singled out and groomed to infiltrate American life.

Not to spy for the motherland, but to work for

the *Organizatsiya*. When the time came for Petrov to become useful, Gordon had helped to set him up as Pete Kinsey on the East Coast and Paul Wheeler on the west.

Sickened by the scope and enormity of the operation, she stared at the man she'd thought of as family. "I trusted you."

Sudden shouts from outside the office spurred Gordon to action. He pushed Kate aside and ejected the disk. Shots rang out and Kate's blood froze.

Then the door burst open. Brody charged in, weapon drawn. A half dozen more gun-toting men in dark vests with FBI in bold yellow print across their chests piled in.

Someone shouted, "Don't move!"

Kate tore her relieved gaze from Brody and realized instantly what Gordon was attempting to do as he seized the ejected CD.

"No," she shouted and flung herself at him. She heard Brody yell, "Don't shoot!"

She tried to wrestle the disk out of Gordon's grasp.

Too late. His manicured nails dug rivets into the silver coating of the disk as they toppled sideways to the ground.

Then there were hands dragging her up and twisting her arms behind her. She cried out as pain from her already sore shoulders gripped her. Panicked, she sought Brody through the sea of Federal agents.

But to her dismay, he was gone.

* * *

"No, you don't." Brody captured Mr. Lanski by the scruff of his neck. He'd seen the man flee the scene in the commotion created by Kate tackling Gordon.

The owner of Lanski's Imports struggled to get away but Brody planted his knee into the older man's kidney. Effectively subdued, Lanski went down to his knees with an oath. Brody cuffed him and pulled him to his feet.

Dragging the heavy Russian back and then handing him over to a Federal agent, Brody assessed the situation and realized that while he was going after Lanski, Kate and Gordon Thomas had been taken into custody and led away.

He raced out of the building in time to see the car they'd said she was in drive away. He stood in the middle of the chaos in the street created by the raid and tried to get himself back under control.

Boy, the way Kate had dived at the man had nearly given Brody a heart attack. For a split second he'd feared the Feds would shoot and ask questions later. The thought of losing her again filled him with dread. And realization.

Deep in his heart he knew she wasn't guilty no matter how bad it might still look even after she'd tried to keep Gordon Thomas from tampering with the disk. Brody'd move heaven and earth to prove her innocence.

Man, she was something. Pride lifted his heart.

She still had that spunk he admired. And she was so brave. He loved her for so many reasons.

Thank You, Lord.

Now, he only hoped she'd give him another chance. If giving up being a law officer was the only way she'd have him, then he'd gladly turn over his badge and his weapon.

The trip to the Federal building went by in a blur of tears. She didn't know what to think about Brody's disappearing act. Had he thought she'd been with Gordon by choice? Her heart twisted in her chest.

She was ushered to a small, two-way mirrored room where two agents questioned her endlessly about Gordon, Paul and the disk. She told them everything she could remember. They took notes and seemed pleased with the information she had.

Now, alone, she shifted uncomfortably in the hard metal chair and tried to still the shaking of her hands, but the effort took too much energy. The tomblike quiet in the cold, sterile room stretched her nerves until she thought she'd scream. She'd been left alone in the room with the large mirror for—she glanced at her watch—forty minutes.

The rattle of the doorknob being unlocked sent a shiver of apprehension galloping down her spine. The door swung open and Brody walked in. Her heart leapt, then plummeted at the hooded expression in his eyes. She shifted her gaze away. She didn't want to face his accusations again. She'd break down for sure.

The scraping of the metal legs of a chair brought her chin up.

Brody sat down across from her. "The disk was ruined. The information irretrievable," he said matter-of-factly.

"I tried to stop him." She rubbed her temples. "He killed Paul. He tried to kill me... I trusted him."

Brody's gaze narrowed slightly. "Why did you trust him?"

In her mind, she went back to the day she'd found Paul bleeding to death on the floor of his living room. "Paul said Gordon's name right before he died. I thought Paul had wanted him, was telling me to trust Gordon." Placing her hands flat on the table, she sat up straight as realization hit. "But Paul was trying to warn me."

Brody's expression softened and he reached out to take one of her hands. A tender melting happened somehow in the vicinity of her heart.

"Maybe, maybe not," he said. "He may not have known who was behind his attack. We'll never know."

The pressure of his palm gave her comfort and made her sad all at once. She wanted to cling to him, to confirm her love for him was real. Instead she slipped her hand away. She couldn't take any more hurt and rejection. "Why are you here?"

"You're free, Kate. Thomas confirmed you

weren't involved and he's confessed to ordering the hit on Paul and the attempts on your life, but he won't say anything else."

Relief swept through her.

"Even after being offered immunity for murder, he won't roll on his comrades. More afraid of them than prison. Without the solid evidence of the disk, there's no way to charge him with anything more. The information you gave will be helpful in the Feds' investigation into the *Organizatsiya*. Lanski was also brought into custody and will be charged with kidnapping. By all accounts, the import business is legit."

The news that she was exonerated from any wrongdoing was welcome and needed. She should feel vindicated. She wasn't the bad person Brody believed her to be. But as she stared at his ruggedly handsome face, emptiness filled her. She didn't know what Brody felt and without the man she loved in her life, her future seemed pretty desolate.

She fought against the stinging in her eyes. She'd thought peace would come with the truth about Paul, but it hadn't. Closure yes, but not peace. She didn't understand. What was she missing? "But why are *you* here?"

His mouth twisted with humble tenderness. "Because I'm an idiot and I want to beg for your forgiveness."

Her mouth went dry. The first quickening of hope tightened her chest. Could it be true?

Once again he took her hand, turning it palm up and curling his fingers over hers. The gesture, at once possessive and tender, made tears burn the back of her eyelids. "I should have trusted you."

"I understand why you didn't," she said softly.

He shook his head. "I should have believed in what I felt for you."

She swallowed hard, barely daring to let the hope rise any further. "What…what do you feel?"

He leaned forward, crowding away the air between them. Her heart stalled as she looked into his eyes and saw the answer to her question. Barely able to breathe, she waited for the words.

"I love you, Kate. Will you give me another chance? A chance to love you?"

Everything inside her wanted to scream "Yes!" But how could she? Just because they loved each other didn't change the fact that he was a sheriff, risking his life every day, and when push came to shove, she couldn't live like that.

She thought about her parents, about how her father risked his life every time he went on a mission. She thought about how the worry slowly destroyed her mother until finally when her father left, her mother sank into despair and a bottle. She closed her eyes against the pain of having to deny Brody's love. "I'm not brave enough to live that life."

The metal clunk of something hitting the table caused her to open her eyes. In front of her lay his badge and his black, ominous-looking gun. Knowing instantly the significance of his gesture, her gaze jumped to his. "No. I can't ask you to do that. I *won't* ask that of you." She pushed the items toward him. "This is who you are."

Brody's hands cupped her face. "Look at me," he demanded.

She made a noise of distress and shook her head. It hurt her to think he'd be so selfless for her. Especially after realizing how ruthlessly she'd been used.

"Kate, listen to me."

The compelling tone in his voice forced her gaze to lock with his. His earnest and loving expression scored her clean through.

"You are the most courageous woman I've ever known. You can handle anything. I'm not going to lie to you. Being a law officer is risky, but so are other professions. So is crossing the street or driving a car. You can't live your life in fear. You told me God would protect you. Then trust that He'll protect us both."

His words were an echo of the thoughts she'd had earlier. Anticipation and joy fluttered like the gentle wings of a butterfly, raising her hope till she thought she might float. "Do you trust Him?"

A thoughtful gleam entered his gaze. "I don't get what purpose my father's death served or the purpose in my being shot. Pastor Sims talked about God's grace, God's undeserved favor. I'm struggling to get my mind around that. Around how in my weakness His strength is perfected." Slowly, he nodded his head. "But yes, I do trust. Trust that He brought us together. Trust that He'll watch over us. And in time I hope I'll understand this whole grace thing."

His words gladdened her heart and filled her with satisfaction. He was on his way to reconciling his relationship with God. Something good had come out of her ordeal. Could something else good come from such a mess?

Something clicked inside Kate, shifted into focus. If he could reconcile with God, could she reconcile herself to a life of risk?

Brody was right that there were risks in any profession, in any lifestyle. Going the safe route hadn't given her what she'd wanted.

She really needed to reassess what she wanted out of life. Was safe and secure really what she longed for? Would those two elusive concepts satisfy the hunger in her heart?

She drank in Brody's face, memorizing every line, every angle. Deep in her heart, she knew this time around she would choose love and walk in faith that God would continue to be her shield.

"Kate, I need you."

Overwhelmed with love for this man, she leaned forward until their lips were nearly touching. Gazing into his eyes, she let her heart shine. "I prayed for peace and God sent me you."

A smile lit up Brody's eyes. "Will you marry me, Kate? Let me stand watch over you for the rest of your life?"

Joy, pure and good burst from her heart, filling her soul. She touched his cheek, the soft pads of her fingers rubbing against the stubble darkening his jawbone. "Yes. Oh, yes."

With a growl of approval, Brody captured her lips.

Kate reveled in the love and passion igniting between them. No matter how risky life as a sheriff's wife would be, she was confident that the peace and security that could only come from God would sustain her through the years at Brody's side.

This time around, she would be certain to hold on to love.

Forever.

* * * * *

Dear Reader,

Thank you for taking this journey with Kate and Brody as they sift through the layers of deception to find the truth, and in the process find love. So often we have to sift through the layers of deception that the world heaps on us to get to the truth of God's love. And in doing so, we bare many scars.

My prayer for you is that you'll let God heal your wounds and hurts as only He can. It's hard work figuring out what to believe when the world entices us with money, power and pleasure, but remember always that your Heavenly Father loves you and will always embrace you as you turn to Him.

May God bless you,

Questions for Discussion

1. Out of all the books you could have chosen, why did you choose Double Deception? Was it the cover? The back blurb? The author?

2. Kate was stunned when she learned her husband had a secret life. Have you ever been surprised by revelations from loved ones? How did you handle the revelations? Did you pray about them? Why or why not?

3. If you were in Kate's shoes, would you have sought the truth? Would you have gone about it differently? Or would you have charged ahead as Kate did?

4. Sacrifice was an important part of this story. Have you ever had to sacrifice something important to you? How did you feel about it?

5. Brody returns to the faith he'd lost after his father's death. Have you lost someone and questioned or lost your faith? What brought you back to God?

6. Did the villain surprise you? Were there hints that you can pinpoint, or was it a complete surprise?

7. Kate thought she would find peace from knowing the truth, but where does real peace come from? Does living a safe and stable life ensure safety and stability?

8. Brody challenged Kate not to live in fear. Is there something you are living in fear of? Over and over again God's word tells us to fear not. Confess your fear to God and ask for His peace. Read Psalms 56:3.

9. Was this the first book you've read by this author? Would you read more from her? Why or why not?

10. What are your most vivid memories from this book? What lessons about life, love and faith did you learn from this story?

DOUBLE JEOPARDY

And those who know your name put their trust in you; for you, O Lord, have not forsaken those who seek you.
—*Psalms* 9:10

To my children; you are my joy and my blessing.

PROLOGUE

March

Gunfire!

The plush private suite on the top floor of the Palisades Casino and Resort in downtown Atlantic City, New Jersey rocked with the deafening noise of gunfire, echoed by the screams of its once-privileged occupants.

The woman's heart slammed painfully against her ribs and a cry burst from her lungs. The tray of glasses she held fell to the carpeted floor with a thud, the liquor soaking the rug. The stench of alcohol mixed with the smell of gunpowder. A potent combination.

She dove behind the freestanding bar. Crouched and shuddering with terror, she clapped her hands over her ears to muffle the retort of weapons firing and the sounds of men dying.

"Oh, God in Heaven, please help me," she prayed, rocking on her heels. She didn't know why she was

praying. Did God even exist? But if there was a time to glom on to any hope that He was real, now was that time.

A man's body dropped to the floor beside her. She gasped. Jean Luc Versailles, the owner of the Palisades, groaned. Thankfully he wasn't dead, but a deep crimson stain spread across the white dress shirt beneath his tuxedo jacket.

Adrenaline pumping, she grabbed him by the arm and struggled to drag him closer to the relative safety behind the bar. Tears clogged her throat and ran down her cheeks. He had always been nice to her.

"You have to get out of here," Jean Luc said with a croak, his voice expressing the pain reflected in his dark eyes.

"You're hurt," she said inanely, her mind trying to recall her first-aid training from high school P.E. Like that had prepared her to deal with a gunshot wound.

Pressure. She had to apply pressure to stop the bleeding. Gagging from the sight and smell of blood, she yanked two bar towels from the shelf beside her and pressed them to his shoulder. She cringed as more gunshots filled the air.

His hand fastened around her wrist like a vise. "My jacket pocket. Get my wallet."

Keeping one hand firmly on the towels, she slid out his black leather billfold from the inside pocket of his tailor-made jacket with her free hand.

"Now what?" she asked.

He closed her hand tightly around the billfold and thrust it against her stomach. "Take the money. Use it. Disappear." He let go of her and pushed himself up to a seated position, the bar at his back. "Escape through the wall panel. Run and don't stop. Go."

Acutely aware of the massacre taking place on the other side of the bar, she whispered, "I can't leave you. We need the police."

"No police." He struggled to his knees, swayed slightly, and reached around her. From behind several liquor bottles he pulled out a large silver gun.

She shrank back, wishing she'd called in sick today. Wishing Jean Luc hadn't invited Raoul Domingo to his private suite. Wishing she were anywhere but here.

But wishing never did any good.

His dark gaze pierced her. "On three."

"What about you?"

He got a foot beneath him. "Just go. One. Two." He staggered to his feet, the gun raised in his shaky hand. "Three!"

Self-preservation, survival instinct, whatever, took over. She scrambled to her feet and in a half-crouch ran toward the mirrored wall.

The sight reflected there made her stumble. Her heart thumped in her chest. Anticipation wound a tight knot in her gut.

Any moment the blast of a bullet would slam into her. But she didn't want to die here today. Every muscle in her body, tightened in readiness, made movement painful.

She flung the potted fichus out of the way and pushed desperately at the edge of the mirrored wall.

A slight click and the wall opened. She squeezed through into Jean Luc's opulent private bedroom in the hotel. The blur of red satin and black leather assaulted her already heightened senses as she dashed for the door leading to the hall on this floor.

Cautiously she peered out.

The corridor was empty. Too afraid to wait for an elevator, she rushed to the stairwell and descended the stairs as rapidly as she could without flying face-first into the concrete walls. She hit the outside door with her whole body and stumbled into the hotel staff's section of the underground garage.

Through the sea of employee cars she saw no one, friend or foe. She raced toward where she parked, fumbling to get her key out of her pants pocket.

Her little blue hatchback was a welcome sight. With shaky hands, she unlocked the door, slid into the driver's seat and started the engine. The gears ground as she shifted into Reverse and almost simultaneously pressed on the gas.

The small car shot backward. She slammed on the brake and shifted into Drive. Her foot pounced on the gas and the car rocketed forward, the tires squealing as she zipped around the curved lot and jetted out onto the dark, deserted street. This late at night people were either at home asleep or inside one of the many casinos along the strip.

She drove, hardly paying attention to the direction she headed until she came to a screeching halt at a red light. Her breathing came shallow and fast. She checked the rearview mirror. As far as she could tell, no one had followed her.

Hopefully she'd had enough of a head start that she could stop somewhere and figure out what to do. Where to go. She needed to go to the police.

Because she'd witnessed murder.

Jean Luc had said no police. But Jean Luc was dead.

Her stomach roiled with terror.

Nothing she'd ever faced in her life had prepared her for this.

She pulled the car into the parking lot of a fast food joint. The bright fluorescent sign illuminated the inside of the car. She'd thrown Jean Luc's wallet on the passenger seat.

Now she picked up the supple leather and thumbed through the contents. Her eyes widened at the number of hundred- and thousand-dollar bills inside the wallet. She swallowed hard.

He'd planned on dying when he'd given her the money.

Heart aching at his sacrifice, she let loose with fresh tears. He'd been a kind and thoughtful employer.

He'd once said she reminded him of his little sister. She didn't know if that was true but she had liked him and admired him.

A pang pierced her heart.

He'd given his life to set her free.

And doomed her to a life of fear.

Did she dare take the time to go back to her loft apartment? Was there anything there worth grabbing? Thanks to Jean Luc, she had enough cash to start over anywhere she wanted.

Only…she couldn't forget the image she'd seen in the mirror seconds before she'd made her escape.

A gun firing at Jean Luc, his body crumpling to the floor.

The expression of hatred on the man holding the gun that delivered the fatal bullet would forever be seared on her brain.

A man she recognized.

The cold eyes of Raoul Domingo would haunt her nightmares.

Where could she hide that was far enough out of reach from New Jersey's most feared mob boss?

Lieutenant Lidia Taylor, Chief State Investigator for the Atlantic County Major Crimes Squad, walked out of the interrogation room with frustration pulsing in her veins. Yes, Jean Luc Versailles's Thai girlfriend, Nikki Song, confirmed that the casino owner had set up a meeting with Raoul Domingo for that night. But knowing about a meeting and proving Domingo was a murderer were two different things.

"Good work," General Investigator Section Detective Rick Grand, Lidia's partner, stated when he met her in the hall, his voice full of respect.

"It isn't enough. I've already got D.A. Porter breathing down my neck on this."

"I have two resort guests who will swear they saw Domingo and his gang get in the elevator," Rick replied.

More frustration kicked Lidia in the gut. "That still doesn't put him in the suite or the gun in his hand. We need to find that girl on the video." The hotel's security camera had shown a woman running out of the hotel employee entrance a few minutes after Versailles's death.

Rick smiled like a Cheshire cat sitting on the moon. "I have a lead on another person who might be able to put Domingo in the same room with Jean Luc."

Lidia stilled. "Details."

"Housekeeping had a maid scheduled to attend to Jean Luc's private room right about the time Domingo entered the elevator. The maid never returned to finish her shift."

"Who else knows about this?"

Rick shrugged. "Just you and me. And housekeeping."

Exhaling an adrenaline laced breath, Lidia said, "Find me that maid before Domingo does."

"Hey, Taylor," called the desk sergeant, Morales,

from the end of the hall, his weathered face glowing with interest. "I've got a live one for you."

Lidia followed the heavyset officer to the public waiting room.

A long-haired blond woman sat in a hard plastic chair near the vending machine. Her frightened blue gaze kept darting to the door as if either expecting someone to come in or as if she were contemplating running out.

"Can I help you?" Lidia asked as she stopped in front of the woman, blocking the exit.

Slowly the young woman stood. Blood splattered the front of her gold and black uniform. The same uniform worn by the hotel staff at the Palisades Casino. Anticipation hit Lidia like the business end of a Taser.

The woman spoke, her voice low and shaky. "My name in Anne Jones. I want to report a murder."

ONE

May

"Really, Patrick, this won't be as disruptive as you imagine. The new computers and software are very easy to navigate. They will just take a little getting used to."

Patrick McClain stared at the Web site for the fancy new system as Sharon Hastings, the Economics Department staff administrator, pointed to the computer monitor sitting on her desk.

Sharon was efficient and talented at her job, but whenever Patrick entered her domain of scattered files and stacks of papers, he had to wonder how she accomplished anything. The array of clutter made him itch.

Patrick twitched his shoulders beneath his tweed sport coat. "What's wrong with the computers we have now?"

In her mid-sixties with graying hair held in a loose bun at her nape and rows of sparkly beaded necklaces hanging down her front, Sharon was a throwback to the seventies, despite her tech savvy. She sighed with a good dose of patience that always brought heat to Patrick's cheeks.

"The school received a grant to buy the new computers. We need to update and stay with the times," she stated calmly.

He understood, but that didn't mean he had to like the change. All of his work was on his computer. "This is going to be a nightmare."

Sharon's lined face spread into an understanding smile. "Don't worry. We have temps coming in to do the software integration. You won't have to do a thing until you have the new notebook computer in your hand. This will be very freeing and much more time-efficient, since you will be able to take your computer home with you and work there instead of coming on campus every weekend."

Taking a cloth from his sport coat's front pocket, he removed his glasses and cleaned the lenses. He thought about his apartment in Boston's Back Bay. His name was on the lease and he did sleep there occasionally, but he didn't consider the stark walls and stiff furniture home.

No, the house he grew up in was home.

But his mother had made it clear recently that she didn't want him coming "home" so often. She'd lamented that it was time for him to get a life. And for her to start living again.

Whatever that meant.

"Well, I just hope whomever you have working on this is competent," Patrick stated and replaced his glasses onto the bridge of his nose.

Sharon inclined her head. "I'm sure they will be." A knock sounded at the door of Sharon's office. "Come in," she called.

The door opened and a young woman, devoid of any hint of makeup, who looked to be in her early twenties, stepped inside. Her short burgundy-red hair spiked up in all directions and her big violet-colored eyes showed hesitance and wariness as she glanced at Patrick. She wore an ill-fitting dress suit and though the drab brown fabric hung off her shoulders, Patrick's gaze fell to the hem of her skirt where her shapely calves were emphasized by heeled pumps.

"I'm sorry, I don't mean to interrupt," the woman said in a soft voice.

"We were just finishing," Patrick offered, feeling the need to banish her uncertainty.

She smiled slightly, and the soft curving of her mouth unexpectedly grabbed at his chest. She turned her gaze to Sharon. "Mrs. Hastings?"

Sharon stood and came around the desk to offer her hand. "I am. And you are…?"

"Anne Johnson. The admin office sent me up."

"Ah, my temp. Did they explain the project to you?"

"Yes."

"Perfect. I was just telling Professor McClain about the new computer system."

A strange lump formed in Patrick's stomach. This young, fresh-faced student was not his idea of a competent person to handle such sensitive material.

He gave Sharon a sharp-eyed glance. If she noticed his disapproval she ignored it. Instead Sharon pretty much dismissed him by pulling Miss Johnson toward the computer to show off the new notebook-style system that would be arriving within the next few days.

The cell phone attached to his belt vibrated. He glanced at the caller ID. His sister. He needed to take the call, but he wanted to stay and learn more about this temp who would be working on the computer issue.

"I'll be going now," he said, unsuccessfully trying to hide his irritation at being ignored by the two ladies.

Sharon nodded distractedly. Patrick met Miss Johnson's wide-eyed stare for a moment before she hastily dropped her violet gaze. The impact of those interestingly colored eyes left him slightly off balance. He frowned some more. He didn't like being off balance.

He stepped out into the corridor and flipped open his phone. "Meggie?"

He listened to his sister's tear-filled tirade. Finally he interrupted, "Meg, have you talked to Dr. Miller about this? Hon, you know how the subway upsets you, so why do you insist on taking it?" He tried to keep the frustration from his voice, but couldn't quite manage it.

"No, I'm not upset with you. Things here are a bit…stressful."

He acknowledged her suggestion that he see a psychologist for stress management. "I'll take that into consideration. Promise me no more subway rides. Take a cab or walk. Isn't that one of the reasons you moved to Manhattan so you could walk instead of sit in a car?

"I love you, too, sis."

He hung up with a sigh. As proud as he was of his little sister for forging out a life in the art world which she was passionate about, he couldn't help but worry. Her obsessive-compulsive disorder flare-ups seemed to be more frequent the more she tried to push herself to overcome the disorder. But at least she knew he'd always be here for her.

As he headed back down the hall of the fourth floor of the main building on the lower campus of Boston College, Patrick's thoughts turned back to the new computer system and he decided he'd *double* backup all of his work, just in case. He was *not* going to trust the wide-eyed Miss Johnson with his life's work.

Lidia entered the outer office of the District Attorney, Christopher Porter, in the old courthouse of Atlantic City. The wood paneled walls and wooden desk made the small space seem cramped. In the corner next to the filing cabinet, where a woman in a blue sweater and navy slacks sat with an open drawer in front of her, a limp palm tree tried to bring some color to the room.

The woman turned as Lidia noisily closed the door behind her.

"Lieutenant Taylor?"

Lidia nodded and flashed her badge at the mousy brown-haired woman. Her pale face and unrefined features were dominated by wide hazel eyes. The name plate on the desk read Jane Corbin.

"You may go in, he's expecting you," Jane said, her voice low and timid. She adjusted her sweater over her ample chest and turned back to the filing cabinet.

So much for chitchat. Lidia gave one solid knock on the wood door before entering. Porter sat at his desk, his gaze on a report in front of him. His salt and pepper hair caught the late afternoon sunlight streaming through the window behind him. He looked up and pinned her to the floor with his intense gray eyes. "Hello, Lieutenant. Have a seat."

Lidia sat across the scarred pine desk. Porter didn't waste time with pleasantries but went right to reviewing the details of Domingo's arrest.

Domingo's DNA matched the blood found at the crime scene. They had him on tape entering the hotel and exiting through a service door during the time of the murders. And they had an eyewitness. It couldn't get better than that.

For over two hours, Porter shot off questions and she shot right back with answers.

But no matter how much he pushed Lidia, he wouldn't find any flaw in the investigation or the arrest of Domingo. They'd done everything by the letter of the law. No way would Domingo walk on a technicality from the homicide division.

From this point on, the burden to convict lay with the D.A.'s office.

Tired and hungry, she finally barked, "Enough." If she didn't get out of the musty office she was going to scream.

Porter started, his sharp gray eyes widening slightly. He wasn't accustomed to her abrupt manner but in time, if they continued to work together, she had no doubt, he'd get used to her.

"All right. Fine. For now." He closed the file lying in front of him with a snap. "We have a solid case. As long as our witnesses continue to cooperate, we should see Domingo behind bars by summer's end."

"They'll cooperate," Lidia assured him with confidence. The three witnesses all claimed to have held Jean Luc Versailles in high regard. All three were reluctant to come forward but thankfully were doing the right thing.

"They're secure?"

Frustration twisted in her gut. "Two are in WIT-SEC. One refused, but is in hiding. We've maintained contact with all three."

"I'm pushing to have the case moved up on the docket. But you know the system."

"Yeah, like molasses in a freeze."

Porter gave her a sidelong glance as he closed and then picked up his briefcase. "Where are you originally from?"

"Michigan."

"Ah."

"Ah?"

"You have a way about you that's different."

Heat crept into her cheeks. "O-kay."

"I like it," he said.

His grin disarmed her. He really was handsome. How had she not realized that before? Sharp, cool and calm under pressure. His thick graying hair once had been very dark but the lighter strands were attractive. She liked the way the corners of his eyes crinkled when he smiled.

Lidia mentally stepped back and assessed the situation. He was a widower, like herself. They were colleagues, working toward a common goal. She'd seen him at church a few times. All pluses. Before she could talk herself out of it, she asked, "Want to grab a bite to eat?"

"Love to." He held the door open for her.

A confused mixture of pleasure and angst stretched through her system. "Great." Lidia walked out of the office and in the hall, very aware of Porter's hand at her elbow.

She couldn't believe it. She had just asked the

D.A. out to dinner. She hadn't been on a date in at least five years and had no intention of starting a relationship beyond the confines of work.

So why was she so looking forward to the evening?

Two days after she'd first stepped onto the campus of Boston College, Anne found herself lugging Professor McClain's new notebook to his office on the second floor. She hefted the box a little higher so she could knock on the professor's door. She waited a moment before knocking again. When no reply came, she shifted the box to her hip and tried the door handle. Locked.

"Great," she muttered and bent to put the box on the floor. Once free of the encumbering box, she shook out her arms and stretched her back. She'd sent the good professor a note telling him she'd be delivering his computer at five o'clock, long after his last class of the day ended.

She checked her watch. Okay, so she was a few minutes early. Still.

She leaned against the smooth green-painted wall to wait. At least the halls were empty and peaceful. So far her job as a BC temp was going well. Boston College lay in the suburb of Newton, eight miles outside of Boston proper. Newton Center had lots of coffee houses and wonderful trinket shops. Plus a commuter train stop that could take her into Boston when she wanted. She really liked the area. Too bad she wouldn't be staying long.

And she hadn't come here without doing a little research. The current campus site on Chestnut Hill had been built in the early 1900s and featured examples of English Gothic architecture that Anne found fascinating. She'd spent countless hours wandering the walking paths that meandered through lush lawns and tall maples and evergreens to stare at the buildings.

There was something so…moving about the majestic structures with their cathedral-like shapes made of stone and mortar. Where she'd grown up houses were made of wood or tin. When she'd moved to the city, she'd found only a concrete jungle that both intimidated and awed her.

In this New England setting, she was content with her life. No matter how short her time here would be. She smothered the anger that sprouted. What was done was done, she had to learn to live with it.

A movement at the far end of the long, empty hallway made her push away from the wall. A man stood in the shadows at the top of the stairs. She couldn't make out his features. He didn't look tall enough or broad enough to be the professor. She squinted. "Professor McClain?"

"Yes?" a deep voice came from right beside her shoulder.

She jumped with a squeak and whirled around to face the professor. Tall, overbearing—and for some reason comforting. "What…?" Her gaze swung back to the shadows. No one was there. "Did you see that guy?"

"Who?" His gaze moved past her toward the stairwell.

Foreboding chased down her spine. She hadn't imagined the man in the shadows, she was sure of it. She tightened her hold on her purse, feeling the outline of her cell phone. Her lifeline. "No one, I guess."

Behind his glasses, Patrick's dark blue eyes regarded her with puzzlement. "Are you okay?"

She liked his eyes, liked how a darker shade of brown rimmed the irises, like layers of rich chocolate cake. "Yes. Yes, I'm fine. Do you always sneak up on people?"

One side of his mouth twitched. "You sound like my sister-in-law, Kate. She's always accusing me of sneaking up on her. I can't help it if I'm light on my feet."

Anne gave his long, lean frame a once-over. "Dance classes?" she joked.

He shrugged and she thought his cheeks turned pink but in the waning light coming from the high window above the classroom doors she wasn't sure. "My mother thought her boys should be graceful."

"Cool mom," she commented as she bent to pick up the computer box. "Where I come from, boys would rather be hog-tied than sent to dance class."

"Here, allow me," Patrick said and bent as well,

his hands covering hers on the box. Warm, big and strong.

"Where are you from?" he asked.

Slowly she withdrew her hands and straightened, aware of a funny little hitch in her breathing. Must still be the adrenaline from the man in the shadows making her forget herself.

"Al—L.A." She'd almost slipped up. That wouldn't be good.

"You're a long way from home."

He had no idea.

"Uh—" Patrick muttered as he stood with the box in his arms. "The door keys are in my pocket."

"No way am I going fishing," she stated and backed up a step. Three months ago, she would have expected that sort of line from practically every man she dealt with but not here, not now. Not the professor!

Patrick pinned her with a droll stare that made her think perhaps she'd overreacted. He balanced the box on one knee while he dug the keys from his coat pocket and held them out to her. "Here."

Taking the keys as embarrassed heat crept into her cheeks, she unlocked the door and pushed it open. Following Patrick inside, she looked around the office, not surprised to see a clean, clutter-free desk, faced by two perfectly aligned chairs and a filing cabinet with neatly written labels on each drawer. All button-down and tidy, just like the professor.

Patrick set the box on the corner of the desk. "I've backed up all my files. Twice."

She arched an eyebrow. "Really? On what?"

He went around the desk and opened a drawer to produce two floppy disks.

"Unfortunately your new computer doesn't take floppies."

His complexion paled. "It doesn't?"

He really was technologically challenged, which she found endearing. "CDs and thumb drives. Tomorrow I'll bring in a portable USB floppy drive."

He took his glasses off and began rubbing the lenses with a cloth. "That will solve the problem?"

"I'll have to save the files onto a thumb drive." She plucked a silver letter opener from the pen holder on the desk and went to work opening the box. "Until then, we can fire her up and see how she runs."

"You've given my computer a *female gender?*"

"We can call your computer a boy if you'd rather." She tugged on the white foam protector and slid the black notebook computer out of the box.

"The female pronoun is fine, like a ship. Just as potentially deadly and much too unpredictable."

"The same way guys view women," she stated and reached in the box for the cables.

"Excuse me?"

His affronted expression made her hold up her hand and amend her statement. She supposed it wasn't a fair statement, nor was it completely true. "Not all, just some."

He set his glasses back on his nose. "You're not old enough to have such a bleak outlook on the male gender."

She blinked. "Not old enough?"

"You're what, all of twenty?"

Her mouth twitched. "I'll take that as a compliment. Though I'm not sure you meant it as such. And I'm actually thirty." She ignored the fact that her current driver's license stated otherwise. What would it matter if he knew the truth?

He cocked his head. "Really? Indeed."

"Yes, indeed." She plugged the cable and cords into the right spots. "Here we go." She opened the lid of the laptop and began acquainting him with all the bells and whistles.

"So I can actually write on here with this little stick? And the computer types it in?"

She nodded, finding his amazement and wonder quite charming. "The stick is called a stylus and yes, the computer converts your writing to text. And," she said with a dramatic flare, "the lid folds all the way back so it looks more like a clipboard than a laptop, which makes writing on the pad that much easier."

"I think I'm going to like this."

Though there was a smile in his voice, his stoic expression didn't change. Odd. And odder still, she so wanted to see his smile.

She picked up her purse. "I'll leave you to play with your new toy. I'll come back tomorrow and download your files off that dinosaur." She gestured to the archaic computer taking up most of his desk.

He walked her to the door. "Thank you. I appreciate your up-to-date knowledge."

She hid a smile. He'd have a coronary if he knew that the basics of her knowledge came from a year of living with Rob, the computer geek, and the rest from the stack of manuals she'd been devouring over the last few weeks.

She was nothing if not a quick study. Would have been nice if the skill had helped with her acting career.

Moving to the Big Apple at seventeen to follow her dream of the Broadway stage hadn't worked out so well. She'd been just another pretty girl among a thousand other pretty girls, some with talent, others not so much. She'd been somewhere in the middle, but playing bit walk-on roles hadn't paid the bills.

Her dream of the theater had faded and reality had set in. Clearly she'd had to adjust her plans and had found a way, besides acting, to survive.

But then again, the professor clearly didn't suspect she was anything other than what she presently appeared to be. Maybe she wasn't such a bad actress after all. That had to count for something.

"Uncle Raoul."

Raoul Domingo stared at his nephew Carlos and tightened his grip on the phone at his ear. He wanted to hit something or someone. But being incarcerated meant he had to hold on to his temper.

At least until he got out of the joint.

He still couldn't believe that female cop and her pretty boy partner had had the gall to bust in to his home in the middle of his dinner and cart him off in handcuffs.

As if he'd ever see the inside of a courtroom. No way! His men would make sure of that.

And then Raoul would settle the score with the two of them—especially the lady cop.

The Plexiglas window separating him from his nephew was dirty and scratched from years of standing between visitors and the inmates of New Jersey State Prison. Knowing their conversation was probably being recorded, he chose his words carefully so they couldn't incriminate him. He asked, "Have you taken care of that little detail?"

"Not yet."

Carlos squirmed under Raoul's furious stare. Raoul wanted to reach through the glass and wrap his hands around his nephew's throat. "Get it done."

"We're working on it," Carlos assured him, his pockmarked face growing red.

"Work harder."

Carlos nodded. His gaze shifted around and he cupped a hand around the receiver. "We've got another issue."

Raoul's nostrils flared. "What?"

"My—uh, *friend* says there's another pigeon in the nest."

Acid churned in Raoul's gut. Another witnesss? How could that be? Trinidad had sworn the hotel was secure the night they'd visited Versailles, but apparently Raoul had been mistaken in trusting Trinidad. The man better come through now or he was dead meat.

"Tri—"

Raoul put his finger to his lips. "No names."

Carlos grimaced. "Yeah. Uh, we're out tracking."

Raoul wanted out of this stink hole so bad he could smell the tantalizing scent of freedom on his nephew. "Happy hunting."

TWO

Patrick paced the thick brown carpet of his office while the clicking of Anne's nails on the keyboard drilled into his head. She certainly knew her way around a computer and she seemed much more competent than his original assessment. Even so, it rankled knowing someone else had the power to destroy his work.

He didn't like uncertainty. He liked being in control. Had grown used to it since the day after his father died.

He'd become the man of the house, the guy his younger siblings turned to for advice or help and whom his mother relied upon to keep their world rotating even if the axis was now a bit skewed.

Patrick worried about his siblings, though Brody, who should be the one most messed up, had found a wonderful wife and now lived a great life. He'd somehow accepted the past and learned to live with the tragedy of their father's death.

Ryan had been too young to have been traumatized by their father's murder, but Patrick could see how much not having a father had pushed Ryan into his quest for material wealth. Patrick had a feeling Ryan thought having money would give him what he'd lacked as a child. Patrick wasn't so sure.

And then there was little Megan. Patrick adored his sister, but she most of all was messed up and not merely from the trauma of losing her dad, but she suffered from obsessive compulsive disorder, which was a bad combination with her fiercely independent spirit. As soon as she could, she'd left home to find her own place in the world.

Sometimes Patrick felt lost without his siblings underfoot. But he'd found a way to express his feelings in his work.

What if Anne lost something despite the CD and the little device she called a thumb drive? What if she inadvertently opened one of his files and read his writings? Would she laugh?

He could only pray that…

What a lame sentiment. As if God would listen.

No, Patrick couldn't rely on God to help, no matter how much his mother or his brother, Brody, tried to convince him otherwise.

So the best he could do was monitor computer-wizard Anne's progress.

A knock interrupted his thoughts. He opened the office door to a young Asian man, slim in build with dark, penetrating eyes that made Patrick think of onyx stones.

"Professor McClain?"

"Yes. Can I help you?"

The young man stuck out his hand. "My name is Cam. I'm transferring from MIT. I'll be taking your class, Macro Economics of the Irish, this summer." For a man with a slight frame, he had a strong grip.

"Wonderful." Why was he here now? Students didn't normally come knocking. Obviously this was an overeager overachiever. Not many of them around anymore. Too many students seemed jaded and uninterested in more than how to make a quick buck. "Do you have the list of required textbooks?"

"Yep. I'm all set. Just putting a face to the name on the syllabus," Cam stated with a pleasant smile. "I—"

"Oh, bummer!" Anne's voice interrupted.

Patrick glanced at Anne. She was shaking her head, her gaze fixated on the new computer screen. "Problem?" he asked.

She nodded but didn't look toward the door.

Wanting to end the interruption, he turned back to Cam and asked, "Is there anything else I can help you with tonight?"

Cam shook his head, his gaze riveted on Anne. "No, thank you."

"Okay, then." Patrick stepped into the man's line of vision.

Those obsidian eyes shifted to meet his gaze. "I'll see you in class, Professor."

As Patrick shut the door behind his new student, a chill skated across his flesh. There was something odd about Cam, something in the way the black of his eyes seemed depthless. Overeager, overachiever and off balance? He'd have to watch the guy. Patrick didn't want a Virginia Tech tragedy happening at Boston College.

Shaking off the strange notion as nothing more than his worry over his work, he turned his attention to Anne. Her bright red, spiked hair didn't look nearly as stiff tonight, as if she'd run her fingers through the points, loosening their rigidness.

Her high forehead creased with concentration and her lips moved without audible sound. The jacket of her ill-fitting brown suit hung off her shoulders, making her look slightly stooped.

"Why the bummer?" he asked as he came to stand at her side.

She sighed as she sat back. Her right hand reached up to massage her neck. "I zipped your files together and changed them to RTF. I just ran a program to import them to the new system and the computer didn't like it."

"That doesn't sound good." Patrick tried to keep a quiver of panic from seeping into his tone. If he lost his work now, he'd have a hard time retrieving it.

"It's not," she replied.

Heart beating in his throat, he asked, "Have I lost anything?"

"No."

Breathing more normally now, he relaxed slightly. "What exactly is wrong and how do we fix it?"

She turned her purple gaze on him. "Your old computer software program is not talking nicely to the new software program. During the transfer, the formatting was lost. I can go in manually to each file and correct the formatting. It will just take some time."

"How much time?"

"A day, two at the most." She clicked open a file. "See."

The text on the screen was from one of his fall lectures, that much he could tell, but the words were all jumbled with paragraph breaks and tab spaces and what looked like hieroglyphics. He pointed to the screen. "What are all those?"

"Computer language. The new system has converted some of the letters and symbols. It's easy enough to read through and correct by deleting and replacing each symbol. But I can't do a global search and replace."

"This is bad," Patrick stated and plucked his glasses off his face to rub with a cloth he withdrew from his pocket.

Anne stood and placed a hand on his arm. "It's not dire, just time consuming."

The spot where her hand rested on his arm fired

his senses beneath his sports coat. He cleared his throat. "You'll have to come back tomorrow then?"

"Yes. And I think I should start first thing in the morning, if you don't mind?"

Staring at the smooth, elegant fingers on his arm, he said, "The morning will be fine. I have a department retreat off campus until late afternoon."

She removed her hand and began shutting down the computers. Patrick replaced his glasses and watched her movements. Efficient, graceful. Competent. Not at all like he'd first thought.

When the office was locked up for the night, Patrick handed his office key to Anne. "Can I walk you to your car?"

She put the key in her purse. "Actually I'm headed to the cafeteria. But thank you, Professor."

"I'm not really a professor." Now why had he blurted that out?

Her eyebrows rose. "You're not?"

"I'm only an associate professor." Heat rode up his neck.

She gave a small laugh. "But you're still a professor."

"True, just not a full professor."

"Okay. And you're telling me this…why?"

"You can call me Patrick."

"Oh. Well, then. Good night, Patrick," she said, giving him an odd look before hurrying away.

Patrick could just imagine his father shaking his head and saying, *Smooth, boy-o.*

A sadness that always burned just below the surface bubbled, reminding Patrick of all he'd lost. Reminding him of all he could lose if he ever let himself care too deeply ever again.

Anne paid the cafeteria cashier for her meal of egg salad sandwich, side garden salad and a bottle of water. One of the perks of temping at the college was the food discount in the cafeteria, though under the harsh fluorescent lights the egg salad had a greenish tinge that wasn't terribly appealing. But she'd had one a few days earlier and had enjoyed it, so she wasn't going to let a little green rob her of her dinner.

Halfway through her meal, she had the strange sense of being watched. Her gaze swung over the few other late evening diners and landed on the student who'd come to Professor McClain's door. Cam, he'd said his name was, stood near the vending machine, his lean, wiry frame still and his black eyes boring holes right through her.

She frowned, hoping to convey her displeasure at being stared at.

He turned abruptly and put his money in the machine. Once he had a can of soda in hand, he moved out the door and into the dusky night.

A shiver of recognition slithered along Anne's arms, prickling her skin. She was sure he'd been the man standing in the shadows yesterday.

Was his claim of putting the professor's face to his name true? Was Cam really a transfer student or someone more sinister? Had she been found? Would she have to run again? Where would she go? How far would she have to flee to be safe?

"Stop being paranoid," she muttered to herself.

But just in case, she'd like to be safe inside the four walls of her apartment.

Gathering her belongings, she quickly left the cafeteria. The balmy June air bathed her, sending the last of the air-conditioned chill of the cafeteria away with a shiver.

Glancing around to be sure no one followed, she hurried to her four-door sedan parked beneath one of the tall parking lot lamps.

As she drove, once again taking a different route to her street, she pulled out her cell phone and pushed the speed-dial number for the one person who wouldn't think she was totally off her rocker for being paranoid.

"It's me," Anne said to the woman who'd picked up the line.

"What's the matter?" The sharp edge of concern echoed in Lieutenant Taylor's voice.

"Nothing, I think. I don't know. I'm just getting antsy."

"You wouldn't call just because you were antsy."

"You said to call if anything seemed out of sync. This student…I don't know. He gives me the creeps. There's something vaguely familiar about him."

"Do you have a name?"

"Cam. That's all I got. He said he's a transfer

student from MIT. He's taking one of Professor McClain's classes this summer."

"I'll check into it." There was a moment of silence. "How's it going with the professor? Is he as stodgy as his profile says?"

Anne hesitated. Stodgy? After spending so many hours with him, that wasn't a word she'd use to describe him. Cute for a geek. Adorably nerdy. Definitely charming in an odd way. Maybe too charming. Too easy to get caught up in. *You can call me Patrick.* "He's an academic. Just the titles of his published articles make me yawn."

An indelicate snort met her statement. "Don't get attached. You'll be leaving there soon."

Anne sighed. "I know. Thanks for the reminder." As if she could forget. "How soon?"

"Hard to say. The D.A. has you scheduled to testify right before closing arguments so you won't have to come back to New Jersey until then."

"How's the trial going so far?"

"Slow. I'll be in touch. And, hey…"

"Yes?"

"Everything's going to be all right. You'll get through this, you know. You're strong."

The reassurance soothed some of Anne's tension. If only she felt strong. "Thanks."

"Call if anything else strange happens. You can always reach me at this number."

"Will do."

Anne clicked off and tried for some deep, calming breaths as she pulled her car into her parking space right in front of her building door.

Inside the safety of her studio apartment, Anne was greeted by a large white Persian cat with only one eye and a pink collar sporting a dangling, sparkly tiara charm.

Relaxing her voice, Anne said, "Hello, sugar." She picked the cat up and snuggled her close. For a moment Princess allowed the contact before squirming to get away. Anne set the cat back on the floor with a sigh. Sometimes she wasn't sure if the cat loved her or not.

A few days after moving to Boston she'd gone to the humane society looking for a guard dog and ended up with a cat. The minute she'd seen the feline, she fell in love with the ball of fluff named Princess and had brought her home.

Princess marched straight to her bowl, tail stuck in the air, and meowed.

"Ah, we're hungry." Anne opened a can of food and left Princess to her dinner.

Making her way over to the Murphy bed, Anne kicked off her shoes and stretched her toes. She hated heels, but the role she was playing required sensible pumps and the itchy dress suit. Thankfully bare legs were an acceptable style. The thought of nylons made her shudder.

She changed into soft cotton pajamas and crawled

under the down comforter. Her mind wouldn't quiet down however. Her thoughts kept churning through the morass of danger that lurked. Was Cam a student or a henchman for Raoul Domingo? Would one of them slit her throat as she slept? As she came out of the school building? Went to the grocery store? Would she ever feel safe?

And what of the professor? And how much she enjoyed being around him?

Thinking about Patrick was more productive than angsting about the threat she couldn't control.

There was something very steady and reassuring about him that drew her in and made her wish he could see her as she really was.

But he might not be so nice to her then.

The social-status-conscious "associate" professor wouldn't want to socialize with a woman who had barely passed high school and had grown up in a trailer in the backwoods.

She punched the pillow with a groan. The sooner she got his computer up and running, the sooner she could move on to another project and another professor before her time was up in Boston.

She couldn't afford to get too chummy with anyone.

Or "attached."

She was pretty sure she could keep from revealing her past, but she wasn't sure that she could keep her lonely heart from wanting what she couldn't have.

A friend. Love. A life without fear.

* * *

As one day turned in to two days of deleting, re-placing and reformatting, Anne's eyes stung with grit and fatigue stiffened the muscles in her neck and shoulders. She'd figured out how to convert the old computer software into a language the new software could easily and readily read, but just to be on the safe side she'd been reading through each file and would occasionally find a trouble spot that she had to manually correct.

Though the subject matter of economics wasn't something she found interesting, she'd certainly learned a lot. There was one file that looked huge and she'd been saving it for last.

She glanced at the computer clock. She should be able to finish with the files and get the docking station set up before Patrick returned to his office.

She clicked to open the file, "Turned Up Side Down" expecting to see more charts, theories and statistics, but instead she found herself staring at a work of fiction.

A novel. Written by Patrick McClain.

Both curiosity and the desire to make sure the file hadn't lost all of its formatting urged her to read.

Fascination kept her glued to the words.

Soon she was hooked into the story of a young boy who loses his father and must step into the role of man of the house.

She laughed at the antics of the boy and his sib-lings and fought tears of empathy for the characters.

She reached the last page with a satisfied sigh, knew she'd seen some formatting issues but had been so engrossed in the story that she hadn't wanted to stop reading to fix them.

She'd have to read through it again. She rubbed at her eyes. It would be easier if she could read the words from a hard copy. She began printing off the book, while her mind raced with thoughts of the story and Patrick.

She realized she knew very little of his private life. Was this book autobiographical or purely fiction? If autobiographical, she was in deep trouble.

Weren't damaged hearts notorious for falling for their like?

After his meeting with the department chair, Patrick headed to his office, expecting to find Anne waiting for him with his computer ready to go and trusting his files to be intact.

Instead he found his office door wide-open and Anne sitting in his chair, her fingers clicking on the keyboard. Off to the side his printer hummed as it rhythmically spat pages into the tray.

Patrick couldn't help the little glow of approval in his gut for how hard the woman worked. A very admirable trait. She definitely had surpassed his expectations, her fashion choices notwithstanding.

Tonight, though, she wore another ill-fitting, conservative dress suit, and her spiked hair seemed especially…barbed. Her normally creamy complexion held a hint of makeup and beneath her dark lashes, circles of fatigue marred her delicate skin.

She glanced up. Her wary smile made him feel as if he'd walked in on something he shouldn't have.

"Hello." He stepped through the doorway and hovered near the desk.

"Uh—hi. I'm sorry, I had hoped to be done by now. This last file has been sticky."

"No problem." He glanced at the printer. "What's this?"

"Your book."

Distress grabbed his throat as he reached for the top page. He barely glanced at the words. His agitation increased until shock and rage choked him.

She was printing his book.

"How could you?"

THREE

The sharpness of his voice made Anne push the chair back, creating more distance between them. He suddenly looked too broad and too muscular for the herringbone sport jacket and tan pants he wore. "Excuse me?"

He crumbled the paper in his hands. "You read my personal file."

Very carefully, she stated, "I've been checking all the files for formatting errors and I simply needed to print this one out and read it again because it's so big. I thought you were aware of what I needed to do."

"Well…I didn't…you shouldn't have," he sputtered.

Gone was the mild-mannered, geeky professor, replaced with a hard-jawed stranger and the storm clouds gathering in his dark eyes warned he was about to blow a gasket.

Yet every line in his face and every nuance of his body spoke of self-control.

Anne stood, her legs steady and her mind calm. Facing an irate academic was nothing compared to the business end of a gun. "Your book is good. Really good."

"This was private." He grabbed the papers from the printer tray and dumped them into the wastebasket.

"No," Anne cried, latching on to the can. "Look, I'm sorry. But don't do this. You have talent."

He tugged on the can until she let go. "Finish what you need to and get out."

Reeling as if he'd slapped her, she could only stare at him as he turned on his loafer-clad heel and left the office, trash can in hand.

"Fine," she muttered, her own anger sparking brightly. She'd only been trying to help. She didn't need him. They were just ships passing in the nightmare of her life.

Quickly she finished setting up the docking station for the laptop. Monday she'd have to ask Sharon to help Professor McClain set up his email with his passwords and such, because obviously they weren't going to be able to work together anymore.

When she was done, she locked up behind her and hurried out of the darkened building. She pushed open the main entrance doors that faced the lot where she'd parked, to find a man sat on the top stair. She hesitated as fear snaked around her, squeezing her lungs, until she realized who sat there.

"Professor?" she managed to squeak.

He stood. "Call me Patrick, please." His features appeared more angular in the glow of the overhead path lights. "I'm sorry. My behavior was inexcusable."

Touched by the humble sincerity in his voice, she admitted, "You were in the right."

"I shouldn't have growled at you."

"I shouldn't have read and printed off your book without asking you, since it clearly wasn't part of your teaching material."

"Regardless, that gave me no right to treat you so poorly."

She arched an eyebrow. What just went down was his idea of treating her poorly? Okay, was the man a saint or just so well-bred that showing anger was considered bad manners?

She'd take his idea of poor treatment any day over the way her father had treated her mother.

Anne shuddered at the memories flipping through her mind. Her father had been a mean, pious drunk and her mother a passive enabler who'd been too tired from caring for five kids to do more than crawl into her own bottle of gin.

Anne's subsequent experiences with men weren't much better. Her first boyfriend, Johnny, had had a temper that earned him the nickname bruiser on the football field. He'd treated her no less gently.

She'd hoped when she escaped the backwoods into the Big Apple she'd find decent guys who would treat her with respect. There'd been Drew, Simon and Greg. Not one had met her high expectations.

Not willing to blithely walk away from this rare gem in her life, she said, "How about we let it go and you walk me to my car." She dared to loop her arm through his.

There was a moment of stiff hesitation before he covered her hand on his arm. "I would be happy to."

Trying not to notice the ribbons of comforting heat unfurling through her veins, Anne's gaze searched the parking lot for her car.

She mentally paused. Something wasn't right. Three of the parking lot's overhead lamps were out. Her car wasn't under any of the ten remaining lit lamps.

Coincidence? She wanted to think so, but a deep, gut-wrenching awareness lifted the hairs at her nape.

You're being paranoid, she scolded herself. Still, her footsteps faltered.

"Anne?"

She halted. "Are you parked over here?"

"I'm in the faculty lot behind the building."

He'd think she was nuts if she told him she was afraid to walk to her car because the light she'd parked under was out, and knowing how much he valued logic, she said, "It would make more sense if we go to your car first and then you drive me over here. That way you don't have to double back. And the school exit is right there."

He dipped his head in thoughtful acknowledgment. "That does make sense."

Anne breathed a sigh of relief as they turned around, but she couldn't stop the chill chasing its way across her flesh as she flung a glance over her shoulder toward the darkened parking space where her car waited.

From the back of the sedan, a man watched with growing anger as Anne and the professor stopped for a moment before walking in the opposite direction and disappearing around the corner of the building. He swore graphically as he unfolded himself from the back seat and got out of the car.

He wouldn't be grabbing anyone tonight.

Since the car had held little information, he knew tonight's work was a bust.

But that didn't mean he couldn't send a message that would give the little rat something to think about.

"I hadn't pictured you as the Mini Cooper type," Anne commented as Patrick shifted into Reverse and backed the small coupe out of his parking spot. "I'd have thought you more of a Volvo guy."

He grunted in acknowledgment. "I bought it for my mother when she expressed interest in driving, but then she changed her mind," he replied, his tone echoed with resignation as he drove toward the front parking lot.

"And you ended up with the car." She stretched her legs, surprised by the amount of room in the vehicle. "Your mother doesn't drive at all?"

"Not at all. Any place she wants to go that she can't walk to or ride the T to, she has someone take her."

"That someone being you?"

He shook his head. "No. She has a whole network of people to chauffeur her around."

Anne couldn't fathom that type of dependence on others.

The headlights of Patrick's Mini Cooper splashed across Anne's car. She sucked in a shocked breath.

"What in the world…?"

Patrick's exclamation of surprise chased the fear sliding down her spine.

The front and side windows had been reduced to jagged holes with sharp glass teeth, a flat tire made the car sit low to the ground and list slightly to the left. The taillights and headlights littered the ground with pieces of colored plastic and glass.

"Oh, thank you, Jesus," she breathed out, grateful she'd heeded the internal alert that had warned her not to walk to the car in the dark.

"You're thanking God for someone vandalizing your car?"

She couldn't make out Patrick's features but she heard the incredulous tone of his voice. How did she explain something she didn't fully understand?

"Do you believe in God?" she countered.

There was a moment of tense silence before he near growled, "Yes."

Abruptly he got out of his car and walked toward her smashed up car, leaving Anne with the distinct impression that he'd had to think about his answer.

Did he really believe? In his heart or just his head? Why did it matter to her?

Don't get attached. She had to remember that.

She got out and walked over to the destruction where Patrick was now examining the tires.

"Slashed."

A feeling of violation choked Anne.

Patrick unclipped a cell phone from the belt at his waist and reported the vandalism. "The police are on their way."

"Thank you for calling them and for being here," she managed to say around the lump in her throat.

"Let's wait in my car." Patrick touched her elbow, the pressure reassuring as he led her back to the coupe.

Once they were settled in, he said, "Well, this was bound to happen."

"Excuse me?" Did he know? How could he? Unless…

"What college do you know of that doesn't have to deal with some negative elements? I just hope it doesn't escalate into something worse."

Anne sighed and let her forehead rest against the side window as she stared out at the night sky. "Let's hope not."

"Not that I'm discounting the vandalism to your car, but I'm glad no one was hurt."

So was she.

Two blue and white Newton police cruisers pulled up and two sets of officers evacuated the cars.

Patrick went to meet them.

Anne took the opportunity to make a call.

"Anne?" Lieutenant Taylor's voice brought her a measure of comfort.

"My car was broken into. Professor McClain called the police and they've arrived."

"Was there anything in the car that had your personal information on it?"

"No, I don't think so." She tried to mentally picture the contents of the car. The candy bar wrapper from the other day. Her travel coffee mug in the holder. Nothing else.

"Good. That's good. Don't worry, Anne. There's no way anyone could find you. I want you to call me when you get home."

"Okay." She hung up, praying that her trust was well placed.

She got out of the car, her gaze searching the dark shadows of the college.

An older officer approached her with a notebook in hand. The name on his badge was O'Sullivan. "Miss, we need you to check to see what's missing."

She shook her head. "There wasn't anything in the car."

"Do you know of anyone who has a grudge against you?"

She swallowed. Yes, but she was sworn not to say anything. "I've only recently moved to the area. I know hardly anyone."

"Have you had any troubles here?"

"No, everyone I've met has been very nice." She thought about the student named Cam. She debated mentioning him, but she'd trust that he was already being investigated.

"Hey, O'Sullivan, we've got two more cars here with the same type of damage."

O'Sullivan flipped closed his notebook. "Well, that puts a different spin on the situation. You weren't a target, only a random victim."

Anne's shoulders sagged with relief. Random she could deal with.

Patrick, who had been talking to one of the other officers, stepped closer. "Does she need to file a report tonight or can she come to the station tomorrow?"

"Tomorrow's fine. I'd make sure you call your insurance company right away and have them tow your car to a repair shop." The officer turned back to Patrick. "How's your brother, Brody doing?"

"Good. Soon to be a dad."

"You tell him congratulations. Does Gabe know?"

Patrick shrugged. "Not sure."

Interesting that the police knew Patrick's family. She wondered what the connection was.

Anne left the two men talking to walk to the passenger side of her car, glass crunching under her heels. She opened the glove box. Empty. Her heart stalled then pounded in painful beats as she hurried back to the officer.

"The insurance card and the registration are both gone." She couldn't keep trepidation from creeping into her voice. The pertinent information on both items listed a post office box address in the downtown branch of the Boston Post Office. She clearly wouldn't be going to the post office anytime soon.

O'Sullivan's brow creased and his light eyes showed concern. "Give me your address and I'll have Johnny and Mic secure the premises before you arrive."

She swallowed back a flutter of panic. She couldn't very well tell them that she couldn't be traced by the information, which would only lead to questions she couldn't answer.

Better to be safe and let the officers check her apartment. She gave O'Sullivan her address.

"We'll follow the officers," Patrick stated and put his hand on the small of Anne's back.

She took comfort from his strength and allowed him to escort her to his car. Once they were driving out of the parking lot, she dropped her head back on the headrest. The need to confide in Patrick rose sharply, but she forced it down.

She couldn't tell him who she was or why she was here; doing so could jeopardize not only her life but his.

Patrick pulled up behind the police cruiser and watched the two officers enter Anne's building. Very few lights glowed from the many windows of the brick structure. The black metal fire escapes made darker slashes in the shadows.

Near the front door two huge arborvitaes grew at least ten feet in the air, blocking the two side lights and providing good cover for someone waiting in the dark to ambush a person going in or out.

Patrick wasn't usually prone to such suspicious thinking. One of his younger brothers, Brody, a sheriff on Nantucket, was the one who'd followed in their father's footsteps by going into law enforcement. But Patrick figured the events of the night must have triggered some latent cop genes.

In the dim light of the moon coming through the windows of the car, Patrick could make out the tightness around Anne's mouth and the worry marring her brow. Protectiveness surged, surprising him with its intensity.

Being protective and responsible for others was part of who he was, but this was…different.

He refused to analyze the possible explanations now and instead covered her hand with his.

She met his gaze and gave him a wan smile. "I'm sorry you have to deal with all of this."

"It's not your fault, and I will be here as long as you need me." And he meant it, which surprised him even more. He liked life to be predictable and uneventful, which didn't seem to happen around Anne.

The two officers came out of the building and approached the car. Patrick gave Anne's hand a reassuring squeeze before they got out to hear what the officers had discovered.

"The place is clear. We checked the halls of each floor and the back of the building. There's no way for anyone to get inside without the access codes," the taller of the two, Officer Nelson, said.

"Will you patrol the area anyway?" Patrick asked, aware that Anne had rounded the car and stood slightly off to the side.

The shorter officer, Buggetti, nodded. "Sure. We'll stay in the area tonight and put a request in for regular drive-bys."

"Thank you, gentlemen." Patrick shook the officers' hands.

"Thank you, officers," Anne echoed as they passed by her on the way to their vehicle.

When the patrol car disappeared from view, Anne turned to Patrick. "Thanks again for everything."

"Uh, sure," Patrick responded. Her words were a dismissal but he wasn't ready yet to leave her; logic dictated that he made sure she got into her apartment safely. "I'll walk you in."

"You don't have to. The officers said all was fine."

"I know I don't have to. I want to."

She blinked, surprise shining in her violet eyes. "Okay. Well, that's fine."

He followed her inside the brick five-story walk-up. All was quiet as they climbed the linoleum covered stairs to the third floor. At the fourth door to the right, Anne stopped and unlocked the door before turning to face him.

"Again, thank you. I'll be by Monday to show you how to use the docking station and help you set up your password accounts," she said.

"How will you get there?"

"Uh— Transit. Or a cab."

She looked scared, tired and in need of a shoulder to lean on. Not to mention a ride. Amazingly he wanted to be that shoulder even though doing so would only complicate his life.

Time for you to get a life, Patrick.

Maybe it was time for that. But did he really want to start with Anne and the burden of responsibility he already felt toward her?

Spending time with her didn't mean he was looking for a romance. They could be friends. They could both use a friend. And friendship wasn't a burden.

He placed a hand on the door frame next to her head. "I'll come pick you up. But in the meantime, is there anywhere you need to go this weekend?"

"No, I just plan to veg out. Well, actually, on Sunday morning I plan to go to church."

Patrick straightened, his chest knotting. "Is it close by?"

She shook her head. Her pretty eyes studied his face. "Would you be willing to take me?"

He took in as much air as his cramped chest would allow. Take her to church? To a house of God?

But he'd offered to take her anywhere she needed to go. Was he now going to put conditions on that offer? His honor wouldn't allow it.

"Yes. I'll take you to church."

Standing in the shadows outside of the apartment building, the man stood waiting to see which lights went on so he'd know which apartment the woman lived in.

Following the cops and the other pair in their little car had been a stroke of luck. He couldn't have planned it better.

Ah, there was the light. Third floor, fourth set of windows. The front door of the building opened and the professor came out. The man pulled back into the shadows until the Mini Cooper was out of sight.

With a cheeky grin, he took out his enhanced state-of-the-art PDA computer system and uplinked to a sophisticated server that, in his hands, would very quickly give him the information he needed.

He might as well have a little fun with his prey before he killed her.

FOUR

Sunday morning arrived with a beautiful forecast of a sunny day topped with a cooling June breeze.

"What do you think, sugar?" Anne asked Princess, who sat on the edge of the Murphy bed, her one eye regarding Anne and the blue polka-dot skirt she held up for inspection. Anne shrugged and turned back to the closet. "Maybe too flowing."

She sighed and fingered the drab business suits she'd been wearing every day to the college. She really didn't like the itchy suits, but she had a role to play. And today was no different since Patrick would be coming soon to pick her up to take her to church. She hoped he'd like the place and the service. She'd been a tad apprehensive when her super, Mr. Bonaro, had recommended it. But she'd instantly felt welcome and safe among the congregation.

A ripple of anxiety and excitement went through her and she jumped on the bed, grabbing Princess along the way. The cat squirmed and then settled into the crook of Anne's neck.

"I really shouldn't be doing this," Anne told the cat. "But I couldn't resist. There's something about Patrick that I like."

Princess meowed and scrambled out of Anne's arms, jumped off the bed and skidded to a halt at the front door where she pawed at the crack underneath. Anne hurried to the door, hoping Patrick hadn't shown up early. She couldn't see anyone through the peephole.

Swallowing a bout of trepidation, Anne cracked open the door. Her stomach rolled. She put her hand over her mouth as she gagged. A rodent laid in the middle of the hall, its neck broken.

"Gross!" She slammed the door shut.

After getting control of her stomach, she called Mr. Bonaro and demanded he come right away.

With a glance at the clock, Anne grabbed a brown dress suit and quickly dressed. She prayed that the super would get rid of the rat before Patrick showed up. Having a dead rat on her doorstep wouldn't make a good impression.

Just as she slipped on her heels, there was a knock on the door. She peered out the peephole. The super.

She cracked opened the door. Vigilo Bonaro barely reached Anne's shoulder. His stooped sixty-plus years frame looked frail but Anne had seen the man heft the full garbage cans in the back alley like they weighed nothing. His wrinkled face was screwed up in disgust. In his hand he held a dark plastic bag that hung heavy with the body of the dead rat. "I got it." He held up the bag.

"Did the…animal have teeth marks?" she asked, avoiding looking at the bag.

He shrugged. "I no inspect it." He nodded his head toward Princess, who'd come to sit at her feet. "Your cat, she bring you gift, no?"

"No. Princess is an indoor cat." She shuddered. "But I'll bet the guy in 3B's terrier could have done this. That dog is always running loose."

"I ask him next time I see him," Mr. Bonaro assured her.

"You don't think there could be more of them around, do you?" Her gaze searched the corridor.

Mr. Bonaro shook his head. "No." He shrugged. "But just in case, I call exterminator."

"Great. I appreciate you taking care of it."

He nodded and ambled away with the plastic bag swinging at his side.

Anne shuddered with revulsion. She quickly made sure Princess had food and water and then grabbed her purse and headed downstairs to wait on the street.

Just as she stepped outside, Patrick's Mini Cooper pulled up. He got out and came around the car to open the door for her. She drank in the sight of his tall, lean build clothed in pressed slacks and an oxford button-down shirt and tie. His dark slightly damp hair curled adorably at the ends and his strong, clean-shaven jaw made her want to reach out and draw her finger along that straight line.

"Good morning," Patrick greeted her, pulling her out of her momentary stupor.

He held open the passenger door. As she passed him she caught a whiff of his aftershave. A pleasing, clean spicy scent.

"Hi. Sorry. I'm still waking up," she said and slipped inside the car.

When he was settled in the driver's seat, he said, "Where to?"

She gave him directions. She thought about telling him of the rat incident but then decided not to taint his morning as well. She wanted him to be open to God's word, not thinking about her living conditions. She was having enough trouble banishing the image from her own mind.

She prayed that the rodent wasn't a bad omen of things to come.

Patrick walked slowly with Anne toward the Newton Community Church entrance. The old stone building stood on a parcel of land on the edge of town. Lush lawns and a beautiful garden made the whole scene picturesque, too perfect to be genuine. People gathered along the walkways, greeting each other with smiles and well-wishes. Had he stepped into the land of the Stepfords?

Several people said hello to Anne as they passed and she introduced him. Patrick nodded his greeting as the knot on the tie at his neck seemed to pull tighter with each passing moment.

He just wanted this over with so they could leave as soon as possible. He didn't want to have to engage in conversation with these seemingly happy people. He didn't want to be here. Church brought back too many memories.

Memories of times with his father as the family headed off to their church.

Memories of how his father would loop his arm over Patrick's shoulder and walk beside him across the park to the building where they worshipped.

Memories of the day he'd been told of his father's death. He'd run off, across the park to the one place he'd always felt peace. The church.

He didn't feel peace in or out of church anymore. He probably never would and pretending he did only made the ache in his soul that much sharper.

But he'd said he'd take Anne anywhere she wanted to go, so here he was.

Anne led him to a row of padded chairs.

"Do we have to sit up front?" He scanned the outer aisles, wishing he could slip out the side door.

Her big violet eyes widened slightly. "No, I guess not. I just always do. We can move back if you'd rather."

He sighed and sat. "This is fine."

Still standing, she stared at him with concern. "Are you sure? I don't mind moving back."

He took her hand and tugged her into the seat

next to him. Her soft, supple skin against his palm warmed him. He loosened his grip, expecting her to withdraw but instead she hung on, confusing his senses and ringing an alarm in his brain that he chose to ignore because her touch both soothed and distracted him.

For this moment he would allow the closeness and emotional connection arcing between them. It blotted out the heartache of loss that was lurking always below his surface and was trying to rise even now. He squeezed her hand and she smiled, distracting him more.

The inside of the chapel was as beautiful as the outside, with high arches and multicolored stained-glass windows. A stage at the front of the sanctuary was equipped with musical instruments. Four standing microphones and a portal pulpit off to the side. Much different than what he was used to. There were no candelabras, no pipe organ or altar. Maybe this was a concert and not a church service.

Wouldn't that be great. He could handle that.

Anne slipped her hand away as the young woman sitting behind them passed Anne a program. He missed the contact of Anne's hand and declined the program offered to him. Within a few moments all the seats filled and a group of people took their places at the equipment on stage. Patrick pulled at his tie.

The band began to play and the singers joined in.

Over the heads of the singers the words of the songs were projected onto the wall.

Hymns.

Patrick recognized the words and the tunes but the songs had been rearranged to an upbeat, contemporary tempo.

Fascinating.

Beside him, Anne's voice rang clear. He listened, mesmerized by the quality of her tone. There was something different about the way she sang as opposed to the way she talked. He tried to decipher what it was, but soon found himself listening to the words and watching serenity steal over Anne's expression.

The songs of God's love and grace resonated with some chord inside Patrick. Emotions and feelings he'd long ago rejected rose, refusing to be batted down. He wanted to run from the room, he wanted to break down, he wanted to kneel before God and ask, "Why? Why did you let my father die?"

Controlling his emotions and his feelings was something Patrick had mastered as a young boy, but it took every ounce of self-possession to get them under control now.

He would not feel. He would not allow God back into his heart. He hurt too much. His family had suffered too much.

When the music ended and the pulpit had been moved to the front of the stage by a man roughly Patrick's age, whom he accurately guessed was the pastor, Patrick turned to stare out the window at the green grass and blue sky. He didn't want to be there, didn't want to hear what the man had to say about God. Patrick would tune the pastor out, like he did Pastor James whenever Patrick gave in and allowed his mother to drag him with her to church.

Movement in his peripheral vision drew his attention to Anne. She had a notepad and pen in hand and was writing. She wrote the reference of Job 5:7.

Patrick remembered the story of Job. God allowed Satan to test Job's faith by taking everything away from him.

Anne continued to write, and against his better judgment, Patrick began to listen to the message. The pastor's voice had a fluid rhythm and his inflections smoothed Patrick's unease.

"Each of us will face real pain, disappointment and loss."

A deep, biting sensation in Patrick's midsection caught him by surprise. He refrained from clutching at his gut.

"The world says you are either loved by God and saved or you are hated by God and made to suffer adversity. Job's friends told him that all adversity comes from sin. But God answered that belief with His own words and rebuked Job's friends. We must know and accept that adversity is part of human life, which faith overcomes."

Patrick dropped his gaze to his shoes; his breathing turned shallow. Faith. He'd had faith once. Had deeply trusted God. But then God had betrayed that trust. How could this pastor say that faith overcame adversity?

"When we lose someone we love, our lives are changed. Change is a part of life. But healing begins when we acknowledge that loss and risk loving again."

Patrick's chest constricted until taking a breath became impossible. He had to escape.

Patrick lurched to his feet and stumbled to the side door where he escaped into the fresh air. Sucking in big, gulping breaths, he tried to reason out the logic of his reaction, but his mind refused to focus on anything other than the words reverberating inside his head.

Faith overcomes adversity.

Risk loving again.

Accept adversity.

He rubbed at his temples. He couldn't accept what happened to his father because doing so would force him to face the loss. Facing that loss would rip him apart.

He had to remain strong for his mother and siblings. He'd become the man of the house after his father died. Everyone had expected him to be brave and not show his pain. All of his father's fellow officers had encouraged and approved of Patrick's strength. Patrick didn't know how to be anything else.

Our lives are changed.

No kidding.

"Patrick, what's wrong?"

Anne's concerned voice forced him to regain control of himself. Squaring his shoulders, he turned to face her. The tender regard in her gaze nearly made his knees buckle. He wanted to reach out to her for comfort, but he didn't know how. He'd always been the one to offer comfort and support.

"I'm fine. You should go back in. I'll wait at the car."

She touched his arm, her hand searing him to his soul. "You're not fine. Did you have an asthma attack? I could hear how hard you were breathing."

If only asthma were the problem. But he nodded. "I couldn't breathe for a moment. I'm really fine now."

She squeezed his arm before dropping her hand. "We can leave now."

"You should stay and finish the service."

"The service is almost over anyway, and I'd rather be with you."

The corner of his lip curled up and gladness touched his heart. "I like the sound of that."

"Do you have plans for the rest of the day?"

"No." Mom had gone to see Brody and his wife Kate for the weekend. He had no one else to spend time with.

"Would you be up for a trip into Boston, maybe take the Duck Tour?"

The water and land tour via a World War II amphibious landing vehicle was a popular Boston tourist attraction. "I haven't done that since I was young." They'd gone as a family when he was six. He cherished the memory.

"I've been wanting to do it ever since I moved here, but just haven't taken the time. So are you game?"

He glanced at her. Spending the day with Anne sure beat going home to an empty apartment or back to his office to wallow in the emotions the church service had stirred up. "I'd love to."

Her pleased smile knocked his senses for a loop. *Risk loving again.*

But love came with risk. And loss. He didn't want to ever feel that pain again. It was only logical that he kept an emotional barrier between them.

Excitement bubbled inside Anne's chest as she and Patrick boarded the bright yellow amphibious landing vehicle. She couldn't believe she was spending the day with Patrick.

The outside of the beast was metal and, according to the brochure, watertight. A canvas awning attached to two poles on either end offered shade to the occupants. Inside, rows of padded bench seats waited.

She and Patrick sat toward the front. He gave her the window seat, which she appreciated since the view was better. His shoulder brushed against hers as they settled in. She didn't scoot farther away, instead shifted ever so slightly to increase the contact. He felt so good next to her, a shield she could finally hide behind.

The tour guide, or rather conductor as he preferred, dressed in a wild display of sixties attire, introduced himself as Sergeant Pepperz, with a Z. He had an uncanny resemblance to John Lennon, wire-rimmed glasses and all.

"Welcome ladies and gents. I'm your guide on this magical, mystery tour through historic Boston. I'll dole out lots of little-known facts and we'll have a groovy time. But first I need you all to practice your duck call. I see by the blank looks that you aren't familiar with our duck call. What do ducks say?"

Anne and Patrick glanced at each other. Someone from the back shouted, "Quack."

Sergeant Pepperz pumped his hand in the air. "Exactly. Let me hear everyone. On the count of three. One, two, three."

"Quack!" Anne lifted her voice. She nudged Patrick in the ribs. "Come on, say *quack*."

"Quack," he repeated dryly.

She laughed and turned her attention back to the conductor.

"When we pass through an intersection, I'll blow my whistle and you all respond with a resounding quack. And when we pass another duck tour, we quack. And when we pass a police officer, we quack."

"You think this is silly, don't you?" Anne remarked.

"When I was six it was fun. Now, not so much."

She shook her head. "What do you do for fun?"

He took off his glasses and began to clean them with a cloth from his pocket. "I write."

"That book is done, right? Are you working on another?"

"I have a few short stories," he replied, keeping his gaze averted.

She didn't understand why he'd be self-conscious about his work. "I'd love to read them."

He slipped his glasses back on. "I wouldn't want to bother you."

Laying a light touch on his arm, she said, "It wouldn't be a bother."

The amphibious beast began to move. "This is so cool," she exclaimed.

"I'm glad you're enjoying yourself," he replied.

Anne searched his expression trying to determine if he were enjoying their time together. The man was a mystery. A source of conflict and complication. She really shouldn't be with him now, except she didn't want to be alone, either. She was tired of being alone.

He looked composed and attentive, which made her all that more curious about his reaction in church earlier that morning.

"Did you enjoy the service this morning before your asthma attack?" she asked, watching closely to gage his reaction. She didn't really think he'd had an asthma attack, but something sure had gotten to him.

He shrugged. "It was fine."

"I thought the message was a good one, focusing on God's faithfulness through troubled times." She certainly could attest to that.

Without God, she probably wouldn't still be alive. He'd proved Himself to her.

His jaw tensed. "I suppose. But I'm not so sure that faith is all it's cracked up to be."

Curious, she stared at him. "Why would you say that?"

"Because faith doesn't change anything. Not really. People can pray until they're blue in the face but what good does it do? Is evil wiped out? Are the problems of this world taken away? No. So why bother?"

His jaded take on faith left her feeling very sad for him. Something or someone had set him against God. Maybe a prayer not answered in the way he wanted or in the time frame he wanted? She reached out and touched his hand. "I'm sorry you're hurting."

He slipped his hand away. "I'm not hurting." He pointed to a structure on their left. "Here's Trinity Church."

The vehicle rumbled past the beautifully constructed building, and though Anne oohed and ahhed over the architecture as their conductor gave a brief history of the church that dated back to 1733, she couldn't help the sadness settling in her soul for Patrick.

He tapped her shoulder and pointed at the botanical gardens that were coming up. She clapped her hands when she saw the beautifully crafted swan boats full of tourists gliding through the man-made lake.

They continued on through the streets of Boston, taking in the many sights. Soon they were heading down a little incline straight into the Charles River.

Anne laughed with glee and was thankful the lunch they'd shared before the tour had been light. She'd hate to be caught with a bout of motion sickness in front of Patrick.

She glanced back toward the shore from which they'd come and her gaze landed on a man sitting in the very back of the boat.

Her breath stalled in her lungs. Cam, the Asian man from the college, sat three rows back.

FIVE

Anne quickly jerked around to sit forward. Her whole body tensed.

"Patrick. Is that Cam in the back of the boat?"

"What?" He turned his head to look. He shrugged as he returned his gaze to her. "I don't know. Could be."

"Why is he here?" Her uneasiness crept along the length of her spine beneath the suddenly over-warm suit.

"Taking the tour?"

"Do you think he followed us?" She fought back a fisson of panic.

"Are you all right? You've gone awfully pale," Patrick said, his voice low and concerned.

"I want off this boat."

Patrick took her shaky hands, his touch solid and secure. She tightened her hold on him.

"Tell me what has you so spooked."

How did she tell him she had a creepy feeling

about his would-be student? Had he been the one to vandalize her car and was now stalking her? Was this all to do with what had happened in Atlantic City or not?

She decided to confide some of her fear to Patrick. She really needed a shoulder to lean on, but couldn't allow herself anything more than a superficial support. She was tired of being alone and scared. "It just seems odd that Cam came to your office, and then my car was vandalized, and now he's here on this tour with us."

Patrick's brow furrowed. "I'll be right back."

Before Anne could protest, Patrick got up and moved toward the back.

Anne shifted in her seat to watch Patrick talking to Cam. She couldn't hear their conversation but she could see Cam shaking his head and introducing Patrick to the girl sitting at his side.

Anne adjusted her view to see a beautiful Asian woman she hadn't noticed before. Patrick shook Cam's hand before returning to his seat.

"Sir, I'm going to have to ask you to stay seated," called the conductor.

Patrick acknowledged the sergeant with a wave then turned to Anne. "He and his sister are taking the tour. She's here visiting. There's nothing sinister going on."

Heat stole into her cheeks. "Oh. Still…what are the odds that they'd take the same tour we are?"

"Is there something you're not telling me?"

There were a lot of things. Things she couldn't fully confide to him no matter how much she enjoyed his company. Or that affection for him had taken root in her heart.

She was becoming attached and wishing she could lean on him. Spending the day with him had obviously been a mistake.

One she would have to be careful not to repeat.

"I overreacted. The big city and all. Back home we always heard stories of how dangerous cities could be. I guess somewhere in my brain that belief was ingrained."

He looked puzzled. "I thought you said you were from L.A.?"

Uh-oh. "Yes, sort of," she hedged. "A small town. You know there's tons of them on the outskirts. The suburbs." She quickly adjusted her focus outside the boat to the ramp coming up. "Here we go."

The vehicle made a smooth transition back to land. She chatted nonstop about the sights coming into view. Bunker Hill, the *USS Constitution*, the famous bar used in the opening credits of the TV show *Cheers*.

If Patrick was bothered by her jabbering or her inconsistent disclosure about her life she certainly wasn't going to give him a chance to comment.

When the tour was over, Anne kept a running commentary going on about all they'd seen as they left the city and headed back to Newton and her apartment building.

He parked the car and walked around just as she opened the passenger door. She took his offered hand, aware of how well their hands fit together. "Thank you for everything."

"You're welcome. May I walk you up?"

Uncertainty lanced through her. There were so many reasons why she should say no. Distaste from the lingering image of the dead rat, her paranoia on the tour, the way her heart beat by fits and starts every time he was close.

But what harm could come from him walking her to her door?

Maybe a kiss?

The thought sent her already volatile pulse boomeranging through her veins.

She really should say no. Her gaze drifted to his mouth. "Yes, you may."

He followed her up the stairs to the fourth floor. At her door, she halted and tried to steady her breath. "Again, thank you."

"It's been a while since we ate. How about we order a pizza?"

The request was unexpected and way too pleasant. "You want to stay? For dinner?"

Mentally picturing the room behind her and trying to recall if she'd picked up her clothes from the night before, Anne remained still. Her breakfast dishes still lay in the sink. When was the last time she'd cleaned the bathroom?

Patrick stepped back. "I've overstepped myself."

"No, no. It's just…" Her life was a disaster. What did it matter if he discovered she wasn't the world's best housekeeper? She wasn't trying to impress him. She should be protecting him from herself, her past, but… She pushed open the door. "I apologize now for the mess."

Princess let out a loud meow and her tail swished. She regarded Patrick with distain before prancing over to her dish and meowing again.

"Her dinner's late," Anne explained as she shut the door behind them and out of habit threw the bolt into place. Turning back to Patrick, the room she'd lived in for these past three months seemed to have shrunk.

"You feed her and I'll order the pizza," he said.

He moved purposely toward the cordless phone on the scarred old oak coffee table in front of the worn plaid upholstered love seat, her only seating except for the two cane-back chairs pushed up to the small, round dinette table in the corner.

Anne paused on the way to the cupboard. She had a refrigerator full of food. "Would you mind if we don't order out? I'll fix a salad and garlic bread."

Midstride, he pivoted toward her. His long legs carried him to her side in just a few steps. "Not at all. I'll help."

The little kitchen space barely accommodated her let alone his larger masculine frame. She squeezed past him and bent down to fill Princess's bowl. "No, that's okay. You're the guest."

"Self-invited."

She straightened, pivoted and bumped against him. Every nerve ending shimmied like a firefly's dance. "I'm glad you stayed," she said, hoping to relieve any regret he might have for asking.

Through the lenses of his glasses, his deep mocha-colored eyes were unreadable. His gaze dropped to her mouth. She moistened her lips, which was pretty difficult considering how dry her mouth had gone.

"What would you like me to do?"

His softly spoken words sent suggestions cascading through her brain.

Kiss me.

Hold me.

Love me.

She bit down hard on the inside of her cheek to trap the ridiculous words from escaping as her mind scrambled to clear her thoughts.

No. No. No. She didn't want him to kiss or hold her. Well…okay, maybe she did just the tiniest bit, but she certainly wasn't looking for love.

Her life was too unsettled and unpredictable.

Don't get attached.

It was good advice. She had to remember it.

She stepped back, her foot landing on Princess's tail. The cat screeched. Anne jumped.

Patrick raised an eyebrow. An interested gleam in those fabulous, chocolate-brown eyes. "A little edgy?"

She could almost taste chocolate melting on her tongue. She made a noise to affirm his statement and to banish the imagined sensation of rich cocoa.

He rubbed his hands together. "Should I get started on the bread or the salad?"

Bread?

Salad?

"Oh, right." Dinner. He'd been asking how he could help, not…what she'd thought. She wasn't sure if she was relieved or disappointed.

"It'd be great if you'd tackle the bread."

She brushed past him to grab the loaf of sourdough sitting in the fruit basket. "There's a knife—"

She turned and he was there again, inches from her. She inhaled the lingering aroma of his aftershave that now mingled with his musky, masculine scent. She stifled a sigh and resisted the urge to rub her cheek against his like a cat looking for affection.

Pushing the loaf of bread into his chest until he stepped back, she continued, "Let me get the knife."

From a small drawer she retrieved the serrated bread knife, then slid open the cutting board, effectively trapping herself between the stove, the cutting board and him. He took the knife and laid it on the cutting board next to the bread while he slipped out of his jacket. His white dress shirt fit attractively against his wide shoulders and lean torso.

She turned away and set the oven to broil. From the cupboard behind her, she took out garlic powder and set it on the cutting board. She was able to open the refrigerator door wide enough to grab a stick of butter and the salad fixings, plus the cold cooked chicken she'd picked up the night before. Making do with the small amount of counter space between the sink and the stove, she prepared their salad.

They worked in silence, the rasp of the bread knife filling the kitchen in tempo to the chopping of her paring knife as she cut vegetables. The unfamiliarity of the domestic scene started a low hum of yearning in her soul.

Her father had never helped in the kitchen. That had always been "the woman's" place to him. Anne tried to recall ever jointly making a meal with any of her ex-boyfriends. She couldn't.

Takeout or microwavable had been the norm until recently. Ever since she'd moved to Boston, knowing that everything in her life was going to change.

Witnessing a murder had a way of doing that.

When the salad bowl was filled, he stepped aside so she could set the bowl on the table. Patrick put the bread in the oven. A few minutes later, with their bread toasted and their salads served, they sat at the round table.

His long legs tangled with hers for a moment before they settled into comfortable positions. At first, Anne tried to keep her knee from resting against his leg, but soon she relaxed and enjoyed the warmth.

"Did you mean it?"

Anne chewed a tomato she'd just popped into her

mouth. The acidic fruit burst with flavor. She swallowed. "Mean what?"

Patrick weighed his words. "That you liked my book."

A smile tugged at the corner of her mouth. She leaned forward for emphasis. "Yes. Very much so. That's why I printed it because I got so caught up in the story that I'm sure I missed some things that needed to be fixed."

The bemused expression on his handsome face was endearing. "You didn't throw it away, did you?" she asked.

A muscle in his cheek twitched, but his mouth didn't. "The printout, yes, but the file is still on my computer."

"Have you sent it out to any publishers?"

"No."

The reply came out quickly and in a tone that conveyed the very idea was preposterous.

"Chicken," she teased.

His eyes darkened and not with amusement. "You're the only person who even knows about the book, let alone has read it."

And both by default and without his permission.

She instantly sobered. "Which begs the question why? Why would you keep a talent like yours hidden?"

"It's private."

"The answer to my question is private or the whole subject is private?"

He thought. "Both."

Considering she had enough issues in her own life that she deemed private, she could understand, even respect his answer. But that didn't mean she agreed with the keeping of secrets. And for some irrational reason she wished for there to be truth between them. At least on some level.

"Do you enjoy jazz music?"

Thrown by the abrupt change in topic, she had to think a minute. "You mean music with saxophones and breathy vocals?"

Patrick's mouth quirked upward. "Yeah, something like that."

"Yes. I think so. Why?"

"I have tickets to a jazz concert tomorrow night. Would you like to join me?"

Unexpected warmth at his request spread through her chest. "I would. Thank you."

The pleasure in his gaze touched her like a caress. "Great," he said.

A tingle of excitement lit her senses and caused her heart to thud against her ribs in an erratic beat. Her gaze dropped to her plate. She'd just accepted an official date with the professor.

So much for keeping her distance.

Scullers Jazz Club on Soldier Road in downtown Boston overlooked the Charles River and showcased the Boston skyline with huge floor-to-ceiling windows. Rich mahogany walls, intimate seating for small parties and a stage with a lush red curtain backdrop created an ambiance few clubs in Boston could compete with. Patrick liked its cozy, less crowded atmosphere. And tonight was the first time he'd ever brought a woman here with him. He hadn't ever wanted to share this very personal passion for jazz with one before. Doing so now was a bit unnerving.

A brunette hostess showed Patrick and Anne to a table near a window where they could enjoy the view as well as the stage.

"This is lovely," Anne remarked as she sat in the chair Patrick pulled out for her.

He took his seat. "Scullers has the best jazz in town."

She picked up the menu but didn't open it. "Do you come here often?"

"Yes, depending on who's playing."

"I wouldn't have pictured you as a jazz fan—more of a classical kind of guy."

"I'm full of surprises," he quipped, enjoying how beautiful she looked tonight with her normally spiked hair a bit softer somehow. Though she still wore the baggy brown dress suit she'd worn to work that day, in the soft ambient light, the brown complemented her complexion in a way it didn't in the harsher fluorescent lights of the college.

She smiled. "Yes, you are full of surprises." She opened the menu. "What would you suggest?"

"The tenderloin over mashed garlic potatoes," he said decisively.

She shut the menu. "Sounds good."

For a moment silence stretched between them.

"Have you seen any good movies lately?" Anne asked.

Grateful that she'd started the small talk with something easy, he told her about a foreign film he'd watched recently.

"You speak French?" she asked.

"No. The movie had subtitles."

She looked impressed. "I've never watched a film with subtitles. Is it hard to follow?"

"You get used to it."

The waiter came over and they ordered their meals.

The conversation strayed to books.

"I read Christian romance novels," she announced.

He knew what romance novels were but Christian ones? He'd bet his mother would like them, if she hadn't already discovered them. He'd have to ask her. "I didn't know there was such a thing. I read more literary works, myself. I want to be challenged, provoked to think."

She leaned forward, her expression showing earnest interest. "Don't you ever read just to enjoy the story? Most of the literary books I've tried are sad and depressing. Wouldn't you rather read more up-lifting and hopeful books?"

"Well, I do read—" he couldn't believe he was going to confess this to her "—horror, for pleasure."

She blinked "*Horror?* You find that pleasurable?"

"Okay, maybe pleasurable isn't the right word. But they keep my interest."

She made a face. "I've read a few and couldn't sleep for weeks."

A mental image played across his mind of Anne curled up on a couch engrossed in a novel and biting one nail as she turned the pages. She'd be so cute, needing someone to comfort her from the scary story. He shook away the image.

"To each his own, I guess," he replied and silently told himself to get a grip. Just because they were out now and the evening was going nicely, didn't mean he should be thinking about spending more time with her. It wasn't like they were dating with marriage in mind. This was just two people out for a little dinner and music. Nothing more.

"I suppose." She gazed past his shoulder, her eyebrows drawing together.

He turned to see what made her frown. "What's wrong?"

Her expression cleared. "Nothing." She shook her head, clearly embarrassed. "I thought I saw Cam again, but I was mistaken."

"He sure bugged you, didn't he?"

"I think the vandalism to my car unnerved me more than I'd thought."

Protectiveness seared through him. He reached across the table and took her hand. The warm, soft skin felt so good within his grasp. "Your reaction is understandable."

She flexed her fingers around his. "Thanks."

The waiter interrupted. "Here we go, two tenderloin dinners."

Reluctantly letting go of her, Patrick sat back and tried to focus on the savory food.

During their meal they chatted about sports and playfully argued over who would win the upcoming World Series. When their meal was devoured and their plates cleared away, Patrick used the excuse of improving his angle toward the stage to scoot his chair closer to Anne.

An excited buzz filled the air when the MC stepped to centerstage and introduced the musicians.

For the next hour, they were treated to some amazing jazz and Patrick reveled in the music as much as watching the play of emotions dancing across Anne's face.

When the last song ended, they stood to clap along with the other patrons.

"That was wonderful," she exclaimed. As they left the club and walked to his car, she added, "Thank you for inviting me."

"You're welcome." He was glad to know she enjoyed herself. He really relished her company, and delighted in the easy way they talked without awkwardness.

When they reached his car, he held open the passenger door. For a moment Anne seemed frozen, her gaze on a Hispanic man standing in the shadows near a closed store.

"Anne?"

She wrenched her gaze back to him. Her whole body shuddered. "I'm sorry. I don't know what's the matter with me. I keep freaking myself out."

Once she was settled in the seat, he leaned in close. "I'm not going to let anything happen to you, okay?"

Though she nodded, anxiety lingered in her violet colored gaze. She didn't believe him. Why?

Was she really only paranoid because of the car break-in or was there something else she wasn't saying?

And how did he get her to trust him enough to tell him?

"Would you like to come in for coffee?" Anne asked, not wanting the evening to end. She'd thoroughly enjoyed herself, regardless of her minipanic attacks. First imagining she'd seen Cam in the crowd and then later thinking the man on the street was staring at her. She really had to get a grip or Patrick would think she was certifiable.

"Coffee would be great," he replied as he walked with her to the door of her apartment building.

Once inside her apartment, Patrick took a seat at the dining room table and she set the decaf coffee to brewing. She pulled out some scones she'd picked up earlier in the day from the bakery at the end of the street. Putting them on a tray, she turned on the oven to warm the pastries up.

The phone rang, the sound jangled along Anne's nerves.

She stared at the instrument. Only a very small, select few had this number. She didn't even have an answering machine because there was no point.

"Are you going to answer?" Patrick asked after the fifth ring.

Meeting his quizzical gaze, she stood. "Yes. Of course."

If she didn't answer, Patrick would ask questions. Questions she wasn't at liberty to answer. Though spilling her guts to him was very tempting. She could really use a voice of reason to keep the nightmares at bay.

She moved across the room and lifted the handset from its cradle.

Before pressing Talk she took a bracing breath. "Hello?"

Heavy breathing met her greeting.

She let loose a disgusted noise in her throat and clicked the end button.

"Problem?" Patrick had risen. Concern etched lines in his face.

"Crank call." She set the device back in its base.

"Probably bored teens. I can remember doing stuff like that. We'd randomly dial and then usually make some dumb joke, like did you know your refrigerator was running? You better hurry before it gets away."

"So you were a bit of a troublemaker, eh?" He raised an eyebrow.

She couldn't tell if he was teasing her or simply stating the obvious. "You could say that."

"Where are your parents?"

"Back home."

"What brought you out here?"

She didn't like the bend in the road this conversation was taking. "You know, I have a friend in the publishing industry. I could send him your book. Get some feedback."

He held up his hand. "No way."

She didn't understand why he'd refuse. Why write something if you didn't want to see it published?

The phone rang again. With a jerk, she grabbed the receiver and punched the talk button. "Yes?"

More heavy breathing.

Anne's jaw tightened in annoyance. "Listen, you. This isn't funny." She clicked End without waiting for a reply.

Keeping the phone in her hand, she moved to the kitchen area and set the phone on the counter.

Patrick stacked the dishes on the rack by the sink. "You could always have your number changed."

She sighed. "I'm sure it's just kids."

She didn't need any more changes. And if it wasn't

kids calling, she'd have bigger problems than changing her phone number to deal with.

When the phone ran for the third time, she picked up before the second ring. "Yes." Resignation laced her voice.

A dry chuckle that sounded anything but teenaged made the hairs on her arms raise. Then a voice, dark and dangerous whispered in her ear, "Have you ever heard the scream of a dying rat?"

Fear rammed into her skull, rendering her speechless. Anne fought back smothering panic as the world receded into a pinpoint where only Patrick's face kept her sanity intact.

The voice, so wicked and close, continued, "It's very satisfying."

The dark night air was just warm enough for people to leave their windows cracked open. A boon for the man dressed in black as he slid the bottom floor window up just far enough to slip through. He didn't worry about prints. His soft leather gloves wouldn't leave any. Blending into the shadowed interior, he made his way toward the door underneath which a beam of light threw just enough glow to navigate the room's furnishings.

Cautiously he cracked the door and peered into the hall. The dull overhead lights illuminated the empty corridor. Making his way silently through the building to the door of his target, his breathing slowed in preparation for entering the apartment.

He took out his tools and used them on the apartment's lock. Before opening the door, he unscrewed the hall lights so there'd be no change in shadows when the door swung forward. Once inside the apartment, he slinked toward the bedroom, having already assessed the apartment during the day when the target hadn't been home. He moved to where he knew his prize awaited.

A figure slept under the cover of a sheet. The man swiftly placed his hand over her mouth as she jerked awake. Her hands flayed the air and her feet kicked. From the sheath at his side he pulled out a large knife. The woman clawed at his gloved hands.

He leaned in close. "You should have kept your mouth shut."

With one clean arc, the man sliced through the woman's throat and her fighting ended.

SIX

The squad room door burst open.

Glad for the interruption, Lidia jerked her gaze from the case file in front of her. She'd been working a double domestic homicide that looked open and shut. The teenage son amped up on meth had shot both parents with the father's hunting rifle.

The kid had passed out afterward and didn't remember a thing. Not unheard of, but the weapon had been wiped clean.

Which was odd. Odd enough to make Lidia suspect there had been another person involved.

Rick, unusually harried, came straight to Lidia's desk. "We've got a situation."

"Yes, we do." She tapped the file.

"Not that. On the Domingo case," he stated, agitation clouding his eyes and edging his tone.

Lidia's lungs slammed against her ribs, trapping her breath. "Tell me."

"One of our witnesses has turned up dead."

Please no. Oh Lord, please not Anne.

She swallowed a shudder of pure dread. She never should have let herself become emotionally involved with a witness, but the young woman had struck a latent parental instinct Lidia had been helpless to deny. "Details."

Rick laid out a series of photographs. No words were needed.

Lidia closed her eyes.

Such a waste.

Patrick watched the color drain from Anne's face and her body go rigid. Her violet eyes glazed over with shock from whatever she'd just heard. Something was wrong. He took the receiver from her slackened fingers and put it to his ear. Dial tone. He clicked off and set the phone aside before taking Anne by the hands and leading her to the love seat.

"Anne," he said softly.

Her gaze shifted slightly toward him. She blinked several times. Her body did one long shudder and her eyes cleared.

"What was that?" he asked.

Her color returned but the tight lines around her mouth spoke of how disturbing she found the call. "Just another prank."

He didn't believe that just a prank call could upset her so badly. "Tell me what was said."

She shook her head. "It's late. You should go." She stood abruptly.

Whoa, what had her so spooked? Whatever it was, he didn't want to leave her like this. She'd started to relax during dinner. He still could hardly fathom her praise of his writing. But now she was distressed again and trying to keep her emotions from showing.

"You're upset. You shouldn't be alone. Is there someone you can call to come stay with you or somewhere you could go?"

Two little lines appeared between her eyebrows. "No. I'm fine. I'll be fine." She moved restlessly into the kitchen, wiping down the counters.

Concern arced through him. But he couldn't stay with her. There was only the one Murphy bed and not even a sofa, just the love seat that had seen better days.

In fact, so much of the furniture in the small studio had seen better days. It looked like she'd shopped at the local thrift store. He suddenly realized there were no personal items or photos or anything that gave him insight to Anne.

He didn't feel like he really knew her and thinking about it, she'd been very close-mouthed about her past. Why?

She stopped moving and stared at him expectantly. There was no other option than to do as she'd asked.

But that didn't mean he was going to abandon her. It wasn't in his nature.

* * *

As soon as the door closed behind Patrick, Anne rushed to her purse and dug out her cell phone. Somehow, someway, her location had been compromised. And clearly the car vandalism *hadn't* been random.

She speed-dialed the only person she trusted but voice mail picked up. Unsure what to make of that, she tried to keep the panic at bay as she left a message.

There was one other number she could call. Scrolling through the cell's phonebook, she found the number she needed.

A man answered on the second ring. "Klein."

"This is Anne Johnson."

"Hold."

The line went quiet.

The adrenaline that had pumped through her veins after the initial shock from the call now slowly drained, leaving her weakened. She sank onto the love seat, pulling her knees to her chest. Princess jumped onto the cushion beside her and let out a loud meow before rubbing her head against Anne's updrawn legs.

Taking comfort in the cat, Anne tried not to let her mind dwell on the sinister words still echoing inside her head.

Being summoned so commandingly to the D.A.'s office put Lidia in a bad mood. She stepped into the outer office just as Jane was hanging up the phone.

Jane grimaced. "You can go in, but he's in a foul mood."

Lidia snorted. "So am I."

She pushed open the door and entered. Porter stood facing the window. "How could you let this happen?"

Lidia stopped short. "Excuse me?"

Porter turned and glared at her before taking his seat behind his desk. Fatigue or stress darkened the skin around his eyes. "You said you had the witnesses secure. Now we've lost one."

Holding on to her patience, Lidia planted her hands on the D.A.'s desk and leaned forward. "First, you don't order me to your office like some flunky law clerk and then snap at me. Second, I told you one witness was in hiding and refused our protection. That witness has paid a stiff price."

And though she had her own methods of keeping tabs on those involved in the investigation, she added, "Third, if you want to know about the other two key witnesses you should be talking to the U.S. Marshals assigned to their cases."

He rubbed a hand over his jaw. "You're right. I'm sorry. This case is falling apart."

Remembering the cryptic message she'd received late last night from Anne had taken a chunk out of her confidence, but she had to hope for the best. Had to trust that God would see this through. "This case is solid even without the one witness."

He shook his head, his troubled gaze meeting

hers. "The video placing Domingo in the hotel has disappeared."

Feeling as if she'd just been rammed in the gut with a night stick, she sank into a chair. "How?"

His mouth pressed into a thin, angry line. "Honestly I think we have a leak somewhere in the system."

Lidia digested that information. If someone had access to the evidence, they could realistically gain access to the case files. "We have to warn the marshals. All the witnesses could be compromised."

Porter sighed with resignation. "It's already happened."

The bottom fell out of Lidia's soul. She prepared herself for the worst. "Tell me."

Abandoning a woman to her fate might not be in Patrick's "nature," but he certainly wasn't built for an overnight vigil of Anne's apartment while crammed inside the Mini Cooper.

The sun was just peeking over the horizon. Cold and stiff, Patrick rolled his shoulders and checked his watch. Nearly six. Anne probably wouldn't come out for at least another hour. He contemplated walking down to the café at the corner. He could really use some coffee. Instead he leaned his head back.

A knock at his window startled him awake. He hadn't meant to sleep. He bolted upright, bruising his knees on the steering wheel and bumping his head on the roof.

At the window beside him stood Anne. All in one piece and smiling. A welcome sight. Her gray business suit hung off her slim frame and gaped at the sides where she bent slightly to look in at him.

He rolled down the window. "Morning."

"Hi. What are you doing?"

"Waiting for you."

Her eyebrows rose. "Have you been here all night?"

"Yes," he admitted.

"Wow," she said, her voice and expression both incredulous.

Not sure he could get out and then back in, he said, "Hop in. I'll drive you to the college."

As she came around to the passenger side, Patrick's gaze scanned the street and sidewalk. People starting their Monday morning.

A man with a dog came out of the building next to Anne's. The dog, a big mastiff, pulled at his leash, nearly dragging the poor guy off his feet. Shouldn't have something you can't control, Patrick thought.

The man and dog passed another man who stood slightly turned away. Something about the wiry, darkhaired fellow struck a chord in Patrick. He couldn't make out the man's features because he had a Red Sox's hat pulled low over his eyes.

Anne slid into the seat. "I can't believe you slept in your car all night."

Keeping an eye on the man, Patrick started the engine and turned the heat to full-blast. Cold air flew at him from the vents, but as the car rolled down the street and picked up speed, the night's claim on the car receded and warmth filled the interior. "It was a bit uncomfortable."

She touched his arm. "I'll bet. Especially for a guy your size."

The unexpected tender gesture tightened his chest and drew his attention. "I didn't expect you for another hour or so."

Her hand slipped away, leaving in its place a warmed spot. "I started out early enough to familiarize myself with the transit train and then the bus," she explained while she held both hands up to the heat vent.

Patrick's gaze searched the rearview mirror for the dark haired man. He was gone. "Makes sense. But I said I would give you a ride."

"You don't have to chauffeur me around, you know."

"I don't mind." He checked the rearview mirror, again. A green American made car pulled out behind them. Two men with sunglasses sat in the front seat.

"You have your own life. I don't want to be a burden," she stated.

The car stayed behind them for several blocks. "You're not a burden."

She sat quietly for a moment as if trying to comprehend his words. "The body shop said I'd have my car back in a few days."

"Great." When he turned to get on the road that

would take him to the college, the car didn't take the on ramp. "Then for the next few days, I'm your guy. I mean your driver."

Pink bloomed in her cheeks, mirroring the heat he felt creeping up his neck at his own fumbling.

"Really, Patrick, you don't have to."

He glanced at her. "Do you *not* want me to?"

The troubled expression in her eyes tore at him. "It's not that. I just feel bad, like I'm inconveniencing you."

"If I were inconvenienced I wouldn't offer. But if you would rather I back off, I will."

"No, actually, I wouldn't."

He glanced over at her again, searching her gaze, hoping she wasn't just being polite, but the sincerity in her expression tugged a small smile from him. "Good."

They drove in silence for a moment. When he checked his rearview again, he couldn't be sure but he thought he saw the same American made car three cars back. He chastised himself for being overly suspicious. There were a million of the same make and model all over the place. There was no reason he should suspect they were being followed.

He could feel Anne's gaze assessing him.

"Where do you live?" she asked.

"Not far from BC." He maneuvered around a slow-moving delivery truck.

"We could stop so you can freshen up and change."

He cast a brief look her way, surprised by her words. "That's okay."

"No, it's not." She waved a hand to emphasize her words. "Look at you. You're a mess."

Because of her teasing tone, he didn't take offense with her assessment. He felt like a mess. "Gee, thanks," he teased.

She worried her bottom lip for a moment. "I don't mean to insult you, but this isn't you. You can't go into work like this."

With a shrug, he replied, "It doesn't matter."

"What will people say?"

Her affronted tone made him pause and chance a curious glance at her. "I don't know. Should I care?"

Her eyes grew big. "Yes. You've a reputation to maintain. You're an associate professor. You can't show up to the college looking like you slept in your car."

Her concern sent pleasure rippling through his system. "But I did sleep in my car."

"Which begs the question why?" She turned in her seat to fully face him. "Why did you sleep outside my apartment?"

An odd sense of self-consciousness attacked him. How did he reason out the need to protect her, even to himself? With the truth? He didn't really have much choice. "You were pretty upset last night. I wanted to make sure you were safe and to be here if you needed anything."

The affection in her expression made him swallow quickly.

"Really? That's so sweet." She touched his arm again, her hand pale and delicate against his tweed coat. "I mean, I don't think I've ever had anyone do anything so nice for me before."

He liked how her words made him feel approved of and appreciated. "It's not that big a deal."

She tightened her hand, her fingers firm on his arm. "Yes, it is. To me, it is."

Keeping one hand on the wheel, he covered her hand with his own. The contact melted him inside. "Thanks."

"For what?"

He lifted her hand and brought her knuckles to his lips to place a featherlight kiss there. "For making me feel so good."

"How'd...how'd I do that?"

"Just by being you."

Her gaze dropped and she slipped her hand away. Her withdrawal sent disappointment curling through his heart. He had the distinct impression that he'd somehow upset her with his words.

Now why would that be?

A stone wall encapsulated the many buildings of Patrick's apartment complex. As they drove through the parking lot, Anne caught a glimpse of a pool surrounded by a wide concrete patio with several lawn chairs and sets of tables with chairs.

Patrick parked near the entrance to the third building. She followed him into the entryway which was tiled with gray stone and the walls were textured in rich tones of blue and cream.

The elevator was mirrored and soothing classical music played from speakers concealed in the ceiling. They exited on to the top floor.

Patrick led her to the twentieth apartment near the opposite end of the building.

He unlocked his door and pushed it open. "Welcome."

She stepped over the threshold into a stylized dwelling that could have easily been a feature for a modern living type of magazine. To the left of the front door was the kitchen that sported sand-colored granite counters, white appliances and a beige flecked tile floor. To the right she glimpsed the powder room with the same flooring, white fixtures and ecru colored hand towels.

The living space had a cream carpet. Lots of cream carpeting and cream walls. A light brown leather sectional dominated the middle of the room and faced a beige-toned stone hearth fireplace. A round pine table and four matching chairs sat near the wall beside a light, finished shelf system with high-tech sound equipment. "It's...uh." Very vanilla. With caramel sauce. "Very nice."

"Thanks. I'm comfortable here."

Her gaze was drawn to the only bit of bright color in the main living quarters of the apartment. A display of photos in pine shadow boxes lined a wall. She went to inspect the images. "Is this your family?"

He came to stand beside her. "Yes." He pointed to a ruggedly handsome, smiling man with his arm slung around a beautiful, laughing redhead. "That's my brother Brody and his wife, Kate. They're expecting their first child around Christmas. He's a sheriff in Havensport, on Nantucket."

Patrick motioned to a picture of a young woman with curly dark hair holding a bouquet of red roses. Her serene smile and kind eyes seemed to stare straight at Anne.

"This is Megan, my sister. She lives in New York City and runs a trendy art gallery. Not long after our father was killed she came down with a bad case of strep, which triggered OCD. The doctors said because her immune system was weakened from grief, she became susceptible to the disorder."

Empathy played a sad melody through Anne's heart. "That must be hard on her."

"It is, but she's coping." He tapped the next picture. "And this is the baby, Ryan." Patrick walked away from the wall toward the kitchen. "Would you care for some coffee?"

"Please."

The man in the photo had a roguish gleam in his dark eyes that was far from infantile. "What does Ryan do?"

"He's an investment broker," he said as he made the coffee. "And very successful for how young he is but he's always been that way. Once scheme after another, trying to make his fortune. I have to admit his entrepreneurial spirit has served him well over the years. He'd set up lemonade stands at the park across from our home and rake in enough cash to pay for us all to go to the movies every Saturday night."

"So he doesn't hoard his cash?"

Patrick gave an equivocal gesture with his hand. "Yes and no. He's generous but smart. He'll be set for life by the time he's fifty, yet…"

"Yet?"

"I worry that he'll miss out on living if he stays so focused on accumulating wealth."

His concern for Ryan endeared him to her. She wished she and her siblings had been as close-knit.

The last portrait was of an older couple. Patrick's parents. "Your mother is stunning."

Patrick set a mug on the counter for her. "Yes, she is. That picture was taken the year before my father was killed."

His words, stated so matter-of-factly, curled around her heart and squeezed. Flashes of his novel came back to her. A deep, penetrating sadness welled inside, blurring her vision.

Keeping her voice even, she asked, "How did he die?"

When he didn't immediately answer, she turned to find him watching her with the oddest expression she couldn't decipher.

"I'm sorry. I shouldn't pry."

He gave his head a quick shake as if to clear his thoughts and then picked up his mug of coffee but didn't take a drink, just stared into the dark liquid. "In the line of duty. Sort of."

He glanced up. In the depth of his eyes she saw his hurt and anger, but then it was quickly banked by his normal stoic expression.

"He'd picked Brody up from school late one afternoon. On their way home a call came over the radio. Dad responded."

He couldn't have said what she thought she just heard. "With your brother in the car?"

"Yes."

Empathy and anger roared through her. Tears burned the backs of her eyes. "How old was your brother?"

"Twelve."

She looked back at the photos, giving herself a moment to clear the clogged tears from her throat.

"Dad was all about duty and honor. I think he thought he was invincible. He left Brody in the car while he went into the situation."

Her stomach lurched. "Did Brody stay in the car?"

There was no mistaking the spurt of rage in his eyes before he blinked it away. "No. He saw my father die."

Images streaked across her brain. The remembered noises, the smells. The horror. She couldn't imagine a child witnessing a murder. Witnessing the death of a parent. She ached for this family that was torn apart by tragedy.

"How awful," she whispered, wishing there were words to express her sympathy.

He briefly closed his eyes. When he opened them the remoteness in his gaze left her breathless. "It was awful. For all of us."

"You said Brody is a sheriff."

He gulped from his mug before answering. "That's right."

"Amazing that he'd choose law enforcement."

"I think he still wants justice for our father's murder."

Her breath hitched. "They never caught the guy?"

"No. There were no witnesses. Brody only saw the man's back as he ran away."

If Anne ever had a doubt about the path she'd chosen, to testify rather than take Jean Luc's money and disappear, those doubts had just been laid to rest.

Someone had to stand up for the rights of the victim. Someone had to bring the criminal to justice. For Jean Luc, that someone was Anne.

Too bad someone hadn't been able to do that for the McClain family.

She wanted to wrap Patrick in her embrace and somehow, someway heal the wound so evident in Patrick's heart.

But she didn't believe she had that power.

She didn't believe Patrick would let her. So all she could do was say a silent prayer that God would bring this hurting man peace.

SEVEN

Patrick made his way across campus back to Carney Hall where Anne was now helping the English department with their computers. He hadn't liked leaving her there, but logically knew she'd be fine. There was no reason for him to be feeling like he needed to stick by her all day.

Even so, he just couldn't erase the fear he'd seen in her eyes last night after that phone call.

This morning she'd seemed calm and hadn't said a word about the call. Instead she'd been very interested in his family.

Talking about his father's death still hurt even after all these years but he'd become good at controlling the pain. He was sure Anne had no idea how hard it had been to answer her questions.

As he approached the building, he glanced toward the public parking lot. He paused as his gaze landed on a familiar car. Near the end of the last row, there was a car matching the one that had followed them earlier this morning.

Patrick's gaze searched the grounds, taking in the smattering of students and faculty.

Patrick noticed a man in a gray business suit wearing sunglasses step from around the corner of the building and ascend the stairs into Carney Hall.

Wait a sec! An image of the car with the two men in sunglasses flashed through his mind.

Coincidence? Not likely.

He rushed inside and took the stairs to the fourth floor two at a time. Business suit guy leaned against the wall just outside the office where Anne worked.

He'd taken off his sunglasses, his face smooth, young. A student who'd taken a fancy to Anne? In a business suit? No way. There was something strange about the man.

"Hey." Patrick headed toward the guy. The man turned and started walking toward the opposite staircase.

"Hey, I'm talking to you," Patrick called out.

The man picked up speed. Patrick sprinted forward. "Stop. Who are you?"

The man paused and turned with an exaggerated sigh. "Back off, sir."

Patrick halted a few steps from the guy, frowning. "Why are you following Miss Johnson?"

"Who?"

"You know very well who. I've seen you twice today. Too often for it to be coincidence."

The guy shrugged. "Don't know what you're talking about."

"Did you smash up her car?"

"No."

"Make prank calls to her?"

"No."

His impassive expression grated. "I don't believe you. I'm calling the police." Patrick pulled out his cell phone.

"That wouldn't be a good idea, sir."

Again with the *sir*. "Why not?"

"You don't want to get mixed up in this, Professor McClain."

How did the guy know who he was? Patrick straightened to his full six feet. "Are you threatening me?"

"Just giving some friendly advice." The man turned to step down the first stair.

Patrick pushed him up against the wall. "Don't walk away from me. I want to know who you are."

The guy pushed back, sending Patrick stumbling. He regained his balance and came at the guy again, taking him once again to the wall and putting his forearm at the guy's throat.

He pressed. "Who are you?"

Suddenly another man came vaulting up the stairs and body-slammed Patrick in the side. Pain exploded in his ribs and the air swooshed out of his lungs but he refused to loosen his grip.

Instead he sent the second guy sprawling on the floor with a kick.

Down the hall a door banged open.

Anne made a strangled sound and rushed forward. "Whoa, guys!" She laid a hand on Patrick's arm. "Stop, Patrick."

Confused by her words, Patrick turned his gaze on her. "Anne, get out of here. Call the police."

"Tell your boyfriend to back off now," the guy getting up from the floor said.

Not sure he could hold both men off and still protect Anne, Patrick let the first guy go and swiftly moved to stand in front of Anne. His heart slammed against his chest as he readied himself to defend her.

"Please let me handle this," Anne said close to his ear.

Shocked by her reaction but not willing to take his eyes off of the two men, Patrick asked, "Anne, what's going on?"

The second guy, the older one of the pair, said, "Miss Johnson, a word."

"She's not going anywhere with you," Patrick growled, his confusion mounting.

Anne took his fisted hand. "I never meant for you to get involved in this."

"In what?"

"Miss Johnson." The second guy's tone rang with warning.

She held up her free hand. "I know. I know."

Patrick turned the full force of his attention on Anne. Her eyes were wide, and a gamut of perplexing emotions crossed her pretty face. Doubt, anxiety, guilt.

A loop of unease wove through his chest, making his already bruised ribs ache. "Anne?"

Her mouth scrunched up and her gaze darted between the other men and Patrick.

Squeezing his hand, she finally let out a groan. "They're U.S. Marshals."

The shock hit him in the solar plexus. "What!"

"Miss Johnson!" the two men exclaimed simultaneously.

She positioned herself with her back to the men. Her eyes pleaded with Patrick to understand.

He didn't.

"I'm not who you think I am."

"Here we go…" the first guy muttered.

"Not here," the second guy ground out. "You cannot do this here."

Head spinning with bewilderment, Patrick tried to grasp the mean of the situation. "Marshals?"

"Yes, marshals." She lifted her head and stared him in the eyes. "I'm in the witness security program."

Staggered by that revelation, Patrick took a step back from Anne.

She released his hand, her eyes filling with tears.

"You've been lying to me this whole time."

* * *

He was taking this badly.

Anne had hoped she could make it through the trial and not have to say anything to Patrick. She should have heeded Lidia's warning to not get attached to anyone.

But she had grown attached and now she had to deal with the consequences. If she was going to come clean with him, she might as well go the whole way.

She relaxed her throat and allowed her natural voice to come through. "Yes, I've been lying to you. Kind of."

He scoffed. "Kind of?"

"It was necessary." She turned to the two agents who'd introduced themselves to her as soon as she arrived this morning. The younger agent had said his name was Ford, like the car, and the older agent was Morris. "Tell him."

"It was necessary," Agent Ford stated dryly.

She made a face. "Thanks, that helps."

Agent Morris stepped closer. "Can we please take this out of the hall?"

Anne led the way to the office she'd been working in. She faced Patrick. "The only thing I haven't been truthful about is my name. My name is really Anne Jones."

He crossed his arms over his chest and peered at her through the lens of his glasses. "That accent is not from Los Angeles."

Heat burned in her cheeks. "Now I never said I

was from Los Angeles. I said L.A. Which also stands for Lower Alabama."

He gave her a pointed looked full of sarcasm. "Right." He took off his glasses and wiped them with a cloth from his breast pocket. "I'm trying to wrap my brain around this. Your name is really Anne Jones and you're in the witness security program because…"

Remembering what his brother had gone through, she knew he'd understand. "Because I witnessed a murder."

He stilled, his long tapered fingers curling around his glasses. "Whose?"

Hoping he didn't bust the lens out of the frames, she said. "My boss. And several other men."

Patrick seemed to digest the information as he addressed the agents. "Is the murderer behind bars?"

Agent Morris answered, "For now. He's being held without bail through his trial. Anne is a key witness for the prosecution."

Patrick put on his glasses. "You're going to testify at the trial?"

"Yes. The agents say in less than three weeks." She held his gaze, losing herself in the chocolate depths.

"You're willing to risk your life to do this?"

The intensity in his question made her feel as if her answer was very important. "It's the right thing to do. I need to see justice done for my boss."

He nodded, his eyes taking on a determined gleam. "Where did it happen?"

"New Jersey. I worked at the Palisades Resort as a cocktail waitress while trying to get my big break on Broadway."

He arched an eyebrow. "You're a cocktail waitress?"

"No. I mean I worked as one to pay the bills, but I'm an actress."

"Indeed. And very good."

"Please don't take this all personally. I never meant to hurt you." This was what she was afraid was going to happen if she let him close.

His voice softened. "You could have told me."

"That's just it. I couldn't."

"And still shouldn't," Agent Ford interjected.

"I'm going to be straight with him," she stated, wishing the two agents would give them some privacy.

"And get both of you killed?" Morris said, his brown eyes challenging.

She frowned as doubt attacked her. "You said yourself that I was being paranoid. That the car, the rat and the calls weren't related."

"Rat?" Patrick touched her shoulder.

She grimaced at the memory. "I found a dead rat outside my apartment door."

Patrick moved closer to Anne, a protective gesture that wasn't lost on her. She'd never had a man be her champion before. He made her feel special, a feeling she decided she really liked.

"They all were related, weren't they?" Patrick demanded to know.

The two agents exchanged a glance. "We don't know. Domingo has a huge network," Morris stated.

"Then why did you tell me earlier I was safe and to go about my day?" Anne demanded.

Again the exchange of nonverbal communication between the agents. "There is no reason to believe your whereabouts have been compromised. We've been assigned to watch over you. If anyone does come after you, we'll intervene."

"You're using her as bait," Patrick nearly shouted.

"Of course not," Morris said, but there was a note of insincerity in his tone that raised the hairs on Anne's arm.

"But I'm going to suggest we relocate you," said Agent Ford.

Her stomach churned with anxiety and frustration. "I don't want to leave."

"If you change details. Add more men. It's only three weeks," Patrick countered.

"A lot can happen in three weeks," Morris said.

"And nothing might happen," Patrick replied.

The agents again exchanged glances. Morris moved toward the door. "I'm going to have to call this in. I'll tell them you want to stay but I won't recommend it."

"You don't have much choice if I leave the program," Anne stated, hating to play this game. This was her life they were talking about. "Agent Ford, would you mind leaving us for a moment?"

The agent nodded and left on the heels of his partner.

As soon as the door shut behind the agents Patrick settled his gaze on Anne. "You can't go back to your apartment."

Logically she knew he was right. Her stomach knotted with frustration. She liked her new life. She was beginning to know a few people at church and really enjoyed the town of Newton.

Unfortunately the agents were right, too. If she stayed out in the open now, she could put other people in danger. She sighed. "I suppose I should let WITSEC take me to a safe house."

"Or you could come home with me."

She blinked at the unexpected offer. "Your place?"

He shook his head. "Not my apartment. My mother's home."

She stepped back in stunned surprise. "No. I couldn't put her at risk."

He advanced a step and took her hands. "Listen to me. You'll be safe at my mother's. I'll make sure of it."

"How?" The man was a professor, not a bodyguard.

"My family has strong ties to the police department in Boston. I just have to say the word and we'll have protection."

"But would that be enough?"

"I'd stake my life on the Boston PD. Trust me."

His warm cocoa gaze drew her in, testing her heart, teasing her senses. She did trust him. Trusted that he believed he could protect her, that the friends of his family in the police department could provide her protection.

But if an assassin were really determined to kill her, could even the most dedicated and brave police officer be able to save her?

"I can't ask this of you," she whispered.

"You're not," he stated firmly, his expression determined.

Swallowing the doubts and fears, she nodded and placed her hand within his. She could only pray it wouldn't be the death of her. Or him. Or his family.

"Of all the underhanded, reprehensible things to do!" Lidia's fist pounded on the desk, the pain of the impact barely registering. She took a deep breath, but her constricted lungs wouldn't allow in more than a fraction of the air she needed.

"Take a seat, Lieutenant," said Special Agent in Charge Joseph Lofland.

He sat behind his wide oak desk, his tie perfectly knotted, his light brown hair neatly trimmed. Only his gray eyes conveyed the anger that Lidia felt. "Morris and Ford were following orders."

"Who ordered them to announce their presence?" she fumed.

"We want Domingo as much, if not more, than you," replied Lofland. "Showing her detail was a strategic move. She was never in danger."

"The girl reached out like she was told and your people let her leave the security of the WITSEC program."

"Any witness in the program is free to leave at any time. Anne Jones chose to reveal her identity."

"After your boys bungled their job," Lidia retorted and flopped down in to the leather chair opposite the desk.

Beside her Porter put a calming hand on her arm. He always had that effect on her. "Now we have to figure out how to keep Anne safe while not in the program and bring down Domingo."

She nodded, acknowledging his words. The only reason Lidia wasn't expounding on her anger was she knew that Anne was safe. One of her own NJPD people was watching her. And now according to the report that had just come in so was all of the Boston Police Department.

"And what about Maria Gonzales?" Lidia asked, thinking of the maid who'd also come forward with her account of seeing Domingo and his thugs enter the suite. Maria had been in the private bedroom at the time and had heard the voices in the hall.

She'd chanced a peek out just to have something to gossip with the other housekeeping staff. She'd already noted the other high stakes players that had entered the suite so when Domingo and his men had arrived she'd been disappointed. No call girls or anything that would suggest more than just a game of cards.

Except, not too much later, as Maria had finished changing the sheets on the bed, she'd heard the sound of gunfire. Terrified, she'd hid in the closet and had escaped after the massacre. But she'd recognized Domingo and seen him limping out of the suite, blood dripping down his pant leg.

She had left the hotel and hidden out at her sister's in Queens and luckily Rick had found the woman before Domingo got wind of her.

"Please tell me you are watching her back."

Lofland seared her with a quelling look. "She is in good hands. Unlike Miss Jones, Maria is content to spend her days in a safe house."

Lidia's mouth twisted as his undertone of censure hit her. Neither she nor the FBI had been able to convince Anne to sit tight in protective custody until after the trial.

No, Anne had an independent streak that reminded Lidia of herself at that age. Twenty-five years ago. A lifetime ago. Now, nearing fifty, Lidia was ready to retire rather than exert her independence any more than she had to. That was the beauty of youth. A person had the energy and conviction to stand their ground, just like Anne had insisted she wasn't going to sit twiddling her thumbs and wait. So she'd entered the program and taken the job at the college, changed her appearance and settled in.

Only Anne had let herself get involved with Associate Professor McClain.

Lidia should have seen that coming. The two were exact opposites. And didn't opposites attract? Just look at her and Porter.

Lidia refused to think about the budding relationship with the D.A. when she needed to focus on the case.

She sat forward. "Look, is there anything either of you can do to speed up the court proceeding? The quicker we get Anne to testify the better."

Porter shifted, drawing Lidia's attention. His gaze held hers. "I'm pushing as hard as I can. But you can imagine Domingo's lawyer is pushing just as hard to delay the trial as much as possible."

Lidia snorted. "Yeah, so he can have time to get rid of the witnesses. All the more reason the judge should move things along."

"In light of the most recent events, I'm sure that the attorney general will step in and advocate with the court," Lofland stated.

"Let's call Dirkman and get on the fast track," Lidia demanded.

EIGHT

"Are you sure my coming here is okay?" Apprehension weaved through Anne's veins. She hoped she wasn't making a mistake.

"Yes, I'm sure," Patrick replied, taking Anne's hand and squeezing it in reassurance as he led her up the front steps of his childhood home. "I've already spoken to my mother and she is looking forward to meeting you."

"What about Princess?"

"Don't worry."

Anne wrinkled her nose and hugged the feline closer. *Easy for him to say.*

He opened the big wooden front door and ushered Anne inside. The scent of vanilla and sugar filled the air.

The bright cheerfulness of the home hit her full force, making her ache for such a life as this home represented. Family, love and respect. A place to be safe and comfortable. A life she could only dream about.

A gleaming hardwood floor stretched beneath her feet and extended into the living room to the left and the formal dining area to the right. A staircase with a polished mahogany banister led to the second floor. She could see the tiled floors and granite counters of the kitchen straight ahead.

The living room was a profusion of color against dark fabrics and wood paneled walls. Throw rugs and pillows of assorted shapes looked artlessly placed, yet the whole effect was very welcoming. All sorts of fresh flowers in vases of various styles filled every available space.

Anne's gaze landed on the gilt-framed oil painting above a beautiful mantel and fireplace. The McClain family stared back at her.

A handsome, uniformed man with dark hair and intense ebony eyes stood in the background. This picture was similar to the one in Patrick's apartment.

Flanking Mr. McClain on either side were two similarly dark-haired sons. Patrick stood a foot taller than the other boy, whom she assumed was Brody. Behind the ever present glasses, Patrick's eyes showed an amused sparkle that she had yet to see.

Though the young Patrick didn't have a smile on his face, he did lack that somber, stoic expression she'd grown accustomed to on the adult man.

Mrs. McClain sat in front of her husband, her long, ebony hair cascading over one shoulder and her crystal-blue eyes sparkling. A young girl stood beside her mother, their resemblance uncanny. Both possessed high cheekbones and fair skin. Megan Mc-Clain had also inherited her mother's blue eyes.

A small boy sat on Mrs. McClain's lap. Must be Ryan. His childish grin and the impish light in his dark eyes were captivating. She could only imagine how much more devastating this younger McClain must be as an adult male.

Such a lovely family. Sadness touched Anne's heart. This family had lost their father and husband not too many years after this portrait had been taken.

Such a senseless loss.

She didn't understand how God allowed such tragedy. But who was she to question Him? She didn't know His plans. His ways were beyond her comprehension. She could only hold on to her faith in a loving God and trust. Trust that He had a reason that couldn't be seen by the human eye.

Patrick tugged on her hand, urging her to follow him. His earnest, eager expression tripled her heartbeat.

Was he as nervous about her meeting his mother as she was? What if Mrs. McClain took a dislike to her? Could Anne take the rejection? Would his mother not want a cat in the house? What would Patrick do then? The questions ran through Anne's mind, tormenting her with insecurity and doubt.

They headed down the hall to the kitchen, and with every step Anne's pulse picked up pace until the moment she crossed the threshold, where a woman with a long, dark braid was just taking out a tray of cookies from the oven.

Mrs. McClain's bright blue eyes lit on her son and then on Anne. She gave them a welcoming smile that twisted Anne up inside. Anne's own mother had never smiled with such warmth. Tentatively Anne smiled back and her blood slowed to a more normal rhythm.

Mrs. McClain sat the tray on the counter, wiped her hands on her apron and then moved to hug Patrick before turning her attention to Anne.

"I couldn't believe it when Patrick called. What a horrible thing for you to have to go through. But you're here now and we'll keep you safe."

"Mom, there's just one thing I forgot to mention."

Colleen raised her eyebrows. "Yes?"

Anne met his gaze. Mirth danced in his eyes.

"We'll have one other houseguest."

Anne suppressed a flutter of misgivings.

Patrick pointed to the animal in Anne's arms. "A cat named Princess."

Colleen smiled and reached out to pet Princess behind the ears. The cat snuffled into Mrs. McClain's hand and began to purr. "That's fine."

"I didn't think you'd mind," Patrick stated.

"Thank you." Though Anne wasn't so sure that she'd made the right decision. She couldn't stop the guilt flushing through her.

She shouldn't be here. This kind woman didn't deserve to have Anne's presence burdening her life.

"I don't think I should stay here. I appreciate your kindness but I should go." She turned to Patrick as anxiety clogged her throat. "I really should."

"We've already been through this. I thought you were going to trust me," he said, his voice soft. His eyes held a hint of hurt.

Anne wanted to, but doubts still lingered. What if something happened to these kind people because of her? She couldn't live with that.

"Is Princess an indoor or outdoor cat?" Mrs. McClain asked.

"Indoor," Anne replied tentatively. "You aren't allergic to cats, are you?"

"No, dear." Mrs. McClain took Anne's hand and drew her to the kitchen nook. "Let's sit. Patrick, would you take Princess to Megan's room?"

Patrick held out his hands expectantly. Anne hesitated. Without Princess she felt even more vulnerable and alone. But Patrick was here and his mother was so nice. She held Princess up to eye level and said, "Be a good girl and go with Patrick." She handed her over and watched in amazement the way the feline curled against his chest.

He winked and walked out of the kitchen.

"Anne. May I call you Anne?"

She nodded, liking the compassionate and forthright way Mrs. McClain had about her.

"Would you like some iced tea?"

"That would be lovely. Thank you," Anne responded.

This was a woman of no nonsense. Anne could imagine she'd had to have been a strong woman to raise four kids by herself after their father died. Anne hoped some of that strength would rub off on her.

"I can understand your reluctance," Mrs. McClain stated in a calm and soothing tone as she sat a pitcher of tea on the table along with three tall glasses. "But please believe me when I tell you that you'll be safe here." She took a seat opposite of Anne. "The McClains have many friends within the Boston Police Department. Patrick's already arranged for around-the-clock surveillance while you're here."

Looking into this woman's kind and caring eyes Anne wished she'd had a mother as vibrant and committed. Her own mother had been tired and broken by life the last time Anne had seen her, over five years ago now.

Not for the first time Anne wondered how her family was doing. The minute she'd had her high school certificate she'd left the small Alabama town and never looked back. She'd been determined not to end up like her mama or her older sister, married to a jerk and with too many kids to feed.

Anne chose to believe Mrs. McClain, chose to put her safety in their hands. *Please, Lord, don't let me be making a mistake.* "I don't know what to say, other than thank you, Mrs. McClain."

"Please, call me Colleen."

Patrick joined them at the table.

"Aren't you heading back to the school?" Anne inquired as he made himself comfortable on the bench seat beside her. His big, warm body pressed along her side, providing her support and strength.

"I'm taking a vacation day."

His mom nearly choked on her tea. "That's a first."

Anne couldn't help but feel thrilled to know he was staying because of her. Too tired and frazzled to decipher or analyze his actions or her reactions, she would just go with it.

"So, Anne, tell me about yourself," Colleen said, her curious blues studying her. "Patrick said you're from lower Alabama. I've never been to that part of the country."

Trapped between the physical wall of the kitchen nook and the impenetrable wall of Patrick, Anne tried not to squirm. What she'd told Patrick still held true. She didn't want to talk about the past.

So instead she would focus on the last part of Colleen's statement. "Alabama's pretty in its own way. Lots of character. The town I grew up in had about one hundred people. We could go for miles without coming across another living soul. The Conecuh National Forest was our playground. Hide-and-seek among the plain pines and we'd skip rocks on the ponds. We'd pretend our old coon dog was captured by the Yankees and we had to rescue him."

"Weren't you afraid of the wildlife?" Colleen sat

forward. "Aren't there alligators and snakes in the swamps in the South?"

Anne shrugged. "You leave 'em alone, they pretty much leave you alone."

"So your brothers…or sisters played in the forest with you?" Patrick asked.

Anne pressed her lips together. She didn't want to discuss her family but she'd stirred the pot with her remark about playing in the forest. She slanted him a glance. "Two of each. During the hot days of summer we would float down the lazy Conecuh River on inner tubes."

She laughed softly, remembering. "My older brother, Tommy, once fell off his tube. He couldn't swim. None of us could. I still remember him floundering around until Josie, the eldest, shouted to him to stand up. That part of the river was barely knee deep.

"And then once, my younger sister, Mimi…I think she was four at the time, found a baby skunk out in the woodshed. She thought it was a cat. Mama 'bout had a fit. But Mimi was not going to let that baby go. Until it sprayed her after she pulled its tail. She smelled for a good month."

Colleen looked puzzled. "You have an accent. I hadn't noticed it before."

Anne winced. She hadn't realized she'd slipped into her natural voice.

"When was the last time you went home?" Patrick asked.

"A long time."

"It sounds like you miss your family," Colleen commented.

Deep in some part of Anne that she tried not to look at, she did miss them. But she couldn't go back. She'd burned that bridge when she took off. She could still hear her daddy's raging voice as she ran down the road toward the highway saying if she left, she'd better stay gone. A year after she'd run off, she'd written a letter asking if she could come back. Her letter had been returned unopened.

And she'd known she'd never be welcomed back.

"I miss the outdoors. And I miss the simplicity of life," Anne admitted.

Colleen nodded in understanding. "Sometimes I think it would be easier to live in the days when there weren't so many cars and so many things distracting us from enjoying each day."

"Exactly. My family didn't have much. Almost no one did in the South. We worried about our needs not our wants, if that makes sense."

"It does," Colleen agreed. "Today people are so caught up in having the latest and greatest. I'm not saying there isn't value in all the technological advances but whatever happened to sitting down and writing a letter? No one writes letters anymore. If you want to communicate, you have to have a computer or a BlackBerry."

Patrick groaned. "Mom."

"What?" She stared at him. "You agree, right?"

He sighed. "I did until I met Anne."

Colleen raised her eyebrows. "Really? Do tell."

"She showed me how change can be worthwhile. That taking a chance on something new, something different, could be a good thing."

The glow of attraction Anne saw in his eyes entranced her, drew her in, making her lean slightly toward him. "Sometimes risk is necessary."

His gaze dropped to her mouth. "Yes, it is."

"It takes courage to change. To be open," Anne said.

"This is true," Patrick agreed.

He was so close, she could see herself in his eyes. "Like going to church?" The words popped out before she could stop them.

His eyes darkened and shuttered, closing her out. He leaned away. "I suppose."

"Church?" Colleen asked.

Anne's cheeks burned as Colleen eyed her with intense interest. "Patrick was kind enough to drive me to my church yesterday."

A pleased gleam entered Colleen's blue eyes and a smile touched her lips. "That's wonderful." She turned her piercing gaze to her son. "Maybe she can convince you to give God another chance?"

Patrick flinched. A tense silence filled the room. Anne didn't understand the dynamics going on but there was no mistaking the deep anguish etched in the lines of Patrick's face.

More than anything Anne wanted to soothe his hurt, but even with God's help, she didn't know how.

Later that evening after sharing a meal with Patrick and his mother, Anne stepped out into the sanctuary of the backyard. A brick patio extended about five feet, then a lush lawn, broken only by wood-rimmed flower beds and four distinctive trees that ended at a dark-stained fence encircling the yard. Over the patio, an arbor had been constructed and wisteria curled around the wooden slats.

According to Patrick, gardening was Colleen's passion. The immaculate landscaping gave credence to his words.

"You okay?" Patrick joined her beneath the arbor. His dark hair captured the illumination from the garden lamps. He'd removed his jacket and rolled up the sleeves of his button-down shirt. He'd also lost his tie and the top two buttons at his throat were undone revealing the rim of the undershirt beneath.

She drank in the sight of him in the evening twilight. "Yes. Being here is better than I expected."

His mouth quirked. "It's only been one day."

Bending to sniff a perfectly formed rose, she answered, "True." She straightened. He was so close, his masculine scent wrapped around her senses. More heady than the flower's perfume. "Are you staying here or going to your place?"

He leaned against the supporting beam of the arbor. "Would you like me to stay?"

She did, but she couldn't find the courage to say so. Trying to act nonchalant, she said, "It's up to you."

"Then I'll stay."

A warm radiance flowed through her. She tried to cover the reaction by changing the subject. "I really like your mother."

Colleen had a force of character that could only come from within, which could only come from a foundation of faith. After that uncomfortable moment when Colleen's remark had stirred the soul-searing pain that Anne had witnessed at the church, they'd managed to move the conversation forward to other topics, mostly due to Colleen's forthright personality.

"She likes you, too," he replied.

Questions burned on her tongue. Would he close her out again if she asked about his relationship with God? But she couldn't ignore what she'd seen or the way she'd ached inside for him. She'd come to care too much for him. "So what do you think about giving God a second chance?"

NINE

"I don't think about it."

This was way worse than she thought. His heart had hardened. Was there a chance she could soften him toward God, open Patrick to possibly reconciling with Him? "Did you grow up going to church?"

He crossed his arms over his chest. "Did you?"

She pulled her gaze to his. Countering her question with one of his own was an avoidance tactic. She didn't want to tell him about her childhood, but she guessed he wouldn't open up unless she did.

Trust had to be earned.

There had been some ugliness in her past that made her cringe when she thought about it. Her parents hadn't lived by the faith they professed, which she supposed could have turned her completely against God, but hadn't. She could separate their actions from God. She knew enough about free will and human nature to know that what one professed with their mouth was not necessarily what was in their heart. She wanted her faith to be in her heart not just her words.

"I did grow up going to church. Every Sunday. In fact, the whole town went. Part of the culture of the South. All hundred of us would gather in the brick building and sing and listen to Reverend Tulane give his very impassioned sermons." She closed her eyes as memories flashed through her mind. "I can still see him standing at the altar in his black suit, waving the Bible as he talked about forgiveness, repentance and the love of the Lord."

She opened her eyes and gave a small laugh. "As a child I loved the stories in the Bible, but that's all they were to me. Stories. Because how could what the reverend said about God changing lives be true if on Monday Mama and Daddy weren't any different than they were on Saturday?"

"What were your parents like?"

Oh, she didn't want to go there. Shame heated her skin, making her overly warm. Their worlds were so far apart. Could he understand the kind of poverty she had experienced?

Taking a seat on a wooden bench, she tried her best to forge ahead. "Daddy worked at the cotton mill. Mama stayed home with us kids, not because she wanted to, mind you, but there were very few jobs in our little corner of the world and the men got them. That's just the way things worked."

Patrick sat next her. "You said you have four siblings?"

"Yes." She took a deep fortifying breath before continuing. "We lived in a run-down trailer outside town. Town, being a relative phrase. A Piggly Wiggly and a Gas-N-Go were about the extent of it."

"And you left when?"

If he found her description of her childhood home distasteful, he had the good manners to keep it to himself. She laced her fingers and rubbed the palms together. "Just before my eighteenth birthday."

"What college did you attend?"

It was a legitimate question coming from a professor to his computer tech. It was a shame-inducing question coming from Patrick, the professor, to Anne, the hick from the sticks. But the Anne that had witnessed a murder and was being given a new chance to be someone else wanted to make up some fantastic tale that would awe and impress.

She could say she'd danced at Radio City Music Hall, sang at Carnegie Hall and performed in a play alongside some Tony award-winning actor. She could say she'd made her mark on Broadway instead of going to college.

She'd glimpsed deeper inside of him through his book than he presented to the rest of the world. And what she'd seen made her decide he deserved the truth—even if the truth offended his sensibilities.

"I never went to college. I have my high school certificate, that's it."

He studied her for a moment. "Then how do you know so much about computers?"

"Books. And I dated a techno geek when I lived in Manhattan."

"Amazing." There was no mockery in his tone. "That's right, you'd said you wanted to be an actress. So you headed to the Big Apple like a lot of other people."

"I did." He might as well hear it all. "I arrived in New York with just the clothes on my back and not a cent to my name."

"Why like that?"

She stared at the stars twinkling in the night sky, remembering how as a child she would wish upon the brightest light. "Because I ran away."

"From what?"

She blinked and dropped her gaze. "A bad relationship. The nearest high school was thirty miles away and big enough to have a decent football team. I started dating the quarterback. Everyone, my parents included, were sure Johnny had a good future ahead of him and thought I was lucky he'd picked me. My parents liked him."

She drew in a breath and gathered herself. "Johnny abused me. When I couldn't take the beatings anymore and broke it off, my daddy was livid. He thought I'd ruined my one chance to have a better life. We fought."

She made a face. "I said some things to him and my mama that were mean but true. Daddy backhanded me, like I'd seen him do to my mama, and I left. I did not want to end up like them."

He slid his arm around her shoulders, the gesture unexpected but oh, so nice.

"That's rough. And you haven't ended up like them. You made a conscious choice to live differently. That's admirable."

The warmth and concern in his voice comforted and thrilled. He wasn't disgusted by her Southern back roads beginning. "Yes." She had made different choices, though not always smart ones. "But not as rough as you losing your father."

He ignored her statement. "So how did you end up at the casino?"

She'd let his avoidance slide for now. "Acting's tough. New York's even tougher. I met a girl who got me connected in Atlantic City. The job paid well and Jean Luc was a good employer."

His arm tightened slightly. "And you saw him die."

She leaned her head on his shoulder as memories assaulted her mind. She shuddered. "It was horrible. So much worse than the movies ever make it seem. I thought I would die, too."

"I'm glad you didn't," he said.

His tender voice, almost a murmur, sent a pleasant shiver down her spine. "God spared me."

He jerked slightly at her words. "How did you get out alive?"

"I prayed and then Jean Luc fell literally to the ground beside me. Before he died he told me of a secret panel in the wall and gave me some cash to run with."

Patrick drew back to look into her face. "You didn't run?"

She lifted her head. "I couldn't. God gave me my life. I had to do what was right. I had to tell the police how Jean Luc and the others died."

"God didn't give you a chance, Jean Luc did."

"Only after I prayed. I know that sounds lame and far-fetched and even naive. But I know in my heart He's real and with me always. I can't pretend to understand Him or why there's so much bad in the world. I can only trust."

"You're noble and courageous, Anne Jones."

The awe in his voice and the gentle way his eyes caressed her face entranced and enflamed her. Affection unfurled and her heart jangled with a breathless anticipation. He was so much more than he appeared, so full of compassion and honor. A man who stirred her interest and made her feel special.

A giddy sense of excitement fluttered through her when she realized his attention wasn't brought on by her looks or what he thought he could get from her, but rather because he saw the person inside.

A delightful shiver ran up her spine. She shifted closer and turned more fully toward him. Attraction flared in his dark eyes, but he made no move to answer her silent plea. She pressed closer, tipping her head back, offering him her mouth, hoping he'd take advantage of the moment.

He touched her face, his hand gentle. He traced her cheekbone. Ran a finger lightly over her lips. Her blood quickened.

"It's getting late. We should go in."

His softly said words confused her until she realized he was slowly easing her out of his arms. She blinked back disbelief. Embarrassment flamed in her cheeks.

He stood and held out his hand. She slipped her palm over his. His strong fingers wrapped around hers securely and he led her into the house. She wanted to ask him why he hadn't kissed her, but she couldn't form the words.

He led her upstairs to the door of his sister's room where she'd be sleeping.

Even with the soft light of the hall, his expression was unreadable. "There are federal agents and police officers surrounding the property. I hope you will try to sleep well."

She nodded, unsure what to say or how to feel. He released her and walked further down the hall to disappear inside another room.

In a haze of confusion, Anne went into the bedroom.

A cat's meow distracted her. Princess sat regally on the foot of the bed, her white coat blending into the white fluffy comforter. The cat released another meow.

Taking the feline into her arms, Anne nuzzled her face into the soft fur. "Well, at least you love me."

The cat squirmed to be released.

"Or not." Anne loosened her hold and Princess jumped back on to the bed to settle on the pillow.

Anne tried to ignore the hurt in her heart as she readied herself for bed. But as she crawled beneath the covers, she couldn't help chastising herself for not heeding Lidia's warning. *Don't get attached.*

Unfortunately for Anne, she was attached. Too bad Patrick wasn't.

Patrick sat in his old bedroom, staring out the window that overlooked the park across the street. Below on the road he could see the federal agent's unmarked car and in the opposite direction the Boston Police cruiser. And there were another set of each at the back of the house in the alleyway. There was no reason he shouldn't be snoozing away.

No reason other than the woman sleeping just down the hall.

His heart squeezed tight as the image of her up-turned face and inviting eyes tortured him. He'd had to use every ounce of self-possession not to give in to kissing her. But she was vulnerable right now. She was hiding from people who wanted to kill her. The last thing she needed was for him to take advantage of her in such a susceptible state.

Admiration for her bravery and integrity filled his heart. From her humble beginnings to a witness for the prosecution.

Pretty amazing.

Her faith in God seemed so misguided, though. Coincidence had saved her life. Yet...there was something so compelling about the way she trusted with her whole heart and soul.

Not Patrick.

His trust had been broken long ago, and there was no way God could ever earn that trust back.

The next day Anne helped Colleen in her garden, planting perennials and annuals Anne had never heard of before.

"You and Patrick seem to be getting along very well."

Anne sucked in a breath at the unexpected comment and inhaled a cloud of dirt from the spade she'd jerked upward at the same time. She coughed, then sputtered, "Uh, well. Yes."

Colleen sat back on her haunches and pushed at stray strands of hair that had come loose from her silver clip that secured the long, dark hair at her nape. Her jeans were faded and her red blouse streaked with dirt. "He's a good man. He's taken on so much responsibility over the years that he hasn't taken time to really live his life."

Anne's pulse beat double. "Because of his father's death," she ventured.

"He told you. That's good. He usually doesn't like to talk about it."

Anne thought about the remote and detached way he'd related the story to her. He hid his feelings behind that stony demeanor, but she now knew better. His book contained all the emotions he refused to show.

"He became the man of the house when he was still a kid. He just goes from one responsibility to another."

Anne closed her eyes as guilt chomped through her, leaving teeth marks across her soul. "Like me."

"Yes, frankly."

Wretchedness burned in her chest. No wonder he'd rejected her last night. She was just another burden to him. "I'm sorry."

Empathy and compassion blazed in Colleen's gaze. "We all do what's needed of us. He's helping you because then he feels needed."

There was no stopping the throb of despair welling inside. Was Colleen warning Anne not to get emotionally involved? It was too late for that. "I understand."

"Do you? I wonder."

Anne cocked her head. "What does that mean?"

The calculating gleam in the older woman's eyes confused Anne. "He may be telling himself he's doing this to help you, but I recognize the way he watches you."

She swallowed, almost afraid to guess what she meant. "Watches me?"

Colleen's mouth curved into a knowing smile. "I know my son. His feelings run deep, but he's so used to keeping his emotions under control that I've often worried he'd never allow love into his life."

"Love?" Anne squeaked.

"I may be jumping to conclusions."

Taking a deep breath to ease the tightness in her chest, Anne slowly exhaled before answering. "Yes, I think you are."

"I raised my boys to respect women and to not toy with their affections," Colleen said, her motherly voice coming through strong.

Anne's gaze jerked up. "Patrick isn't toying with my affections."

Colleen narrowed her gaze. "But are you toying with his?"

Aghast at the suggestion, Anne vigorously shook her head. "Of course not. Patrick's a great guy. I wouldn't hurt him for the world."

Colleen seem to be satisfied. "Good. I'm glad to hear that."

Anne wasn't sure what to make of the exchange. Was Colleen warning her off or trying to play matchmaker?

Colleen stood and dusted the dirt from her knees. "I've always believed that when Patrick finally gave his heart to a woman, she'd have to be a special woman."

Well, that ruled her out. Anne dropped her gaze to the hole she'd dug, wishing she could crawl inside.

A hand on her shoulder lifted her gaze.

"You're a very special woman, Anne Jones."

Colleen winked and then went inside, leaving Anne reeling from her words.

Definitely matchmaking.

Darkness blanketed the house, but the man knew there were other men standing guard. Two outside and two inside. He'd been monitoring their activity and now the time to act had come. As always dressed in black, he crawled military fashion across the dry grass toward the dining room window where an old, full rhododendron would provide him cover as he cut through the glass and entered the house.

Once in the dining room, he paused to listen. The soft sound of rubber soles on linoleum told him at least one guard was in the kitchen using only the moon's illumination as light. The man edged toward the arched entry that led to the living room and the stairs. This time he had both his sheathed knife and a gun with a silencer in a holster at his shoulder as his weapons.

He took the stairs two at a time, careful not to step near the middle where the wood might creak and give him away.

As he reached the landing, an inky shape, bulky and close, rammed into him, sending him off balance and down a few steps.

"Stop!" came a shouted command as the stairwell was flooded with light.

With a quick yank, the man drew his gun and fired two shots at the federal agent descending the stairs. Realizing that he'd miscalculated, the man abandoned his quest. The target would have to wait for another day. Being caught was not an option.

He ran down the stairs as the agent who had been in the kitchen skidded to a halt, his weapon drawn, but the man was ready and fired off a shot that hit the agent square in the forehead.

The man hit the light switch, throwing the house back into darkness just as the front door banged open. The man sprinted to the dining room and out the window. He heard the shouts of the remaining agents. Not taking the caution he'd used in approaching the house, the man ran headlong for the copse of trees at the edge of the property where his car waited.

Within minutes he disappeared down the highway.

"Dirkman wants the witnesses brought in for a run-through before they take the stand," Porter told Lidia as she entered his office and took a seat in the leather chair across from his desk.

They seemed to be doing this a lot lately. He'd call, she'd come to his office and then they'd head to dinner. She found herself looking forward to the evenings when she wasn't working. She hadn't done that in years.

Tonight they were on the job.

It was standard practice to prep witnesses before the trial, but Lidia couldn't help anxiety from twisting inside her gut. Somewhere in the system they had a leak. A leak they had yet to plug. A surge of anger rode a high tide through Lidia's blood.

One witness was dead. Nikki had been right. They hadn't been able to protect her. Guilt and frustration stabbed at Lidia's conscience. She should have tried harder to get the girl to agree to protection. Maybe she wouldn't be dead now.

Anne was no longer in the program but stashed in Boston, in a civilian's house no less, though thankfully safe for the moment. But for how long?

Unfortunately the safe house where the third witness, Maria Gonzales, had been was ambushed last night. Maria made it out alive thanks to the surviving two out of the four original agents guarding her. She was now safely hidden in another secure location. One only she, Porter and Lofland knew about.

"Can't you go to the witnesses?" she asked, fearing that bringing them in before their scheduled time would only put them in more danger.

He nodded. "That's what I was thinking. I was hoping you'd come with me."

An unexpected flush of happiness cascaded over Lidia. She'd planned on demanding to accompany him, but this...this was so much better. He wanted her with him. They would make a good team. A work team.

She knew better than to think further than the immediate. Life took unforeseen turns that could leave a person floundering.

But she still couldn't help the burst of pleasure from making her smile. "I'd love to join you."

TEN

Lidia and Porter arrived in the wee hours of the morning at the two-story corner house with green trim across from a park. They were greeted by tall, dark and tweed. Patrick McClain, she guessed correctly.

They showed their identification and were admitted.

The house, shrouded in darkness except for the hall light, exuded a kind of comforting warmth Lidia sorely lacked in her own life. The place she called home was a small ranch in the suburbs with about as much charm as a carport.

This was a good place for Anne to be, Lidia decided as she and Porter followed Patrick to the kitchen. Anne sat at the kitchen nook table with another woman. A lit candle on the table glowed brightly, the light bouncing off the flowered walls and outlining the two women with halos of illumination.

Anne jumped up and came to hug Lidia. Lidia tried not to let the emotion welling up take hold, but it was good to see the young woman looking so much better than she had when Anne had told her story of watching Jean Luc die.

Lidia held Anne at arm's length. "You changed your hair."

Anne touched the short layers of red. "The new me," she quipped.

The older woman stood, and Anne introduced them. Mrs. McClain's frank, assessing gaze washed over Lidia.

"Mrs. McClain." Lidia held out her hand.

Accepting her hand, Mrs. McClain inclined her head. "Lieutenant."

Lidia introduced Porter. "This is District Attorney Christopher Porter."

Porter stepped forward to shake hands with Mrs. McClain and then her son. "Thank you for allowing us to come at such an odd hour."

"We understand," Mrs. McClain assured them. "I thought the kitchen table would serve you best."

Lidia and Porter exchanged glances. The layout of the house with the kitchen at the rear and then the yard beyond made a much safer place to conduct their interview. Less likelihood that a sniper on a roof could find a clean shot.

"Perfect," answered Porter.

Anne slid back into a seat. Porter took the seat opposite her and laid his briefcase on the table.

Lidia turned to the two McClains. "Would you mind giving them some privacy?"

Mrs. McClain nodded. "I'll go back to bed. Patrick, please lock up after our guests." She kissed her son's cheek before padding out of the room.

Lidia arched an eyebrow at Patrick. She could see by the stubborn jut to his jaw he didn't like having to leave Anne. Lidia could appreciate his protectiveness and obviously, despite her warning to Anne not to get attached, the two had developed feelings, but she had a job to do. "Professor?"

He inclined his head. "I'll be in the living room." To Anne he said, "Call me if you need me."

"I will," she said, her eyes wide and fixed on him.

When he left, Lidia came to the table. "Anne, why do you have purple eyes?"

Anne grinned. "You said to change my appearance."

"That I did." Shaking her head, Lidia sat down and gestured for Porter to begin.

Two hours later, Porter seemed satisfied. "You've done well, Miss Jones."

Lidia took Anne's hand. "The morning of the trial, a team of U.S. Marshals will escort you back to New Jersey."

She blinked. "You won't be with me?"

Lidia shook her head. "No. But I will be at the trial as the arresting officer."

"Miss Jones, don't be disturbed if during the court proceedings you grow emotional," Porter commented as he gathered his notes together and slipped them into his briefcase.

Anne bit her lip. Anxiety curled in her abdomen. "It will be hard to see Mr. Domingo again."

"You won't be alone," Lidia said, drawing Anne's gaze. "We'll be there. And I have a feeling the professor won't be letting you out of his sight."

Anne shook her head. "I'm sure he'll be glad when this is over so he can get on with his life."

Lidia's expression clearly stated she thought Anne didn't know what she was talking about. "Oh, come on. The minute I walked in here and saw the way that man looked at you, I knew. The man has it bad for you."

A quiet laugh of disbelief escaped even as her heart beat an erratic tattoo in her chest. "No. You're wrong. He doesn't...does he?"

Lidia slid a glance at Porter. They seemed to communicate without words. Curious. Anne suddenly had the distinct impression that there was something going on between the two. Good for Lidia. She deserved some happiness.

Anne squeezed Lidia's hand to gain her attention. Giving her a pointed look, she said, "I could say the same about you."

Lidia's eyes widened and red crept up her neck. "Okay. Enough." Lidia released her hand and stood. "We'll see you in a few days."

Anne followed them to the front door. Patrick came out of the living room where he'd apparently been reading. He shook hands with Porter and Lidia before they left.

The full impact of what she was doing hit Anne.

In a few days she'd be sitting on the witness stand facing the man whom she saw kill Jean Luc Versailles. She shivered all the way to her toes.

"Cold?" Patrick asked as he slid his arm around her shoulders.

Not now. Anne raised her gaze to his. "Just nervous about the trial."

He nodded. "I don't blame you. But you're doing the right thing. And I'll be with you every step of the way."

Relief and gratitude swept through her. She needed him to be with her like she'd never needed anyone else in her life. Boy, was she glad to have his support.

She tried to read his expression, to see past his defenses into his thoughts, but she couldn't. Did he care for her even a little or was she really just a responsibility he'd taken on like any other?

Please, Lord, let this...this thing between us be more than mere responsibility or neediness.

Did she dare pray for love?

"You're going to have to control that temper of yours, Raoul," Evelyn Steiner remarked.

Raoul tolerated the female lawyer because she was sharp. Sharp eyes, sharp intellect and sharp tongued.

Today, she'd pulled her graying-brown hair so tightly into a bun that even her features were sharp.

He'd always found having a woman lawyer both amusing and useful. People tended not to believe that a lady like Evelyn, with her thousand-dollar pumps and Chanel suits, would defend a man whom she thought anything but innocent.

Ha! Evelyn was one of the shrewdest and craftiest people Raoul knew. That's why he paid her the big bucks.

Now sitting across from her in a private room where there were no guards listening, Raoul relaxed his hunched shoulders. First thing he was gonna do when he got out, after he smeared that smug look off that lady cop's face, was have a massage.

There was this little blonde over in Newark who could make a man scream with those strong hands of hers. "Yeah, yeah. I know. Keep it cool in court. But it's never going to get that far."

Evelyn raised a perfectly shaped eyebrow. "You know something I don't?"

Raoul smirked. "Can't have a trial if there ain't no witnesses."

Narrowing her stone-cold eyes, she said, "Don't go mouthing off. The D.A. is aiming for the death penalty. You need to be focused."

She cleared her throat. "I've filed a motion for continuance but that's been denied. I've filed a motion to suppress two of the witnesses because they can only put you and your two boys in the room, but the judge is being stubborn. So much hangs on this one girl."

She pulled out a file. "Anne Jones from Alabama. I'll do what I can to discredit her, but there doesn't seem to be any skeletons to dig up. In fact, she's too perfect. From a dirt poor family. Left for New York after high school. Had a few boyfriends, but so far nothing to hold against her. By all accounts, she's a hard worker and a decent person."

The image of the blonde running toward the mirrored wall, her blue gaze colliding with his in the reflection, flashed in Raoul's mind. Rage tightened his throat, once again tensing his shoulders.

She wasn't supposed to have been there. He'd been told only of the two card players that would make up the foursome.

Had Raoul known about the waitress he'd have taken her out first. Women had a way of messing everything up.

Raoul leaned forward, piercing Evelyn to her seat. "You let me worry about the girl. You just do your legal magic, like a nice little puppet."

Evelyn's lip curled. "Careful, Raoul. That client/ lawyer privilege only goes so far."

Molten fury clouded his vision for a moment. "Are you threatening me?"

Her lips thinned into a semblance of a smile. "Making sure you know that respect goes both ways." She waited a heartbeat before continuing. "Now, let's get you prepped. Just in case."

Raoul deliberately banked his roiling temper. When this was over, there would be several female skeletons for the grave diggers.

Anne paced the backyard of the McClain home. She was supposed to be planting more flowers in a bed near the garden gate, but she found staying in one spot difficult.

The late afternoon sun touched her where the sleeveless top and shorts she'd borrowed from Megan's drawers exposed her skin. The heat of the patio bricks on her bare feet brought a measure of comfort, and the aroma of roses, wisteria and earth worked to calm her stretched nerves.

She was to testify tomorrow. Lidia and the D.A. were confident that with Anne's testimony Jean Luc's murderer would be brought to justice. Patrick promised to support her through the trial, but the question that kept running across her mind was what would happen after the trial?

Would she go back to New York and continue her pursuit of a career on Broadway? Did she even want that now?

If not that, then what? What would she do with herself? And would Patrick be in the picture? Or once he was no longer needed, would he gladly walk out of her life?

Her head began to pound with the confusing and upsetting thoughts.

She felt trapped in the backyard. The balmy

spring air added to the sensation of oppression, like a huge hand of heat pressing down on her, making her sweat. She wanted to go for a walk, to be out in the open and not be afraid.

But she had to get through the next few days. She went back to the flower bed and tried to clear her mind as she put the plants into the ground.

Just as she was finishing with the last plant in the flat, Patrick came into the yard. He wore brown slacks and a striped button-down shirt with the sleeves rolled up. His work clothes. He stared at her, his gaze assessing and interested, before walking across the patio to the flower bed.

Growing uncomfortable under his intense study, she asked, "Did Sharon get your password accounts set up?"

He nodded, his head tilting one way and then another as he peered at her through the lens of his glasses. His eyebrows went up. "Your eyes. They're blue."

She grinned sheepishly. "I was wearing contacts before."

"Ah." He waved his hand to her hair. "Are you really a redhead?"

She shook her head, touching the sheared ends. "I was born a towhead actually."

"The purple was unique, but blue eyes suit you."

She couldn't help a little quaver of anticipation

deep inside of her. "I hope that the real me will be okay."

"Of course," he replied. "My brother Ryan will be joining us for dinner tonight."

"Oh. That's unexpected." She wasn't sure how to feel about meeting one of Patrick's siblings and becoming that much more enmeshed in his family. Surely heartache only lay down that path.

"Yes, well. That's Ryan. He's heading out of town and called to say he'd be stopping by. Mother has informed our guards already."

"That's good, because we certainly wouldn't want Ryan to be mistaken for an assassin," she quipped.

Patrick's eyes darkened with concern and a frown appeared between his eyebrows. "No, we wouldn't."

Whew! The man needed to lighten up. She looped her arm through his. Her heart seemed to rush to the places all along her side where she touched him. Talk about overheating. "Ease up there, Professor. It's going to be a good night," she pronounced.

Because come tomorrow she had a serious job to do. And she needed him to be ready to catch her if she botched it.

"It was really nice meeting you, Ryan," Anne said as the youngest McClain was about to take his leave after a delicious dinner and extremely enjoyable evening. Anne's sides hurt so bad from laughing; she could hardly remember the last time she'd had such a good time.

Patrick and Ryan were more different than any two brothers could be. Where Patrick was calm and reserved in tweed, Ryan's hip designer clothes, and hyperenthusiasm and charm both entertained and overwhelmed.

And watching the way Colleen handled each son according to their temperament was a lesson in parenting that Anne had never witnessed before.

Colleen drew out Patrick and reined in Ryan simultaneously. It was truly fascinating.

Ryan gave Anne a crushing hug. "You be strong."

Colleen had asked Anne's permission to reveal her story, since her presence affected their family. Anne couldn't see a reason to keep it a secret.

Anne laughed and gently eased out of his arms. "I will. You have a safe trip. I'd much rather be heading off to Maui tomorrow than New Jersey."

Ryan's dark eyes gleamed. "Maybe one day Patrick can take you to the islands."

For a moment Anne went speechless and she could feel blood flooding her face. Did matchmaking run in the family, or what?

Jaw set in a tight line, Patrick put his hand on Ryan's shoulder and maneuvered him toward the door. "Have a safe trip, little brother. Let us know when you get back."

Colleen stepped between them. "Boys, mind your

manners." She kissed Ryan's cheek. "Be careful and call when you land."

Ryan's smile softened. "I will, Mom. I'll bring you back something fun and pretty."

"Just come back," the McClain matriarch commanded.

Ryan waved and disappeared out the front door. Anne avoided checking Patrick's gaze as she made her way to the back patio. She still couldn't believe his brother's bold statement. It was one thing for her to hope that the future would include Patrick but another entirely for someone else to put that hope to voice.

The night sky twinkled with a million stars, making the heavens glitter. The air had a bite to it. Anne was glad she'd put on the sweater set along with the long skirt she had had brought over from her apartment. She planned on wearing the outfit tomorrow at the trial because it was feminine yet modest.

"I'm sorry for Ryan's big mouth," Patrick stated when he came out of the house and joined her in the backyard.

Waving away his concern, she said, "He's a kick. I enjoyed him."

"Indeed," Patrick replied, his gaze on something over her shoulder.

She turned to see what he found so interesting. The back gate was cracked open. A cold shot of alarm trapped her breath somewhere between her lungs and her throat.

"Go back inside," Patrick ordered as he stalked toward the gate.

She reached out to stop him. "Don't!"

Too late. He went out the gate. The world slowed as she waited, standing there alone in the garden, fearing that Patrick wouldn't return. Knowing that if anything happened to him, it would destroy her.

In a moment of intense understanding she realized she loved him. Oh, man.

She sank to the ground. Each passing second that Patrick didn't return felt like a knife twisting in her abdomen.

There was a movement near the gate. She gasped. Then Patrick materialized out of the shadows and rushed to her side. Giddy relief brought tears to her eyes.

"What's wrong?" He gathered her in his arms. "Are you hurt?"

Shaking her head, she touched his face. "No. I just got scared. You left and I was alone and I was afraid you wouldn't come back and I thought he'd gotten you and—"

"Shh." He put a finger to her lips. "I'm here."

For a moment she soaked in his presence, allowed the comfort, the support, he offered to wrap around her like a protective shield, because she feared all too soon, once the trial was over and he resumed his life, he'd be only a memory and she'd once again be alone. Forcing herself to rein in her emotions, she asked, "Did you see anything?"

"Our guards are all where they should be. I told them about the unlatched gate. They'll keep a watch out."

"Good. I feel so silly for panicking."

He helped her to her feet. "You have reason for being on edge. But soon it will be over and you can start your life over again."

She so wanted to ask if he'd be a part of her new life, but the words stuck to the roof of her mouth. Now was not the time to see where their relationship was headed. She knew better than to make decisions in the midst of a crisis.

So much hinged on the next few days.

Her life and the love growing in her heart for Patrick.

ELEVEN

Carlos sat in the metal chair in the prison visitors' area across from his uncle, and was thankful for the Plexiglas that separated them. Carlos hadn't even told his uncle the bad news yet.

"Uh, well, one pigeon got away," he said. He cringed at the molten rage filling his uncle's face.

"What are you going to do about it?" Raoul ground out.

Carlos swallowed back the panic churning in his stomach. "That one can't be caught again. At least not yet. The handlers are being very hush-hush."

Raoul leaned forward, his palms flat on the metal shelf in front of him. Carlos could see the beads of sweat along his uncle's forehead. Carlos wished he had the guts to tell his uncle to take a flying leap but...Carlos couldn't. He had no doubt Uncle Raoul would make him pay if he dared. And when Raoul called in a debt, people suffered. Carlos didn't like pain and didn't want to suffer.

Carlos kind of hoped his uncle would stay behind bars, but for men like Raoul, laws didn't matter and prisons weren't enough to curtail power. So Carlos would do what he must to stay in his uncle's good graces, and thus stay alive unharmed.

"Don't worry, Uncle. We've got time before hunting season is over. We'll snag a big bird and dine for weeks," Carlos said, trying to sound self-assured and confident.

"You get that bird, nephew, fast. Or the last thing you'll need to worry about is food."

Carlos shuddered. "I will, Uncle. I will."

From the farthest corner of the garden, deep in the shadows the man watched as Patrick walked the woman into the house.

Frustration kicked him in the gut. He hadn't anticipated that the woman would come out into the yard at the exact moment that he'd slipped in. She'd been too far away to slit her throat without giving her a chance to sound an alarm.

He'd had a pitiful few seconds to decide to hide without relatching the gate.

He planned to kill the woman and get away without being caught. One miscalculation wasn't going to change that. He'd just have to adjust his plans.

He knew the schedule of the security teams outside. He'd been watching them for the past two nights. He had timed his approach to coincide with the police officers' change in shift and then crept along the darkened alley to wait another hour for the feds' shift change. He'd taken advantage of that precise moment to slip through the gate.

But then she'd walked out. Closely followed by the professor.

Too bad McClain had noticed the gate so quickly and put the men outside on the alert. Dumb luck, that.

Now the man would have to wait longer until they were settled in their cozy little beds before he could do away with the woman. One quick slit of his knife and she wouldn't be talking to anyone ever again.

Easy enough.

Now he just had to wait.

Patrick sat at the desk in the upstairs den, his home computer up and a new story staring at him, waiting for the words to flow across the screen. But he couldn't process his thoughts into any coherent idea. All he could think about was Anne.

At every turn the woman left him off-kilter and holding his breath to see what other surprises she had for him. And he really couldn't say he resented or re-gretted the roller-coaster ride she was taking him on.

His mother liked her, more than the few other women he'd brought home over the years.

And Ryan had gushed all over Anne like a lovestruck puppy. But then again, that was Ryan. He charmed the women and then left them wanting more. Though Anne had seemed to enjoy Ryan's attention, Patrick had realized quickly that Anne hadn't taken Ryan very seriously.

Interesting.

Patrick had to admit he was relieved. The burst of possessiveness had caught him off guard when Ryan had hugged Anne. His brother's overly demonstrative way had always boggled Patrick's mind, but tonight it had downright irritated him.

Rubbing at his gritty eyes, he glanced at the clock. Only a few more hours before the marshals would arrive to escort Anne back to New Jersey. Patrick stretched and decided he'd better at least try to rest so his brain would be alert for tomorrow. He shut down his computer, and then headed to bed.

After the trial, he'd see where this relationship with Anne was headed. He wasn't sure in what direction he wanted the relationship to go but he did know he wanted her in his life. The only question was, would she want *him* in her life?

Anne couldn't sleep. She tossed and turned, disturbing Princess who hissed a warning of discontent every time Anne shifted. Finally Anne decided to give up on sleep for the night. She slipped out of bed and wrapped the warm robe Colleen had pulled out of Megan's closet around her and stuffed her feet into a pair of fuzzy slippers.

She shuffled to the window and stared out at the moon so high in the dark sky. Light spilled over the street below, outlining the Boston Police cruiser and the federal agents' four-door sedan.

Anxiety burned in her stomach. They were on the home stretch now and she couldn't wait for this all to end.

A noise behind her raised the hair on her nape. The doorknob turned. Patrick?

The dark silhouette of a man, who clearly was not Patrick, entered and closed the door before stealthily moving toward the bed. She pressed into the darkened corner of the room. Her heart thudded in her chest.

Stifling the scream building inside of her, Anne edge along the wall toward the door. Her side collided with the dresser. She winced as the dark figure whipped around. A long knife glinted in the moonlight.

Anne let loose a scream.

Just as Patrick began to doze off a woman's scream split the air.

Jolted awake, he bolted from his bed and out the door. He didn't hesitate, running straight for his little sister's room. Anne's room.

He burst through the door and hit the light switch. His gaze landed on Anne, pinned against the dresser and struggling with a man dressed in black wielding a nasty looking knife in his tight fist.

He recognized the wiry, dark-haired man. He'd seen him standing on the street outside Anne's apartment the morning he'd picked her up for church. The assassin the FBI had feared.

Adrenaline and rage pumped through Patrick's veins and thundered into his ears. Undeterred by the weapon, Patrick lunged at the man, using his shoulder to push the man away from Anne. They landed with a thud on the floor.

The intruder rolled away and jumped to his feet, the knife swooshing through the air in an arc.

Patrick came to his feet, blocking the door and keeping himself between the assassin and Anne. "Go, Anne. Get the agents!"

The man jabbed his weapon at Patrick with practiced precision, trying to force him back.

"No!"

Anne's scream galvanized Patrick into action. He swiped the sweater that Anne had worn earlier from the back of the small vanity chair, and wrapped it around his left arm. Using the bulk on his forearm as a shield, Patrick moved in, closing the gap between him and the intruder.

The assassin thrust the knife forward, slicing through the protective sweater.

Patrick barely felt the sting of the knife. Calling on old lessons, he took advantage of the moment to use the knuckles of his other hand in a downward arc to rap forcibly across the forearm of the hand that held the knife, hitting the radial nerve and causing the man to drop the weapon with a pain-filled yelp.

Before the man could make another move, Patrick followed with a sharp jab of his foot to the side of the man's right knee, eliciting a scream as the leg buckled, bones snapping. The man dropped to the floor, withering in agony.

The pounding of footsteps echoed in Patrick's adrenaline-laced mind. Hands pulled him back as he continued to lunge forward, intent on causing the villain more harm.

Two police officers maneuvered him out of the way.

"Patrick, Patrick. Let them take care of this," Anne's voice urged, her gentle hands holding his arm.

"You're okay?" Patrick blinked as the rage receded. His breathing came in labored huffs. The room became a sea of uniformed officers and federal agents. He looked into Anne's clear blue eyes. The concern and tenderness there calmed his racing heart.

She nodded. "But you're bleeding."

Bright red blood seeped through the sweater she'd planned to wear the next day to court. "Minor compared to what could have happened."

Reality hitting her, Anne shuddered. He could have been killed defending her life. Her heart pitched and a mix of guilt and gratefulness spread over her. She didn't deserve such a wonderful knight in… black silk pajama bottoms and a red T-shirt.

An officer spoke into the mic at his shoulder. "We

need a bus." He gave the dispatcher the address for the ambulance.

A federal agent stepped over to Patrick. "Good job. You broke his leg."

"Would have liked to have broken his neck," Patrick muttered.

The agent's lips thinned. "If you had we wouldn't be able to question him. At least this way, the man's at our mercy."

Patrick grunted. The agonized curses and moans of the fallen man filled the air. Anne turned away, not wanting to feel compassion for the man's pain. He'd tried to kill her, but even that knowledge couldn't snuff out the empathy twisting in her heart.

"Anne? Patrick?" Colleen McClain stood in the doorway, her long hair unbound and her robe held tightly at the neck. Her worried gaze took in the scene in the room.

"We're both okay, Colleen," Anne answered.

"Patrick, you're bleeding." Colleen rushed forward.

"Just a scrape, Mom," Patrick assured her.

Colleen searched his face before turning her gaze to Anne. "You two should wait downstairs for the medics. I better go put on a pot of coffee since none of us will be sleeping much tonight."

Patrick stared after his mother. "That was odd."

Anne pulled him toward the stairs. "Something other than a man breaking into your house and trying to kill me?"

"Yes. My mother."

Anne led him into the living room and made him sit on the couch. "What was odd about your mother?"

"She didn't try to take over."

Anne sat beside him and averted her gaze from the bright red stain spreading through the sweater, instead she focused on his face. The color had leached from his skin. Was he going into shock?

She needed to keep him alert and talking until the paramedics arrived. "Is your mother usually the take-charge type?"

He shrugged. "The motherly type."

Didn't he realize how blessed he was to have a mother so willing to be a parent? "I don't understand what the problem is."

"She left me in your care."

Anne stilled. That hadn't been lost on her. His mother had clearly given the reins of his care to her once she realized his injury wasn't life-threatening. "I guess she feels I'm capable of keeping you sitting while we wait."

"You were holding off that guy pretty well. You have some well-disguised muscles."

Muscles or not, Anne had never been so frightened in her whole life or had fought so hard. As terrifying as witnessing a brutal murder had been, being attacked had been worse. "I'm glad you came when you did. And as for muscles, climbing trees as a child and carrying trays filled with drinks may have built up some strength, but what you did took skill. You didn't learn those moves in dance class."

"Mom may have thought we all needed to be graceful, but dad thought we needed to know how to fight."

"So that was some kind of martial arts?"

"No. Good old-fashioned street fighting."

"Very effective," she said, impressed and a bit awed. Every day that passed Patrick allowed her glimpses of the amazing man he was beneath the professor persona. "Did your siblings learn as well?"

He inclined his head. "Yes. I made sure they all were taught just as I had been. That's what my dad wanted."

"Is it because of your father's death that you've given up on God?" Surprised at herself for her boldness, she held her breath.

The soft light of the table lamp bathed his pale features in a warm glow but the shuttered expression in his eyes frosted the air. "God betrayed me. Betrayed all of us."

She silently sent up a prayer of guidance. She wasn't equipped to help him come to terms with God's ways. "I don't know why your father had to die, but I do know God didn't do it."

"He's in control, right? Omnipotent, all powerful?"

Bitterness laced his words, but also a deep hurt that made her ache inside.

"But he gives us free will. Your father chose to

respond to the call. He chose to get out of the car." She winced. She was mucking this up. She didn't want him to think that blame rested solely on his father. "The man who shot him made a choice. We all make choices. And every choice a person makes has a ripple effect and touches other people's lives."

"I've heard this before." He waved his uninjured hand, his expression dismissive. "It still doesn't explain why God didn't intervene. Why God chose to ignore my prayers of safety for my father."

His pain gutted her. Hadn't she had that same thought when she first entered the McClains' house? She wished she could make Patrick's hurt go away. "I don't have an answer to that. All we can do is choose to love and to trust."

He seemed to weigh her words, his eyes staring into hers as if searching for something. What else could she say? Her own faith was so tender and full of discovery, how could she possibly help him to accept God's love?

A commotion at the front door drew their attention. The EMTs arriving. Patrick stood as an officer directed a young African-American woman over to attend Patrick's wound.

Her name tag read, Keller. "Hello, sir. Let me take a look."

Knowing now was not the time to pursue their discussion, Anne watched as the EMT unwound the bloodied sweater from Patrick's arm. Anne's stomach pitched at the sight of the gash slicing across his forearm.

"This is shallow. You won't have any permanent damage," remarked Keller. She turned to wave at an officer standing by. "CSU is going to want a picture of this."

The office nodded and hurried away. When he came back, another man followed carrying a camera. He snapped off several shots of Patrick's arm, before Keller shooed him away. Keller then used butterfly bandages to close the wound. "Keep it dry until you can get in to see your regular doctor."

Loud yelling split the air as the would-be assassin, strapped to a gurney, was carried down the stairs by two other EMTs.

"I have rights!" the man screamed. "I want my lawyer!" As they passed through the hall toward the front door, the man spit at Anne and Patrick.

"Lovely," Anne stated dryly.

One of the FBI agents approached. "We've identified your assailant. His name's Rico Trinidad. We'll find his connection to Domingo. In the meantime, we need to move you to a more secure location."

Disappointment and dread slumped Anne's shoulders. She didn't want to leave, but she knew for the McClains' sake she should.

"Why?" asked Patrick. "You don't honestly think anything else will happen tonight, do you?"

"We can't be sure. This location was compromised," explained the agent.

Patrick shook his head. "She's not going anywhere. You'll have to figure out a way to keep her safe here."

Anne couldn't believe Patrick still wanted her to stay even after the intruder. She wanted to question him, ask him why? Did his feelings run deeper than responsibility? But those questions would have to wait until the right time. Now was not that time.

After the trial, when their lives could go back to some semblance of normal. Then she'd ask and she'd tell him of her feelings.

The agent turned to Anne. "Miss Jones?"

"I'll stay," she said softly.

The agent nodded. "Then I will post agents inside as well as outside."

"Fine," agreed Patrick and then put his arm around Anne and directed her toward the stairs. "We have a few hours."

Anne scoffed. "Yeah, like I'm going to sleep now."

He touched her cheek. "Let me check on Mom and then if you can't sleep we can sit in the den and watch a movie."

Liking that idea, she nodded. "That would be great."

He squeezed her shoulder before heading back downstairs. Anne entered her room and sank on to the bed as exhaustion settled in. "Princess?"

She'd last seen the feline scurrying under the bed when that monster had entered her room. Lifting the ruffled duster, Anne peered into the darkness. One bright eye stared back at her.

"I don't blame you, sugar. I want to hide, too."

But come tomorrow she'd be out in the open, exposed and sitting on the hot seat.

A few minutes later, Patrick appeared at the door. "A movie?"

Anything to distract herself from what lay ahead. She followed him into the den and sat beside him on the brown leather sofa across from a wide-screen Plasma television. They selected a comedy. But even before the opening credits ended, Anne's eyelids grew heavy.

Patrick slid his arm around her shoulders and drew her against him. She let her head rest against his shoulder and as sleep claimed her she thought how much she wished she'd never have to move from this spot again.

But wishes never came true.

Patrick's heart swelled with tenderness for Anne as she slept pressed against his side, the short ends of her hair tickling his chin. He'd come so close to losing her tonight. Just the memory of that knife held so closely to her graceful neck brought terror creeping up his spine. No matter what, he was not going to let anything happen to her. He'd move mountains to make sure she testified at the trial.

Part of him acknowledged that his desire to see justice done in this case wasn't totally due to Anne, but because he wished someone had come forward to testify in his father's murder. Maybe then, Patrick would find peace with his father's death.

Reverend James would say peace only came from God.

Anne had said, *All we can do is choose to love and to trust.*

He was afraid he'd never find peace, because he couldn't find love or trust inside himself.

Carlos couldn't believe it. Trinidad had screwed up. His uncle was going to be furious now. Heads would roll. Probably Carlos's first. He shuddered with dread and fear. His uncle had left him in charge and expected the pigeon's neck to be wrung before Raoul even stepped into the courtroom.

Rubbing a hand over his pockmarked face, the roughened skin scraping across his callused hand, Carlos knew there was only one way to get out of this mess. He had to take control of the situation and take the woman out before she reached New Jersey. Otherwise, he'd have to face his uncle's wrath and the prospect of Raoul revealing Carlos's secret.

Suzie, Carlos's wife, would leave him in a heartbeat if she knew he was still gambling. She'd bash his head in if she found out just how deep in debt he'd gotten himself. Carlos was only able to keep Suzie in the dark because Raoul kept the creditors at arm's length. They were probably just as scared of Raoul Domingo as Carlos was.

Because Raoul Domingo held more power than could be contained behind a set of prison bars.

Carlos made two phone calls and then left his uncle's warehouse before the sun started rising over the eastern horizon.

He was going hunting.

TWELVE

As the sun rose, Patrick woke Anne. Her sleepy eyes and messed hair were so adorable. His sister's robe engulfed Anne's slighter stature. He slipped his arm around her waist and steered her past two FBI agents to Megan's room so she could ready herself for the trial.

Careful of his wound, Patrick dressed and shaved before stepping back into the hall.

Because the two agents posted on either side of Anne's door still stood guard, he assumed that Anne had not emerged yet. With a nod, the agents acknowledged Patrick when he approached the door and softly knocked.

A moment later, the door opened and Anne stepped from the room. She was wearing the baggy brown dress suit he'd first seen her in, her brown textured purse slung over her shoulder. Her eyes were purple again, with a decidedly determined gleam. But instead of the spiky hair she had worn previously, her red hair had been blown dry and lay in feathered wisps around her face, emphasizing her delicately carved bone structure.

"Good morning," she said with a smile.

His heart rate picked up. They'd only parted for a short time, why did he feel so electrified to see her again? "You ready?" He held out his good arm for her.

"As I'll ever be," she replied and looped her arm through his.

They descended the stairs with the agents fast on their heels and found his mother sitting at the kitchen table sipping coffee. Across from her sat a man dressed in black with a white collar.

Patrick stopped short. "Reverend James?"

The reverend rose and shook Patrick's hand. "Your mother called." He smiled, the lines at the corners of his green eyes crinkling. "You must be Anne. Colleen was just telling me about you."

Anne slid her arm from Patrick and shook the reverend's offered hand. "I am."

"Colleen also tells me you are a believer."

Patrick felt his insides bunch and twist. "We'll be leaving soon."

"There's time for Reverend James to say a blessing over Anne," Colleen said, her gaze pinning Patrick to the floor.

"I'd love that," Anne said, her gaze on Patrick.

He stared into her eyes, into her heart that was full of faith. The expectant look on her face clearly asked him to cooperate. Forcing back the bitterness that tried to rise, he inclined his head. Only for Anne would he stay.

As Reverend James prayed over Anne, Patrick couldn't stop the memories of his father's graveside service when the reverend had spoken about God's redeeming love.

Patrick had stared at the brown wooden casket, hating that his father was stuck inside that box, hating that God had allowed his father to die and hating that now Patrick had to be the "man of the house" as so many of the other mourners kept murmuring to him when they came close.

Patrick took a step back as clarity stole his breath.

He hated God for taking his father. He hated his father for taking that call. But mostly Patrick hated that he'd had to sacrifice his life for his family.

The need to bolt grabbed him by the throat. How could he have such a selfish thought? He backed up another step, needing space.

Anne glanced up, her questioning gaze trapping the breath in his lungs.

We all make choices.

But he hadn't had a choice. Had he? He'd done what was necessary. What was expected.

"Mr. McClain?"

Patrick pivoted to stare at the agent who'd stepped quietly into the kitchen. Mentally scrambling to gather his chaotic thoughts in order and show some coherency, Patrick led the officer farther down the hall. "Yes?"

"The marshals are here."

Focusing on the situation, Patrick nodded and then moved to the trio in the kitchen. He touched Anne's elbow. "Excuse me," he said.

Reverend James raised his head with a sheepish smile. "Sorry, I tend to be verbose."

Patrick didn't comment, but he exchanged an amused glance with his mother.

"We need to leave," Patrick explained.

Colleen gave Anne a fierce hug. "You be strong."

There were tears in Anne's eyes. "I will. Thank you for everything."

"I'll see you again," Colleen assured her with a twinkle in her eye.

Anne said goodbye to the reverend then walked out the door with the agent. Patrick followed her to the big, black SUV waiting at the curb. Two men stood by the hood. As they approached, the men flashed their IDs.

"We'll be driving to the airport in Spencer and flying from there to New Jersey," the marshal named Fritz said.

"Why out of Spencer?" Patrick asked. The town was a good two-hour drive away.

"Logan's too busy. Would be too easy to take out a target in a crowd there," explained the other marshal.

"That makes sense." After last night, Patrick was glad the marshals were taking such precautions.

Fritz moved to the driver's side while the other agent, Mitchell, opened the back door for Anne. She climbed in and slid to the other side of the leather seat. Patrick made to climb in behind her but the agent held up a hand stopping him. "Sorry, sir. Only Miss Jones."

Anne scrambled to the door. "No. He's coming with us."

Frustration beat a steady rhythm at Patrick's temple as the agent adamantly shook his head. "We have our orders, miss."

"Have you talked to Lieutenant Taylor? She is expecting me to accompany Miss Jones," Patrick prodded.

"I can't let you ride with us, sir. But there's nothing I can do if you choose to follow us and purchase your own plane ticket to New Jersey," the agent said with a pointed look.

"Well enough." Patrick met Anne's nervous gaze. "I'll be right behind you all the way."

She gave him a wan smile.

The agent shut the door. She wasn't visible behind the tinted glass. Patrick waved and then headed to his car.

He was not going to let the SUV out of his sight.

Anne fiddled with the leather seam in the seat at her side as a way to keep from jumping out of the moving car. She inhaled. The SUV still had that new car smell. She wondered if she were the first to be transported in its luxury.

She glanced at the stretch of highway behind the vehicle, making sure that the little green Mini Cooper stayed within sight. She'd thought they'd lost Patrick as the agent had maneuvered his way out of the early morning commuter traffic of Boston, but every time she was on the verge of telling the driver to slow down, the Mini Cooper would pass a car and slide in behind the SUV.

The agents in the front seat didn't seem inclined to talk so Anne didn't bother. She wasn't in the mood to talk, either. They'd been driving for over an hour. The metropolitan landscape had given way to a more rural scenic drive along MA-9. Rolling hills, farms, an occasional town passed by as they zipped along.

Anne liked the name of the one they'd just passed. Cherry Hill. It sounded quaint and looked even quainter, like a good place to visit one day if she got the chance.

By the end of this day, she'd have some semblance of her life back and could return if she wanted.

A virtual hive of bees attacked her stomach at the reminder of what was coming. She should have eaten before leaving the McClains' house. She opened her purse and dug down to the bottom where she found a protein bar.

A loud pop startled Anne. She dropped the snack. The vehicle jerked and weaved. Terror streaked through her. She screamed and braced her hands against the front seat. Another loud pop. The front windshield exploded in a shower of glass.

The world spun. Anne felt a sharp pain as her head connected with the side window. The seat belt pulled painfully at her ribs, squeezing the breath from her lungs. The last thing she saw as darkness closed in was the side of the road dropping out of sight.

Patrick saw the rear tire of the SUV transporting Anne blow out. The vehicle swerved and rocked and then the windshield exploded. His heart seized momentarily in his chest, before banging against his ribs in a chaotic beat.

They'd been shot at! From where?

Patrick slammed on the brake. The little car fishtailed as the tires gripped the blacktop. Horror clogged his throat as he watched the big car in front of him spin toward a drop-off on the edge of the road.

The black car disappeared over the side. Patrick came to a roaring stop, flung open the door and jumped out. He ran to the spot where the SUV went over. "Anne!"

The vehicle had landed on its top. He saw no movement from within. Patrick's world narrowed to a pinprick. Dread slammed into his heart.

He scrambled down the side of the ravine, rocks sliding beneath his feet. Heaving with shocked breaths, he slid to his knees beside the car. He checked the agents. Alive but unconscious.

Fearing what he might find, Patrick yanked on the back door, the metal groaned as he pried it open. Anne hung upside down, the seat belt holding her fast to the seat. "Anne! Oh, come on, baby, be alive." Now that he'd found her, he couldn't live without her.

He squeezed inside to check her pulse. Alive! But strapped in.

His own wound throbbed but he ignored the pain. He could only think of her. He had to get help. He reached for his phone on his belt and let out a moan of frustration. His cell phone was on the passenger seat in his car at the top of the hill.

Helplessness, anger and panic ran a course through his system, firing off all his nerves. Grasping her by the shoulders, he gently pulled her from the wreckage.

He threw his head back and yelled toward heaven, "God, please. Help us!"

A spray of gunfire hit the dirt inches from Anne's body. Patrick threw himself over her. He had to get her away from the vehicle. If a bullet hit the engine, they'd all be dead.

A different noise drew his attention. A car screeched to a halt on the road above. Suddenly a man appeared over the rim of the hill.

Cam? His student? With a gun in his hand.

They were dead now. Patrick rose, ready to meet this threat head-on.

Cam skidded down the side of the hill. "Get back down!" He held up a shiny badge that reflected in the sunlight. Patrick squinted, not believing what he was seeing.

Patrick crouched down as relief swept through him. "You're a cop?"

"Yes, Professor." He inclined his head toward Anne. "Is she alive?"

"Unconscious. So are they." Patrick indicated the men in the front seat. "We need to get them to a hospital."

Cam nodded and pulled out a cell phone to give dispatch their location. His gaze searched the area as he squatted beside Patrick. "Did you see the assailants?"

"No. It all happened so fast. I think the shots came from that cluster of trees." Patrick pointed to a spot where a grouping of maples shaded the highway.

"I'll be back," Cam said and made his way around the SUV and toward the road.

After a long, silent stretch that pulled at Patrick's nerves, a succession of gunfire broke the air. Patrick waited, feeling vulnerable in the open.

Cam returned, his gun returned to his holster. "I took out the sniper as he was fleeing. It was Carlos Jaramillo. Domingo's nephew."

"Good. That's good." One more assassin down. How many more would they have to fight? "Who are you?"

"Cam Trang. NJPD. Lieutenant Taylor arranged for me to keep an eye on Anne." He winced, his almond-shaped eyes regretful. "I missed too many lights in town and got caught behind a slow-moving truck or I'd have been here sooner."

"Your being here wouldn't have stopped it." Anger tightened Patrick's jaw until it ached. "How could this have happened? This Carlos character was already here. Waiting."

Cam's lips twisted with frustration. "There's a leak in the system. The route the agents were given was only known by a few so it will be pretty easy to track."

Track right to Domingo, Patrick was sure.

A few minutes later, EMTs arrived along with several police and federal agents. Anne and the two marshals were put on gurneys and lifted up the hill to be put into the back of a waiting ambulance. Patrick climbed inside next to Anne. He held her hand, rubbing the skin lightly. She had to be okay. She didn't deserve this. She was just trying to do the right thing.

Lord, I don't understand. She trusts you. Is this some kind of punishment for me?

Anne would tell him God wasn't punishing him. She didn't believe that He worked that way. Patrick wasn't sure what to believe.

The ambulance took them to the nearest hospital in Harrington, just thirteen miles from Spencer, their original destination.

At the hospital Patrick paced the hall outside the room where the doctor examined Anne. Cam stood a few feet away, talking on his phone. Thankfully the federal agents had had enough clout to have Anne taken directly to a private room. Now Harrington police officers stood watch at both ends of the corridor and outside the room.

A nurse opened the door. "Mr. McClain, she's awake and asking for you."

"Thank you." Relief flooded Patrick in a rush. He entered the room. Anne lay in the bed, her eyes open and she smiled at him. Her face sported a dark bruise over her left temple. Patrick's veins throbbed with anger at the men who did this.

The doctor, an older man with gray hair and a lean face, held a clipboard in his hands and nodded to Patrick.

Pulling a chair up to the edge of the bed, Patrick sat and took Anne's hand. He didn't know what to say so he kissed her knuckles and relished the warmth of her palm in his.

Cam stepped into the room. Anne gasped and Patrick quickly explained who Cam really was.

"Wow," she said softly. "I knew there was something up with him."

"Dr. Holt, how is her condition?" Cam asked.

"Stable. She has a slight concussion and bruised ribs from the impact."

"When can we move her?" Cam asked.

"I wouldn't recommend it for at least three days. Now if you'll excuse me, I have other patients." The doctor left the room.

Anne squeezed Patrick's hand. "The trial."

Patrick nodded and addressed Cam. "Can you have the D.A. postpone the trial?"

"I was just talking with him. He'll ask the court for a postponement but is unhopeful the judge will comply because the trial was pushed forward at the request of the state."

"So what will happen if the trial isn't postponed?" Anne asked.

"The D.A. will have to make his case without your testimony."

Anne struggled to sit up. Patrick reached to help her. She groaned and gripped his arm. "But I'm the only one who saw Domingo kill Jean Luc."

Cam nodded, his expression grim. "Yes. But there is a witness who can place him in the suite just not put the gun in his hand."

"Who?" Anne asked.

"A maid, Maria Gonzales."

"I know Maria. She's a nice woman." Anne turned her gaze to Patrick. "I have to get there. I can't let Domingo get away with murder."

"You heard the doctor. You're not in any shape to be moved for a few days," Patrick said, wanting to protect her from any more pain.

Her eyes pleaded with him. "I *have* to go."

He understood her need and admired her determination. "Cam, we're going to New Jersey."

Cam came closer, his dark eyes concerned. "Are you sure?"

Anne nodded. "Yes."

"I'll call Porter and let him know we're on our way."

"No." Patrick shook his head. "There's a leak somewhere. I'm not taking any more chances with her life. Just the three of us."

Cam considered him for a moment. "We'll have to figure a way around the agents in the hall."

"A fire alarm," Anne suggested.

Patrick glanced at her. She shrugged. "That's how I got out of detention in high school. Pulled the alarm."

"I'm afraid to ask why you had detention in the first place," Patrick said.

She grinned, a spunky light in her eyes. "Let's just say the home ec teacher ran screaming from the room and leave it at that."

He rolled his eyes. "Deal." To Cam, he said, "Do you think it will work?"

A sly gleam entered Cam's almond-shaped eyes. "We can't put other patients' lives at risk, but I can distract the agents."

"Okay, then." Patrick rubbed his hands together. "Let's make a plan."

After much talking and debating the options, they decided on a course of action. Since Anne was in a hospital gown and her own clothes were cut up from when the nurses removed them from her body, Patrick went in search of something for her to wear. Cam left to make arrangements for a plane at the airport at nearby Southbridge. Anne could only wait until the men returned, but she used the time to pray.

Patrick came back carrying a set of green scrubs.

"Where'd you find them?" she asked.

"In one of the E.R. doctors' rooms." He came to her side. "Okay, how are we going to do this?"

She held out her hand, amused by the flush of color riding up his neck. "Let me deal with this. You go see how Cam's doing."

He frowned. "Won't you need help?"

"I'll manage," she said, unwilling to have him dress her like a child. That was not the way she wanted him to view her.

"I'll be back," he stated and walked out.

"Yeah," she laughed softly. Not exactly Arnold Schwarzenegger, but he'd do. She wiggled out from beneath the sheets, gritting her teeth against the pain in her rib cage. With excruciating care, she slipped the pants on and then the top. Before tying the ends together, she touched the deep purple bruise on her chest. It could have been so much worse. "Thank you, Lord, for watching out for me."

The door opened slightly. "You okay?" Patrick called from the other side.

"Just a sec." She finished dressing. "Come in."

Patrick entered, followed by Cam. The smaller Asian man pushed a wheelchair in front of him.

"How did you get that?" she asked, as Patrick gently lifted her from the bed to set her on the seat of the wheelchair.

"I found it on the next floor down. No one will miss it for a while," Cam said. "The nurses have a shift change in about five minutes. That's when we should do this."

Patrick put his hand on her shoulder, a soothing heat spread through her at the contact. "Not too late to back out."

She covered his hand with her own. "I'm not backing out."

"All right then. Cam will distract the officers and I'll wheel you to the staff elevator, which will take us to the back parking lot. My car is right by the elevator door."

Anne took a shallow breath and winced as she slowly let it out. "Let's do this."

THIRTEEN

As on any day in which a trial commences, the courtroom bustled with activity, much like the stage where a dramatic production was enacted. The curtain was up and the players on their marks.

It was the last day of the trial, and the prosecution's key witness wasn't coming. Her transport had been ambushed and then she skipped out on the agents assigned to guard her. District Attorney Porter had used every argument possible to delay the proceedings, but his motion for a continuance so late in the hearing was denied.

If the Boston Police could get the would-be assassin who hit the McClains the night before to turn on his boss, they could add attempted murder to Domingo's charges.

Domingo's lawyer's motions for dismissal were also denied.

Porter would have to be satisfied with the little

solid evidence they had and the unsubstantiated testimony of Maria Gonzales.

Lidia sat on the bench behind the prosecutor's table where District Attorney Porter and one of his assistants were preparing for their closing remarks.

Across the aisle, Domingo sat beside his shark of an attorney, Evelyn Stein. The smug expression on his beefy face grated on Lidia's nerves. The man was going to get away with murder. It just wasn't right.

Lidia burned with anger. Someone had given the secure route the marshals were using to Domingo's men. Thankfully Anne lived, but she wouldn't be coming to testify. She could only pray Anne was safe.

Lidia leaned forward and touched Porter's shoulder. He shifted to look at her, his jaw set and his eyes grim. "You're doing great," she told him.

His expression softened. "Thanks. I'm glad you stayed."

After she'd given her testimony, she hadn't left as she usually would. Right now, her other cases would have to wait. She was here for Porter. She squeezed his shoulder and sat back. Making her support obvious was a big step. She wasn't sure where the relationship would lead, but for now she was where she was needed and that felt good.

A commotion at the back of the courtroom drew her attention along with everyone else's. The judge banged his gavel. Court security placed their hands on their sidearms.

Lidia jerked to her feet in stunned surprise as Professor McClain wheeled in Anne Jones. Lidia's heart contracted at the sight of the ugly bruise on Anne's delicate, young face. She wore scrubs and no shoes.

Porter jumped to take advantage of Anne's arrival. "Your Honor, we'd like to call our last witness to the stand."

Evelyn rose, her strident voice ringing off the walls. "I object, your honor!" Beside her, Domingo's agitation was palpable.

Judge Turner narrowed his eyes. "On what grounds?"

"Prejudicial."

Irritation etched lines around the judge's mouth. "Overruled."

"I demand a recess," Evelyn bit out.

"You demand a recess?" Judge Turner's bushy gray eyebrows rose nearly to his hairline. "Not in my courtroom, you don't, Ms. Stein."

"May we approach the bench, your honor?" Evelyn asked, her voice modulated.

With a quick flick of his wrist, the judge motioned the lawyers forward.

Lidia took advantage of the moment to go to Anne's side and gave her a gentle hug. "What are you doing here? We were told you wouldn't be able to leave the hospital for a few days and then that you slipped away from your guards."

Anne glanced up at the professor. "We thought it best not to let anyone know I was coming."

"Good thinking." Anger burned in Lidia's gut. Someone with trusted information had betrayed the justice system. She fully intended to capture their mole.

Lidia's attention strayed to the animated conversation taking place at the front of the courtroom. Looked like Ms. Stein wasn't thrilled the key witness had shown up after all. Then Lidia's gaze shifted to where Domingo sat, his dark eyes trained intimidatingly on Anne.

Lidia instinctively moved to block Domingo's view. The worm's evil had touched Anne enough already.

After a moment, the two lawyers returned to their respective tables. The judge said, "Call your last witness, Mr. Porter."

"Here we go," Anne murmured, her hand shaky as she placed it over her heart as if to calm the organ down.

"You'll be fine," Lidia assured her as she and Patrick stepped aside so that a deputy could take control of the wheelchair.

Anne was wheeled to the front of the room and sworn in. Lidia resumed her seat and Patrick sat beside her. He never took his earnest gaze off Anne.

Lidia leaned over and whispered, "You love her, don't you?"

He started. A moment passed before he answered, as if he were searching his heart. "Yes. I do."

Regret and empathy settled in Lidia's chest. "Thought so."

She had a feeling that the professor and Anne hadn't contemplated their future after the trial. Anne's only safeguard would be to reenter WITSEC. Lidia wondered how deeply the professor's feelings went. They'd have to run very deep for him to give up everything to follow Anne.

And if not, Anne was in for a lot more heartache.

Reconvening two hours later, Judge Turner addressed the jury from his massive chair behind the tall oak bench. "Jury, have you reached a verdict?"

A man, who represented the other eleven jurors, rose. "In the case against Raoul Domingo in the murder of Jean Luc Versailles, we the jury find the defendant guilty of murder in the first degree."

From her place near the back of the courtroom, Anne closed her eyes with relief. The trial was over, finally. Domingo could appeal, but at least for now, there would be justice for Jean Luc. Domingo would go to jail and Anne could resume her life.

Her heart had been beating a steady gallop since the moment she'd first entered the courtroom and thumped against her rib cage so hard during her testimony she was surprised no one heard it through the microphone that had been placed beside her.

She hadn't wanted to look at the man who'd murdered Jean Luc, was afraid she'd falter in her statement. But one look at Patrick and his faith in her had given her the strength to face Domingo as she related how she'd seen him pull the trigger of the fatal shot that killed her employer.

And now that the verdict had been handed down, she turned her gaze to the convicted murderer who swore at his attorney as two uniformed officers struggled to restrain him. Domingo lifted his gaze and searched the crowd until he spied Anne. A shiver slithered down her spine as those black eyes narrowed.

"You're dead!" Domingo shouted. "Don't ever think I'll forget!"

Patrick stepped in front of Anne, blocking her view. "Don't listen to him. He's going to jail for the rest of his life." Patrick reached for the handles of the chair. "Let's get out of here."

She didn't protest as he pushed the chair out into the corridor. The marble floors gleamed and the wood paneling shined. High arched windows let in light and warmth from the summer sun, yet Anne felt chilled. Domingo's threat rang in her ears. Would she ever feel safe again?

"Miss Jones?"

A man in his mid-fifties wearing a red tie and-white shirt beneath a navy suit, which attractively framed his square build, approached.

"Special Agent Lofland," Anne acknowledged him.

"We need to talk," he said. "Professor, would you please join us." Lofland indicated for them to follow him through the marbled foyer of the courthouse. He headed toward a set of doors.

Patrick pushed the wheelchair, his expression grim. What was he thinking? Did he sense the lingering danger? Would he want to continue to protect her? Would he be glad to see their association end or would he want, as she did, to see where their relationship could go? He was so good at hiding his thoughts, his hurts. Anne's heart ached.

Behind them the courtroom doors burst open and the D.A. came out, mobbed by reporters.

"There's Miss Jones!" someone cried out. The flock of reporters veered away from the D.A.

"This way. Hurry," urged Lofland as he ushered them through a door into another corridor. Behind them the door shut and locked automatically. The gaggle of voices and even pounding on the door faded as Patrick wheeled Anne into yet another room. An interrogation room. The unadorned white walls, tiled floor and metal table with several chairs unnerved Anne.

"Professor, would you take a seat, please," Lofland asked as he pulled up a chair to face Anne.

"What's going on?" she asked, her voice shaking slightly.

"The trial may be over, but not the danger to your life," he said, his intense eyes showing compassion.

"He was convicted," Patrick stated, his brown eyes dark with concern. "Domingo will be in jail. It's not like he's part of the Italian mafia."

Lofland inclined his head. "True. But Raoul Domingo still has a powerful network and men that are loyal to him."

Anne tried to quell the rush of dread and fear flooding her system. "So what are you saying?"

"The only way the government can guarantee your continued safety is if you reenter the WITSEC program."

Anne swallowed. "And if I don't?"

"You, and anyone—" Lofland turned his gaze meaningfully onto Patrick "—you associate with will be in danger."

Anne's shoulders slumped. She had feared as much but had hoped, prayed it wouldn't be so. She glanced at Patrick. Her heart pounded. He looked stricken.

Patrick rose. "Can't you break up his 'network'?" He started to pace. "Surely there's some other way."

"There isn't. And we are working to break up his operation but it takes time. Time that Miss Jones can't afford to remain in the open," Lofland said.

A future with Patrick wasn't a possibility. She'd put him in enough danger. Had put his family in enough danger. She couldn't do it any longer. She resigned herself to a life, alone and in hiding. "How soon must I leave?" Anne asked.

"Now." Lofland eyed Anne and then Patrick with a speculative gleam. "We could arrange for you both to go."

Patrick stilled, his expression arrested in surprise. "Both?"

"If you want. But you'll have to leave everything behind and won't be able to contact anyone from your former life."

Anne's heart twisted as she watched the agent's words sink in him. Patrick's gaze met hers. She finally knew what he was thinking. His family was everything to him. His life too full to give up for her.

She knew he cared. She wasn't an idiot. No man would protect her the way he had if he didn't care. But he didn't love her. She was just a responsibility that he should now be free of.

Thankfully she hadn't told him her feelings. He never needed to know that she'd fallen in love with him. She raised her chin. "No. Patrick won't be coming. Just me." She gazed at Patrick. "Do you think your mother would take care of Princess?"

He blinked. "Of course. But you can't—"

She held up her hand to stop him. "I'm looking forward to starting over again. Maybe a brunette this time with green eyes," she said, forcing herself to sound upbeat.

"Anne," Patrick said softly, his voice full of pain.

"Don't. I'm going to be okay. I made a choice when I decided to testify. I knew there'd be sacrifices. How many people get to have a clean slate and a chance to reinvent themselves? Life's an adventure. I'm looking forward to it." Her voice cracked on the last word. She turned her gaze quickly back to the agent so Patrick wouldn't see the tears in her eyes. "Can I say goodbye to Lieutenant Taylor before I leave?"

"I'll have her sent in." Lofland stood. "I'll give you two a few moments."

Anne wanted to protest. She didn't want to have to say goodbye to Patrick but she stiffened her resolve and forced a smile.

As soon as the door closed behind Lofland, she said, "Thank you, Patrick, for all you've done. I couldn't have made it on my own."

He sat and pulled the wheelchair close, taking her hands. "I wish things could be different. I wish I was free to go with you, but I'm not. I can't leave my family and you can't stay."

Her heart fragmented into a jigsaw of pieces with sharp edges that cut and wounded her from the inside out. Agony surged, but she held it back. She couldn't let him see her pain. She needed to let him go without making him feel guilt for unintentionally hurting her.

"I'm not asking you to come with me," Anne stated firmly. "Whatever we feel for each other was born out of a crisis situation. It would never last for us." If she told herself that enough, maybe one day she'd actually believe it. But her heart knew the truth. He was the only man she'd ever truly love. "But, please, promise me you'll consider sending your book into a publisher or an agent."

Sadness entered his gaze. He touched her cheek. "I'll miss you."

Gut-wrenching pain blasted through her middle. She pressed into his palm. "You'll forget all about me."

"I'll never forget you," he vowed and tilted her face up so that their gazes met. "Never, Anne Jones."

He didn't care about her enough to sacrifice for her. Could she blame him? She'd brought nothing but trouble to his doorstep. "Anne Jones doesn't exist anymore," she whispered.

"She'll always exist in my heart," he countered and leaned forward to capture her lips.

She kissed him back with all the love in her heart. Love that she would never voice. Sweet torture. Blessed pain.

She pulled away, her breathing nothing more than ragged gasps. "Goodbye, Patrick."

He looked as if he wanted to say something. But, she closed her eyes and turned her head away, cutting him off before he could speak. "Please, go now."

As if on cue, the door to the room opened and Lidia stepped in, her face animated with excitement. "We found the leak. District Attorney Porter's secretary, of all people."

"That's good to know," Patrick said, his voice flat. He rose from the chair, his back straight and his eyes desolate. He nodded to Lidia and left without looking back.

"Oh, honey." Lidia gathered her into her arms. Anne let loose the anguish filling her soul.

And knew she would never be the same.

FOURTEEN

Three Months Later

"You're out here moping again?"

Patrick slanted his brother, Brody, a quelling glance. He might be outside in his mother's garden and he might be sitting with Princess on his lap while he contemplated the stars, but he was not moping. "You don't know what you're talking about."

Brody stepped in front of him, his sheriff's uniform retired for the night and in its place, he wore faded jeans and a Boston Red Sox T-shirt. His dark hair curled at the ends as it always had as a kid. "Ha! Mom says you've been moping for months. Ever since you let Anne go."

Patrick tightened his jaw. He'd had to let Anne go. Asking her to stay would have put her life in danger. "Leave me alone."

Brody's expression turned serious. He put a hand on Patrick's shoulder. "That's the problem, bro. You *are* alone and have been for too long."

"What? You aren't making sense." He shrugged off Brody's hand. "Shouldn't you be inside with Kate?"

"She and Mom went baby-stuff shopping. That'll take a while." Brody sighed as he sat next to Patrick on the bench beneath the arbor. "Let me give you some unsolicited advice."

"You do know the definition of unsolicited, don't you?" Patrick didn't wait for a response. "Unasked for and unwanted."

Brody chuckled. "Yep. Exactly. You, big brother, are so smart you're dense."

Patrick rolled his eyes. "What does that mean?"

For a moment Brody remained silent. Patrick hoped that was the end of his brother's chatter.

"Patrick, you need to let go."

Turning to face Brody, Patrick asked, "Let go? Of what?"

Brody's solemn dark eyes filled with determination and concern. "You stepped in when Dad died and we all appreciate it. We all love you. And we want you to know that your job is done. We no longer need you to be a father to us. We need you to be our brother."

Everything he'd been for the past fifteen years rebelled at the notion. "Were you elected as the spokesperson?" Patrick groused.

"Yes. And, dude, you need to get a life."

The ground beneath Patrick's feet seemed to shift,

making him feel off balance. "That's easy for you to say. You left. You have Kate."

Brody's left eyebrow rose a fraction. "I left because it was too painful here. I have Kate because God intervened in my life."

Patrick scoffed. "Now you sound like Anne."

Brody touched Patrick's shoulder again. "Until you let go of your hate and anger toward God, you're never going to be free. You're going to be stuck in this role you've saddled yourself with and always be alone."

Patrick's gut clenched. He set Princess on the ground and then stood, hoping to ease the pain rolling through him. He didn't want to hear his brother's words. Didn't want to acknowledge the truth squeezing his heart. "Have you forgiven God?"

Brody leaned his elbows on his knees. "Yes. I have. Kate has helped me understand that no matter what our circumstances, God is always God. He doesn't change. I'm not saying it's easy. But the hate and anger can eat your soul if you're not careful."

That was true. Patrick could feel the darkness chomping through him. He hadn't been aware of it until Anne had whirled into his life. And now hearing Brody confirming the knowledge made his heart race with possibilities. "But what about Mom?"

Brody stood, his expression patient. "Mom's okay. She's been waiting for you to move on so that she could."

Patrick paced the patio as he worked through the

concept. He thought he'd been doing the right thing by always being here for his mother. Always being available for his siblings. *We no longer need you to be a father to us. We need you to be our brother.*

We all make choices, Anne had said. Patrick had chosen the role he'd thought necessary when he was a teen. But now? Now he needed to choose a different path.

Patrick stared up at the stars, seeing the twinkling lights through a blur that wouldn't be wiped away by cleaning his glasses. For the past few months he'd been miserable and missed Anne so much there were times when it was a physical ache in his chest.

Let go of your hate and anger toward God.

A sensation of fullness grew inside of him, a deep rising of emotion that clogged his throat and pushed at his lungs.

Brody slipped an arm around his shoulders. Patrick moaned as the tears he'd never shed for the loss of his father burst out. He cried in his brother's arms as the grief that had been buried beneath the hurt and betrayal for so many years gushed out.

All we can do is choose to love and to trust.

As the tears subsided and a calmness he'd never experienced before settled in, Patrick lifted up a prayer asking God to give him another chance.

Now all he had left was the impossible task of finding Anne.

* * *

Lidia hated the paperwork part of her job. Filling in forms, making sure all the t's were crossed and the i's dotted wasn't just a cliché, it was a reality she knew could make or break the case when presented in a courtroom.

Today she was putting the finishing details to the report of a burglary/homicide at a convenience store on the strip. Summers were always bad with the teenagers out of school, bored and looking for a thrill. She would be glad when the schools opened again in a few weeks.

"Hey, Taylor!"

Lidia sighed at the all-too-familiar desk sergeant's bellow. Morales never just picked up the phone to buzz her. No, he had to yell through the station house like he was calling some errant child on the playground. She got up and stretched her back before heading in the direction of the sergeant's desk.

"Got a live one for you," the sergeant joked, his craggy face breaking into a grin.

Morales liked his joke. The joke was getting old.

Lidia followed the direction of the sergeant's pointed finger. She blinked and then moved forward. "Professor?"

Professor McClain met her, his hand outstretched, his gaze determined and desperate. "Lieutenant. Thank you for seeing me."

"What are you doing in New Jersey?"

"Is there somewhere private we could talk?"

"Sure." She led him down a hall to an interrogation room. Once inside, she leaned against the wall, curiosity eating away at her patience. "What's up, Professor?"

"I have to find Anne. I should never have let her go. I'm miserable without her. Agent Lofland won't help. You're my only hope."

Stunned didn't describe the reaction running through Lidia. A bit of anger, a bit of joy and a huge dose of protectiveness for Anne made Lidia's gaze narrow. "She was pretty broken up when you left her."

He scrubbed a hand over his face. "I know. I made an enormous mistake. I'm willing to do whatever it takes to be with her. I just have to find her."

If his expression wasn't so sincere and his eyes so beseeching, Lidia would have dismissed him off the bat. But compassion and the need to see love triumph compelled her to say, "I don't know if I can help you but I'll see what I can do."

Patrick sat at his desk in his office, his hand placed atop the pages of his manuscript. A cover letter addressed to a literary agent waited for Patrick's signature. An addressed envelope sat off to the side. He just lacked the courage to go through with it.

He was trying hard to let go of the role he'd had for so long and step out of the comfort zone he'd lived within.

His first step had been to resume going to church.

The church that Anne had introduced him to. When he sat in the pew near the front he could almost imagine her sitting there beside him. He was learning about God, slowly coming to terms with his father's death.

His second step had been to tell his family about his book. They'd been excited and encouraging.

He was still hopeful that his third step would one day come to fruition. But as yet he'd been unsuccessful in locating Anne. He stopped by the federal building every other day to ask Agent Lofland for help.

And every time he was told the same thing—that her whereabouts were confidential. Patrick had hoped that Lieutenant Taylor would be able to help, but it had been three weeks and no word.

Today he was determined to mail off his manuscript.

His desk phone rang. Glad for the distraction, he answered, expecting Sharon, but was surprised to hear Lieutenant Taylor.

"Professor, I think you need a vacation."

His heart jumped. "A vacation? Where?"

"I hear Disney World is a fun place."

Hope rose, making his palms sweat. "Okay. I could do Disney World."

"Mondays seem to be a less crowded day. And at two in the afternoon Cinderella's Golden Carousel is a must."

"Thank you for that tip."

"You're welcome. And, Professor?"

"Yes?"

"God bless you."

Patrick checked his watch. Five minutes to two. He stood in front of the beautifully ornate Golden Carousel. The lilting music played and children laughed, filling the air with the delighted sounds of the happiest place on earth—Disney World.

Patrick wasn't sure what he was supposed to be looking for. His nerves were stretched tight as he searched the crowd, looking for Anne.

Would she still have the spiky red hair or would she have changed? Would she have purple or blue eyes? Would he ever be able to find her in the crowd of determined and pleased park-goers?

The Florida sun beat down on his head, so welcome after the cold that had breezed into Boston the past week.

Maybe he was on the wrong side of the carousel? He walked in a clockwise direction, his gaze scanning the carousel, the line, the other rides. When he was back to where he started he checked his watch again. Ten minutes after.

His spirit plummeted. He was never going to find her. He moved to sit on a bench that faced the carousel. He'd wait all day if that's what it took. He wasn't going to give up now.

A family with a toddler and a girl of about six stopped close by.

"Mommy, look. There she is," exclaimed the little

girl and pointed toward one of the many female Disney characters. The family walked off toward a ride.

A character, Geppetto, Patrick was pretty sure, strolled past.

Patrick's gaze searched the crowd. But how on earth would he ever recognize her?

"Patrick?"

The voice so familiar came from his right.

He sprang to his feet, his gaze swinging to the woman who stood a short distance away. For a moment he was stunned speechless, then his heart leaped and joy washed over him as he took in the short dark hair with a red bow, that framed wide green eyes and ruby-red lips. The blue and yellow dress hugged curves he'd been dreaming about.

"Snow White," he stated in stunned disbelief.

"Follow me." She gestured to him with a white gloved hand.

Keeping a discreet distance, he followed her as she led him toward the ride named after her character. She lingered a moment near the entrance to greet the many children and adults who wanted to hug Snow White. Then she glanced at him, again motioned for him to follow.

Patrick hurried to catch up as she rounded the corner of the building. When he came around the corner she was nowhere to be seen.

But then he noticed an open doorway. He stepped through into an orange colored hallway with exposed pipes.

And she was there waiting for him.

"What are you doing here, Patrick?"

Wanting nothing more than to take her into his arms, he forced himself to remain still. He had a hurdle to cross first. "I want to ask for your forgiveness and if I can have a second chance."

Her hand went to her heart. "Nothing's changed."

He stepped forward and gathered her hand in his. "I've changed, but my love for you hasn't."

The adorably stunned expression on her face tugged at his heart. "Yes, I love you," he repeated.

"But your family. Your career," she protested, her eyes growing watery.

"They understand. There are universities in Florida, too. But the real question is, do you love me?"

A tear crested her lashes and fell. "Yes," she whispered. "Oh, yes."

His heart soared. "Then nothing else matters. You are my priority. As long as we're together. We'll work things out."

A smile of pure joy lit her face. She threw her arms around his neck. "I'm so happy to see you. I've been praying that God would bring us back together."

Patrick pressed his lips to her mouth and said, "He's answered both of our prayers."

EPILOGUE

Lidia fiddled with the buttons of her long, leather jacket and struggled to resist the urge to check her lipstick as she waited outside the courthouse for District Attorney Porter. Few clouds dotted the clear September sky and the fall leaves were beginning to turn. She pulled the corner of her collar closer against the crisp bite of the air that announced the coming change in the weather.

She leaned against a stone pillar, hoping to avoid the notice of the circling media and other bystanders waiting for the D.A. to emerge after prosecuting a gruesome murder case against a renowned psychologist. Lidia had no doubt the sicko-pycho would be found guilty; she'd led the investigation and it was airtight. And with Porter's amazing skill as a prosecutor, the guy would be put away for life.

The doors to the courthouse opened. The defense attorney, a polished, younger up-and-coming man with political ambitions, came out and was immediately descended upon by the reporters. From where Lidia stood she couldn't hear the lawyer's statement, but she could guess he was dissing the justice system and probably purporting his client's innocence.

Her gaze shifted back to the open door as Porter came outside. A smile tugged at her heart as well as her mouth. She loved to watch him in action. Cool, calm and full of honor. Not only was Christopher Porter turning out to be a considerate and attentive companion, but she respected and admired his prowess in the court.

The man had stolen her heart.

As he threaded his way through the jumble of media who'd also caught sight of him, his gaze searched for someone. She waved. His expression softened. And her smile widened. He'd been looking for her. He pushed his way through the crowd toward Lidia.

As he approached, she stepped away from the pillar and headed to her cruiser parked at the curb. Pretending to be his escort had served them well as both a means to keep the media from sniffing out the truth of their relationship, and also to show the NJPD's support of the district attorney.

Once they were secure inside the vehicle and on their way, Lidia asked, "How did it go?"

"Well. It's a solid case, thanks to you and your team. We reconvene in the morning for closing arguments."

"That creep should get the death penalty." She

thought of the victim, a twenty-year-old college student who'd come to the doctor for help, only to end up dismembered and dumped in the ocean.

"Agreed."

Mentally shaking off the image of the victim, she said, "On a better note, Domingo's dead."

Porter lifted an eyebrow. "Really? Details."

Lidia grinned at his use of her phrase. "A shank to the kidneys. He bled out before the guards could get to him."

"Can't say that I'm sad."

"No. You reap what you sow in life. He may have held a lot of power on the outside, but, apparently, not on the inside."

"You do know what this means, don't you?"

"Of course I do." Giddy anticipation bubbled through her.

"Then let's go see Lofland."

"My thought exactly," she stated as she headed the car toward the Federal Building. "Anne and the professor can come out of hiding."

She couldn't wait to tell them.

Patrick entered the two-story town house he shared with his wife, Anne. Around him splashes of color permeated every inch of space. But it wasn't a chaotic collection of hues and tones but a blending of personalities and styles. Brown and beiges, leather and stone for him with complementing accents of plush fabrics in shades of red, purple and green for her.

The aroma of warm bread and roasting meat tantalized his hunger. "Hello?"

"In here," Anne called from the kitchen.

He couldn't wait to see her. Every day when he came home from the University of Florida, where he taught freshman economics under the name Professor Kelley—having taken his mother's maiden name—Patrick held his breath, praying that today wasn't the day their whereabouts had been compromised. The fear bordered on fanatical but there was a real threat that one day someone would find him or Anne and their lives would be shattered.

He entered the kitchen and took a moment to stare at his wife. Her darkened hair had grown to touch her shoulders and accentuated her creamy skin. She wore a loose ruffled blouse and shorts. Her pink-tipped toes were bare. Every day she grew more beautiful and more precious to him. The sacrifices of walking away from his career and his family had been well worth her love.

She turned her blue-eyed gaze toward him, her eyes shining with happiness. She'd gotten in the habit of taking the green contacts out at home. "How was your day?"

He rolled up the sleeves of his oxford button-down shirt. "Good. Glad to be home. My stomach wants to know what's for dinner."

"A celebratory meal," she announced. "Pot roast, potatoes, carrots and French bread."

He slid his arms around her waist and pulled her close. "What are we celebrating?"

"I received my first A today in my English class."

She had enrolled at the university as a freshman. A big step. But as yet hadn't picked a major.

"That does deserve celebrating," he said and bent to capture her lips as pride for her swelled inside his chest.

A knock at the front door startled them apart.

"Are you expecting someone?" he asked.

Anne shook her head, her eyes wide. "Could be a neighbor," she said, but her voice lacked conviction.

Patrick hated the awful feeling of uncertainty that around any corner, at any knock, their lives could be torn apart by a vengeful madman. "Stay here," he said and went to the door.

Peering through the peephole, he caught his breath. He took a step back. His heart hammered against his ribs. Anxiety twisted his gut.

"Who's there?" Anne whispered to him as she came to his side and slipped her hand into his.

"Lieutenant Taylor and District Attorney Porter," he replied. What could their appearance on his and Anne's doorstep mean?

Anne quickly unlocked the door and yanked it open. With a squeal of delight she flung her arms around Lieutenant Taylor. "Oh, my word," Anne exclaimed in a rush of words. "What are you doing here? Come in. I'm so happy to see you."

His wife obviously had a different reaction.

The officer laughed and hugged Anne back, then allowed herself to be dragged inside.

Porter followed at a more sedate pace. "Professor."

They shook hands, but Patrick's voice deserted him. He closed and locked the door behind their guests.

"We have news," Porter stated, his lined face relaxed, not at all grim or concerned.

That was a good sign, wasn't it? "Please, sit," Patrick invited.

When they were seated, Taylor and Anne on the couch, Porter on the love seat and Patrick in the side chair, Patrick asked, "What news do you bring?"

"Domingo is dead," Lieutenant Taylor announced.

An oppressive stone of dread that constantly rode Patrick's back lifted. He nearly slid off the chair.

"Does that mean—" Anne blinked as tears filled her eyes. "We don't have to hide anymore?"

"That's right. The New Jersey police have worked diligently to break up what was left of his network. The threat to your life died with Domingo," Porter explained, his voice light.

Anne held out her hand to Patrick. He clasped her delicate fingers within his, feeling the slim wedding band that matched the one on his finger. He knew exactly what he wanted to do. He wanted to give Anne the wedding she deserved, in a church with family and friends around. The little ceremony in Vegas over the Fourth of July weekend had been nice and corny and wonderful, but now they were free to live. Really live.

He pulled Anne to her feet so they stood facing each other. He stared deep into her eyes, seeing himself reflected in the crystal-blue depths. "Anne, will you marry me again? This time in Boston?" he asked, totally unconcerned that they had an audience. "With our family and friends as witnesses."

Her smile outshined the sun. "Yes. Oh, yes."

* * * * *

Dear Reader,

I hope you enjoyed the journey that Anne and Patrick made through this book. Anne had a tough choice to make, one I hope that I would have the courage to make if I were put into her shoes. Though at first her faith was tentative at best, Anne allowed God to work in her life and she was able to help Patrick see that God loved him, even though he felt betrayed by God. Patrick's unresolved grief tainted his view of himself and his life, thus causing him to close off his heart to love.

I think too often people, Christians especially, fall prey to the fallacy that having faith will guarantee a smooth-sailing life without any heartache. And when trouble comes, as it inevitably does, we're quick to blame God rather than turn to Him for comfort. God's word is clear that trials will be a part of our lives, but through those trials, we have the opportunity to grow in our faith. I pray that as you and I face difficulties we will look to God for comfort, peace and guidance.

May God bless you always,

Questions for Discussion

1. What made you pick up this book to read? Did it live up to your expectations?

2. Did you think Anne and Patrick were realistic characters? Did their romance build believably?

3. If you were faced with the choices that Anne had, how do you think you'd respond?

4. How much of Anne's background shaped who she was? How much of your background shapes who you are?

5. Talk about a time in your life when you were faced with a difficult choice. How did your faith help you through this?

6. Patrick hadn't grieved for his father's death as a boy. How did this affect his life?

7. Is there something in your life that you haven't grieved that is affecting your faith?

8. Patrick thought he had to fulfill a certain role in his family: how did this affect his life? Is there a role you have in your family? How does this affect your life? For Patrick, his role needed to

change so that he could find happiness. How can your role change to make your life more enjoyable?

9. Did you notice the scripture in the beginning of the book? What application does it have to your life?

10. Did the author's use of language/writing style make this an enjoyable read? Would you read more from this author?

11. What will be your most vivid memories of this book?

12. What overarching lessons about life, love and faith did you learn from this story?

We hope you enjoyed these classic
Love Inspired stories.

Love Inspired stories show that faith,
forgiveness and hope have the power to
lift spirits and change lives—always.

Love Inspired

**Uplifting romances of faith,
forgiveness and hope.**

Enjoy *new* stories every month from
Love Inspired, Love Inspired Suspense
and Love Inspired Historical!

Available wherever books and
ebooks are sold.

SPECIAL EXCERPT FROM

Love Inspired
SUSPENSE

*Someone doesn't want Sonya Daniels
to find out the truth about her past.
Read on for a preview of HER STOLEN PAST
by Lynette Eason from Love Inspired Suspense.*

Sonya Daniels heard the sharp crack and saw the woman jogging four feet in front of her stumble. Then fall.

Another crack.

Another woman cried out and hit the ground.

"Shooter! Get down! Get down!"

With a burst of horror, Sonya caught on. Someone was shooting at the joggers on the path. Terror froze her for a brief second. A second that saved her life as the bullet whizzed past her head and planted itself in the wooden bench next to her. If she'd been moving forward, she would be dead.

Frantic, she registered the screams of those in the park as she ran full-out, zigzagging her way to the concrete fountain just ahead.

Her only thought was shelter.

A bullet slammed into the dirt behind her and she dropped to roll next to the base of the fountain.

She looked up to find another young woman had beat her there. Terrified brown eyes stared at Sonya and she knew the woman saw her fear reflected back at her. Panting, Sonya listened for more shots.

None came.

And still they waited. Seconds turned into minutes.

"Is it over?" the woman finally whispered. "Is he gone?"

"I don't know," Sonya responded.

Screams still echoed around them. Wails and petrified cries of disbelief.

Sonya lifted her head slightly and looked back at the two women who'd fallen. They still lay on the path behind her.

Sirens sounded.

Sonya took a deep breath and scanned the area across the street. Slowly, she calmed and gained control of her pounding pulse.

Her mind clicked through the shots fired. Two hit the women running in front of her. Her stomach cramped at the thought that she should have been the third victim. She glanced at the bench. The bullet hole stared back. It had dug a groove slanted and angled.

Heart in her throat, Sonya darted to the nearest woman, who lay about ten yards away from her. Expecting a bullet to slam into her at any moment, she felt for a pulse.

*When Sonya turns to Detective Brandon Hayes
for help, can he protect her without both of them
losing their hearts?
Pick up HER STOLEN PAST to find out.*

*Available August 2014
wherever Love Inspired books are sold.*

Love Inspired
SUSPENSE
RIVETING INSPIRATIONAL ROMANCE

Emma Landers has amnesia. Problem is, she can't remember how she got it, why she's injured or why someone wants to hurt her. When she lands on the doorstep of former love Travis Wright, she can barely remember their past history. But she knows she can trust him to protect her. The handsome farmer was heartbroken when Emma left him for the big city. But there's no way he can send her away when gunshots start flying. Now Travis must keep Emma safe while helping her piece together her memories—before it's too late.

A TRACE OF MEMORY
by
VALERIE HANSEN

THE DEFENDERS

Protecting children in need

**Available August 2014 wherever
Love Inspired books and ebooks are sold.**

Find us on Facebook at
www.Facebook.com/LoveInspiredBooks

The Wrangler's Inconvenient Wife
by
LACY WILLIAMS

With no family to watch over them, it's up to Fran Morris to take care of her younger sister, even if it means marrying a total stranger. Gruff, strong and silent, her new husband is a cowboy down to the bone. He wed Fran to protect her, not to love her, but her heart has never felt so vulnerable.

Trail boss Edgar White already has all the responsibility he needs at his family's ranch in Bear Creek, Wyoming. He had intended to remain a bachelor forever, but he can't leave Fran and her sister in danger. And as they work on the trail together, Edgar starts to soften toward his unwanted wife. He already gave Fran his name…can he trust her with his heart?

WYOMING
Legacy

United by family, destined for love

Available August 2014
wherever Love Inspired books and ebooks are sold.

d us on Facebook at
w.Facebook.com/LoveInspiredBooks

LIH28274

Love Inspired

A reclusive Amish logger, Ethan Gingerich is more comfortable around his draft horses than the orphaned niece and nephews he's taken in. Yet he's determined to provide the children with a good, loving home. The little ones, including a defiant eight-year-old, need a proper nanny. But when Ethan hires shy Amishwoman Clara Barkman, he never expects her temporary position to have such a lasting hold on all of them. Now this man of few words must convince Clara she's found her forever home and family.

BRIDES OF
Amish Country

Finding true love in the land of the Plain People.

The Amish Nanny

by

Patricia Davids

Available August 2014 wherever
Love Inspired books and ebooks are sold.